Parts of Robert

Felix Anderson

Special thanks to Steven Porter of Stillwater River Publications
for his invaluable editorial advice.

PARTS OF ROBERT

1.

Monday, May 10th, 2010, at 11:15 a.m. Angela Winslow forwarded a name and address to me: Robert Simmons, 34 Roxbury Lane, apartment 4D.

Angela works with *Heart and Hands,* a non-profit organization that delivers food and medication to elderly or ailing LGBTQ community members in Southern California. Two months earlier, I relocated to Los Angeles from Pennsylvania after receiving a grant from the E. Y. Eldon Foundation to research the life of novelist Erich Jacobson, who lived and worked in L.A. from 1936 to 1946. The research focused on documents in various local university archives and, to a lesser extent, on interviews with people connected to Jacobson or else who had letters, diaries, or other records belonging to family members acquainted with him. The work and a lack of social contacts in the area left me some free time that I opted to spend purposefully.

According to Angela, Robert typified the average *Heart and Hands* client. "You'll pick up his groceries and medication," she told me the day she added him to my roster. "He hasn't any family and very few friends left, so a little conversation wouldn't be amiss."

Christopher Isherwood described the observant narrator of his *Berlin Stories* with the famous line: "I am a camera." Six weeks of quizzing people about Jacobson had accustomed me to behaving like an extension of my phone's voice recorder, regarding people solely as repositories of information accessible by a few pertinent questions and abundant listening. This approach served me well both with my interview subjects and my *Heart and Hands* clients. Four years of gender history in college had left me curious to hear firsthand what queer life had been like in their youth, while they, grateful for the attention, praised me and my listening skills to Angela.

"How old is he?"

"Seventy-five," she said.

"Fairly young," I said.

"A heart condition and arthritis restrict his mobility. I told him to expect you around three."

"Okay."

"As you'll see by his shopping list," she said, "he's very particular about brands."

"I'll remember."

The text listed Hearth Fire whole wheat bread, Shell Stream low-fat almond milk, Tropic Morn orange juice, Bradshaw's strawberry jam, Velma's vanilla biscuits, a liter of Shale House ginger ale, seven single serving-sized bottles of Gunter's nutritional shakes, chocolate flavor, and assorted fruits and vegetables.

I returned the phone to my pocket and my attention to the third of ten overstuffed boxes containing the personal and professional papers of Paramount Pictures executive Oliver Castle, housed in the media archives at UCLA. Castle had lured Jacobson to L.A. with an offer to adapt one of his novels to the screen and kept him on salary for the next two years, revising the script according to a volley of ever-changing and often capricious suggestions, until Paramount executives overrode Castle's dedication to the project and cut Jacobson loose.

Castle, in contrast to his vacillations as a script advisor, had been something of a hoarder in the matter of his records. The boxes covering his prime period at Paramount, 1935 to 1943, divided the years into four boxes devoted to three months each; I focused on the ten containing records for the duration of Jacobson's employment under Castle, February 1936 to April 1938. The hours I spent with each depended on the volume and nature of their contents and my ability to restrain my curiosity whenever an intriguing yet unrelated issue cropped up in them. UCLA also housed material from other industry figures who dealt with Jacobson after Paramount dismissed him, and Castle's papers had been providing an expanding list of still others absent from the scant biographical information on Jacobson, like fellow Paramount scribe Gus Cavanaugh, whose papers also resided at UCLA, all of which extended my field of search well beyond my initial expectations.

Unsurprisingly, the archive soon began feeling like the proverbial second home, and my daily life settled into a routine only slightly less intractable than that for an average job. I arrived between nine and nine-fifteen every morning, sat at a table with a box before me, and read through as much of its contents as possible, pausing to copy the odd page or pages to my phone before breaking for lunch anywhere from eleven-thirty to one depending on the morning's yield. Usually, I ate at a nearby sandwich shop called Between the Sheaves, the name a tortuous pun on the familiar phrase "between the sheets," the sheaves in question being the sheaves of wheat that became bread slices for the sandwiches. The name tried the patience of both patrons and employees, judging by the martyred expressions on the kids behind the counter when newcomers asked for an explanation and the sheepishness of the regular customers near enough to hear their exchange, yet the quality of the food convinced most people to overlook the pun. I generally spent forty-five minutes to an hour eating and reviewing the material copied to my phone, gradually forming a more detailed picture of Jacobson's life before returning to UCLA for more reading until three-thirty or four in the afternoon.

Joining *Heart and Hands* altered the latter half of this routine two or three times a week. Angela or my clients forwarded requests around noontime, and I ran the errands in the afternoon, usually between one and three. Depending on the number and duration of my missions I either returned to the archive for a few hours or headed back to the tiny rooms the Eldon Foundation provided for me, where I incorporated my day's findings into everything I had already uncovered.

The day I received Robert's grocery list, Castle's box three had relinquished nothing about Jacobson, yet quite a bit about Gwen Ryan, a starlet Castle had been grooming for leading roles for over a year before she became pregnant by a studio electrician and eloped with him. The old studios tended to regard their talent as products, objects to buy, sell and use at their discretion. Consequently, when a product like Gwen exhibited an independent streak by falling in love, especially with someone lacking publicity value, it infuriated those overseeing their careers. Gwen's saga began with a memo I read at nine-thirty and continued, with Castle alternately despondent and furious, until I exerted enough willpower to leave off at one-thirty for lunch at Sheaves and, afterward, run my errand.

The market proved unusually crowded at two-fifteen. I collected the items on the list, stood in the check-out line for ten minutes, and at five minutes to three, turned into the parking lot fronting Robert's building.

Thirty-four Roxbury Lane had been constructed forty-five years earlier, consistent with then-current standards of opulence, yet on a tighter budget than those standards required. Large, cursive letters reading *Roxbury Place* hung high on an orange stucco wall above rows of windows backed either by frowsy drapes or grey metal blinds. A ragged rhododendron hedge concealed the foundation, parting to allow access to a plate glass door with *Roxbury Place* and the number 34 stenciled in flaking gold paint on the upper half. The door admitted me to a lobby with faded red fleur-de-lys wallpaper; a worn red wall-to-wall carpet; two palms in red lacquer pots embossed with gold fleur-de-lys; wall sconces dripping with faux crystal pendants; and a matching chandelier dangling by a brass chain from a shallow, recessed dome in the ceiling. I padded across the carpet to the elevator and ascended to the fourth floor.

Cream-colored woodwork framed more fleur-de-lys wallpaper and crystalline sconces along the fourth-floor hallway, silent except for the muffled grumble of TV sets in the closed apartments. Turning the first corner, I found a door with a brass 4D on it and knocked.

"Coming," a low, gurgling voice said, a necessary assurance since a full minute then elapsed between my knock and the same voice speaking against the door. "Who is it?"

"Paul Heywood from *Heart and Hands*," I said.

The door opened. Robert Simmons leaned on a polished wooden cane, wearing a green plaid shirt, blue cardigan sweater, baggy grey trousers, short black socks, and brown plaid slippers. He had sparse, pale yellow hair, loose ruddy skin sprinkled with age spots, chestnut eyes, and a pleasant smile with teeth slightly discolored but not false. Hunched over the cane, he stood about eight inches shorter than me.

"Come in," he said, shuffling to one side to let me through.

"Yes, sir," I replied as I stepped across the threshold.

"And you may drop the 'sir.' The last thing I need is impertinent reminders of my age."

I laughed and paused in the entryway while he closed the door.

The apartment reduced the building's exterior aesthetic to a small rectangle. The entryway, large enough to accommodate five people standing close together, had a worn black-and-white checkerboard linoleum floor. Two plastic trellises, threaded with plastic ivy, jutted from the side walls to form a second doorway marking the entryway from the living room. Opposite, more checkerboard linoleum began at the door to the kitchen. Gold wall-to-wall carpeting covered the intervening living room, its worn fibers evoking an unswept threshing floor. Pine deodorizer and bay rum mingled in the hot, stuffy air.

Robert closed the front door, turned to me, and pointed his cane at the shopping bags. "What are those?"

"Reusable bags," I said. "*Heart and Hands* adopted them last year, according to my supervisor. They're more environmentally friendly."

"Commendable," he said. "Do they go back with you?"

"That's what makes them reusable. Why? Did you want them?"

"Good grief, no. I have a stack of old grocery bags under the sink. I use them for garbage, though I doubt I'll have enough trash to fill them for another ten years."

He hobbled between the trellises into the living room. I followed.

A window on the right-hand wall, framed by parted beige drapes, admitted a shaft of afternoon sun that, reflecting off the gold carpet, enhanced the room's narrowness. A green sofa stood against the left-hand wall, with an old cherry wood coffee table before it and an open door just past it. Equidistant from both window and sofa, a recliner with a swivel base and worn green upholstery faced a fifteen-year-old television on a cherry wood occasional table. A taller pine table with a small square top stood next to the recliner, holding a half-empty glass of ginger ale, a copy of Chekhov's stories, and a pair of reading glasses with thin silver frames. A tiny dining area behind the recliner had only a delicate cherry wood writing desk topped by a few pieces of unopened mail, a white ceramic lamp with blue delft designs, a laptop computer currently turned off, and a framed black-and-white photo of Robert in his late twenties or early thirties, striking a self-conscious pose in a dark suit I dated to the late 1950s. Nondescript landscapes in cheap white wooden frames hung over the sofa and on either side of the window.

An overstuffed bookcase covered the far wall. Following him past the bookshelf on our way to the kitchen, I noticed a preponderance of plays and theater histories along with classic novels and more short story collections. Glancing to my left through the door on the other side of the sofa, I glimpsed a narrow room containing an old cherry wood bed with a white spread and a cherry wood side table with a brass alarm clock, a box of tissues, and a grey ceramic lamp shaped like a Doric column.

The kitchen consisted of another, tinier rectangle. A beige countertop ran along the far wall, with a sink in the middle, drawers, and cupboards directly beneath, and two cupboards above, the upper two separated by the width of the sink. A small semicircular shelf jutted over the sink from the base of each cupboard; three brown pill bottles stood on the right-hand shelf. The counter ended on the left at a small beige stove with a dull copper teakettle on the back burner. Two feet away, against the left-hand wall, a matching beige refrigerator stood beneath a clock shaped like an antique copper pastry mold. A dishwasher anchored the other end of the counter, while on the right-hand wall, a window with gauzy yellow curtains over-looked the rear of the building: a short strip of grass with three stunted palm trees, bordered at the back by the neighboring apartment complex. A little table with a yellow Formica top, thin aluminum legs, and two matching chairs with padded vinyl seats stood before the window. A beige can opener, a white microwave, a wrought iron stand like a miniature coat rack holding four plain blue coffee mugs, a black and chrome toaster, and a pine bread-box had been neatly portioned along the counter.

"Set the bags there." Brandishing the cane again, he indicated a spot between the coffee mugs and the toaster.

"Would you like me to put everything away for you?" I asked.

"You're very kind." He sat with a grunt on a chair at the table. "The produce goes in the refrigerator, of course, though you can leave the pears on the counter."

I transferred his Romaine lettuce, one green pepper, two tomatoes, and a celery rib into the vegetable crisper and stood the Shell Stream and Tropic Morn cartons on a lower shelf, alongside a bottle of Chef's Special raspberry vinaigrette salad dressing and a jar of Bridger's heart-healthy mayo, both half empty. A plastic jug of Bountiful Bog cranberry juice, a glass bowl half full of fruit salad, a partially depleted cheese wedge covered in plastic wrap, an unopened package containing two chicken breasts, and six eight-ounce cups of black cherry yogurt labeled Bub's Little Yogurt Tubs completed the refrigerator's spare contents.

As I shut the door and returned to the counter, he tilted his head and asked, "Are you, by any chance, a student?"

"Why do you ask?"

"You look like one."

"I do?"

"The glasses and reserved manner exude an unmistakable aura of studiousness. Then there's the subtle dishevelment of your clothes and hair, indicating a preoccupation with cognition over appearance." I realized for the first time how often I leaned my head on my hand while reading Castle's papers, which undoubtedly played havoc with my hair. And I never paid particular attention to my wardrobe, except on special occasions. He continued. "If I were casting the role of a youth beginning his climb through the academic hierarchy, you'd be ideal, a balanced blend of intellectual and leading man."

"Thanks," I said.

"I hope I haven't overstepped. When I was young, you could appreciate peoples' appearance without there being any sinister undercurrents, not that those undercurrents didn't exist. We've forgotten it's possible to enjoy human looks for their own sake, the way you can enjoy the seashore or a giant oak."

"This is the first time I've been compared to the seashore," I said, "or a giant oak."

"I'm glad you have a sense of humor. It eases my embarrassment."

"I'm not offended. I know what you meant." I placed his pears on the counter.

"I'm not embarrassed about that. It's needing your aid. I got around pretty well until a month ago. Even after my heart attack, I was out and about in a couple of weeks, with the help of my cane."

"What changed?" I folded the empty bag, laid it aside on the counter, and removed the loaf of whole wheat Hearth Fire from the top of the second bag.

"Put that in there," he said, indicating the breadbox.

The box released a stale, yeasty smell when I opened it. I slid the Hearth Fire inside.

"I changed, thanks to the arthritis," he said. "Three weeks ago, I fell leaving the market. A young couple helped me up, and I managed to get home. But I had some bad bruises, so I got checked out, and they found a clot. Now blood thinners have taken their place among the pills for my heart and arthritis. I'm surprised I don't rattle like a maraca when I walk. My doctor suggested assisted living. Then I heard about *Heart and Hands*. I'm cooped up either way, but I'm used to this apartment, and I'd rather not leave unless I have to."

"Understandable."

"When I was young, I walked everywhere. Until this happened, even taking the bus at least gave me a change of scene."

"I can't give you a change of scene, but don't be embarrassed about my being here. I wouldn't have volunteered if I weren't happy to do it."

His turned speculative again. "Why did you volunteer?"

"I'm new to L.A. I haven't made any friends yet, and I had the time." I unpacked a bag of dried papaya, a box of prunes, Bradshaw's jam, Velma's biscuits, and Gunter's shakes from the second bag. "Where do you want these?"

"Leave the fruit on the counter. I'll bring it into the living room later."

"The living room?"

"I nibble on it while I read. The biscuits and shakes go in the cupboard in front of you. The jam goes in the other. My diet has left both quite bare; just don't refer to me as Old Mother Hubbard."

"Why would I do that?"

"The digital generation," he said, grunting. "It's a children's rhyme, one of those attributed to Mother Goose in centuries past. Look it up sometime."

I placed the biscuits and shakes in their appointed cupboard, on a shelf beside five other boxes: two of Field Treasure whole grain cereals, one wheat squares, the other bran flakes, one of Field Treasure wild rice, one of Snapdragon unsalted crackers, and one of Cozy Cup apple-cinnamon teabags, the front of which pictured an anthropomorphic tabby cat holding a steaming teacup in its paw.

"What do you do that provides you so much free time?" he said.

"I'm here on a research grant."

"What are you researching?"

"A mid-century children's author," I said, "Erich Jacobson."

His brows contracted. "I like to think I'm well-read, but I don't recognize the name."

"He's somewhat obscure. He wasn't even a writer by profession."

"What was he?"

"A psychoanalyst," I said, "one of the second-generation analysts after Freud striving to legitimize analysis as a therapy. He didn't start out writing children's books, either. From 1928 to 1934, he published three mysteries featuring Gustave Pedersen, a psychiatrist who solved crimes."

"What were the titles?"

His polite but relentless questions soon altered our talk to a truncated version of my in-person pitch to the Eldon officials: and, as always when someone questioned me about my project, the effort to remember its key points revived a trace amount of the anxiety attending that initial interview.

"*A Cold Corpse, Fisherman's Secret,* and *The Midnight Sun Murder,*" I said, reaching up to place his jam in the second cupboard, which also contained three cans of Fine Flake tuna fish, a jar of Hive Gold honey, six cans of Cal's Cardio low-salt, low-fat soups in various flavors, cans of Summer Glory fruit and fruit cocktail, the same brand's low-salt vegetables, and small bottles of dried thyme, tarragon, dill, and oregano. "They sold well, but Pedersen never caught on with readers the way other detectives of the time did, like Hercule Poirot or Philo Vance."

"And he lived in Los Angeles?"

"He was born and lived most of his life in Denmark. He was only in California from 1936 to 1946."

"During the war," Robert said.

I lifted the Shale House ginger ale from the bag.

"Leave that on the counter, too," he said. "What brought him here?"

"An executive at Paramount Pictures liked *The Midnight Sun Murder* and invited Jacobson over in 1936 to adapt it as a screenplay, but after two years, they scrapped it. If they'd made it, it would've been the first mainstream film concerning psychoanalysis, predating Hitchcock's *Spellbound* by a decade."

"You really know your subject."

"No other way to get a grant," I said.

"Writing for films must have been quite a change for an analyst."

"Not really," I said. "A volume of his letters came out in 1974. They're the starting point for my research. In one of the letters, he says that he hoped by turning the novel into a film, he might demystify and therefore help popularize psychoanalysis, which was partly his intention in writing the novels."

"Why only partly?"

"He also loved literature for its own sake and fancied the idea of being an author. His feelings about scriptwriting were more mixed. He wasn't married and only expected to be here for a few months. And like many then, he was fascinated by American movies and curious to see how they were made."

"From a layman's viewpoint or a psychoanalyst's?"

"Both, from what he wrote to friends. The letters include some devastating analyses of the people he encountered in the industry. On the other hand, he loved the weather and spent a lot of time at the beach."

"Unsurprisingly."

"He also accumulated a wide circle of acquaintances: coworkers from Paramount, local analysts, and people outside both spheres."

"Is that why he stayed ten years?"

"Not entirely. The Paramount executive, Oliver Castle found the scripts problematic. According to him, Jacobson had difficulty reconciling the esoterica of psychoanalytic theory with the pacing movies demanded. Castle kept him revising the script for two years."

"Why did Castle keep at it so long?"

"It was a personal project for him. He was in analysis himself, and from what he says in the memos I've read, he was hoping to make the first film dealing seriously with the subject. The few psychiatrists in films up to then tended to the sinister: Dr. Caligari in 1919 and one called Dr. Kammer, played by George Zucco, in *After the Thin Man* in 1936. Then, in 1938, Fred Astaire played a musical comedy analyst in *Carefree.*"

"And Paramount was willing to pay for all this revising?"

"Castle had him work on a few other scripts to justify keeping him on salary, but Jacobson says in his letters only a few bits of what he wrote ever ended up onscreen."

"Not uncommon for novelists under the Hollywood studio system. A similar fate befell Aldous Huxley, F. Scott Fitzgerald, and William Faulkner."

"Though they did receive a handful of screen credits," I said.

An unspoken yet unmistakable commendation of my familiarity with the arcane subject of novelists in old Hollywood flashed across his face. "True," he said, "probably because they were more famous. What happened with the script he was there to write?"

"The studio decided the problems were insurmountable and shelved the project. But by then, the war had started in Europe, which kept Jacobson from returning home."

"What did he do? I assume after they abandoned his adaptation, he was out of a job."

"He tried interesting other studios in it, to no avail. In the meantime, he joined a local analyst in his practice, Dr. Peter Cork."

"So he spent the war years here, making a decade in L.A. all told."

"Only I'm not convinced all has been told. That's where I come in."

"How?"

"Jacobson returned to Denmark as soon as he was able, in 1946."

"Even though he liked the climate and had a practice going?"

"He didn't like being an expatriate. He says in one of his letters that despite the glories of Southern California, he could only ever be at home at home."

"A construct worthy of Gertrude Stein," he said. "Go on."

"He married a graphic artist of British descent, Ingrid Beyer, in 1950 and devoted his attention to re-establishing his practice. Then, in 1953 he began writing children's fiction. From '53 to '56, he published four books about a herring named Harold, illustrated by his wife."

"What were their titles?"

"*Harold Herring and the School of Fish, Herring Overboard, Harold Herring in Hot Water,* and *Harold Herring meets Electra Eel*; at least, those were the English titles."

"They're why you're researching him?"

"Yeah. My mom had the Harold books when she was a kid. I found them in a box in our attic when I was seven, and fell in love with them."

"I see."

"Like I said, nobody knows why he turned from crime to children's literature. He and Ingrid wanted kids, but they never had any even though, as he claims in a letter, their physician declared them both fertile. The consensus is Harold emerged from his frustrated desire to be a father."

"A consensus from which you dissent?"

"Wanting to be a parent may have played a part in Harold's birth, but I've a hunch his time here also had something to do with it."

"Is this hunch based on anything definite?"

"A few vague remarks about 'complications' in his letters from 1944 and 1945," I said. "Jacobson was usually very forthright in his correspondence."

"Probably the result of being an analyst, bringing other people's buried truths to light."

"I think the coyness camouflaged something serious. It's not too far-fetched to connect that with his turn to a genre he'd shown no interest in before."

"And this is all untilled ground in literature's generally overworked terrain?"

"An analytical interpretation of his books appeared in 1976, but so far, nobody's considered the possible influence of the Los Angeles period on his work. The people at the Eldon Foundation agreed with me, and here I am."

"A fascinating tale," he said. "How are you going about your investigation?"

"I'm combing the major studios' archives and the personal papers donated to local universities by industry people who dealt directly with Jacobson. I also have contact information for descendants of some of Jacobson's friends and posted an online request for anyone with documents relating to his life here. Then there are the psychoanalytical association records."

"No wonder you're rumpled. I wish you luck. And I hope to hear more as you continue."

"Thanks."

"With that going on, what made you devote your free time to *Heart and Hands*?"

"It's a way to meet people."

"There are more conventional ways to meet people."

"True. But driving from one archive to another, I noticed a lot of older people around who looked lonely and . . ." I stopped and folded the second bag.

"You felt sorry for them?"

I flushed. "I didn't mean . . ."

"Don't worry about it. I feel sorry for myself sometimes. Oscar Levant once said self-pity is the only pity that counts. I've come to agree."

"Who's Oscar Levant?"

"A character actor in movies," he said. "His heyday was roughly in the period you're researching. He started out as a concert pianist and later became a fixture on TV talk shows. I loved his acting when I was young. I still love it when I catch one of his films on TV."

"Why do you agree with him about self-pity?"

"Because each person alone knows exactly what they endure. And since there's nobody to mourn me after I'm gone, I get to do it while I'm alive, like Tom Sawyer and Huck Finn crashing their own funeral."

His bemused expression belied the grim words.

I changed the subject. "Anything else I can help you with?"

"Not for the present." He stood with the aid of the cane. "I'll need my heart pills on Friday. Think you'll be picking them up?"

"I've been officially assigned to you by *Heart and Hands*, so unless you request a change . . ."

"Not likely," he said. "You've hooked me with the Jacobson story. Uneasy shall lie the head that wants the truth about Harold Herring."

I tucked the empty shopping bags under my arm. He walked me to the door.

"If you notice any fresh fruit on sale the next time you're in the market, pick some up for me: blueberries, cherries, raspberries, grapes, strawberries. But no more than half a pound. I can only eat so much before they and my digestion spoil."

"Got it."

I opened the door, and he closed it behind me. I descended in the elevator, strode across the lobby, and out to my car, mulling over my first impression of Robert Simmons: bitter, literate, and observant, with a quick if frequently dark humor, all of which indicated an intriguing store of information to explore.

Tuesday morning, I finished Castle's box three. I found nothing concerning Jacobson, and an abrupt, unsatisfying conclusion to the Gwen Ryan matter. Following the failure of several schemes to thwart her marriage and her preganancy—abortion being a viable, if illegal, option for those with enough clout—Paramount dropped Ryan from their contract player list and fired her electrician husband. The documentation on them ceased after that, with the newlyweds and prospective parents out of work.

Despite attempts to redirect my attention to Jacobson, his absence from the papers in box three allowed me to brood over the fate of these long-ago lovers, a mood that carried over to my lunch at Sheaves. Rather than return to the archive and try my luck with Castle's box four, I drove to Glendale for an appointment with a respondent to my online post, who contacted me three days ago claiming he had letters written by his grandfather that mentioned Jacobson as an acquaintance, though he refused to divulge their contents over the phone. Arriving at his address, a mousy little man with stringy brown hair and a tatty mustache confronted me with four envelopes, brittle and discolored like autumn leaves, clutched in his hand and the question:

"So, how much you guys pay for shit like this?"

"I don't have the resources to buy material," I said. "The best I can offer is an acknowledgment in my monograph, if and when it's published."

He chased me off with a barrage of abusive epithets and, after several hours stuck in traffic, cursing him in return, I arrived back at my apartment and spent the evening scouring the internet for more about Gwen. Eventually I learned that Ryan and her electrician, Edgar Devon, relocated to Oakland where Devon opened an appliance store and repair shop. They begat four more children and died in their eighties, surrounded by children and grandchildren, all of which sent me to bed at ten-thirty with my curiosity sated and my spirits gratified.

Friday morning, on the way to box four, I described my encounter with the greedy rodent to Hilda, the patient Virgil who guided visitors through the infernal depths of the archive.

"You get people like that now and again," she said. "If he had anything truly substantial, he'd have let you read one or two to get you interested."

Friday afternoon at one, I stood before the door to 4D in Roxbury Place, holding a little white pharmacy bag.

"You're prompt," Robert said. "Would you care to come in for a while?"

"Sure. I'm officially free of the archive for the weekend."

He escorted me to the kitchen, where he removed the bottle from the bag, peered at the label, and placed it with the other bottles on the shelf over the sink. "Would you like a drink? I'm not allowed alcohol, but I can offer you ice water, almond milk, or ginger ale."

"Ice water will be fine."

"Sit," he said.

I sat at the kitchen table. He filled two glasses with water and grabbed a handful of ice cubes from the freezer to add to mine. He set my glass on the table and fetched the second bottle, containing a single pill, from the shelf over the sink. "This is the moment I decide whether I wish to remain alive or not," he said.

"Don't talk like that."

"Sorry," he said, amused and, I thought, touched by my unease. "I forgot you're still too young to appreciate such dark humor."

He opened the bottle, dumped the pill into his hand, and glared at it before flicking it into his mouth and chasing it down with a swig of water.

"How often do you take them?"

"Twice a day, afternoon and night," he said after swallowing the water. "They're my penance for the sins of gluttony, ironically committed in my salad days." He dropped the empty bottle into a metal garbage pail lined with an old shopping bag, standing between the dishwasher and the table.

"Is your diet better now?"

"Depends on how you define 'better.' It's healthier, as you've no doubt deduced from my shopping lists and your peering into my cupboards: cereal, almond milk, toast, frozen waffles, jam, juice, tuna, low salt soup, unsalted crackers, salads, chicken cutlets, breaded chicken breasts, turkey burgers, rice, fresh or canned veggies, yogurt, Gunter's shakes, herbal tea, and ginger ale, week after week. Afternoons I snack on Velma's biscuits or fruit, and on special occasions, I splurge on pasta with tomato sauce."

"There's some cheese in your refrigerator. Are you allowed it on your diet?"

"In moderation. Essentially it's to flavor my turkey meatloaf. Sometimes

I mix it with bread crumbs to coat my chicken parts. I'm also handy with herbs and spices, a talent I acquired in my immediate post-college years when all I could afford were the ordinary and inexpensive."

"You're able to work around the restrictions, then?"

"Oh, absolutely," he said, "though it's been a while since I really looked forward to the taste of a meal."

"You don't seem like you were ever overweight if the photo on your desk is any indication."

"I wasn't. The food I loved settled in my pulmonary system rather than on my waist. It might've been better if it'd turned to fat. I couldn't be heavy in my work, and I'd have saved the bother of pills and doctors."

"What did you do?"

"I was an actor, though, like every actor, I took different jobs to make ends meet."

"That's why you treated me like a casting director the other day," I said.

"Seeing real people as potential characters becomes second nature very quickly," he said, "maybe too quickly."

"Were you famous?"

"If I had, I wouldn't be inhabiting this sun-drenched shoebox. I did theater and minor roles in movies and on TV."

"I'd love to see them."

"They're hardly worth it."

"Why?"

"I was mediocre, at best. I preferred the stage, perhaps because stage appearances are ephemeral, like everything in our world."

"Would you mind if I searched for them online?"

He assumed an expression similar to the one he had while contemplating his pills. "I should've kept my mouth shut."

"I'll withhold comment if they live down to your judgement."

"Fair enough."

The pastry mold clock read 1:45 p.m. "I should get going," I said. "I've got another delivery."

"Just as well. It's almost time for *Grandview Park*."

"You watch soap operas?" I asked.

"Only *Grandview*, and only from a perverse sense of loyalty," he said.

"What loyalty?"

"I was on it for five years."

"Really? When?"

"1961 to 1966," he said.

"That long ago? How long has it been on?"

"Since 1955. Fifty-five years isn't unheard of for soap operas. *The Guiding Light* ran on CBS for seventy-two years. It started on radio in the 1930s and went off the air in the early 2000s."

"Wow. What was it like being on *Grandview*?"

"Not bad. Onscreen, I suffered from an unrequited love for my brother's wife. Off-screen, I enjoyed a long-standing affair with the actor playing my brother."

"I'd like to hear about that."

"Remind me to tell you the next time you come."

Interest in this projected discussion, shining through his cynicism, confirmed my first impression of him as a source of information.

Saturday and Sunday, I again ignored my Jacobson studies to watch hundreds of online clips headed "Robert Simmons—Actor." They showcased an able, personable performer from his late twenties to his late sixties, in parts ranging from a young hoodlum in an old crime drama to a discomfited senior citizen in a tactless ad for a hemorrhoid ointment that had certainly been posted for its kitsch appeal.

Monday afternoon, I arrived at 4D with two full shopping bags.

"Ah, supplies," he said. "You know where the kitchen is."

"I found your hemorrhoid commercial," I said, passing between the ivied trellises.

"Good lord." He closed the door and followed me to the kitchen.

"It was kind of funny," I said.

"You can't imagine the teasing I got. From total strangers, too. How did you find it?"

I set the bags on the counter and began storing his groceries, starting with a fresh loaf of Hearth Fire. "Everything's available on the Internet."

"True," he said. "The good go to heaven, the bad go to hell, and the embarassments go online."

"Do you use your computer much?"

He eased onto a chair at the kitchen table. "Just to pay bills and track my bank balance, and play music while I read. And order a book or two."

I set his dried papaya on the counter. "I spent most of the weekend reviewing your credits."

"I'd think a young scholar would have better things to do than engage in intellectual self-flagellation."

"Sometimes." I inserted his Velma's biscuits, Field Treasure wheat squares, and Cozy Cup tea bags into their cupboard. "I caught your appearance on *Dewey's Place*."

"What the hell's that?"

"A drama from the 1960s," I said, "about a family who own a restaurant in Chicago. You played a drunk on an episode in 1967." I aligned his seven Gunter's shakes beside the cereal and tea bags, listing other bits of his resume I had plucked from cyberspace.

"Thankfully, it's all a blur," he said. "I remember nothing but a series of studios with dozens of technicians; actors who imagined being filmed granted them immortality; and scripts top-heavy with plot points in circulation since the Roman Empire."

I stood his Shale House on the counter, folded the empty bag, and set it aside. "You weren't as bad as you said."

"Nor was I as good as I could have been, which is the same as being lousy."

"Now, who's self-flagellating?"

"Not me," he said. "What did it amount to? Enough money for this place and a few images lost among millions of others of equal disinterest. My best work was on stage, which was gone the moment I did it."

"Do you have any clippings from your theater work?"

A brief smile enhanced his resemblance to the photo on his desk. "Your charm and persistence must aid your research considerably."

I piled his lettuce, tomatoes, and green pepper into the crisper. "My information usually comes from documents written by dead people. Getting them is more a matter of persistence than charm. What about the clippings?"

"I'm afraid even your persistence fails where they're concerned. I saved reviews and photos in my proud youth, but when I realized where my career was going, I decided I didn't want any reminders of where it'd been."

I displayed a hefty bunch of grapes. "These were on sale, so I picked them up per your instructions."

"They look delicious. Put them in the fridge."

I laid the grapes on a shelf beside something square wrapped in wrinkled foil. A package of fresh basil followed the grapes; after that, two zucchini, a dozen eggs, a pound of low-fat ground turkey, seven black cherry Bub's Tubs, and a Chef's Special raspberry vinaigrette. "You're the first of my clients to order zucchini," I said.

"In my New York days, I had a fling with a chef in an Italian restaurant. That's where he worked, of course, not where we had our fling. He taught me to prepare an excellent zucchini frittata, though nowadays I only use egg whites and a bare minimum of olive oil and parmesan."

I stacked four packages of Ice Floe frozen vegetables in the freezer. "Was this while you were sleeping with the actor playing your brother?"

"No, Paolo came after I'd left the actor and the show."

"You promised to tell me about both the next time I was here."

"You're really interested?"

"Absolutely," I said.

"Okay," he said, responding like someone who had long since scattered even his fondest memories to the wind. "Let's move to the other room. These chairs aren't suited for lengthy anecdotes, at least not where my arthritis is concerned."

I removed the final item from the bag: a tube of Green Gleam, a toothpaste with a strong mint flavor and pale green tint that, according to a moss green banner on the top of the box, had been manufactured since 1935. "Where do you want this?"

"Leave it on the counter," he said, standing. "I'll bring it to the bathroom later. I was going to make tea if you'd like some."

"Why don't you let me make it now that I know where everything is?"

"You're my guest."

"I'm here to assist you. Go get comfortable, and I'll have it ready in a jiffy."

"Drop a spoonful of honey in mine."

Preparing the tea, I felt the same anticipation that tweaked me whenever I opened a fresh box at the archive. The hot water drenched the Cozy Cup teabags, releasing an aroma of cinnamon and apples that I sweetened by stirring a teaspoon of Hive Gold into each mug, and I carted them to the living room.

Robert had swiveled his recliner to face the sofa. I set his mug on the table by his chair, next to his glasses and a worn paperback copy of Goethe's *Faust*. I placed mine on the coffee table and sat on the sofa opposite him.

"*Grandview Park* was more fun than I expected," he said, "and not just because of the affair. They started me on a year's contract, which stretched into five. At that point, I'd have been grateful for the year."

"Weren't you doing well?"

"About as well as ninety-eight percent of the actors in New York ever did, or do. I'd been hunting acting jobs for five years, ever since I graduated college. I scrounged a few bits and walk-ons in plays and on TV. Mostly I worked in department stores or as a busboy or a waiter, and never for the better places in town."

"Were you looking to get into TV?"

"God, no," he said. "But I didn't turn it down because it was work and because there was considerable overlap between stage and TV at the time. Do you know that about half the shows from television's first fifteen years were done in New York?"

"Yes."

"Then you probably know they were done live, which made stage-trained actors a useful commodity."

"Because they were more accustomed to live performances," I said.

"And stage actors, in turn, sought TV work for the money and exposure. A lot of younger stage people then hopped directly from TV to movies."

"James Dean, Eva Marie Saint, Jack Lemmon," I said, and in response to his wondering look, added: "I've seen films of their TV work."

"Another point in your favor," he said. "I joined *Grandview* without any expectations beyond a regular salary, luckily for me since the show saddled me with a lot of sentimental tripe about a black sheep who fell prey to shady deals and had the hots for his brother's wife. The material was so inane the only way to preserve my sanity was to adjust my acting to match it, so I became the hammiest, campiest cad imaginable."

"And they kept you on for five years?"

"Hammy and campy is what the audience wanted. Back then, day-time television was aimed at overworked housewives. The evening schedule sought to attract their overworked husbands and restless children."

"Surely it wasn't all that bad."

"No. The prime-time dramas like *Playhouse 90* and *Studio One* that hired those up-and-coming stage actors had theatrical quality productions and scripts," he said. "Sadly, though, their period was brief. Practically every-thing today is a soap opera. Even the news is hammy and campy."

"You really think so?"

He sipped his tea and nodded. "When I was a boy, there was a radio comedian on named Fred Allen who had a permanent antipathy towards network executives. He once joked about a subspecies of executive he called a 'Molehill Man.' According to him, the Molehill Man arrived in his of-fice at nine to find a molehill on his desk and had until five to turn it into a mountain. Molehill Men are everywhere now. Preachers, pundits, and assorted lower-case messiahs fill modern media's infinitely available space with the entire bag of theatrical tricks, from the oldest and hoariest to the most sophisticated, turning molehills into mountains that they then pass off as news or commentary, a catch-all phrase that exists mainly to justify the compulsive tongue-wagging necessary for transforming molehills into mountains. The last time you were here, you asked if I'd ever been famous. The most fame I ever won came from chewing the scenery on *Grandview Park*."

"How famous were you?"

"The summer I was involved with black-market penicillin, I received a thousand letters a week. I realized then that rather than entertainment, we were a surrogate family and friends to people who didn't get along with theirs or had none at all. Seven months after joining the show, I was the focus of innumerable aspiring heroines hoping to reform my wayward character. I strove to dispel their ardor by returning a headshot with an impersonal dedication as myself, like 'Glad you enjoy the show. Keep watching.'"

He sighed and shook his head. "You can't imagine those letters. Some were pathetic. Others were psychotic."

"How did you handle them?"

"The pathetic ones got a longer dedication. The psychotic ones got nothing at all. I derived a great deal of comfort knowing my correspondents never suspected that in real life, the cad who made their hearts beat faster slept with other men."

"When did the affair with your TV brother start?"

"The first day, as I recall. My character's brother was a lawyer."

"What was his name?"

"Brice . . . oh, you mean the actor playing him?"

"Yes."

"Grayson Albany. Brice's wife was Judith, played by Margaret Baum." The latter name evoked a smile that persisted through a sip of tea.

"I assume from your expression you liked her a lot."

"I adored her from the moment we met. She and Gray started on the show in 1958 and were already fast friends. Everybody called her Maggie. I shortened it to Mag. The first day, my character arrived on Brice and Judith's doorstep in a thunderstorm, and after two minutes of dialogue that provided the back story for the brothers' childhoods, I confessed to embezzlement and begged him to help me out. This established our dynamic for the next five years. I'd get into trouble, and he'd get me out. When I arrived on set for our first scene, Gray looked at me in a manner that told anyone familiar with the signs he'd be an easy conquest."

"Signs?"

"Did you take any gender or queer history courses in school?"

"Yes."

"Then you undoubtedly know that in the days when being gay was both socially unacceptable and illegal, we relied on subtle looks and gestures for mutual recognition."

"I see. When did you and Grayson hook up?"

"Quicker than immediately," he said. "We finished the episode, I met him for dinner, and we went back to his place and bed."

"What was he like?"

"A good guy, fun, criminally handsome, but in a rut."

"What do you mean by a rut?"

"He traded his talent for security. For all intents and purposes, he led an average middle-class life, with a regular job, a nice apartment, and nice clothes, except for forays into the city's gay nightlife, not that there weren't enough average middle-class husbands enjoying the same extracurricular activity. He knew everything about acting on a soap and became my mentor, a mentor with benefits, you might say. He showed me tricks for memorizing long stretches of dialogue for episodes showcasing our characters, a valuable talent even though we had cue cards off-camera. It was often like performing a different one-act play five days a week."

"Sounds rigorous," I said.

"It was at first, especially considering the quality of the material we worked with. Gray taught me to relax and take it with a grain of salt. Following our first night, after a particularly grueling day, he'd invite me to dinner. Then, we'd go back to his place and release our tensions. A month later, he tendered me a semi-genuine offer to move in with him."

"What made it semi-genuine?"

"He said since I'd only just started on the show, living with him would cut my expenses in half. Of course, it cut his expenses in half, too. It worked out well, though. We enjoyed each other's company without ever forming an attachment strong enough to breed jealousy. He liked going out at night, hunting tricks. Sometimes I'd go with him. Just as often, I'd stay home and read. Then one day, Gray inadvertently found a way to add more interest to our work."

"How?"

"We were doing perhaps the fifteenth scene of me in his office, asking for his help. He was sitting on the corner of his desk, the toes of his left foot touching the floor. He knew the camera was cutting him off just above the waist. He had his right hand on his right thigh, and as we argued, the fingers of his right hand caressed his thigh gently, a gesture that, in private, signaled arousal. He was trying to make me laugh, but I stayed in character. A little later, when I turned my back on him at a moment of high drama, knowing where the camera was cutting me off, I clenched my buttocks two times, fast and hard enough for him to notice from below my suit jacket. I heard him clear his throat before speaking his next line, indicating I'd brought him closer to laughter than he had me. We found treading this particular patch of thin ice on live TV exhilarating, and from then on, we challenged each other to find ways to sneak the true nature of our relationship into our scenes, flaunting our sex lives to millions of viewers in ways only understood by an astute few."

"How'd you manage that?"

"By introducing the signs I mentioned. We'd react to the other's lines with what on the surface seemed like indignation or repentance, but to the initiated indicated seething lust. Then we'd gravitate to the most phallic-looking objects on set. Being a lawyer, Brice's office was rife with pens and pencils. During our scenes there, I'd pick one up and hold it against my lower lip while I talked. Our very straight director interpreted this as a nervous tic that I introduced to show my character's guilty conscience. One day I began a scene fixing a light switch with a screwdriver in my hand."

"Why were you fixing a light switch?"

"They threw in things like that to add what they considered realism. Gray entered, and during our conversation, I kept rubbing my thumb over the handle of the screwdriver. Another time they had a thin, stubby abstract sculpture like an unfinished lamp base on a side table. During an argument, I shifted beside it and casually squeezed the tip in exactly the way Gray liked me to squeeze the tip of his penis. He turned purple, stifling his laugh. But he delivered his lines in the same high dudgeon as at the beginning of the scene, and everyone assumed his twitching neck muscles were a part of his performance."

"What about his turning purple?"

"It didn't matter because we were still broadcasting in back and white. Later in the dressing room, we fell into each other's arms laughing."

"Nobody ever caught on?"

"Not enough to cause a scandal, thankfully. If what we were doing had become public, our careers would have ended. Viewers, sponsors, network executives, and even our director, readily confused the latent sexual tension in our scenes with a portrayal of overt sibling rivalry. Gay men saw through the pose, of course, but the majority of them considered it a coincidence. We received letters from men around the country coyly asking if we realized some of our gestures had other meanings in certain circles, but we never responded. As long as Gray and I were on it, though, *Grandview Park* had a cult following among gays who were home in the afternoon to watch it."

"What about your friends and the people you hooked up with? They obviously knew."

"Yes, but back then, gay culture was sharply delineated from the mainstream, not least because it denoted an illegal activity. Unless you were a professional informer or blackmailer, outing somebody else meant risking the same ostracism and arrest. Our friends knew, and we often recieved free drinks in gay bars for our on-air nerve, but everybody maintained discretion for mutual protection."

"Were there any gay employees on set?"

"Oh, sure. They knew, of course. Mag loved it so much that she took part in it. If anyone hinted at the truth in her presence, she hotly defended us, describing Gray and me as the butchest characters since Wyatt Earp, leaving them more than a little befuddled. Then she'd tell us about it. One time Winston Abrams, the network photographer, was taking publicity pictures with us. His gayness preceded him by a country mile, which allowed us to play around."

"Play around how?"

"We were dressed like a proper 1960s trio: Gray and I in suits, thin ties, and short hair. Mag had a blue satin gown with shoulder straps, pearls, and a bouffant. Wyn, at one point, seated Gray and me on stools, shoulder to shoulder. Mag stood behind us, leaning between our heads. Wyn framed us in a medium close-up, cutting Gray and me off just below our armpits. What nobody saw was that as we sat and smiled, Gray and I had our near hands in each other's laps."

We laughed. "I suppose there's no point asking if you have a copy of it."

"I wish I did, if only to illustrate the story. I never expected to be telling it this late in the game. It was one of *Grandview*'s more widely reproduced publicity pictures. You might well stumble over it in an old newspaper or magazine while doing your research." He sighed. "Mag was another one wasted on that show. She was feisty and smart and had tremendous allure. She'd have been great in the theater."

"She never performed on stage?"

"A few times, but she also preferred security. She was married to a dull little man named Harlow Baum, who owned a string of discount shoe stores in the city. They had a daughter, Deb. The stores didn't bring in much money, at least not enough to support the family in great comfort, so Mag stayed on *Grandview,* earning more than Harlow, which finally ruined their marriage. He started drinking and died of liver failure ten years after I left the show. Five years after that, Deb married and Mag retired. I was Mag's sounding board while her marriage fell apart and her confidante after Harlow died. We stayed in touch after I moved here. I'm sure if she'd lived, she'd be the one bringing me groceries."

"When did she die?"

"Two years ago."

"What about Grayson?"

"What about him?"

"How long were you together?"

"Until I left the show, although as I tried to make clear, 'together' is stretching things when describing our relationship."

"Why did you leave?"

"Ambition," he said. "The New York theatre proved too much of a temptation. When my character caught on, I negotiated a contract that allowed me time off for plays."

"Wasn't that taking on a lot?"

"Not for me," he said with faded pride. "I was able to compartmentalize. When I landed a part, they'd cut back my screen time for rehearsals. Rehearsing fixed the play's text in my memory. Of course, my roles were usually supporting parts with an infrequent second lead thrown in, which meant I had less to learn than the main actors. On the other hand, while the material for *Grandview* was always new, it was a lot less challenging, and we had cue cards. Once the play opened, I'd work on *Grandview* in the morning, perform it live in the early afternoon, forget what I'd just done, and head to the theater."

"Were these the roles you mentioned before?"

"They were the beginning. They strengthened my credentials as a serious actor, especially after I proved to directors, audiences, and myself that I could handle difficult material like Ionesco and Beckett. I was never an ace interpreter, but I acquitted myself well, and the critics largely agreed. The work also fed my ego. I imagined that after a slow start, I had, at last, embarked on the career I always wanted. This increased my resistance to TV. By the end of my fifth year on *Grandview,* I was rushing from studio to stage more often, so I decided to leave after my contract expired. For the next six or seven years, I worked almost exclusively in theater, in everything from Shakespeare to musicals, albeit again playing secondary or character roles."

"How did Grayson take your leaving the show?"

"I think my stretching out emphasized his rut. He had less fun at work without me and our game. Our personal lives also diverged. I spent more evenings performing, which meant he spent more evenings going out alone. After six months of listening to him complain that I'd become boring, I found a smaller, cruddier apartment and moved out."

"Did you ever see him again?"

"We ran into each other every so often, but since he lingered in his rut, we had little to talk about. We lost touch after I moved here. Nine years ago, Mag phoned to tell me he'd suffered a stroke. He died three months later."

"Did you love him?" I said.

"No. I liked him. He was bright and had a great sense of humor. But he was too content with his rut. I think that's why he was always searching for new bedmates. He didn't crave sex as much as he craved variety. As for me, a series of easy lays felt like another kind of rut. I needed the challenge that came from tackling different roles."

The contempt with which he pronounced the phrase 'easy lays' left me curious about the rest of his romantic life, while his readiness to open up eased my scruples about exploring the subject. I waited until he sipped his tea and replaced his mug on the table before posing my next question. "Were you ever in love?"

A thoughtful, somewhat troubled expression contracted his brow. "Yes," he said, "three times."

"Who with, if you don't mind my asking?"

"Not if you don't mind waiting until your next visit for an answer. It's getting late."

"Yeah, almost time to revisit your alma mater." He laughed and leaned on his cane, preparing to stand.

"Don't get up. I'll put these in the dishwasher. You get ready for *Grandview.*" I carted the mugs to the kitchen, picked up the deflated shopping bags, and walked back to the living room. He had swung the chair to face the television.

"See you in a few days," I said.

"Thanks for everything, Paul."

"No problem."

The hall, lobby, and even the street seemed unusually quiet after what I had just heard. Rather than drive home, the habit of chasing leads ingrained by my research steered me downtown to the Argonaut, a secondhand bookstore that also dealt in vintage sheet music, old magazines, and other ephemera. Hilda had mentioned it to me on my arrival as a potential resource for my work.

The Argonaut occupied the second floor of an old, converted factory, a sprawling, block-long building whose brick walls and tall, narrow windows betrayed its age, revealed by the large 1924 chiseled on the cornerstone just opposite the tiny lot where I parked.

Upstairs, a wooden door with a foggy glass panel covered in leaflets touting local theater groups, bands, book club meetings, and support groups opened onto a broad space traversed by long, high shelves, with other shelves pressed against the walls between the windows. Signs, handprinted on white cardboard tacked to the shelves, advertised their contents: history, mysteries, literature, biography, and so on. A glass case displaying first editions, topped by a computer and an old-fashioned brass cash register, stood to the left of the main door.

A guy around my age sat behind the counter, wearing jeans and a green tee shirt, with sprays of shining black hair and bright, attentive cerulean blue eyes at that moment trained on the computer. When the door closed behind me, he turned, smiled, and asked, "Can I help you?"

The smile, crinkling at the corners, momentarily obliterated my surroundings and my reason for being there. "I'm looking for magazines from the early to mid-sixties, with articles on current TV shows . . . current for the period, that is."

He nodded, ignoring my needless clarification, or so I hoped. "This way."

He emerged from behind the counter and started along the inner wall. I followed, entranced by the beautiful view of his beautiful buttocks shifting in his jeans, and enveloped in the trail of his cologne: a dense yet brisk scent that to me recalled a sunny autumn morning back east.

A doorway immediately after the last bookcase led to a smaller room containing two tables stacked with vintage sheet music in protective plastic sleeves, and shelves of boxes bearing the names of old magazines: *Life, Look, Time, McCall's, Collier's, The Saturday Evening Post,* with the dates of the issues inside, some reaching back to the late 1920s. If, according to Robert, the picture of him, Gray and Mag had been widely reproduced, it likely appeared in magazines such as these. I also wondered whether the older issues contained articles on Jacobson and his work, a possibility I held in reserve as an excuse to return.

The storekeeper ran his fingers along a shelf. "These are from the sixties," he said. "Are you looking for a particular show?"

"*Grandview Park,*" I said.

He looked over his shoulder at me, startled. "Seriously? My mom watched that when she was a kid. Are you doing a history of it or something?"

"Not really," I said. "I volunteer with *Heart and Hands.* They're . . ."

"I know them," he said, smiling more broadly. "They make deliveries to older gay people."

"One of their clients was on *Grandview Park.*"

"Cool. I'll have to tell my mom. Who did he play?"

"He didn't say. He was only on for five years, until 1966."

"She watched it then. She'd probably remember him. This might be a good place to start."

He slid a box labeled '*Look*: 1960–63' from a shelf, lowered it to an empty spot on the table nearest us, and removed the lid, revealing a stack of glossy magazines the size of placemats, a common dimension for magazines of that era. He handed me the top issue and, rather than return to his post at the front counter, picked up the second magazine and flipped its pages.

The first two issues yielded nothing. I placed mine on the table to one side and grabbed another from the box. A few seconds later, he dropped his magazine on the one I had discarded and began on another, setting the pattern for a shared search conducted in silence, disrupted on my side by a few furtive yet irresistible glances at the focused gaze he directed toward his magazines and the combination of firmness and gentility of the hands grasping the fragile paper.

Flipping through his eighth magazine, he paused and said, "Here's something." He handed me the issue, open at a page containing a column of print about the show.

"I'm looking for cast photos," I said. "I should've mentioned that before."

"No problem." He consigned the magazine to the discard pile and opened another. "I've thought about volunteering with *Heart and Hands*. What's it like?"

"Great," I said and enumerated the organization's virtues and rewards.

A minute later, he interrupted me. "What about this?" He showed me a group photo containing Robert as a young man, happily awaiting my reaction as if coveting my approval.

"That's good."

I directed him to set the magazine down beside the discard pile. We resumed hunting, laying every subsequent issue with a *Grandview Park* pho- to onto the second pile. An enticing musky scent gradually reached me through his cologne.

We had sorted through the *Look* box and reached halfway through one labeled *McCall's*: 1962–1966 when he turned the magazine in his hands around, saying, "Here's another one."

I instantly recognized the photo Robert described. A slightly awkward tilt to the two men's near shoulders indicated the secret positioning of their hands. "Great," I said, adding the issue to the purchase pile. "This'll be enough for now."

"Cool. I'll check you out." He returned the discarded *McCall's* to their box and carried the others to the front counter. "I'd like to hear more about *Heart and Hands*," he said as he calculated my total. "That's five bucks, even."

I opened my wallet. "I'll tell you about it whenever you want."

"The store closes at six. We could grab a coffee if that's not too soon."

Looking from my wallet into his waiting cerulean eyes felt like watching the jackpot symbols drop into place on a slot machine. "Not at all." I handed him my five dollars.

"Do you know the coffee shop on Eighth?"

"You mean Brewer's?"

He handed me my change. "Yeah. I'll meet you there at six-thirty."

"Great."

"I'm David, by the way."

"Paul," I said.

We shook hands.

"See you in a bit."

"See you."

"Do you want a bag?"

"No, I can manage."

I carried the magazines to my car and drove to my apartment, David's crinkly smile hovering in my imagination, more intriguing than the Cheshire cat's.

Back home, I left the magazines on my computer table, showered, shaved, spent a half hour at the bedroom mirror attempting to ameliorate my academic dishevelment, and at six-twenty approached Brewer's, an up-scale coffee shop with a bohemian ambiance anchoring a block in one of the city's trendiest areas. David, just reaching the main door, had undergone a change similar to mine.

"Hey," I said over his shoulder.

He turned. The blue eyes flashed, and the smile crinkled. "Hey," he said, "right on time."

"I'm a stickler for punctuality."

"Me too." He held the door open for me.

Two major factions comprised Brewer's crowd at that hour: white-collar workers desperate to replenish the energy lost during the day and newly-minted adults gathering steam prior to a night at the clubs.

"They're busier than I expected," David said. "I hope we can get a table."

"Something may open up. I'll keep an eye open."

We stood in line for five minutes when I spied a young couple with hair dyed chartreuse and pumpkin respectively preparing to vacate a table.

"Get me a medium dark roast and head for the window," I murmured and fled before he had a chance to answer.

The surrounding confusion and loud conversation enabled me to slip into one of the chairs at the table, its seat still warm from the previous occupant, before anyone else noticed its availability. Looking out the window, I watched chartreuse and pumpkin argue on the opposite corner and stalk off in different directions before David arrived with our coffees, a dozen sugar packets, cream in two little plastic cups, and two plastic stirrers.

"Good deal on the window seat," he said. "I didn't know if you wanted anything in your coffee, so I got the works."

"Just a little sugar," I said.

I opened a packet and sprinkled half into my cup. He mixed a full packet and a container of cream into his decaf hazelnut.

"What do I owe you?" I asked.

"Forget it."

We stirred our coffees and spent fifteen minutes exhausting the topic of *Heart and Hands* before the conversation lagged.

"I should thank you for helping me this afternoon," I said.

"No problem. I like treasure hunts. I know where everything is in that store, and can look anything else up on the computer. I didn't think any request could throw me, but you managed it."

"You shouldn't have spent so much time with me, not that I'm complaining."

"Why shouldn't I?"

"What if a customer came in and you weren't around?"

"I'd have heard if anybody came in."

"You still might have gotten in trouble with your boss."

He laughed. "Not likely. I practically own the Argonaut."

"Really?"

"Yep."

"Why practically?"

"My grandfather opened it seventy-five years ago. It's been in the family ever since. My dad owns it now. My sister isn't interested in books, at least selling them, so I'm set to take over when my dad retires. Ever since I started running it, he's been acting more retired anyway."

"Is that what you always wanted to do?"

He shrugged. "I never really knew what I wanted to do. Unlike a lot of people, I don't have a grand passion guiding me. I spent my whole life around the place, and it's like home. I also get to read a lot, which I like, and I meet interesting people."

"If you mean me, you may have to revise your opinion before the evening's over."

The cerulean eyes twinkled. "I doubt it. You're friends with an actor who was on my mom's favorite soap, and you're generous enough to spend your free time doing charity work. I learned that a few minutes after you walked in. I'm sure there's more."

"What would you like to know?"

"Do you have a grand passion, or are you just making a living, too?"

"You nearly guessed it before. I'm on a research grant for the next year."

"What are you researching?"

I repeated what I had told Robert, varying the story enough to prevent it from becoming stale. "The Harold books have been out of print for forty years. But there's been internet chatter calling for their reissue, which may return Jacobson to prominence, at least among fans of children's literature."

"And your work would ride the wave of their resurgence."

"I have a hard time imagining my work riding a wave."

"If you learn why he wrote the books, it'll be a standard reference."

"Maybe. Mainly it's a labor of love. If I contribute to Harold's rediscovery, even in a small way, I'll be satisfied."

"Nice," he said. "I don't envy you, though. You'll be buried in documents for months."

"That's one of the reasons I joined *Heart and Hands*. It guarantees me an hour or two of human contact each week."

"Good luck with both. And if you ever need the Argonaut for anything, let me know."

"I will. Thanks."

We covered the ensuing pause by sipping our coffees, after which he said, "So what about the Harold books appeal to you?"

Once more I regressed to the earnest Eldon applicant, even more so than with Robert since impressing David felt almost as consequential as impressing the decision makers at the foundation. I sipped my coffee again, marshaling my thoughts, set the cup down and said, "For one thing, they create a wonderful, freewheeling world for a child to inhabit. Secondly, Harold's a great character, probably best described as a benevolent trickster."

"What makes that the best description?"

"The way he solves problems," I said. "In *Harold Herring Meets Electra Eel,* the other fish tease Electra because she looks like a snake and generates electricity. She responds by hiding out in a little hole in the coral and flashing her charge to scare them off. Harold realizes she's unhappy and devises a number of schemes to lure her out and, at the same time, convince the other fish to accept her. One episode starts with Cindy Sardine looking for her little daughter, who's gotten lost . . ."

"Harold and Cindy don't sound Danish."

"The names were changed for the English editions. Jacobson was bilingual; otherwise, it would have been impossible for him to work here, as a scriptwriter or as an analyst. His publishers insisted he work with a translator, but everything indicates he translated the books alone, and the translator only proofread them."

"Okay. What about Cindy?"

"Her daughter's lost in an underwater ravine, and she approaches Harold and his school for help."

"His school?"

"He traveled with a school of herring who often figured in the plots. The dean was Professor Harding."

"Harding Herring," he said, his grin acquiring an ironic edge.

"They hear Cindy's daughter calling, but it's too dark in the ravine to see her. Harold swims to Electra's den, but since he knows she'd never respond to a plea for assistance, he begins teasing her. When she sticks her head out, he flicks sand in her face with his tail. She chases him, flashing angrily, followed by the school. Harold dives into the ravine, Electra illuminates the spot where Cindy's baby is, and Harold's school friends escort her to safety. Cindy expresses her gratitude to Electra, and she begins wondering if perhaps she might serve a purpose other than to attract scorn. The book climaxes with Harold and Electra foiling a shipload of pirates, but it's too long to go into."

David blinked, replied with a simple, noncommittal "Cute," and sipped his coffee.

I scrambled to repair the damage, only to clutch at commonplaces. "Jacobson writes it better than I can tell it. And for a six-year-old, it's magic."

"What did your dad think about your attachment to Harold?"

"Nothing. His grand passion was to be a cowboy. When I was five he decamped to Montana. My mom had a good job in a real estate office and didn't want to follow him."

"Where did you live?"

"Pennsylvania," I said. "My mom thought he was crazy, but he was adamant and swore he'd convince her to move out there after he became established. The next winter, he was killed in a snowmobile accident."

"I'm sorry," he said and stopped, again at a loss.

"It's strange, I know. I have a hard time believing I missed much with him not around."

"It's good you're not bitter."

"I was when I was a kid. Later, like I said, I wondered if his leaving wasn't a good thing. Can you imagine being raised by a frustrated cowboy? What about your family?"

"My parents are still alive, still married, and live upstate. I was born too late to know my grandparents, though. I'd have loved to meet the one who founded the store."

"How late were you born?"

"My parents had me in their forties. They're in their early seventies now. My sister, Marge, is forty-six. She's married to Brad. He's a pediatrician. They have two kids, Mark and Adrian."

"Does Marge work?"

"She had a catering business before she got married. Brad being a doctor, she was able to retire to raise the kids, but she's talked about going back to it when they're a little older."

"I can tell by the way you talk about them you get along well."

"One of the benefits of a late birth is you're everyone's baby. Marge was nearly an adult when I came along. She was more like an apprentice mother than a sibling."

"You're spoiled, then."

"A little, I suppose. There wasn't any drama when I came out to them at sixteen. And I'm always at Marge and Brad's place on Lake Barrow."

"Where's that?"

"Four hours northeast of here," he said. "They have me up all the time. Of course, I'm a free babysitter. But Mark and Adrian are great, so I don't mind."

"And you eat well with a professional chef in the house."

The crinkly smile peeped over the edge of his coffee cup. "Absolutely."

"Sounds like you have a good life even without a grand passion."

"I think so. Do you have any siblings?"

"No. My mom dated for a while after my dad died but never seriously. Her mom lived about an hour away. We went there every Sunday for dinner until she died, when I was thirteen."

"What about your mother's father?"

"He died when I was two. My mom has a sister with kids, but they were in New Jersey, and we didn't see them as often. My dad has a brother with kids in Idaho. So in terms of family, growing up it was just my mother, my grandmother, and me."

"You must've been lonely."

"I had a few school friends and my reading. What do you like to read in your downtime?"

He opened his mouth, only rather than his answer I heard a woman at the table behind me say, "It's seven-thirty. We'd better leave if we want to get there in time."

"I should get going," I said.

"Why?"

Chairs scraped the floor as the group behind me stood.

"It's late, and I'm starving."

"They have great sandwiches here," he said.

The menu, written in different colored chalk in fancy script on a black-board behind the main counter, listed cold deli sandwiches, bagels, fruit cups, and the like.

"I had a sandwich for lunch," I said. "That's why I'm starving."

"There's a great Italian restaurant on the next block."

I offered an insincere show of hesitation before allowing our casual meeting to become a dinner date.

The Palazzo restaurant had a windowless dining room lit by dim recessed bulbs in the ceiling and votive candles on the tables. A slender, skeletal host installed us at a side table close to the bathrooms, and a chatty redheaded waitress sold us on the day's special, linguini with Portobello mushrooms. We resumed the question of reading habits, and on learning that we shared several favorite books, we began comparing tastes in general. He liked hot, spicy food, swimming and hiking, a spectrum of musical styles, and mornings. I preferred mild food, solitary study, and classical music, and required at least two cups of black coffee on waking before my brain began firing on all neurons. We both avoided red meat, superficial socializing in bars and clubs, drank little alcohol, had minimal interest in movies and TV, and actively resisted the addictive properties of social media.

The dining room thinned to five occupied tables—overhung with faces aflutter in the light of guttering votive candles—by the time our espressos and zabagliones arrived, which we consumed in the ease of our newly struck balance of similarities and differences.

Outside, before heading for his car, he said, "I know it's customary to wait a day or two and phone, but I hate suspense. I had a great time tonight. I'd like to see you again."

"Just what I was thinking," I said.

"Great. I'm going to my sister's for the weekend. How about Monday night?"

"Six-thirty at Brewer's?"

"I'll see you then."

"See you."

We shook hands and parted on the sidewalk.

Lying in bed, recalling what Robert said about the restrictions imposed on gay men the past, increased my gratitude for the natural, spontaneous progress of David's and my flirtation.

Reviewing its highlights soon lulled me to sleep.

2.

Monday morning at ten-thirty, I entered the archive drenched in sweat. "Hi, Paul," Hilda said, walking past with an armful of faded file folders, "getting hot out yet?"

"My car thermometer says ninety-one."

She nodded grimly. "They said it'll be bad for the next few days. Luckily, you have a nice, air conditioned warehouse to lounge around in."

"If you call sitting on a hard-backed chair, bent over a cardboard box lounging," I said.

"It's better than being outside."

"True."

She smiled, bid me "Happy hunting," and marched away with her files.

The conditioned air shielding me from the heat outside also eased the frustration of sifting through the memos and letters comprising the first third of Oliver Castle's box four. None so much as mentioned Jacobson, yet, they vividly demonstrated the extent to which costs and delays obsessed the average film producer, which with the near-hysterical tone pervading some likely explained Castle's resorting to psychoanalysis, a minor, if telling detail that barely compensated for two and a half hours' steady reading.

Robert forwarded his grocery list to me at eleven-thirty, releasing me from the drudgery. I ran into Hilda again on my way out.

"Any luck, Paul?"

"Not really," I said.

"I don't want to discourage you, but you're going to have more of those days than not."

"Am I the millionth frustrated scholar you've had to placate?"

"My supervisors advised me not to keep count. And the frustration's usually temporary; lengthy sometimes, but temporary."

"It's my own fault for dreaming up this project in the first place. See you tomorrow."

"More deliveries today?"

"Yeah."

"Keep hydrated."

"I will."

Walking from the archive to my car, and afterward across the parking lot to the market and back felt like a jaunt through Death Valley, an impression not shared by the local population from what I observed of them through the sweat veiling my eyes. The copy of *Look* lay on the back seat of my car; after settling the bags, I removed Robert's Hearth Fire from the top of one, opened the magazine to his trio photo, and tucked it between his vanilla biscuits and bran flakes, for easier transport and a more dramatic reveal, the drama an innocuous conceit even more excusable, I decided, after my unproductive morning in Oliver Castle's company.

Robert opened his door wearing brown corduroy pants, a blue flannel shirt, and the blue cardigan he wore on my first visit.

"Aren't you warm in those clothes?" I asked.

"It's the blood thinners," he said. "They thin the blood and freeze the soul. That's why the only cold foods I eat are salads, yogurt, and cereal."

He followed me to the kitchen and sat at the table. "Mind if I watch you put the groceries away again? You're the only company I get, except for infrequent appearances by building maintenance. I'd like to make the best of it."

"What about friends?" I placed his Hearth Fire in the bread box.

"Those left to me are in conditions similar to mine, which limits us to phone calls. The research go well today?"

"This was one of my least informative sessions." I rested his prunes and papayas on the counter. "On the brighter side, I have a surprise for you."

"Are you sure that's the brighter side? The older I get, the more sinister the word 'surprise' becomes."

"I'll take my chances." I withdrew *Look* and, with a magician's flourish, handed it over.

Robert grabbed the magazine, goggling at the picture, and leaned back, racked by a deep belly laugh. "Where did you get this?"

"The Argonaut Bookstore downtown," I said, sliding his Velma's biscuits, bran flakes, and a fresh box of Snapdragon unsalted crackers onto the shelf in their appointed cupboard.

"Is that still in business? I used to haunt the Argonaut when I first moved here."

"I have it on good authority that it's been around for seventy-five years."

He traced the bottom edge of the photo with his forefinger. "See where we were cut off so people wouldn't suspect where our hands were? We called it our crotch-crop." The finger drifted to the female face, and his amusement softened to fondness. "Dear Mag . . ."

I lined his Gunter's shakes beside the Snapdragons. "You told me you wished you had a copy. It's yours if you want it."

"The picture's only good to illustrate the story behind it. I don't have anybody to tell it to. You keep it. I'm sure you've plenty of friends who'd get a laugh out of it. And you can assure them you had it from the horse's mouth."

I stood his Shale House ginger ale and a can of Snowdrift shaving cream on the counter beside the prunes and folded the bag. "I found a few other magazines with shots of you from *Grandview Park* if you'd care to see them."

He stared pensively at the one in his hands. "I'll consider it. But you shouldn't have gone to the expense. Let me reimburse you."

"Are you kidding? The whole stack cost five bucks. And finding them may prove more fortunate for me than for you."

"Why?"

"I got a date with the clerk." I placed his salad ingredients in the refrigerator.

"In my day, stores only gave trading stamps with their merchandise," he said. "What's he like?"

I described the cerulean eyes, tumbling black hair, and the high points of our conversation.

"Sounds delectable," Robert said.

"He is, so far. I'm supposed to see him again tonight."

"Why the uncertainty?"

I placed a package of chicken cutlets in the refrigerator. "There's no guarantee he'll show up. You know how it is. You find someone a good prospect at first, and then you think better of it. There's also a possibility that even if he does show up, we won't seem as interesting to each other as we did Friday night."

"Those are the chances you take when you try to connect with someone. I'd say while it may not be a dead certainty, there's every reason to expect you'll find your dreamboat waiting at the coffee shop with your mutual attraction intact. And though it's a trite enough palliative, if he does stand you up, it's a clear sign of poor taste on his part."

"I'll keep it in mind." I began stacking his Bub's Tubs beside the chicken cutlets.

"And the next time you're here, you can tell me whether your chemistry combusted or fizzled . . . as much as you're comfortable telling, of course."

"Deal," I said.

I set a new Bountiful Bog cranberry juice and Shell Stream almond milk—whose logo depicting an open almond shell pouring a river of milk into a tumbler I found oddly erotic—on the bottom shelf of the refrigerator. He watched me and chuckled.

"The first flush of romance is always appealing, even to a flinty old coot like me."

"It's a little too soon to refer to this as a romance."

"Apologies," he said, still amused.

I closed the refrigerator door and faced him. "Maybe you're less flinty than you pretend."

"I hope not. I've never broken character in my life."

"Speaking of romance," I said, folding the empty bag, "you promised to tell me about the three times you were in love."

"You really want to hear about that?"

"As much as you're comfortable telling," I said.

"I didn't bore you enough on Friday?"

"If you hadn't, I wouldn't have met David. Who knows what fringe benefits might attach to another anecdote?"

"Okay," he said. "Shall we have tea again?"

"Hot tea on a day like this?"

"Then I'll have tea. You know where the other beverages are, and I'm sure you noticed the ice cubes in the freezer, though I rarely use them."

He hobbled into the living room. I brewed the tea, poured a tumbler of ginger ale with ice, carried the tea to the table by his recliner, and assumed a seat on the couch, my ginger ale on the coffee table.

"So what sort of guys softened the heart of the flinty young coot you must have been?"

He grinned and nestled into the chair. "To grasp that, you have to understand who I was back then, particularly in high school. That's when I first fell in love."

"You had a high school sweetheart? This is juicier than I imagined."

"I don't know about juicy, but it'll be honest." He sipped his tea. "I was born and raised in Braintree, a town just outside Boston. My proximity to a culturally rich city is important for understanding who I was, and mostly still am."

"What makes that important?"

"Because I grew up at a time when the arts were still considered part of being an educated adult."

"Haven't they always been?"

"No," he said, "and certainly not now. There are two approaches to learning, at least in the Western world. The first is embodied by what's known as the 'Renaissance Man' since it was most clearly enumerated in Renaissance treatises like Castiglione's *Book of the Courtier*."

"An individual who cultivates several different abilities and fields of knowledge," I said.

"Including the arts," he said. "The emphasis on variety in Renaissance Man, for me, reflects the various capabilities of the brain since the brain is, of course, the organ from which we derive our knowledge and talents."

"What's the second view?"

"The second coalesced in response to rational Enlightenment views of the world as a vast mechanism or machine comprised of individual parts performing specific functions. This bore its fruit in the Industrial Revolution with a strict division of labor, and philosophies like Utilitarianism and Pragmatism that cast human civilization in mechanical terms, reducing individuals to creatures whose purpose is, first and foremost, to perform a narrow function within the whole. From the perspective of both philosophy and actual work practices, Utilitarian Man is only expected to learn what he or she needs to know to perform their assigned function day after day, year after year."

"Discouraging whatever other capabilities their brain might possess."

"The opposite of the Renaissance approach," he said. "Of course, the two views weren't born whole in the historical periods associated with them; they merely received their definite expression then. Two millennia before the Renaissance, Plato's *Republic* laid out a society in which the majority of inhabitants are Utilitarian functionaries, ruled by a minority of philosopher-kings possessed of a Renaissance scope of knowledge."

"And even during the actual Renaissance the ideal was limited to an elite, for whom it served as a sign of superiority and a claim to social status."

"Which is how I inherited it," he said.

"I don't follow."

"The Renaissance approach remained the template for elite education even after the Industrial Revolution. When the middle classes began their ascendancy in the eighteenth and nineteenth centuries, they adopted many of the elite's signs of power, including culture. The printing press made literature more widely available, and museums and theater became public spaces, catering to a middle-class clientele. They embraced a similar attitude to education. Think of the basic public school curriculum that lasted into the twentieth century, with alternating lessons in math, reading and writing, science and history. The variety of subjects considered essential for a general education encourages students to exercise various capabilities of their brains, as with Renaissance Man. And, as with Renaissance Man, the arts were a part of the basic curriculum."

"Not uniformly," I said.

"Oh, of course not," he said. "But for most in that class in those periods, they were esteemed among the other human accomplishments covered by the term civilization."

"The attitude you inherited."

"Yes. My parents were of the educated middle-class, and the arts permeated their lives. Books were always near to hand: on their night stands, on the coffee table, and in a bookcase that took up almost the entire north wall of the parlor. Mine's a pale shadow of theirs," he said, gesturing toward the shelves behind him. "They also had an extensive record collection: classical pieces; Gilbert and Sullivan and Victor Herbert tunes that had been popular in their childhoods; and more recent ones by Gershwin and Kern and Irving Berlin. They also listened to the symphony and Metropolitan Opera, both of which were broadcast on network radio then, and regularly attended plays and concerts. In the mornings, I'd find programs from their previous night's event and study them, wondering what it'd been like. And I'd listen, or eavesdrop, on them discussing music, plays, and books, between themselves and with their friends."

"Who were their friends?"

"Oh, a doctor named Truex and his wife Edith, a man named Oswald—our local bank manager—and his wife Judith, Mr. Mullins, the local librarian, and Doug and May Crenshaw, who ran the town's premiere hotel.

Sometimes they'd get together to make up what was called a theater party. Boston was a tryout city then. Do you know what that is?"

"Producers tried out shows in two or three cities before premiering them in New York. It allowed them to polish the rough spots."

"Correct. Things have changed so drastically in my lifetime that I'm no longer sure what's common knowledge and what's esoteric, though with your education, I'm sure the esoteric is commonplace to you."

"A little more than for most people, maybe," I said.

"Anyway, as I said, the arts being a fundamental element of human civilization for those of my parents' era and station, they also figured in their children's education. When I started school, we learned to read with primers like the *Dick and Jane* books, which told simple stories that combined the study of written language with the art of fiction. Later, we studied stories by Mark Twain and O. Henry, and memorized poems like Longfellow's "Evangeline" and excerpts from Shakespeare. We had music classes and a drama club in high school. Respect for culture was also apparent in the number of outlets around then."

"What sort of outlets?"

"Theater was very common, and not just for those lucky enough to live near a city like Boston. The big Broadway hits sent road companies around the country, and smaller communities had semi-professional and amateur theater groups. Mainstream magazines regularly printed short stories by serious writers, and public libraries offered free access to books. Along with the symphony and opera, network radio presented adaptations of important plays, from classics to recent hits, and this at a time when we had only a handful of stations to choose from. I recall in the late 1940s hearing an hour-long version of Noel Coward's *Blithe Spirit* with members of the Broadway cast. Articles about literature, theater, and music were also standard for most magazines and newspapers."

"You were practically destined to become an aesthete, then."

"I suppose. At first, I just followed the example my parents set. I read because I saw them reading and listened to music because they did. The pleasure it gave me made it a habit. There was nothing better than sitting on our back porch on a summer day, lost in a novel; lying on the living room floor after a good dinner, listening to a play on the radio; or being immersed in a Tchaikovsky concerto on a snowy winter afternoon. When I was old enough, they started taking me to shows in Boston, and I devoured every article I saw about books, music, and theatre. Gradually, I developed my own tastes from what I found in our house and what I discovered on the radio and in the library."

"Did they depart much from your parents'?"

"Sometimes," he said, "particularly in music. I adored jazz, which was at the cutting edge of pop music when I was growing up. My parents despised it."

"All music from that era sounds the same to me."

He smiled wearily. "Amazing how everything converges in perspective. Jazz musicians in those days relied heavily on songs by Gershwin and Kern, and other popular composers. My parents preferred the original, straightforward versions, and felt jazz desecrated the composers' intentions. I liked the originals, too, yet hearing them enabled me to appreciate the variants and improvisations jazz musicians grafted onto them, first the swing bands and then the bop groups and singers who emerged after the war. They were staples on radio, broadcasting live from nightclubs and ballrooms, usually late into the evening. I'd stay up past midnight, listening and doing homework."

"What about other aspects of pop culture, like movies?"

"I enjoyed the movies, and some of the comedies and dramas on radio were well written. But I never took them seriously. The best were amusements. The worst existed only to prevent theater screens from going dark or radio stations from falling silent."

"I know what you mean."

"So between my parents, what I was exposed to in school, and what I discovered on my own, the arts expanded from an important presence in life to my primary interest."

"Some people who grow up with the arts rebel against them."

"Only because devaluing what your parents hold dear is a knee-jerk reaction for most kids," he said.

"What made it different for you?"

"The pleasure it gave me was too intense, too ingrained in my daily existence to renounce it, even in the cause of generational independence. Much later, I realized that pleasure derived from the content and nature of the various art forms, both of which are rooted in brain function."

"Isn't it rather obvious that art is a product of the brain?"

"So obvious it prevents most people from seriously considering the implications," he said.

"When did you start considering them?"

"When I read George Bernard Shaw's essay "The Sanity of Art" in college. There, he claims that culture 'heightens the senses and ennobles the faculties,' by which he meant the physical senses and intellectual faculties. Unfortunately, dividing the senses from the faculties in that way prevented Shaw from exploring how art plays into the connection between the two; or perhaps there was too little work done in cognitive science at that time for him to be fully aware of the connection. Only after decades of reading did I appreciate art's heightening and ennobling powers as I experienced them in childhood."

"How did you experience them?"

"I'm sure you know the basics. Our brains collect information via the five senses that we organize into an interior image of the outside world. Contemplating this interior image leads us to abstract ideas or concepts that are applicable to the outside world—numbers, words, shapes, logical propositions, and such. This enables us to do everything from raising plants to building rockets. The nature and content of the arts also result from, as well as mirror, this ability."

"How?"

"As a child, I was only aware of the end point of the process, playing with the images and ideas in my head without considering how they'd gotten there. So what first attracted me to the arts were its contents, the thoughts, and impressions embodied in various media that, as Shaw said, help acculturated individuals develop and ennoble their intellectual faculties."

"The content of art replicated your interior images of the outside world."

"Simply put, yes. Visual art portrayed the shapes, colors, lights, and shadows of faces, landscapes, and abstract designs. Music distilled joy, desire, rumination, fury, fear, and other states into sounds. Actors embodied traits I observed in the people around me: the joviality of Mr. Blake, for instance, who ran our local hardware store, or the doleful didacticism of our math teacher Mrs. Wren. Books, plays, and films depicted places, events, ideas, and emotions, along with their characters' shifting identities and destinies. The allure of artworks in childhood came from recognizing fragments of my everyday experience in them. Later, I realized these reflections illustrated what it meant to exist in a given time or place, along with those human qualities that transcend time and place. For a boy whose brain was still developing and just beginning to speculate about life and his place in it, the cumulative image of the outside world I found in the arts was a crucial resource for pondering the human condition and coming to terms with it."

"What about the nature of the arts?"

"Their nature elaborates on or extends the senses we use to gather information, which was what Shaw meant when he talked about art heightening our senses. Visual art corresponds to vision, stimulating the parts of the brain associated with visual perception. Music correlates to hearing and is structured on mathematics; even more, a study I read about not long ago showed that listening to music stimulates the brain as a whole, not just areas associated with hearing or math. Dance combines music with signals the brain sends the body to coordinate movement. Writing stems from our capacity for language, which to me makes it the most important and all-encompassing of the arts."

"Why?"

"Our brains have the unique ability to associate words with everything—or nearly everything—it perceives, including itself. Good writers utilize words to describe as much of the experienced world as possible, which in turn calls upon readers to actively draw on their past perceptions to interpret the writer's words. If a writer describes a rainy day, the words recall all the rainy days the reader has experienced. If a writer writes about love, anger, or any other emotions, the reader recalls their experiences with them. A writer discussing abstractions like geometric shapes or logical problems calls upon the reader's capacity for abstract, logical thought. By referencing the range of our experiences, written words exercise our brain's power to reflect on them and, by extension, itself. They unite physical and intellectual perceptions, allowing them to heighten our senses and ennoble our faculties at the same time, all of which lends literature a richness that the other arts lack."

"I see."

"Moreover, literature and drama, being primarily narratives, also encourage us to arrange our perceptions in temporal sequences."

"Temporal sequences?" I said, caught off guard by the phrase, something I later learned to expect from Robert.

"Cause and effect sequences playing out in time, the perception of which is key to the functioning of our intellectual faculties. Farming techniques and plans for a rocket go from point A to B to C and so on because both are narratives elaborated by brains able to transform sensory data into connected temporal sequences."

"And since narrative arts like theater and novels chart the effects of events that occur and actions taken by different characters, they help us think temporally."

"Yes, although every artwork encourages some degree of temporal thinking since all represent an artist's actions taken in time."

"How do you mean?"

"Paragraphs of prose, stanzas of poetry, arrangements of notes and instruments in music, the lines, shapes, and colors on canvas or in sculptures, all result from various temporal processes. Appreciating art, in part, means appreciating the cumulative effect of those innumerable individual acts, which in turn means tracing their consequences one upon another: how an adjective alters the meaning of a noun, how the familiar notes of the scale recombine into unique melodies, how a specific placement of lines and shapes and colors creates a distinct impression."

"What about works created spontaneously," I said, "like painters splashing paint haphazardly on a canvas? And Tristan Tzara once created a poem by pulling words on slips of paper from a hat."

"Spontaneous isn't the same as instantaneous," he said. "A spontaneously created artwork is still the outcome of events leading to its existence, and on completion relies for its effect on the interplay of its components. Ultimately, since the brain is the organ with which we perceive ourselves and the world around us, exercising or stimulating it, in part or in its entirety, enhances our experience of being. As Shaw and many other people believed, the arts are an essential resource for that stimulation."

"An intriguing theory," I said.

"I'm sure it's more than theory, though I'm not qualified to flesh it out the way a neuroscientist or a philosopher might. But it's certain the arts developed in tandem with our species, or maybe our species developed in tandem with its arts. Cave paintings and musical instruments predate farming in the archaeological record, and historians use the arts as a yardstick to mark the development of civilizations. When I recall how theatre, novels, poems, pictures, and music affected me in my youth, their power to stimulate thought seems self-evident. All, in their unique ways, encouraged me to view things and people, ideas and emotions from new and often unsuspected angles because they coaxed my brain into working in unaccustomed ways. And, by refreshing my perceptions, heightening my senses, and ennobling my faculties, they supplied a pleasure obtainable from nothing else I ever encountered."

"Leading to your choice of profession," I said.

"Indeed."

"Why acting rather than painting or music?"

"Though all the arts appealed to me, my strongest affinities were for literature and drama. I loved following the vicissitudes of characters and events in novels and plays. Then it became more. I imagined entering the story, interacting with the characters, improvising dialogue, and influencing events. That's the difference between an art lover and an artist. One contemplates finished works. The other feels compelled to participate in the process of creation. When I was thirteen, I arrived at the inescapable conclusion that nothing would make me happier than bringing my fantasies to life, and I decided to become an actor."

"How did your parents react?"

"I never told them."

"Why not?"

"Despite the value accorded the arts, the difference between appreciating art and being an artist translated into a fairly strict social divide, at least for the educated middle-class. Perhaps the profession was too uncertain, its remuneration too elusive to earn respect, or creativity too mysterious to earn trust. Whatever the reason, the same people for whom culture was an essential element in civilization regarded artists as beings apart. Parents discouraged their offspring from pursuing art as a career. Listening to my folks and their friends talk, I became aware of this divide early on, but the allure of acting was too strong not to risk their displeasure. I read every play on their shelves and in our local library, listened to them on radio, and pestered my parents for tickets to every show that played in Boston. When I turned fifteen, they allowed me to take the train to the city alone on Saturdays. I'd spend the day shopping for books and records, attend a concert or play, and a movie too if I had time."

"If you couldn't tell your parents, was there anyone else with whom you could share your passion?"

"No, though you're anticipating the point of this extensive back story."

"You said your school had a drama club. Did you participate in it?"

"Sure. But the appeal for them was the fleeting thrill of playacting, of extending a childhood amusement beyond its proper time, which was probably why the club was tolerated."

"I don't know what you mean."

"The same social division between art and artists held true in school. We studied the arts as an essential human accomplishment rather than a potential career choice. Nobody expected learning to write compositions would make anyone want to become a professional writer, and nobody considered the drama club a training ground for future theater professionals. Lacking the standards imposed by a serious ambition, our drama club gravitated to popular fare, the light comedies, and sentimental dramas popular at the time rather than the material that interested me. So, finding myself at some distance from my peers in general and from those who supposedly shared my interest in theater, I drifted into a solitude sustained by the culture I admired and the dreams I wove around being an actor."

"You must have been lonely."

"I was, but it prepared me for the even wider division between me and other people that opened up after I hit puberty."

"What was that like? I mean, when did you realize you were gay, and how did you come to terms with it?"

"As far as realizing it, prior to the upheaval of puberty, my ideas of love between adults were, for better and worse, derived from the chastely romantic images in films and plays and from observing my parents, who were careful about the extent of the physical affection they allowed me to witness between them. The rush of hormones I experienced hinted at another side to all that, a hint that became definite knowledge thanks to a medical book my parents kept on the top shelf of their bookcase."

"You hadn't read it before?"

"When I was about eight, I opened it up to see what it was, but rather than another exciting story, I found only a dull reference book for home use, so I ignored it. My more technical interest in the human body at thirteen drove me back to it. A section outlining the mechanics of sex revealed the goal for which everything in the movies and plays served as preliminaries, after which I began supplementing those images of romantic love with baldly erotic fantasies of a man and a woman copulating."

"How did you go from that to recognizing your sexuality?"

"Once I understood how people acted on their desires, I applied mine to those around me. Instead of an anonymous couple, I cast real people in the fantasies playing in my private mental theater, mostly schoolmates but anyone in town I found attractive. This led to another inescapable conclusion: for me, only the faces and shapes of men exerted the erotic and romantic appeal on which adult relationships were based. I recall feeling this with some intensity when I came across an old World War II issue of *Life* magazine containing photos of shirtless soldiers in the South Seas. Then, of course, there were the glamorized images of leading men in the movies."

"How did you react? It had to have been more than just following an inclination, like with becoming an actor."

"Absolutely," he said, "thanks to the dearth of practical information. My parents' medical guide mentioned homosexuality only in passing and only to list it as one among several abnormalities. Yet I couldn't deny it any more than my desire to act, so though it was much harder than settling on a profession, I just had to accept it."

"You said you derived your ideas about romantic love from movies. What about books?"

"Those in my parents' library tended to treat the intellectual and moral issues of love affairs. They were too subtle and too complex to be interesting or, perhaps I should say, arousing for a thirteen-year-old."

"Some mainstream novels and pulps at that time featured gay characters. Did you ever encounter any of those?"

"Yes, though certainly not on my parents' shelves. On my trips to Boston, I'd spot the paperback potboilers in the train station and in shops. They sensationalized the subject, with covers depicting exaggerated stereotypes of gay men and copy promising readers a deep dive into a netherworld of people only barely human. I had to summon all my courage to take one from the rack and flip through it, and then only when I was sure nobody was looking. Buying one would have been a waste of money."

"Why?"

"I couldn't risk bringing it into the house. The best I could do would've been to read as much as possible on the train and get rid of it. And from what I read on the sly in the shops, their content wouldn't have been reassuring. They generally presented being gay as a social issue or psychological problem, embodied by grotesque or tragic characters. The mainstream novels took a similar tack, albeit without the hysterical tone of exploitation. A few articles or stories touching on homosexuality appeared in magazines or the newspapers, and on a few rare occasions I overheard my parents talk about it with their friends."

"How'd they react?"

"With everything from subdued revulsion to pity, yet always with the belief that it was a social issue requiring control, like juvenile delinquency and mental illness. But, whether a social or a medical issue, an even stricter divide existed between gays and straights than between artists and other people."

"There was some conflation between artists and homosexuality, too, back then," I said. "Wasn't 'artistic' a common synonym for being gay?"

"Yes, which gave me another reason to be circumspect with my parents, not only about my erotic longings but about my wish to be an actor. Now that I think of it, as a teenager I read only two works with gay themes."

"What were they?"

"First was Noel Coward's play *Design for Living.* It chronicled a three-sided relationship between two men and a woman with hints of sex between the men. Luckily, it was sandwiched within a larger collection of his plays I found in our local library, so I could read it without suspicion."

"Were any of the mainstream novels with gay characters in your library?"

"I don't know. If I was too anxious to flip through one in the anonymity of a Boston bookstore, there was no way I was going to risk reading even the spine of one nearer home."

"What was the second work you read, then, and how did you get hold of it?"

"Coming home on the train after attending a production of *Hamlet,* I found a copy of Gore Vidal's *The City and the Pillar* wedged between two seats. This had come out the previous year and provoked considerable scandal. I paged though it on the ride and smuggled it into the house under my coat. However, both were problematical as guides for a middle-class teenager seeking validation for his identity. Coward's play is a fantasy of the upper classes while Vidal's protagonist murdered the object of his affection."

"What happened to your copy of the Vidal?"

"I got rid of it as soon as I finished it, which was how it probably ended up on the train in the first place. So while there was some information floating around to assure me other men felt as I did and acted on their desires, the consensus cast a shadow over being gay that didn't jibe with the thrill I experienced."

"Akin to the thrill you got from art?"

"Except for one being primarily intellectual and the other primarily physical," he said.

"What do you mean by 'primarily?'"

"Since art forms originate with the physical senses, art can't help being a little sensuous. And while my sexual cravings emerged from a physical need, they were also the starting point for a greater desire to love and be loved, something that has more to do with a meeting of the minds than a collision of bodies. To have even a chance of fulfilling my desire for love, I had to step from under the shadow and accept that I wanted romantic relationships with men alone. Even if I couldn't admit it to anyone else at that moment in my life, I had to be honest with myself, then wait for a chance to seek out the others I knew were out there. Until then, I ogled every attractive male in sight and crafted lengthy erotic productions for them in my imaginary theater."

He sighed and sipped his tea. "There you have a portrait of the actor as a young man, or at any rate as a high-schooler: isolated from others by his attraction to art and his own sex, living life in the seclusion of his imagination. Then Terry Vaughan arrived."

He stopped, leaned his head back, and closed his eyes long enough to worry me. "Robert? Are you okay?"

He spoke in a low, dreamy voice, eyes still closed. "I'm just wondering how in hell I describe Terry to you. I mean for you to really understand."

"Start at the beginning. When did you meet him?"

"The first day of junior year," he said. "I'd spent the summer like the previous two, reading, going to movies, riding the train to Boston, and working a part-time job stacking shelves in the drugstore for our pharmacist, Mr. Carrion."

"Carrion, did you say?"

"I did, and he looked it. His son was a doll, though. He helmed the store's soda fountain." He opened his eyes and turned to me. "You may or may not know drugstores back then were a combination pharmacy and diner."

"I came across photos of some while doing background research on 1930s L.A. They could be pretty fancy, with marble counters and chrome fixtures."

"Ours was plainer but still nice."

"And the counter person wore a white smock or apron and a little paper hat," I said.

"Like the pharmacist, except for the hat," he said. "I spent many a pleasant hour admiring Carrion Jr. in his. When summer ended, I anticipated another dull year trudging down the same plain hallways, sitting in the same plain classrooms, covertly eyeing my less plain male classmates. Walking into English class that first day I was met with a stunning young man sprawled at a desk in the front row. He had short, wavy black hair; an oval face with a hairless chin; round cheekbones that softened rather than sharpened his features; small red lips, and intelligent brown eyes with lids that hung halfway down as if he were half asleep. I'd been admiring male beauty for a while by then, but nothing prepared me for Terry. Are you familiar with Coleridge's poetry?"

"Only the *Ancient Mariner* and *Kubla Khan*."

"There's a short poem of his, an ode portraying Cupid as a tiny creature similar to the fairies of Celtic lore. He imagines capturing the fairy Cupid, dropping him in a goblet of dew, and drinking him down. The final two lines are:

And sure I feel my angry Guest
Flutt'ring his Wings within my breast.

The moment I laid eyes on Terry, I felt the same wings fluttering. I'd never experienced anything like it. At first, I considered it a consequence of a purely physical attraction. I assumed that, as with every other cute guy, I'd spend a few hours imagining him in various sexual scenarios before turning my attention to another."

"Is that what you did with Carrion Jr.?"

"And with passengers on the train, customers in the drugstore, audience members in the theater, the actors onstage, members of the track and baseball team . . ."

"When did you realize it was different with Terry?"

"Soon enough," he said. "The seating assignments landed me beside him, which allowed me to study how he looked in almost every position and every mood, enhancing the details of the sexual scenarios I cast him in when I was alone. Gradually I expanded my scenarios to fantasies of everyday life, illustrating the more comprehensive intimacy I imagined possible with love."

"Such as what?"

"Walking around town with him, eating at the drugstore with him, or going to the movies with him," he said. "They all became objects of a desire as intense as the one to touch him. Happily, I at least had his presence five days a week in English class."

"Did you get closer to the comprehensive intimacy you imagined?"

He nodded slowly. "Three months after school started, I went to the public library to return a book by George Jean Nathan."

"Who?"

"He was a famous theatre critic. I'd seen a repertory revival of Thornton Wilder's *Our Town* in Boston the previous August and wanted to borrow more of Wilder's work. The library had long oak reading tables, and as I neared the theater section, I spotted Terry at one, his gorgeous face bent over a volume of Eugene O'Neill."

"How did you know he was reading O'Neill?"

"I recognized the book. I'd borrowed it not long before."

"I see."

"The possibility of a mutual interest establishing an actual relationship between us hit me harder than the soldiers' pictures in *Life*. The wings fluttered like mad, but I went on, struggling to appear at ease until I stood opposite him and asked if he liked O'Neill. These were the first words I ever spoke to him."

"How'd he react?"

"He looked up quickly, surprised to hear anyone addressing him. When he saw me, his tiny mouth broke into a welcoming smile that weakened my knees. He said: 'Oh, it's you. Hi.' I said: 'Hi. You like O'Neill?' He said: 'Sometimes. He has interesting ideas, but I find him too wordy. Watching his plays, you can feel like you're drowning in dialogue.' I said: 'Have you seen many?' I'd only ever seen *The Hairy Ape* and *Strange Interlude* in performance. He said: 'A few.' I asked which ones, and that began a long conversation during which I learned about his life before he came to town."

"How much life did he have at that age?"

"Enough for me to envy," Robert said. "His family had moved to Braintree from Westchester, New York. He appropriated his interest in the arts from his parents, as I had with mine. He was better read and generally more sophisticated than me, yet the pleasure he derived from the arts was similarly organic, and as we spoke, rather than intimidated, I felt only a desire to learn more from and about him. Our talk segued from O'Neill to current dramatists, particularly Arthur Miller and Tennessee Williams. But while I'd only read their plays, he'd seen them in New York. Two hours later, we'd forged a connection that lasted for the rest of our high school careers, although I was always a bit in awe of him, not only for his looks but for the breadth of his knowledge."

"Was he hoping for a career in the arts, too?"

"He wanted to write novels but didn't rule out the possibility of plays. Quite a few writers then, like Somerset Maugham, were equally well regarded as novelists and playwrights."

"Did you become an item after that?"

"Depends on what you mean by an item," he said. "Once we learned how well-read we each were, we realized we were also the most well-read in the entire English class and possibly the entire school, teachers included. This made us inseparable by default. We spent our free time at school talking like we had at the library and did our homework at each other's houses. I can't tell you what it felt like to be in his room or to have him in mine. We'd race through our homework to hash over our cultural obsessions, which we considered the more important topic. Lacking the theoretical framework for the arts I've sketched for you, we spent hours picking apart individual artworks and artists and debating our likes and dislikes. Still, these talks further sharpened our perceptions by forcing us to pay closer attention to the works in question and our responses to them."

Robert paused to drink some tea. I sipped my ginger ale. The melting ice had deflated its bubbles and diluted its flavor.

"Who were some of the artists he liked?" I asked.

"Too many to mention. He particularly admired the modernist avant-garde that emerged at the turn of the century. He showed me how their work made the arts more self-reflective."

"What do you mean by self-reflective?"

"The art form became the art, rather than a vehicle for it; or perhaps I should say form became substance. Gertrude Stein and James Joyce explored the capabilities and limitations of language. Pirandello and Brecht did the same with theater, Schoenberg and Stravinsky with music, and Picasso and Duchamp in the visual arts."

"You weren't familiar with their work before?"

"Vaguely. Even in the late 1940s, they were still considered the lunatic fringe of the cultural world. Their work was, therefore, difficult to access. Terry gave me a crash course. He let me borrow his copies of Stein and T. S. Eliot and played recordings of Bartok and Stravinsky. He also had pictures from art magazines and gallery catalogs tacked to his walls: works by Picasso, Miro, Magritte, Dali—and de Kooning and Pollock, whose pieces he'd seen exhibited in New York. He showed me how, rather than a lunatic fringe, their chief virtue was a carefully considered rebellion against established dictates of art."

"Some consider lunacy a form of rebellion."

"Doubtful."

"Why?"

"Rebellion is essentially a means to an end, a method of bringing about a desired change. Genuine lunatics lack the ability to comprehend the means and ends necessary for rebellion to work."

"How did you see the modernist rebellion working?"

"You've undoubtedly heard the maxim 'you have to know the rules in order to break them.'"

"Sure."

"Usually, it's applied to writing: grammar, syntax, and other rules of composition, though it's true for every medium. Now, rebellion being a means to an end, you not only need to know the rules in order to break them; you also need a good reason. Picasso and Dali, Dadaists and Surrealists and others of that era—the best, anyway—thought deeply about art, their chosen media, and what they wished to accomplish with it."

"What do you feel they wished to accomplish?"

"The reinvention of reality, or at least its representations. This desire emerged in the nineteenth century with the Impressionists in painting and writers like Mallarme and Whitman flouting traditional poetic methods. In fact, Shaw wrote his essay on art to defend the early wave of modernist avant-garde from attack. The push to reinvent reality became more intense, more virulent, and sometimes violent after the carnage of World War One. The cultural upheavals from the teens to the 1930s reflected a growing belief that society had to change to avoid further pointless massacres, and the only way for it to change was to change its perception of reality. Given its ability to heighten the senses and ennoble the faculties, art seemed uniquely positioned to perform that function, even though, of course, this wasn't what motivated everyone in the avant-garde."

"And this outlook resonated with you and Terry, even though you were both of a different generation?"

"Rebellion was in our nature as teenagers, even more so for me, being gay and an inveterate outsider. Terry showed me how, with their rebellion, that generation of artists accomplished two much more serious and fundamental things."

"What?"

"First, by exploring what literature, theater, music, and the plastic arts could and couldn't do, they refined the power of expression for those arts. Second, by focusing on the substance of their media, those media became objects of appreciation in their own right. They compelled us to regard words, musical notes, paint, and stage scenes as raw sensory data, to be experienced directly, along with all the other sights and sounds, smells and tastes of daily life."

"Thereby refreshing your perception of them," I said.

"Very much. By changing my approach to their work, Terry gifted me with yet another way to approach both art and the world."

"You didn't exaggerate his sophistication. How did he end up in Braintree?"

"His dad was an insurance company executive and got a job with Prudential in Boston. His mother was interested in gardening and wanted to live in the suburbs."

"Did his parents know yours? From what you've said, they should've been as compatible as you and Terry."

"They met as a result of Terry's and my friendship. They were cordial but never close. You know how cliques crystallize and ossify, especially in small towns. They belonged to different social groups."

"Did that impact your friendship with Terry?"

"No. We were always welcome in each other's houses. I think our parents were glad we had someone to share our interests. As for me, if I'd started with a general desire for Terry's company, actually being in it surpassed my wildest dreams."

"You must have been equally attractive to him," I said, "otherwise he wouldn't have bothered with you."

"I contributed my own assets to the relationship, though his seemed disproportionately greater. I showed him around Boston: the museums, bookshops, and records stores, and we'd attend plays and concerts, sitting in the cheap seats. Later, over a cheap meal at a diner and then on the train going home, we'd discuss what we'd seen or heard, fulfilling the fantasies of companionship that grew out of my initial attraction. Also, since my tastes differed from his, I had the privilege of introducing him to artists hitherto unknown to him."

"Like who?"

"I quoted lyrics from pop songs by Cole Porter, Johnny Mercer, and Hoagy Charmichael that I found as insightful and beautiful as anything by great writers in other fields. Once, I recited extensive extracts from Gilbert and Sullivan to support my claim that beneath the jaunty ditties, W. S. Gilbert was one of the sharpest satirists of all time, a judgment I still stand behind. I'd play him the latest records by Art Tatum, Charlie Parker, Dizzy Gillespie, Billie Holiday, Ella Fitzgerald, and other jazz titans who, in those days, were all either at or approaching the apex of their abilities. As he listened, his sleepy eyes widened, and his face lit up with astonishment and pleasure, an expression that perfectly mirrored how I felt when a turn of phrase or musical motif refreshed my perceptions. Considering his erudition, I was intensely proud of those moments."

"Sounds ideal," I said. "You both had a general interest in the arts, yet your tastes were unique enough for you to learn from each other."

"And there were our ambitions. After picking apart others' works, we'd embark on lengthy discussions about ours. He'd outline ideas for stories and novels, and I'd invent roles to play until our dreams merged and we imagined me acting in plays written by him. If puberty hinted at intimacy between two people, I, for want of a better word, termed love, those hours with Terry demonstrated what such a love might mean, day after day, week after week, month after month. When I was with him, the world made sense, and life had meaning."

Robert shifted in the chair and sipped his tea.

"Were you ever actually lovers?" I said.

"After a fashion. I think he was more curious than serious about sex with another male. Neither of us had any practical knowledge. As a topic, it arose in connection with female schoolmates or a woman we passed on the street that he found attractive."

"Whom he cast in his private scenarios," I said.

"To my dismay. He'd poke me in the ribs and leer as if I were a fellow spectator in that particular theater."

"How did you respond?"

"I'd nod without elaborating and wait for him to move on to a more interesting subject."

"What steered him towards you, sexually, I mean?"

"A combination of things, I'd say. He had a wide-ranging curiosity about people, hence his interest in literature. Rather than force human existence into conformity with scientific, philosophical or religious doctrine, he was fascinated by the unique details of individual lives."

"Including homosexuality?"

"As you said, it'd been appearing in mainstream fiction for a while even then, and shortly before I met him, the Kinsey report had revealed the frequency of gay encounters among men who identified as straight. These probably piqued his curiosity. What tipped the scales in my favor was the bond we'd already established. None of our peers, boys or girls, had a comparable interest in the arts, so it was perhaps inevitable he'd turn to me to gratify his sexual needs as well."

"How'd it happen?"

"One afternoon, we were in his room after finishing our homework, discussing the British film version of Oscar Wilde's *An Ideal Husband* starring Paulette Goddard, which had received mixed reviews on its release two years earlier. Following our exhaustive, if callow, critique, we started on Wilde's private life, which had long since been public knowledge. We made an equally callow attempt to determine if and how it had influenced his writing. This was about the time academics assumed the habit of retroactively psychoanalyzing artists. One of us, I forget who, mentioned the Kinsey report, and we traded speculations on the subject. I, as usual, hid the extent of my interest. He stopped talking, which was rare for him, and looked at the floor. Finally, tentatively yet quite seriously, he said: 'Have you ever wondered what it might be like?'"

Robert laughed and continued, "Good God, had I wondered about it? I'd been dreaming about nothing else ever since I saw him in the front row of English class. But I remained cautious and answered 'sometimes,' copying the confessional hush in his voice. He waited a moment, lifted his eyes to mine, leaned over, and kissed me. Naturally, being inexperienced, what followed was rather perfunctory—more kissing followed by me bringing him to orgasm. But loving him made it incredibly profound. Exploring that lithe body, I finally experienced what I'd only been intuiting."

"Was that the only time it happened?"

"No, it became a regular if intermittent part of our friendship, or relationship, or whatever you want to call it, for the next two years. Sometimes an exceptionally intense conversation led us as if by natural progression into bed. Sometimes in class, he'd glance at me with a gleam in his eye, and I knew that later, after finishing our homework, we'd loll about his room or mine, eager and fumbling." Robert closed his eyes and sighed. "I'll never forget him lying naked on his bed. He had lustrous, clear skin with just enough hair to catch the afternoon light and lend it sparkle. If I was proud of introducing him to artists previously unknown to him, I was even prouder of making him come, even though at that age, orgasms require little effort. Afterward, he'd jump up and get dressed, giggling as if what had happened between us was an improper yet frivolous amusement, and we'd go back to being friends discussing theater and literature and our plans for the future."

He opened his eyes, squinting at the sunlight beaming from the window behind him onto the wall around me.

"Did you ever discuss the sexual aspect of your relationship?" I said.

"No. I assumed he avoided the subject because either he was less accept-

ing of his sexuality than I was of mine, or he was straight and just wanted relief. And I liked what we did too much to risk losing it by forcing any issues."

"Didn't that put you in a difficult position?"

"Worse," he said. "It underscored the disparity of our interest in each
other, which I knew would separate us for good."

"Why should it separate you?"

"We were separating anyway. After graduating high school we'd be
going off to college. If, as I suspected, he continued identifying as straight,
embarrassment over having sex with me would likely prevent him from
maintaining the relationship. Unless he admitted to being gay, which didn't
seem to be in the cards, he'd probably go on to lead a completely different
kind of life. So while in other respects I anticipated being an adult, loving
Terry made it my worst enemy. Our entire senior year, I hated being apart
from him. I wanted to sear every detail in my mind—how his fingers ta-
pered, how his hair stuck up after he'd lain in bed awhile, and especially
his voice."

"What about photos?"

"Pictures fix their subjects to a single time and place. I wanted to take
Terry with me as he was then, yet flexible enough to adapt to whatever
changes I underwent in the future, the way married people do for each
other." He snorted. "What a pathetic notion, even for a lovesick teenager."

"Then you lost touch entirely?"

"After graduation, he went to Harvard, I to New York and Columbia.
Still, while I expected him not to write, I always thought I'd hear about him
sometime, some way."

"Why?"

"Our plans," he said. "I believed I had potential, but I was sure he had
and never doubted he'd bring his to fruition. That's what made him irresistible. There was a lifetime of accomplishments bound up in him, waiting
to break out."

"Do you think they ever did?"

Robert shook his head. "I'd have spotted his name on a book or in a theater program. I know practically all teenagers overestimate their destinies.
But what we talked about then felt so real, so true, it makes me wonder."

"Wonder what?"

"Were we just another pair of naïve adolescents, or did we really have
the potentials we imagined, and instead somehow failed them, failed ourselves? I've seen my filmed performances and can believe I had less talent

than I imagined. Perhaps I was better on stage, and taking TV and movie work to survive prevented me from investing as much effort in them. But nothing can shake my conviction that Terry had tremendous ability."

"You might find him online."

He flinched. "I prefer not knowing what happened to him. Age too often means the gradual deterioration of a person and their talents in pursuit of necessities or our endlessly hyped luxuries. I hate thinking about Terry like that. I'd rather remember him as a horny kid, exuberant in his ambitions and in the hours he shared them with me."

He finished his tea and slowly exhaled as if reviving from an anesthetic. "That was the first time I fell in love," he said.

"One down, two to go."

"The second will have to wait. I never expected reminiscing would be this exhausting."

I swallowed the last of my watery ginger ale and carried our empty receptacles to the kitchen. When I returned, he had swiveled his chair to face the TV and picked up the remote, ready for his trip to *Grandview Park*.

"See you in a few days," I said.

"Okay, Paul."

I stopped and turned back between the ivied trellises. "By the way, what was your character's name on *Grandview*?"

He stared at me, nonplussed. "Why?"

"David's mom watched it as a kid. He thinks she might remember you."

He pursed his lips. "Grantland Montague Hunnicutt."

"You're kidding."

"I wish I were. You've never lived until you've spent fifteen minutes stalking the cute counter help at the necktie counter in a crowded New York department store, only to have a rabid fan scream out "Grantland Hunnicutt!" at the top of her lungs just as you're about to bag your quarry."

"At least I won't forget it. A name like that sticks in your mind."

"Like a poisoned dart," he said. "Have fun on your date. And don't spend more than three minutes discussing Grantland."

"Why three minutes?"

"I wouldn't want to be completely forgotten."

Driving home, the sunlight reflecting from the city's glass and concrete tore away the softer hues of Robert's reminiscences, yet what he said about art retained its clarity. The notion of art refreshing one's perceptions neatly conveyed the inexpressible quality that attracted me to music, and books, including the Harold stories, a fortifying reminder after my morning in the archive.

The sultry afternoon had steeped my tiny apartment in stifling heat. I turned on the air conditioner, sorted my mail—paper and electronic—and stood under a cool shower, wondering if my first glimpse of David behind the counter at the Argonaut had been anything like Robert's first glimpse of Terry. I pondered the variety of human attractions, what about a person appeals to another, what we think it means or portends, and how little it enables us to predict. After drying off, I slipped into my underwear, grabbed a bottle of water from the refrigerator, and sat on the sofa, sipping it while enjoying the cool air and the serenity of Gershwin's *Lullaby* on the radio, before dressing for my date.

The temperature had dipped to eighty-seven, and the sun mellowed to burnt orange by the time I returned to my car. Watching the first few lights along the streets and on buildings begin to glimmer, everything that happened during the day waned to the prelude to the next quarter hour.

The Monday evening crowd packed Brewer's even tighter than on Friday, though at six-thirty, I noticed a higher ratio of clubbers to office drones. The chatter, shifting bodies, and stark track lighting provided a striking antithesis to the quiet, sunny emptiness in Robert's place. The line of customers reached the main door despite the speed of the kids behind the counter. Standing only a few paces in from the sidewalk, I glanced about, searching for the cerulean eyes and crinkly smile among a thicket of dowdy strangers, relying on Robert's comments about taking chances when meeting new people and the reflection on David's taste if he failed to show to counteract what felt like an immanent disappointment.

Ten minutes later, as my position shifted to the middle of the line, I spotted David at a table by the far wall, a cup of coffee before him. His left hand rested beside the cup, clutching his phone. He stared at the screen, the glow from which tinted his face and shirt a faint blue. I purchased a decaf latte and wove between the tables toward him, reluctant to disturb his perfectly lit concentration.

"Hey," I said.

He glanced up, a controlled pleasure spreading across his tinted features like a pale delphinium blooming. He tapped the screen—removing the blue wash from his face—and laid the phone on the table. "Hey," he said, "on time again. I didn't do as well in the window seat sweepstakes on my own."

"No problem." I indicated his phone. "Did I disturb you?"

"Just checking orders for the store. Nothing that can't wait."

"How was the weekend at your sister's?"

"Great," he said and sipped his coffee. "Traffic was heavier than usual on Friday. I got there after supper and had to take leftovers."

"What was leftover?"

"Barbecued chicken. My nephews made me play video games before they'd go to bed. I had to fend off a fire-breathing dragon while not spilling barbecue sauce on a five-thousand-dollar sofa."

"How did you fare?"

"I sacrificed my digital doppelganger to the good of the sofa."

"And your standing as a permanent guest."

"Exactly. Saturday, we swam and played croquet. It rained on Sunday, so we stayed on the back porch and played board games. If you're curious, I've got pictures." He lifted the phone challengingly.

"Let's see," I said.

He tapped the screen and lowered the phone to the table before me. "Here we are swimming." The picture showed David submerged to his collarbone in shimmering water, his shaggy hair plastered to his head. A child bobbed on either side of him, one a brunette with blue eyes like David's, the other blonde with brown eyes, their shorter hair also drenched, grinning like water sprites newly born from the lake. He pointed to the brunette. "That's Mark. He's seven." His finger shifted to the blonde. "That's Adrian. He's six." He swept his finger across the screen.

The second image reproduced the first, except for a Border collie swimming in the foreground. "That's Chopin," he said.

"Chopin?"

"Marge is into classical music, too. The kids call him Chop."

The next picture showed two adults in their late thirties seated at a wicker table on a sun-dappled porch. The man had a jovial if nondescript face, green eyes, and thin hair the color of Adrian's. The woman had a white straw sun hat, freckled skin, black hair, and blue eyes like Mark and David, and a crinkly smile—again like David's—set within rounder cheeks. A white ceramic tray on the table displayed two cooked lobsters wreathed in parsley sprigs and fancily trimmed lemon slices.

"That's Brad and Marge."

"I see she made up for Friday's leftovers."

"Not for my sake. She was practicing for my parents' anniversary next month."

"Speaking of your mom," I said, "I found out what my actor friend's name was on *Grandview Park*. Grantland Hunnicutt."

"I'll tell her the next time I talk to her."

The following images depicted David and his nephews playing croquet; David, Marge, Chop, and the kids in a flower garden; Brad, David, and the boys playing a board game on the porch; the boys eating chocolate chip cookies, their lips smeared with melted chips; a close-up of a monarch butterfly perched on a flowering shrub; the two boys and Chop rolling on the lawn; Chop watching the boys on a trampoline; and David sleeping in a chaise lounge near the lake shore, his nephews poised to drop a frog onto his bare forearm.

"Looks like a full weekend," I said.

David exited the picture gallery and tucked the phone in his pocket while I leaned back and sipped my coffee. "Except for the frog. When it landed, my arm jerked up, and catapulted it fifteen feet. I thought I'd killed it, but it rolled back up and hopped into the lake."

"Who took the picture?"

"Brad, at Mark's insistence. Mark also found the frog and had the bright idea of dropping it on me while I was asleep. He's quite a little ruffian at times."

"What about Adrian?"

"He's more studious. Mark being older, Adrian looks up to him and usually goes along with whatever Mark suggests."

"Usually?"

"Sometimes he succeeds in putting on the brakes when Mark gets carried away." David stopped and regarded me as if I had unexpectedly donned the mantle of virtue reserved for chivalric heroes. "I'm impressed. Family photos more often bore people unless you're really good at hiding it."

"If anything, I'm envious."

"Why?"

"I told you the other day I'm an only child. What you have with your sister and her family seems amazing. Or am I idealizing something I don't know much about?"

"No, it's as good as it looks, apart from the occasional flare-up of sibling rivalry between Mark and Adrian or Marge and me. I love having them around . . . or, at least, close enough to keep me from getting lonely."

"I'll keep envying you, then."

He smiled and glanced out the window. Streetlamps and car lights streaked the nightscape with silver. "We should think about dinner," he said.

"Would you mind if we had a sandwich here? I don't feel like eating much when the weather gets really hot."

"Sure. I had a huge lunch anyway. There's a great Indian place around the corner from the Argonaut. I had some chicken Tandoori delivered. You should try it."

My heart leaped at the possibility of a third meeting his suggestion implied and sank at the pretense offered for it. "I'm not a fan of spicy foods. The one and only time I tried Indian, it was like chewing live coals."

He laughed. "I forgot. You mentioned that at the Palazzo. They have milder dishes for less adventurous palates."

"I prefer thinking of my palate as more finely calibrated."

"Whatever it is, I'm sure you'll find something to satisfy it if you're willing to take a chance."

"I'm always willing to take chances," I said, "if I apply an appropriate amount of caution beforehand."

"Don't apply too much, or you'll miss the best ones. If you're serious about trying the restaurant, I'll guide you through the temperature variants. What do you want now?"

I scanned the menu hanging behind the counter and settled for chicken salad on rye. David chose roasted vegetables on a torpedo roll. The crowd had thinned by then, and he returned with our sandwiches, along with little bags of potato chips, after five minutes.

"May I ask you something?" I said, peeling the plastic wrap from my sandwich.

"Sure."

"You said you took over the Argonaut because you never had any other ambition. Wasn't there ever anything you wanted to do?"

He swallowed his first bite before replying. "When I was a kid, I fantasized about becoming an animal handler and an astronaut and everything else kids imagine might be exciting. Growing up around the store, it became a familiar pattern to follow, or maybe it just entered my blood without my noticing. Now I imagine being a grey-haired old man with a strange tourist attraction where people come to handle historical relics called books."

"That's all?"

He wiped his mouth with a napkin. "Your concern is dangerously approaching the paternal."

"I don't mean to be. It's just that most people are striving toward a goal."

He shrugged. "My nephews have me thinking I might make a good father. Other than that, I'm happy with what I'm doing. If Thoreau felt most people lead lives of quiet desperation, I lead one of quiet contentment. Why are we on this topic?"

He bit into his sandwich, awaiting my answer.

"Sorry," I said. "Robert said today he felt he'd failed in his ambition to become a serious actor. It got me thinking about success and failure."

"Just keep in mind that they're relative terms, and the only signs of either are material goods arbitrarily designated as such."

"I'm not sure what you mean."

He swallowed and elaborated. "When I was eighteen, there was a lot of hype about a restaurant called Marvell's. The food was supposed to be the best and was priced accordingly. Reviewers called it 'marvelous Marvell's.' I'd drive by it on my way to work at the store after school, and I started obsessing about eating there. I saved three months to afford one dinner. I invited a friend to go with me."

"How was it?"

"The food was amazing. Afterward, I felt let down."

"Why?"

"I wondered that, too. Then I realized the hype surrounding it led me to expect some kind of transformative experience. I imagined, without being aware I imagined it, that the décor and pricey food would work some magic that'd change me for the better. Instead, I felt exactly like I had before. That stopped me from buying into what most people consider success. I realized it's measured by things whose reputation for quality is more superstition than fact."

"I've never been much of a materialist, but I never considered it in terms of superstition."

"It is, though" he said. "Cars, clothes, gems, and the rest are invested with an innate property called 'quality.' People talk about quality food or quality furniture . . ."

"Sure."

"The thing is, quality is a vague ideal rather than something concrete. As such, it lends itself to the belief that possessing quality goods makes their owner a quality person, just as a four-leaf clover is supposed to shift its innate good luck to its owner. I'm happier reading, being with my family, and watching the sunset over Lake Bellow. So after Marvell's, I decided to value my existence on its own terms rather than hold it up to the questionable standards of outside markers."

"Smart."

"It's been a good guiding principle, although not many people understand when I try to explain, much less agree. Are we done philosophizing?"

"Sorry."

"No problem. After two days of video games and animal stories, it's nice having an adult conversation."

"Maybe I need a few days of video games and animal stories to keep me from being too adult."

"Adulthood is another myth. Each age brings its lessons and problems. Some of us handle them better than others, but nobody ever gains the upper hand. Whoever says otherwise is lying to themselves and everybody else. That's my other guiding principle."

"Another good one," I said.

An uneasy pause ensued. David glanced at the time, sighed, and stretched his arms. "I should get going. The store opens at eight."

"Me too," I said, wondering whether broaching such serious subjects had scared him off another meeting. "Where'd you park?"

"In the lot around the corner."

"That's where I am. May I escort you to your car?"

The crinkly smile reappeared after too long an absence. "Sure."

We compressed our soiled napkins, potato chip bags, and the plastic wrap from our sandwiches into our empty coffee cups, stood, dropped everything into a garbage can by the door, and stepped into the balmy night. We walked with the crowd drifting along the sidewalk until we reached the corner and turned toward the parking lot.

Cars nestled like insects beneath the lot's high overhead lights. The narrow side street, momentarily devoid of pedestrians, heightened my awareness of the noisy avenue several dozen yards away, of David's nearness, and the possibility of losing sight of him for a few days or forever. I halted at the entrance to the lot.

"Something wrong?" he said.

"I hate suspense, too."

"What do you mean?"

"I know we've only seen each other twice, but I can't let you get away without knowing what it's like to kiss you."

He smiled his crinkliest smile. "A bit hokey, but I'll let it go considering you've been hanging around an old soap opera actor. Besides, I've been wondering what it'd be like, too."

We lingered over the kiss for a lengthy minute, after which he pulled back enough to ask, "Where do you live?"

"Baywood Avenue."

"I'm closer."

We hurried to our cars, and I followed him to his building.

The front door to his apartment opened onto a small living room with a kitchen at the right. Opposite, a short hallway led from the living room to a bathroom and bedroom. We kicked our shoes off inside the main door. He discarded his shirt in the living room, revealing what had been submerged in the photo of him at the lake: a compact torso with a thin line of black hair sprouting up from his belt, along his belly and branching across his pectorals like a fuzzy capital T. My shirt landed in the hallway entrance. His pants dropped a few feet farther. Mine crumpled in the bedroom doorway. We scattered our socks and underwear on the rug beside the bed and toppled in an ardent knot on his plum-colored duvet.

Afterward, we lay side by side, panting and staring at the shadows on the ceiling. Something akin to a pair of wings fluttered in my chest.

"So," I said, "that's what it's like."

He turned to me and laughed. We rolled our foreheads together and kissed off and on, exchanging caresses as if verifying what we recalled of each other's bodies.

The next morning we set another date for Wednesday and parted for work.

3.

The heat peaked at ninety-four on Tuesday. None of my *H&H* clients requested deliveries, and so the day assumed the pattern they all had when I first arrived in L.A. I entered the archive at nine and, after trading good mornings with Hilda, renounced further human contact to rummage in Castle's box four. The contents, dated October to December 1936, documented Castle's and Paramount's concerns for the upcoming holiday releases, the mounting hysteria over which relegated Jacobson, a solitary contract writer, and his repeatedly revised mystery to veritable nonexistence.

I broke for lunch at twelve. Conditioned by Castle's Christmas chatter, I expected to find Sheaves awash in Yuletide tunes and décor. Instead, I entered the same astringent interior of white walls and chrome furniture that symbolized cleanliness for most eateries, with the usual, equally astringent lite rock playing on the audio system. I ordered a roast turkey wrap and club soda and sat well away from the sunlight pouring through the large front window, the heat of which mounted a steady offensive against the shop's arctic air conditioning. I ate slowly, searching my email for responses to my posts about Jacobson and replying to a few friends who had emailed me. I returned to the archive at one, read down to the last quarter of box four without results, and called it a day at three-forty-five.

"Anything new?" Hilda asked on my way out.

"Nothing apart from me probably needing a new prescription before

I'm done," I said, adjusting my glasses. "I can't believe I have six more boxes to get through."

"Mr. Castle seems to have been as compulsive about preserving his records as he was about creating them."

"A double-edged sword at best," I said.

"Think of it this way: the more material, the likelier it is you'll find what you're looking for."

"A prediction rather than a platitude, I hope."

Resisting an early return to my empty apartment, I drove ten blocks to The Bean Counter, a coffee shop I had discovered after my third day at the archive: smaller and, in terms of décor, more formal than Brewer's. Three businesspeople—each staring at a computer—two fawning couples, and a woman escorting a boy and girl both under five years old, all sat far apart from one another. Except for infrequent outbursts from the children, the shop remained quiet enough to hear the coffee machines behind the counter hiss and gurgle. Even the employees conversed in undertones.

Adopting the prevailing separatism, I chose a table away from the others, sipped an iced mocha, and studied what I had copied to my phone during the last week, mining Castle's less-than-cryptic prose for multiple meanings to suggest new veins for research. My lack of success quickly led to daydreams of lolling in bed with David and his plush capital T. An hour later, when the post-work, pre-dinner crowd began invading the shop, I guzzled the rest of my mocha and fled.

Still resisting the solitude awaiting me at home, I drove about at random, the radio blaring pieces by Ravel, Offenbach, and Liszt that induced a pleasant, near-catatonic state until, a mile down a less-traveled secondary street, I spotted a restaurant called the Green Rooster. The façade boasted a series of designs from traditional Polish handicrafts that dispelled my lethargy with a surge of nostalgia for my maternal grandmother's home, the interior of which attested to the material goods and domestic skills her mother had brought with her when she emigrated from Poland in the early 1900's. Dishes, figurines and cookware, most of which had been wedding gifts to her mother, along with napkins, handkerchiefs, doilies, curtains, quilts and other items her mother created from scratch and decorated with designs in colored thread, continued to fulfill their functions for my grandmother, or else resided on shelves, or framed within a gallery of family photos, reminding her of both her heritage and her personal past, a service they later performed for my mother and me. Compelled by curiosity and a vain desire to recover the irrecoverable pleasures of Sunday dinner at that house, I pulled into the nearest lot and headed in.

Inside, the outside coalesced into a collection of household implements and craft samplers, all richly decorated like those my grandmother had, albeit enshrined in frames and display boxes, sharing wall space with elegant folk art prints—including one of a rooster rendered in moss green, highlighted by every other color—that lent the restaurant the preciousness of a museum display, unlike the warm, personal historicism my grandmother had achieved. Restraining the urge to share my reminiscences with my server, I ordered two of my favorites, cabbage soup and *pierogies* stuffed with potato and cheese. Their flavors deviated from what my grandmother had learned to prepare from her mother, yet they retained enough familiarity to sustain the comforting recollections of those bygone dinners and point up my solitude without anyone to share either the food or the memories.

A glossy purple dusk had fallen by the time I left the restaurant. I returned to my apartment, turned on the air conditioner, showered, stretched out on the sofa, and phoned my mother.

"Hello, Paul. How are you?"

"Good. How about you?"

"Fine. How's the research coming?"

"Okay, in general. Not so good the last few days."

"Too bad. I'm sure it'll pick up."

"Tedium is part of the process. You'll never guess what I had for dinner: cabbage soup and *pierogies*."

"Where did you get those?"

"I was driving around, and all of a sudden, there was a little Polish restaurant."

"I'm surprised there are any out there."

"This is the first I've seen, not that I've been looking for any." I started to describe it but she cut me short.

"I'm sorry, Paul. I want to hear all about it, but Evelyn and Kate will be here any minute. We're going to the casino."

"Oh. Okay."

"Call me tomorrow. We'll have a long talk."

"I may be busier tomorrow."

"Well, call when you can."

"I will. May I ask you something quick before you go?"

"Sure."

"What happened to all the stuff grandma got from her mother?"

"It's in storage. I keep meaning to figure out what to do with it. Do you want any?"

"I might."

"Then I'll leave it where it is. I've got to go. Evelyn just drove in."

"Have fun, and don't lose too much money."

"We're only playing bingo. Kate gave up slot machines."

"Good for her."

"Have a good night."

"I'll try. Bye."

I hung up, paid a few bills online, banished my phone to the table beside the sofa, and slumped backward, my frustrated desire for conversation manifesting in thoughts of David, my *H&H* clients, and even Hilda. I grabbed my tattered copy of Stewart Daniels' *Analytical Critique of the Novels of Erich Jacobson,* the 1970s study I had mentioned to Robert, from the computer desk. I browsed through it like I had Castle's memoranda at the Bean Counter, on the off chance of stumbling over something I missed during my first six readings. Unable to focus on more than two paragraphs in succession, I tossed the book to the table with my phone, turned on the TV, flipped through fifty-odd stations, turned the TV off, turned on the radio, and played an hour of online word games until, exhausted by the silence and my futile distractions, I crawled into bed at quarter to ten. I lay awake until ten-thirty, appalled to think the day just passed typified daily life for me my entire first month in town.

The next morning, my provisional third meeting with David fixed a definite goal for the day, something toward which all the rest tended, from showering and dressing to studying Castle's minute analyses of 1936 holiday box office receipts at the top of his box five. As with the previous day's pre-holiday memos, my morning's reading imbued lunch at Sheaves with Castle's post-New Year's letdown. Conversely, watching people prance around in shorts and sunglasses heightened my plunge back into January 1936 when I returned to the archive at twelve-forty-five, an illusion that lasted until David messaged me at two-thirty.

Still on for dinner?

Absolutely.

Want to try the Indian place?

Sure. When?

I'll close at six. Meet me at the store.

Okay.

Once our provisional meeting became a certainty, my attention repeatedly drifted away from box five until three-thirty, when I discovered four memos from Paramount production executive William Merrivale warning Castle that Jacobson's latest revision of the *Midnight Sun Murder* script relied too much on analytic jargon. This at least helped explain why the studio dropped the project, even if it failed to shed any light on why Jacobson switched to children's books. I copied the memos to my phone and left for home at four. There, I stood under a cold shower, relaxed for an hour with Scriabin, Grieg, and Borodin on the radio, dressed, and arrived at the Argonaut at quarter to six.

"Hey," David said when I entered. He scampered to the door, locked it to prevent anyone else from entering, and escorted me back behind the counter, where we discussed our days while waiting for the remaining patrons to take the hint and depart.

"Why are you going through Castle's papers if there's so little about Jacobson in them?"

"Since I've no idea exactly what I'm looking for, I can't predict where I'll find it. Whatever complications Jacobson met with may have been in his personal or professional life, or maybe one crossed over into the other."

"Didn't you say he mentioned these complications in letters from the 1940s? He stopped working for Castle in 1938."

"The antecedents could reach back to when he first came here."

"And what are the chances Castle was directly involved or even knew about it?"

"Little, if any," I said, "but he might've mentioned something in passing that could put me on the right track. Jacobson's experiences working for Castle might also connect to information from other sources that could lead me to what I want. That's why I'm begging people for information online. I can't afford to miss any hints."

"I've said it before," he said, shaking his head, "I don't envy you."

The last customer, a tall, thin woman with huge round eyeglasses, purchased two books on Georgian silver and left, after which David turned off the audio system, the air conditioner, and the lights and escorted me downstairs to the street.

Rounding the corner opposite the dated cornerstone, he led me toward a storefront topped by a gold and silver sign reading Brahmin's Banquet.

Inside, a narrow rectangular room reached almost to the far wall, jammed with tables, chairs, and diners.

"I've never seen it this crowded on a Wednesday," he said.

A petite woman in a black satin jacket over a beige blouse, clutching two menus, approached us. "There's a forty-five-minute wait for a table."

David looked at me. "What do you think?"

I shrugged. "This is your turf."

"How long is the wait for take-out?" he asked the woman.

"Twenty minutes."

He turned to me again. "We could get something and go to my apartment unless you had your heart set on dining out."

"Your place is fine."

The woman directed us to a counter away from the main entrance, beside a row of chairs occupied by people waiting for take-out orders, bored and awkward like patients in a doctor's waiting room.

"I was hoping to get you back to my place, anyway," David murmured in my ear.

"You weren't the only one," I murmured back.

He guided me through the temperature gradients of the different dishes, and forty minutes later, we entered his apartment, hot and stuffy like mine after a day of emptiness. He instructed me to place the Brahmin's Banquet bag on the kitchen counter while he fired up the air conditioner. I set it beside an inscrutable chrome appliance like a cross between an old-fashioned over-the-head hair dryer and a squat robot.

"What's this?" I asked on his return.

"A state-of-the-art popcorn popper," he said.

"Not what I'd expect an opponent of superstitious materialism to own," I said.

"Marge and Brad gave it to me last Christmas. Besides, it makes great popcorn, so its value isn't entirely superstitious."

"How's it work?"

"I'll show you later. We can pop some corn and watch TV. *Royal Thorns* is on."

"What's that?"

He stared at me. "Seriously? It's one of the biggest shows around."

"Never heard of it."

"We've got to get your head out of that archive. Mind if I shower before we eat? I'm still grimy from the store."

"No, go ahead."

As the shower spattered in the bathroom, I wandered about, noting details I missed my first time in his apartment: the titles on his bookshelves; the art posters and photos of his family; the furniture, ranging in quality from cheap cube chairs to an oak coffee table before the sofa; and his strangely colored throw pillows, five a subdued taupe, four a dark purple, three a searing acid yellow. An amber bottle on his bedroom dresser informed me his autumnal cologne had been christened *October Mist* by its designer. Searching his kitchen cupboards, I found several products on my *H&H* clients' lists, most notably Field Treasure wheat flakes.

He rejoined me after fifteen minutes, wearing a grey tee shirt and brown plaid lounge pants whose loose material clung to different sections of his legs at each step.

"If anything's gotten cold, we can toss it in the microwave," he said.

We sorted the food and sat opposite each other at his small, round dining table. I tentatively assayed my Tandoori chicken and curried vegetables until, finding after a few forkfuls they left my tongue and inner cheeks unscathed, I dove in with abandon. David followed the shifting calibrations of my palette with a bemused cerulean stare.

"What do you think?" he said at last.

"Good."

"No live coals?"

"No."

"Excellent."

I helped him clear the table, a brief chore with only a handful of take-out containers, napkins, and utensils to contend with. The proximity forced on us by his tiny kitchen drove us into each other's arms and, from there, to his plum duvet. As I traced his T in the afterglow, he glanced at the clock and sat up.

"It's almost time for *Royal Thorns* unless you'd rather stay here."

"And miss seeing that popcorn popper in action?"

He grinned, jumped up, pulled on his shirt and lounge pants, and sauntered into the kitchen.

Ten minutes later, we settled on the sofa, our heels on the coffee table, each with a bowl of fresh popcorn on our laps. He turned on the TV.

Royal Thorns bore out Robert's contention about the ubiquity of soap operas. It boasted higher production values than most; a larger cast; a historical setting—the British Wars of the Roses—and idealized views of

the aristocracy and early modern warfare, yet its structure betrayed its underlying identity: an open-ended narrative with melodramatic plot points
placing its characters in recurrent peril.

Despite David's meticulous exposition of the backstory to the present
episode, I suspected the show's chief appeal for him lay in the frequency
and ingenuity with which its characters, especially the male warriors, appeared in various states of undress. As for me, it played like the wet dream
of a frustrated history buff somewhere in the U.K. Watching the battles and
love scenes drag on, my face settled into a stony, noncommittal expression
similar to the one he wore while I related the rescue of Cindy Sardine's
daughters from the undersea ravine.

Five minutes into a solemn wedding sequence, he tried my silence with:
"What do you think?"

"I think I'll keep my head in the archive."

"Come on."

"Sorry."

"Maybe it's hard for you to get into it because you haven't seen it from
the start. I could show you some of the earlier episodes."

"No, please," I said and relayed my suspicions about the lonely British
history buff, which earned me a laugh despite his determined attempt to
preserve his indignation.

"What about Victor Hart?" he asked.

"Who?"

"The leading man. He's the reason most people watch, anyway."

"Oh. He's okay."

Incredulity raised his voice an octave. "Okay? He's one of the hottest
guys on TV."

"He's just not my type."

"How can he not be?"

"He looks like an action figure from the Westminster Abbey gift shop.
And his eyes are too far apart."

"No, they aren't," he said, again wavering between indignation and
laughter.

I pursued the laughter as relentlessly as I had pursued his passion on the
duvet. "If they were any farther apart, they'd be hanging from his earlobes."

"Shut up," he sputtered, flicking a piece of popcorn at me that bounced
off my nose.

"He must have the peripheral vision of an iguana," I said.

He tilted his head back to laugh. I flicked a piece of popcorn at him, aiming for his open mouth, but only striking the underside of his chin.

Unable to speak for laughing, he flicked more popcorn at me, at which point we left both the Wars of the Roses and our mythic adulthood behind for a game of Popcorn Tag. Starting side by side on the sofa, we soon moved off and around the room, ducking and dashing to avoid being struck while striving to tag each other, our laughter rising to an anarchic ecstasy that every so often coalesced into insults and threats that renewed our determination.

After emptying our bowls, we recycled the ammunition now strewn across the floor and extended our goals to direct contact, each reaching for the other when he paused to scoop popcorn off the rug or attempted to dart out of striking range. We circled the room four times, flicking, reaching, and scattering popcorn everywhere, until finally, I cornered him in the small strip between the sofa and wall. A torch lamp at the far end forced him into a last-ditch attempt at escape by leaping over the back of the sofa. When he sprang, I lunged, grabbed the waistband of his lounge pants, and yanked them to his ankles. The momentum dragged him backward, face down on the floor. I pounced and straddled his buttocks.

"King of the hills," I cried. "I win."

He wriggled and laughed beneath me. "Shit head," he said.

He managed to turn face up, at which point I pinned his shoulders to the floor. He scissored my waist between his knees, pulled me down, and our spontaneous game of tag became a spontaneous second round of sex, albeit a less uninhibited one, as we strove to avoid rug burns.

Wedged between the sofa and wall, under the light of the torch lamp, proved a surprisingly cozy spot to enjoy the afterglow.

"You're helping clean up the popcorn," he said.

"Don't you have a vacuum cleaner comparable to the popper?"

"Maybe this Christmas," he said, "if I'm a good boy."

"And if you and Santa share the same broad definition of that term."

He sat up and pulled on his pants. "Let's get to it before the urban vermin have their own free-for-all in here."

We crawled out from under the lamplight, hunting and gathering popcorn into a small kitchen trash bag.

"Not as fun this way, is it?" he said.

"You started it."

"I know."

When we finished, he tied off the bag, tossed it into a bin under the kitchen sink, and we returned to the sofa, somewhat at a loss to continue the evening.

"I'm too tired for a third go-round," he said. "I spent the afternoon cataloging and shelving a collection of books from an estate sale, and I'm not even a quarter of the way through it."

"Is that a hint for me to leave?"

"No, just to lower your expectations. Unless you want to go," he said, anxiety alloying his exhaustion.

I touched my forehead to his, a gesture referring back to our first night together that from then on served as a talisman of intimacy between us.

"No," I said, "and my expectations have already been exceeded."

"Maybe we can watch something else."

A brief discussion resulted in our revisiting the gay subtexts in Hitchcock's *Rope* and *Strangers on a Train* albeit without the benefit of popcorn.

Ten minutes before the climax of *Train,* the film's images and David's apartment became equally unreal, floating around my faltering awareness like satellites around a dying star. I nodded off to a close-up of Robert Walker and re-opened my eyes on David, leading me to his bedroom.

"I should go," I slurred.

"You're too sleepy to drive. I promise I won't take advantage of you."

"At least you've absorbed some chivalry from that *Thorns* show."

"I've always been chivalrous. You didn't notice because I've been too busy being charming."

"A real prince . . ."

"Do you need to go to the bathroom?"

"Too tired . . ."

He stripped me, tucked me under his blankets, and joined me after his own trip to the bathroom, arms snug around my waist, and I dropped off to the tingle of his stubble against my shoulder.

The following day, to my surprise, I found the exuberance fostering our game of Popcorn Tag not only still alive but thriving in the harsh, hot light of the L.A. morning, like a genie we had released from a bottle to watch over our being together. Showering, breakfasting, or dressing, we had only to look at each other to observe the playfulness the genie commanded seething beneath our thin, adult veneers.

"Will I see you tonight?" he asked as we approached his door.

"You'd better," I said. "I found a great Polish restaurant last night. I want to take you there."

"I've never had Polish food."

"It'll be payback for your help at Brahmin's Banquet. And you can give your fire-proof palate the night off."

"I'm open to a little recalibration. What made you go there in the first place?"

"I'm part Polish on my mother's side. Should I text you or just show up at the Argonaut?"

"Why don't we meet at Brewer's . . . say six-thirty?"

"Great."

The temperature reached eighty-seven before I reached the archive. The middle of Castle's box six led me from the post-holiday morass into the daily morass of studio operations, spiced with petty infighting, typical of a large Hollywood studio and, indeed, workplaces the world over, none of which involved Jacobson. Out of frustration as much as hunger, I broke for lunch early, at ten past eleven. Walking to the main door, Hilda waved to me from where she stood beside another visitor, a short, sad-looking man with a frizzy black beard and a purple tee shirt.

"You're looking bright," she called to me. "Find something good?"

"No," I said. "But I'm making strides in my personal life."

The purple-shirted man watched us, his dour eyes disapproving of Hilda's and my lighthearted exchange or perhaps of the disruption to his talk with her.

"About time you looked beyond the ephemera of the dead," she said to me.

"That's the gloomiest euphemism I've ever heard."

She laughed. "Sorry. The gloom was unintentional. Don't let it spoil your mood."

"Nothing could," I said.

Halfway through a chicken wrap with onion jelly at Sheaves, Lena Crenshaw, one of my four original *H&H* clients, messaged me to pick up her cholesterol meds. After lunch, I headed to the pharmacy and arrived at her apartment by two.

Lena's apartment presented an astonishing study in contrasts, a focused motif of Victorian preciousness—pictures of women in flowing gowns wandering twilit gardens, roseate wallpaper, statuettes of fairies, and a smell of floral potpourri—wholly at variance to its resident, a former nurse with a forthrightness bordering on the dictatorial, expressed by a ragged baritone that sounded as if every word had been marinated in scotch and rubbed against a cheese grater.

"Thanks for coming, Paul."

"No problem." I handed her the pharmacy bag.

"Thanks. How've you been? How's the research?"

"Less than spectacular at present." Absently, I withdrew a bag of chocolate-covered espresso beans from my pocket and popped a couple into my mouth.

"Sorry to hear it." She honed in on the bag with the lustful curiosity of a lifelong gourmand. "What are those?"

"Chocolate-covered espresso beans. Want one?"

"I've never had them before."

"Here."

The first crunch altered her lustful curiosity to gratified surprise. "These are great. Where did you get them?"

"A coffee shop on Eighth called Brewer's. I stopped in for a latte before the drugstore."

She cadged a second bean. "Would you mind picking me up a bag next time you're there?"

"Sure. I'll get one tonight and drop it off tomorrow."

"Don't make a special trip for me."

"I'm going there anyway."

"You really are a coffee addict, aren't you?"

"Actually, I'm meeting someone."

Her chewing slowed. "You mean someone as in a date?"

"Yes."

"Good for you. I was beginning to think you didn't know the difference between a research library and a monastery. What's he like?"

I described David to her as I had to Robert, adding several of the less intimate details I had discovered in the interim.

"He sounds marvelous," she said, "like one of the boys on *Royal Thorns*."

"I should've known you watched that."

"Don't you?"

"No. I'm too busy with Jacobson to watch much TV."

"It's a great show. Of course, I'm an old-fashioned, card-carrying romantic."

"I've noticed."

"Don't get snippy, young man. I've earned the right to indulge my fantasies. And if I were you, I'd be more open to romance before cynicism ages you prematurely."

"I'm trying."

"See that you do," she said, "only don't get so moony you forget my espresso beans."

"I won't."

Entering Brewer's at six-thirty, I found David in a window seat. As I approached, latte in hand, he looked up and flashed a grin that assured me our playful genie had not only survived the morning but thrived in the interim, a third presence marking us off from the regular crowd projecting their mythic images of adulthood at one another. The jokes and laughs shared by those in business suits, worn out from a day of corporate drudgery, and the kids preparing for another night of drinking, drugs, and hookups, lacked the self-sufficient frivolity David and I enjoyed as we compared the monotony of cataloging his estate sale books with that of combing Oliver Castle's papers.

"We should get going," I said after finishing my harangue. "I'm starving."

"And I'm eager to subject The Green Rooster to the same hyper-criticism you gave *Royal Thorns* last night."

"Having standards isn't the same as being hyper-critical," I said, standing. "I have to get some chocolate-covered espresso beans before we leave."

"Don't we get dessert at this restaurant?"

"They're for a client."

I explained about Lena while we gathered our recepticles, tossed them in the garbage, and assumed a place in line for the counter.

"Is it wise to discuss your personal life with your clients?" he asked.

"I don't tell them everything," I said, "or even half."

"What did you tell her about me?"

"Enough."

"Why so vague?"

I looked at him. He stared back challengingly. I faced the counter.

"You're too perceptive," I said.

"And you're too evasive. Come on."

I braced myself and said: "She told me you sounded like one of the guys on *Royal Thorns*."

He reacted as I expected, with happy, derisive laughter, as if a technicality had belatedly granted him the victory in Popcorn Tag.

"Of course," I said, "by her own admission, she's an old-fashioned card-carrying romantic. And though your family may spoil you, I'm enough of an old-fashioned card-carrying anti-royalist not to treat you like a prince."

"You said I was one last night."

"Sleep deprivation impaired my judgment."

He heaved a sarcastic sigh. "Another radical intellectual."

"To the core," I said and bought Lena's beans.

David walked before me and opened the door as a woman our age approached from the other side, her frizzy red hair and emerald green eyes vibrant even against the colorful Pacific coast sunset. Registering David's face, she stopped short and smiled. "Hey," she said, "the mysterious David F. I've been meaning to call you."

David's reciprocal grin lacked the expressive corner crinkles. "Hey, Rene, how've you been?"

"Good."

"Cool. This is Paul Heywood. Paul, Rene Arlington."

"Hi," I said.

"Nice to meet you." The emeralds swept me with the thoroughness of a CAT scan and returned to David. "Where are you two off to?"

"Dinner," David said.

"I won't keep you, then. But it's lucky I ran into you. I'm getting a party up tomorrow night. What about it?"

"I'll check and see," David said.

"Sure. You know my open-door policy. Show up if you feel like it."

"Will do," David said.

Rene headed for the counter. We escaped to the pavement, still smelling of the midday heat. We walked a few dozen feet, David unexpectedly and uncharacteristically quiet.

"A friend of yours, obviously," I said.

"Yeah, I've known Rene since college."

"But you weren't ready to run into her with me."

He shrugged. "I guess I was hoping to keep you my little secret for a while."

"I know the feeling." I looped my arm through his. "She seems okay, though."

"If unreliable at times."

"How do you mean unreliable?"

"She's a procrastinator. We decided it explains her looks. The red hair and green eyes are a simultaneous stop-and-go signal."

I laughed. "Procrastination isn't the worst thing in the world."

"Depends how far you take it. I think she's still sleeping off the nights she had to stay up finishing her term papers."

The bulk of the dinner crowd had left the Green Rooster by the time we arrived, leaving a quiet, relaxed atmosphere for both patrons and servers. David shook off the inexplicable torpor induced by Rene and looked around while we waited for a table.

"Cool place," he said.

"I know. It reminds me of my grandmother's house."

A server beckoned us to our table. I guided David through the menu, after which he ordered chicken in sour cream and dill with egg noodles and asparagus. I chose roasted root vegetables and cabbage rolls. Our server brought the white wine we ordered, and David resumed his inquiry into my Polish background.

I unleashed the memories I had been unable to share on my first visit to the restaurant, relating them with the same halting enthusiasm that I had related my affinity for Harold Herring at Brewer's, aware that my words fell far short of what I felt and searching his face for signs of something more than polite attention. I ended the account of my great-grandmother's accomplishments with:

"She even made rag rugs."

"Rag rugs?"

"They'd braid scraps of material, wind the braids around, and stitch them together. My mom had a few in our house. I had one in my room growing up."

"Were your great-grandmother's things as elaborate as these?"

"Some."

"She was pretty creative, then."

"Creativity was more often expected of people in her day."

"You think so?"

"It's called folk art because rather than sacrifice beauty for practicality, traditional cultures more often than not attempt to merge the two, even when it comes to everyday objects. This was true of the things my great-grandmother didn't make, bowls, platters, and figurines like these," I said, nodding at the displays.

"And your grandmother kept them all?"

"Those that survived the wear and tear of use," I said.

We each reached for a sip of wine, allowing me a moment of silence to ponder Robert's claim about the organic nature of art, an echo of which reverberated in what I had just said.

David lowered his glass first and watched me, the crinkly smile on full display.

I swallowed and said, "What?"

"I'm beginning to understand your attraction to the past."

"Anyone interested in anything can't help being attracted to the past, or some degree of it. The present is the result of what came before, after all."

"I also like how animated you get when you talk about it."

Our server derailed this topic by laying our dinners before us.

"What do you think?" I asked after his first few bites.

He smiled sheepishly. "I wanted to rag it the way you did *Royal Thorns,* but it's too good, even for the thrill of revenge."

"Good. I'm planning on making this a regular stop."

He ate a forkful of asparagus, sipped his wine, and said: "Was your grandfather Polish?"

"No, part Pennsylvania Dutch and part New England Yankee."

"How'd he like living in your grandmother's museum?"

"I don't know. He died eighteen months before I was born. The house had a den with a lot of fishing equipment and stuffed fish on the walls, and he had a little orchard of apple, pear, and plum trees in the backyard. They were his pride and joy."

"He had his own spaces, then."

"Probably why their marriage lasted," I said.

We returned to our entrees. "So," he said, splitting a chicken piece, "want to go to Rene's party?"

His obvious disinclination advised caution. "I'm okay with being each other's little secret for a while."

"The only problem is she's the taproot for the grapevine growing in our little tract of queer society. She's probably phoned and messaged everyone about you by now."

"Then we might as well get it over with."

"You'll have to repeat everything about your research all night."

"I've repeated it so much already I do it by rote anyhow."

"If you get sick of the scrutiny, we can leave early."

"I'm sure it'll be fine."

"If it comes off at all," he said.

"Why wouldn't it?"

"Rene's likely to put off buying food and drinks until the last minute and have to cancel. Then she'll forget to tell a few people, and they'll show up as she's getting ready for bed."

"You think that's likely?"

"Yes. Two years ago, she decided to give a going away party for her girlfriend at the time, Dawn. She was going off to join an archeological dig in Croatia. Dawn had to leave a day early and Rene canceled. But she forgot to tell everybody. Ten guests showed up to find her in a nightshirt and panties, eating a pint of butterscotch ice cream and watching *The Mummy*."

"Are you sure this isn't just hearsay?"

"I was one of the ten."

"What happened?"

"She shrugged and said, 'Sorry, Rene goofed,' and the ten of us went to the first movie we could find."

"If it happens tomorrow, we can go back to your place and pop some corn. Oh, no. She's not one of those people who refer to themselves in the third person, is she?"

"Sometimes. Why?"

"I can't stand that. It's so insufferably pretentious and cloying at the same time."

"Insufferably?" he said with mock awe. "You must really hate it to bring out the heavy, polysyllabic artillery. David will have to watch his step."

"You're lucky I like these cabbage rolls too much to fling one at you."

"Table manners you learned at your grandmother's?"

"I was never in a single food fight until we met."

"Well, that's one thing for David to be proud of."

Our playful genie hovered over the remainder of the meal and accompanied us back to David's apartment, where it again watched over our liaison, though without any further waste of food.

The next day, five memos appeared near the bottom of Castle's box six in which Castle and William Merrivale debated the viability of Merrivale's notion to hire a police psychiatrist as a consultant in hopes of winnowing down the psychoanalytical elements in Jacobson's script to the terse standards of the average 1930's crime drama. Castle, under the sway of orthodox Freudian analysis, convinced Merrivale to abandon the idea. I scanned the memos to my phone and read on with renewed hope, which dissipated as I reached the bottom of box six and dug through the first third of box seven. I left off for lunch at one-thirty and phoned Robert.

"Paul," he said. "I'm delighted to hear your voice."

"I'm relieved to hear yours."

"Why?"

"I haven't brought you groceries in over a week. I was getting worried."

"You're kind to be concerned, but I'm fine. I just haven't been eating as much."

"Are you losing your appetite?"

"I always do when the weather gets hot," he said. "If I run low on anything, I'll let you know. How are you doing with your author?"

"He's still guarding his secrets."

"Assuming he has any to guard. What about David?"

"We're still having fun."

"Good. Keep it up."

"I intend to."

"And tell me everything when I see you next."

"I will."

David and I met at Brewer's at six-thirty before heading to Rene's for seven, his share of our mutual playfulness hidden behind a death mask of stoic composure.

Rene Arlington lived in a ground-floor apartment decorated in a style a college friend of mine termed "futons and fairy lights." The minimal furnishings associated with this style enabled her to cram the space with people, the majority of whom paid as much heed to their phones as each other. The combined glow of phone screens and fairy lights turned the assembly into creatures more of light and shadow than flesh and blood, though enough flesh and blood remained for them to consume the food our host, true to her repute for poor planning, provided in insufficient amounts. Every so often, she coerced a guest into procuring more, her request coyly prefaced by: "Do you mind doing Rene a little favor?" Judging by their prompt compliance, her conscripts had long ago accepted these brief, compulsory periods of servitude as an unavoidable condition of her friendship. Meanwhile, I gritted my teeth whenever I heard her refer to herself by name.

As an outsider and David's date, I attracted the most attention, measured by the extent to which I distracted people from their phones. As he predicted, I spent most of the night eulogizing Erich Jacobson for inquisitors whose responses ranged from mild curiosity to indifference to wild amusement, all ending with my interlocutors returning to the safe haven of the screens beaming up from their palms. Luckily, a few guests had actually read the Harold books and heard me out with interest, while against all odds, one opened up a new, if narrow, vein for my research.

A scrawny, delicate twenty-two-year-old bearing the cumbersome name Rodney Quinn and a job developing genetically modified flowers for an upscale greenhouse called Fantasy Floral, posed the expected questions about my being in Los Angeles and maintained exclusive eye contact with his phone during my answers. When I mentioned Jacobson, he said, to my surprise yet without shifting his gaze: "He was a shrink back in the day, wasn't he?"

"Yes," I said. "Not many people know that."

"My grandmother had a friend who was his patient."

"Really? How do you know?"

"There's something about it in some letters she sent my grandmother. My mom told me about it once."

"Do these letters still exist?"

He shrugged, his indifference increasing in proportion to my excitement. "I think my mom still has them. She keeps a lot of old stuff."

"Do you think she'd let me see them?"

"I'll call her and let you know."

Five minutes later, after acquiring a fresh drink and a vegan éclair from a boxful newly provided by one of Rene's flunkies, I rejoined David, standing alone and awkward after concluding a conversation with two other guests. His friends had welcomed him eagerly, yet the stoic mask persisted, and every now and then, I noticed him searching me out as if worried I might leave without him. I recounted my talk with Rodney.

"Maybe he just wanted your phone number."

"It sounded too specific to be a pretense." I finished my éclair and wrapped my free arm around his waist. "And at present, I'm only interested in Jacobsonia. Wouldn't it be ironic if here's where I end up finding what I was looking for after all these weeks of interviewing people and digging through archives?"

"Yeah," he said, unmoved by the irony. "How're you getting along otherwise?"

"Okay. I've heard a bit more about you, some of it embarrassing but not enough to strip you of your princely charms."

He blushed and stared into his drink. "You're lucky your past's in Pennsylvania."

"Don't I know it?"

The shifting crowd separated us again. Now that they had pumped me dry about my life, I reverted to my voice recorder persona and plied them with questions which they answered as distractedly as they had heard mine. David reached me again after forty-five minutes.

"What do you think?" he asked. "Had enough?"

"What's the rush?"

"We've been here long enough to satisfy Rene. There are other things I'd rather be doing than expose you to biased witnesses of my youthful indiscretions."

"Like giving me your wholly unbiased versions?" He said nothing. I decided to back off until I learned more about the dynamic between him and his friends. "We can go if you want to."

We sought out Rene and said our goodbyes. Rodney interceded before we left. "I talked to my mom," he said. "She says she'll call you in a few days."

"Great. Thanks."

The mask finally slipped as we reached the sidewalk, and returned to being each other's little secret.

"They seemed like a good group, on the whole," I said.

"Yeah, they are. Want to get some pizza?"

"Didn't you eat enough at Rene's?"

"I just grazed. There's a great pizza place three streets down from me."

"Is this another ruse to get me back to your apartment?"

"Only if you want to go."

"I do if you do."

As we ate our pizza, I expanded on my hopes for Rodney's lead.

"You think it's likely a patient would've written much about her treatments?" he said.

"Why not?"

"I can see her being explicit in a journal, but in a letter, especially when you've no control over what happens to it after . . ."

"True. But it's rare to gain any insight into an analyst's style, especially from the patient's viewpoint. Even a few tidbits will be worth it. What're you doing tomorrow?"

"Shelving the last of the estate books," he said crunching the crust of his third slice, "and getting some online orders ready to mail on Monday."

"How many orders?"

"More than you'd expect. Online sales are picking up. I used to do them for an hour after the store closed, but not anymore. It's getting difficult to fill them and deal with the in-person trade."

"Too bad you have to work at all."

"If you're that starved for my company, you could tag along."

I welcomed the invitation along with his bantering tone. "Don't think I won't take you up on that," I said.

"Academics should watch their double negatives."

The next morning I watched him fulfill his duties as owner-in-training of the Argonaut. As promised, this involved shelving books and prepping online orders between waiting on the few patrons who braved the heat to shop. When, after two hours, the fascination waned, I began prowling the shelves for titles of both personal and professional interest from a memorized list that seemed to reach back to when I first learned to read. Scanning the spines or perched on one of the many step stools scattered along the aisles, turning pages, and listening to the classical music he had been chivalrous enough to introduce over the audio system, I had the sense of wandering a literary preserve similar to the private parks where European nobles once hunted, an illusion infrequently shattered by the sounds of the front door opening or a customer approaching, or David walking by with an armful of books.

Once, standing on a step stool in the theater section, checking out titles Robert had mentioned to me, David passed by and clipped my buttocks with his palm.

"You offer such excellent service, Mr. Farmington," I said.

"We always give our customers what they want."

A half-hour later, spotting him on a step stool shelving books on Ancient History, I returned his gesture only to discover a sweaty, grey-haired man in a threadbare corduroy blazer at the end of the aisle watching me.

Twenty minutes after noon, I picked up the lunch David ordered from Brahmin's Banquet, which we ate together behind the counter. Afterward, I spent the afternoon in the magazine room, collecting reviews of Jacobson's novels and a few profiles that, while lacking the personal details I sought, documented how his books had been received in the United States.

The next day, Sunday, I studied the articles more carefully alone in my apartment. They revealed a pattern of contrasts, or contrasting viewpoints, which inspired a new theory that I outlined for David later on at dinner.

"The reviews for the mystery novels focus a lot of attention on the analytical elements," I began.

"Are you surprised? You told me psychoanalysis was still cutting-edge when they were written."

"That's my point. The interest in Freud that was pervasive back then makes both the mysteries and the reviews very dated. The same isn't true for the Harold books. The articles and reviews concerning them usually mention Jacobson's being an analyst, but they're more about the books' intrinsic appeal."

"Meaning what?"

"I think they were more popular than the mysteries—and still are—because they aren't just illustrating an intellectual system."

"Okay," he said. "What's that got to do with what you're working on?"

"Maybe Jacobson intuited that popular interest in Freud might wane at some point, and the Harold books were a way to distance his art from his profession."

"Sounds reasonable," he said. "But do you really think that's what he meant by complications?"

"A change of mind can be stressful, especially when it concerns things you believe in strongly, like your vocation, or in his case, vocations. Unfortunately, it'd also be harder to prove."

"Why?"

"If a definite event made him switch genres, if something happened to him or someone he knew, it might be preserved in records not directly connected to him: letters, diaries, police reports, or hospital records. They probably wouldn't tell the whole story, but they'd narrow my search. If it resulted from a change in his thinking, my only hope is if he wrote an account of it or told someone who recorded it in turn."

"Making it more imperative for you to get a hold of every relevant document," he said, with an "I still don't envy you" look.

Monday to Wednesday, I spent my mornings at the archive, afternoons delivering for *H&H,* and evenings dining with David, followed by the twin delights of sex and play. I progressed from Castle's box seven to box eight, containing documents from October to December 1937. As with those months from 1936, the frenzy surrounding that year's Christmas releases conditioned me to expect holiday decorations everywhere, a persistence of vision I complained about to David during Wednesday's dinner.

"Maybe it's time you gave up Castle and looked somewhere else."

"I'd love to, but I can't risk missing anything. I also have to finish what I start. Stopping before Jacobson's fired from Paramount would be like leaving a movie in the middle."

"You had no trouble doing that with *Royal Thorns.*"

"The exception proving the rule," I said, "and if ever there was an exception *Royal Thorns* is it."

"Okay, okay." He sipped his bottled water and changed the subject. "I spoke to my mom. She freaked when I told her your friend played Grantland Hunnicutt."

"Really?"

"Well, as near as my mom gets to freaking. Seems he was as big a deal as he says he was."

"He'll be glad to hear it."

"She'd like to ask you about him."

"Sure, not that I know much."

"I doubt she expects a full biography. She's just excited he's still around and that I know somebody who knows him."

"Does she want to call me or meet us in town somewhere?"

He sipped more water and cleared his throat. "Actually, she suggested we meet at my sister's for lunch on Saturday. Marge already asked them, and I have a standing invitation. I know it's sudden, but she's really excited. They'll also want to grill you about Jacobson."

"They know his work?"

He nodded. "I didn't know they did until I mentioned him. It's up to you."

He stopped and waited. Meeting his family so soon after meeting him seemed more daunting than my research, yet his barely concealed enthusiasm proved irresistible.

"After those pictures, I've been dying to know what Lake Bellow's like in person," I said.

The crinkly smile broke out. "You'll love it. You'll like them, too. The only thing is it's a four-hour drive. To get there for lunch, we'll have to leave between six and six-thirty, in case of traffic. I know how you are with mornings . . ."

"I'll be okay if I have enough coffee. Just don't expect much for the first hour or so."

"We'll be driving, so it won't matter."

"Then call your sister and tell her we're coming."

The smile broadened, and I wondered at the difference between this and the mask he affected for Rene's party. Apparently, our being one another's little secret mattered less with his family than with his friends, while I felt more like remaining a secret, for a while at least, from them than from the people I met at Rene's.

But, as with Jacobson, I reserved judgment before gathering more information.

4.

The heat wave broke late Thursday night, leaving the air a comfortable seventy-six when I returned to Robert's with food and medication on Friday afternoon. I noted two changes. A grey cardigan replaced the blue, and the plastic ivy had vanished from his entryway trellises.

"I bring sustenance," I said, crossing the threshold.

"In more ways than one." He closed the door and followed me to the kitchen.

"New sweater?" I asked.

"No. I spilled minestrone on the blue one. I'm debating whether or not it's worth attempting to salvage."

"I'll take it to the cleaners if you want."

"Is that part of your duties?"

"All errands are within *H&H's* purview. Besides, you belong in a blue cardigan."

He assumed a seat at the kitchen table. I rested the bags on the counter and began transferring his salad ingredients to the vegetable crisper.

"What happened to the ivy?" I said.

"Saturday afternoon, I decided I couldn't stand how ugly it was anymore and ripped it out in a frenzy, or what constitutes a frenzy at my age."

"What did you do with it?"

"I wish I could've used it to strangle whoever decorated this apartment, but they probably died of a drug overdose sometime in the 1970s. I'm going to throw it out unless you're interested."

"As much as I hate waste, there's nothing I need less than several yards of plastic ivy," I replied, stacking seven Bub's Tubs on the shelf above the vegetable crisper.

"How are things with your bookseller? Still having fun?"

"Very much." I set a pound of chicken breasts next to the Bub's Tubs, and stood a Bountiful Bog cranberry juice and a Bridger's mayonnaise on the bottom shelf.

"I'd surmise from your buoyancy that you've already slept together, probably more than once."

The open refrigerator cooled my flushed face. "You sure can read signs, can't you?"

"Are you going to tell me about him, or would you deny an old coot his vicarious pleasures?"

I closed the refrigerator and returned to the nearly empty bag on the counter. "He's amazing. Handsome, sweet, and wise for his age," I said.

"A description lifted nearly verbatim from Rodgers and Hart's 'Wait Till You See Him.'"

"What's that?"

"A song from the bygone era of Broadway musicals, though Hart's exact words were 'pensive and sweet and wise.'"

I stacked four packages of Ice Floe mixed vegetables and one of Tanner's frozen multigrain waffles into his freezer, at the same time speaking into the cold fog swirling out into the warm kitchen. "He's definitely not pensive, and so far, he's been nothing but sweet."

"How about wise?"

I repeated David's comments about success, failure, and their ambiguous outward signs while folding the empty bag.

"Wise, indeed" he said.

I started on the second bag, describing the last several days: Brahmin's Banquet, Popcorn Tag, the Green Rooster, Rene's party, and hanging out at the Argonaut until, after sliding more Velma's biscuits into their cupboard between his Field Treasure bran flakes and unsalted Snapdragons, I stopped prattling, afraid to tempt fate by revealing more, or perhaps reluctant to trust my instinct to confide in Robert.

He waited while I stared at the boxes on the shelves, arranged with their nutritional information facing outward. "Something wrong?" he said.

I settled on full disclosure. "I felt it, Robert."

"I expect you did."

"No. I felt Coleridge's wings."

"You're really falling, then."

"Can a person fall that quickly?"

"It's unusual but not unheard-of. If you recall, I felt the same the moment I saw Terry."

"I wonder if David felt it, too."

"You'll find out eventually, one way or another."

"Don't make it sound so foreboding."

"It needn't be, if you can resist being carried away by Coleridge's wings."

"I'll try. But it'll be hard. Seeing him with his family...."

"You've met his family?"

"No, but it's imminent."

Robert shook his head. "You'll have to be a little less ecstatic and a little more intelligible."

"Sorry." I arranged his Gunter's shakes next to the Snapdragons. "He showed me pictures of him with his sister and her family."

"How much family does she have?"

"A husband named Brad and two little boys, Mark and Adrian. They also have a border collie named Chopin. The kids call him Chop."

"Chop? He must be a lamb."

"Robert . . ." I said, my head drooping under the weight of his heavy-handed wordplay.

He dismissed the reproach. "I'm as unapologetic about my love of puns as I am about my love of men. Go on."

"This will probably sound crazy," I said.

"Amorous honoraria usually do. Go on anyway."

"When we first met, there was a warmth about him that... that...."

"Suggested an underlying capacity for love?"

The idea seemed crazier when spoken aloud; yet, reassured by his comprehension, I forged ahead.

"Yes. It was in his eyes and smile, in how he stood and spoke and gestured, like it was so much a part of his nature it had to escape any way it could."

"Which may have been an illusion deliberately created by him, or an equally illusory projection of your desires, or a little bit of both."

"And with all the small talk and being together required to get to know each other, it can take a while to find out which it is."

"And even then, you can't always be sure."

"His affection for his family was clear in the pictures. I think that's why he showed them to me." I stacked three cans of Cal's cardio soups on their shelf, placed the Shale House ginger ale beside the papaya on the counter, and folded the bag.

"To exhibit that facet of his personality without actually drawing attention to it. Could be," Robert said. "And what about you? It'd be very unfair if he laid his character bare, so to speak, while yours remains concealed."

I laid the second empty bag atop the first and leaned against the counter. "He said he thought I was a good guy from the beginning because I volunteer with *H&H* and took the trouble to search for your photo."

"Impressive. You've deduced key elements in your respective characters in record time from the subtlest clues. Sherlock Holmes couldn't have done it any better."

"I'm just not sure how comfortable I am being drawn into the rest of his life while we're still getting to know one another."

"Didn't you say meeting his friends resulted from a chance encounter?"

"Yes. I didn't mind that so much. Family's another thing. Strangely, David's attitude is the exact opposite."

"The opposite of what?"

"Mine. He wasn't too keen on introducing me to his friends, and he was quieter than I've ever seen him when we were there. On the other hand, he's over the moon about me meeting his family. I'm a little nauseous."

"Not surprising. If he's as close with his family as he says, he's probably more confident with them, more in control than with his friends. You, on the other hand, are being thrust into his more hermetic relationship with the family, which gives you less control."

"I suppose," I said, "but it still doesn't make it any easier."

"If you're not ready for the family, why are you letting him force the issue?"

"He's not. You are."

"Me?"

"I told you his mother wanted to know who you were on *Grandview Park*."

"Ah, yes: Grantland Hunnicutt, eternal meddler in other people's affairs."

"She remembers him and wants to ask me about you."

"What'll you tell her?"

"I don't know . . . just answer her questions, I suppose."

"Careful. She may still nurture a crush on Grantland and be hoping for some better-late-than-never fling."

"David knew you were gay before he knew your character name. I'm sure he's told her."

"You're not certain?"

"He'd have to tell her I met you through an agency serving the LGBTQ community."

"Any lingering fan frenzy should be diffused, then. But if his mother's the only one interested in me, why are you being thrown in with the rest of them?"

"His parents and sister live closer to each other than to L.A., so his sister hosts all the family get-togethers. Your celebrity value may just be an excuse for them to appraise David's new guy, anyway. He's the youngest, except for his nephews, and I'm assuming they're a little overprotective."

"I'm sure you'll win them over like you won over David. Is there a date set for this confrontation?"

"Tomorrow," I said, nauseous again.

"That is soon."

"David usually spends the night or weekend, but with me along, it'll only be a day trip. And I really want to see the house."

"Why?"

"They live on Lake Bellow . . ."

"Where the hell's Lake Bellow?"

"Four hours north of town," I said. "The pictures he showed me are gorgeous. There's a back porch overlooking the lake, a wide lawn leading down to the water...."

"And spiders and snakes and coyotes," he said, aping my enthusiasm. "Sorry, Paul, but after leaving Braintree, I became an orthodox urbanite."

"I'm also curious to know what his family's like. I'm an only child, and as I told David, I've always envied people with brothers and sisters. You never mentioned any, so I assume you're an only child, too."

"I am, and grateful for it."

"Why grateful?"

"I saw how being gay complicated familial relationships," he said, "at least when I was younger. A lot of the friends I made after leaving home had siblings. Some knew their brother or sister was gay and accepted it. More commonly, they either preserved a tactful distance that precluded any discussion of the gay siblings' love lives or flat-out disowned them."

"That happened to one of my other clients. Her two sisters got married and had kids shortly after leaving school. She's a nurse, and when she'd go home for holidays and birthdays, they'd badger her about getting married and urge her to chase the eligible doctors at the hospital where she worked. Finally, she blurted out the truth. They never spoke to her again."

Robert sighed. "I can't imagine being truly close to a brother or sister only for them to turn against you like that. Do you discuss me with your other clients?"

"Sometimes, but only when it's contextually appropriate, and never by name."

"Good. Not that there's any reason to keep my private life private anymore. To return to your question, being an only child allowed me to be a freer agent. I kept my folks in the dark and got on with it. People were also less likely to allow gay siblings near their children. The straight consensus viewed homosexuals like satyrs, pursuing anything that moved . . . though being undomesticated had its rewards."

"Like what?" I said, unable even to guess his meaning.

"Accepting your sexuality in a disapproving society sharpened your perception of it in yourself and others. You'd study someone for hints they had similar leanings and felt a certain triumph if your conclusions proved correct, especially if they were attractive and you lured them into bed. You also believed the people who shuddered at the idea of two men or two women doing such things had nothing in their lives as exciting. They got married and reproduced. You had the endless thrill of watching for and seizing on everything that spoke to your identity, whether friends, lovers, or culture. There was a perpetual stimulation in being who you were that wasn't always about sex, even though it derived from your sexuality."

"So, for you being gay sharpened your perceptions the same way art did?"

"Which likely accounts for the high number of gay artists. Then again, pursuing that stimulation may just have been compensation for leading a legally and socially restricted existence."

"Would you have considered settling down and having kids if you'd had the ability . . . the legal ability, I mean?"

"Probably not," he said. "Once I realized I was gay and knew it wasn't an option, whatever parental instincts I might've developed atrophied. I was also too focused on my career to give children the necessary attention."

"What about settling down? Do you think you would've been happy in a long-term partnership?"

"You're leading me back to the story of my great loves, aren't you?"

"Honestly, I wasn't. But you owe me another two. I also appreciate vicarious thrills."

"Comparing the thrills we offer each other is like comparing week-old bread to a freshly baked brioche. However, I almost enjoyed a long-term union."

"When, and with who?"

"Scotty Christopher," he said, his tone flat, unlike the dreamy fondness with which he described Terry. "We met after I left *Grandview* in '66. I'd returned to theater full-time, or as much of it as I could get. We worked on the same play."

"Was he another actor?"

"Set designer. He started out in TV, and by the time we met, he was working in both TV and theater, though, like me, his theater work was mainly off-Broadway."

"What play did you work on?"

His face puckered like someone struck by acute indigestion. "*Serve Me the Honorable Marmoset.*"

"What?"

"I know. It's almost as bad as Grantland Montague Hunnicutt. This was a time when experimental theater was in vogue, part of a wider fashion for the avant-garde."

His dismissiveness surprised me. "I'd have thought you'd have been in your glory."

"I'd have thought so, too. But although the 1960s avant-garde was strongly influenced by that of the 1920s and 1930s, the fashion had less to do with art than with a concurrent fashion for rebellion. The atrocities of World War II, followed by the Cold War and its parallel Hot War in Vietnam, seemed to indicate history wasn't just repeating itself but fulfilling the fearful predictions of the post-World War I generation. A similar rebellion against the status quo fermented and, with it, a vogue for avant-garde art. Unfortunately, when such things become fashionable, they often lose their purpose; or rather, their purpose changes to merely enabling people to feel *au courant.*"

"Then you think artists in the 1960s rebelled because rebelliousness was fashionable?"

"Not all of them. But as I mentioned before, great artists break the rules because it's the only way to say what they wish to say. Lesser artists in the

1960s broke the rules for the fun of rebelling, for which they simply copied the most superficial qualities of the earlier avant-garde: a blithe infraction of rules, the more outrageous and shocking the better. And because it was fashionable, it opened a royal road to the fame and profits available with mass-media, a motive Andy Warhol, for one, explicitly avowed, hightened senses and ennobled faculties be damned. They ignored the fact that the best art, even avant-garde art, must be artful, and as such it requires considerable thought and effort to achieve. But because audiences followed the fashion for rebellion, in those days, a work merely had to flout convention to receive a hearing."

"And *Marmoset* was one of these?"

"One of the worst. Characters switched identities from act to act for no reason other than to bewilder the audience. They spoke in non-sequiturs and broke into filthy quatrains sung to tunes retrieved from Arthur Sullivan's wastebasket."

"Arthur Sullivan?"

"As in Gilbert and," he said.

"Oh." I leaned my shoulders against the cupboard behind me and crossed my ankles.

"The play had obviously been written to prove its author's rebel status, and there's nothing duller than a work that exists solely to stroke its creator's ego."

"Why did you do it?"

"My agent convinced me it'd be a sensation, not just for its avant-garde trimmings but because those trimmings included political satire."

"What did that have to do with it?"

"It's hard to understand today, with political satire as common as dust, but in the 1960s, it was extremely popular and controversial, especially after the relative blandness of 1950s pop culture. *Marmoset*'s satire was too carelessly deployed among its other careless elements to carry much force. I had my doubts after I read the script, but I loved theater and saw a chance to have fun with the characters they wanted me to play."

"What were they?"

"In the first act, I was a crooked lawyer clearly modeled on the shysters Groucho Marx played in films. In the second, I was an undertaker reminiscent of another, and by that time obscurer pop culture figure, a mortician called Digger O'Dell from a 1940s radio sitcom, *The Life of Riley*, whose dialogue was laden with *double entendres* concerning death and funerals. In the third, I was a cleaning woman that codified every cleaning woman in every old movie and every TV drama involving one."

"A cleaning woman?"

"We also changed sexes in the third act, again for no discernable purpose other than to amuse the author."

"Were they as much fun to play as you expected?"

"Somewhat, though with all the rigmarole going on, the actors' efforts were barely noticeable. The first thing I did was steer my performance away from Groucho's mannerisms and those of the actor that played Digger, who spoke in a low, macabre monotone. The director insisted on steering me back, and when I pointed out the similarities, he swore there was a huge difference. That's when I began noticing the influence pop culture had even on people who prided themselves on being conversant with high art."

"Wasn't that also typical of the 1960s? Pop culture from the early part of the century was as fashionable as the avant-garde of the same era. Maybe *Marmoset* was a deliberate attempt to mix the two."

Robert shook his head. "Little about *Marmoset* was deliberate. That was the problem. If the author had been in more control of his material, he would have achieved the effects he was striving towards. The same was true of the director. If he'd had clear reasons for borrowing from past performers, it might have been tolerable. Instead, the author, director, and my cast mates went blindly on, giddy with their own inventiveness, never stopping to ask whether what they invented served any purpose. That's how Scotty and I got together."

"He wasn't giddy either?"

"No. Usually, set designers didn't attend many rehearsals. But as if the density of language and characterization in *Marmoset* weren't enough, the action propelled us from place to place faster than in an old-fashioned bedroom farce. The settings changed four or more times in each act. During rehearsals, the director and author repeatedly changed both. Scotty had to be on hand to turn a railroad station into a hospital or a funeral parlor into a race track."

"That must've driven him crazy."

"Less than you'd imagine. *Marmoset* would've been impossible to stage without minimalist sets. Chairs, tables, a dozen wooden crates, and lighting effects suggested the different locales. Scotty merely had to rearrange a chair and table or alter the lighting to comply with the director's requests. If anything, he found it tedious. One day, when the director and author were in a huddle deciding on more of what they called 'refinements,' I was in the wings, dreading the outcome of their latest brainstorm. Scotty came up next to me and said: 'Do you like this play?' I said 'no,' and I can't tell you what a relief it was to finally admit it to somebody in the production. I'd complained about it to friends, especially Mag, but they thought it was funny. Scotty and I shared the foreboding that came with being up to our necks in it."

"You became a refuge for each other."

"Pretty much. He'd caught my eye early on, though. He was weightlessly thin, like he had bird bones, and walked with a diffident shuffle suggesting total self-confident awareness as if nothing could surprise him, which he proved with his instant and precise changes to the sets. He had thin, buttery blonde hair and pale aqua eyes that were always partly unfocused as if he had learned not to pay too much attention to the world around him, and a complimentary, sardonic grin with a slightly unaligned front tooth. The tooth really made the grin, for me. It symbolized his dislocation from the world in general and our surroundings in particular."

"An unconventional portrait," I said.

Robert smiled. "I appreciate your tact. He wasn't conventionally handsome, to be sure. But I found his combination of cynicism and birdlike fragility irresistible. I was also impressed that he noticed my discontent with *Marmoset* amid the general giddiness and flattered that he shared his with me. Once we acknowledged our concerns, we began meeting after rehearsals at an all-night cafe a block from the theater to pillory the director and author and wallow in our misery."

"I assume you wallowed a lot."

"It was justified. I'd been trapped in rotten plays before, but with *Marmoset,* the presentiment of failure was acute. Scotty compared it to being on the Titanic, whereupon I proposed hiring a brass band to play 'Nearer My God to Thee' in the lobby on opening night."

"Was it as bad as you expected?"

"Just about, yet as I said, there were enough fashionable rebels among theatergoers to grant it a three-week run."

"What about the critics?"

"The more discerning saw through the pose. Others . . . are you familiar with the Rorschach test?"

"Psychologists show a patient a series of ink blots, and the patient describes what they see in them, which helps demonstrate how the patient's mind works."

"There were a number of critics and academics for whom artworks, especially any termed experimental or avant-garde, weren't to be appraised for their virtues or faults but rather as Rorschach tests challenging their intellect. They scoured plays and pictures and whatnot for details suggesting profound philosophical ideas and wrote reams of words to explicate them, less to demonstrate the value of the artwork in question than to show how brilliantly their minds worked. There were enough of them around to extend our run."

"How did you and Scotty salvage a romance from the wreckage?"

"A perfect metaphor," Robert said.

"Your erudition is rubbing off."

"I'm flattered, and becoming more erudite can only do you good. The romance began a week before we opened. Until then, the things connecting us were negative: the discomfiture of indentured servitude to a lousy play, savaging the author and director and the actors who followed them like baby chicks. It was fun and essential for our sanity, but it was one-dimensional. One night I was bitching about the director forcing me to copy Groucho and Digger O'Dell without his realizing it. Scotty agreed, and, in doing so, revealed how much of 1940s pop culture he absorbed as a kid. He even recalled the name of the actor who played Digger on radio: John Brown. From then on, we forgot our gripes to reminisce about the movies, books, and plays that shaped our tastes as youngsters. In minutes he changed from someone who merely understood my distaste for *Marmoset* to one who shared my experience of culture as an essential, organic joy."

"Turning the negative connection positive," I said.

"When our talk turned to music, he bragged about his record collection and rattled off names that plumbed the depths of my memory: 'Magic is the Moonlight,' 'Till the End of Time,' 'Stardust,' Billy Eckstine, Ella Mae Morse, Jimmy Lunceford, the Pied Pipers, and the Modernaires with June Hutton. The next night, rather than sit over coffee reiterating our loathing for *Marmoset*, we retreated to his apartment to play records. As we listened, he described growing up in New York, and I talked about Braintree. I even told him about Terry."

"Was that a calculated move?"

"No. Since Terry and I routinely discussed what was happening in music, it was inevitable that what Scotty played would remind me of him. After that, we talked about our more recent pasts in theater and TV. He loved my stories about *Grandview Park*."

"I'm not surprised."

"He'd heard about what Gray and I were up to on air but never actually watched. We had several acquaintances in common, and he'd attended parties Gray took me to, but somehow we never crossed paths. Our mutual interests, along with the music—much of which from that time, as you may know, was relentlessly romantic—ultimately landed us in bed. That planted the seed, so to speak."

"Did Coleridge's wings beat again?"

"Yes, to my surprise."

"Why was it a surprise?"

"I'd been with men since college, though I wasn't promiscuous, and there was my five-year tryst with Gray. But it was never the same as it had been with Terry. I assumed what I'd felt with him had been due to my being an impressionable teenager. That night at Scotty's, I experienced more than a sexual attraction and wondered if he did, too. Unfortunately, preparing for *Marmoset*'s opening left us little chance to explore whatever else might be going on between us. We'd work on the play by day and head to his place for music and sex at night. During that harried week, it was our way to unwind, a healthier alternative to drowning our sorrows in a bar."

"Similar to how things began with you and Gray. What happened after the opening?"

"Scotty started work on another play, *Splendid Transients*. But our evenings were too pleasant a habit not to continue. Every night for *Marmoset*'s three-week run, I dashed from the theater to his apartment, where he had dinner and records waiting."

"What happened after *Marmoset* closed?"

"I'd saved enough from *Grandview Park* not to fall back on my old stopgaps of waiter or store clerk. Also, thanks to *Grandview*, I'd acquired a reputation for memorizing scripts quickly and performing unerringly on live TV, or as unerringly as any fallible human might be expected, which made me a desirable commodity within the industry."

"Weren't most TV shows being filmed by the time you left *Grandview*?"

"Yes. Some were still live. Others were what they called live-to-tape, meaning that, although it was taped, nothing was edited out, except for an occasional cuss word or major malfunction, like if a portion of the set collapsed. Smaller errors remained part of the show. A stage-trained actor with a background in live TV narrowed the margin for errors and helped shorten the production schedule. More importantly, from my point of view, was that TV production was shifting to the west coast."

"Why did that concern you?"

"It limited my options. Only soaps, the evening news, game shows, talk shows, variety shows, and commercials were done in New York. Another long haul on a soap didn't interest me, and I didn't qualify for anything other than commercials, so I relied on them to tide me over between stage jobs."

"They served you well, apparently."

"Especially since they were being filmed as well. I'd do one once, and it'd be repeated over and over at the sponsor's discretion. Each repetition earned me a residual check. They kept me solvent. And since they were filmed during regular working hours, Scotty and I had more evenings free to go out."

"Where did you go?"

"Restaurants mostly," he said. "His professional interest in visual art meant we went to a lot of art galleries, and our shared careers in the theater brought us to a lot of plays. And we went to the ballet, the symphony, and sometimes the opera."

"The opera only sometimes?"

"He liked it more than me, despite my parents' efforts at indoctrination. On the brighter side, many of the jazz and pop musicians we'd grown up listening to were not only still performing but were better than ever. They'd appeared in spots around New York throughout my college days in the 1950s, and whenever I managed to scrape up the price of admission, I'd go hear people like Benny Goodman, Dizzy Gillespie, Peggy Lee, Lena Horne, sometimes alone, sometimes with friends. Later on, I'd go with Gray. But with Scotty, it was more like a date, which enhanced the pleasure of it immeasurably."

"What about movies?"

"We saw quite a few films, though as with music, we were particularly drawn to those from our childhood and adolescence."

"They were part of the 1960's vogue for early pop culture too, weren't they?"

"A big part, mainly due to TV stations and repertory cinemas around the country padding their schedules with them. They appealed to people who had grown up with them, like Scotty and me, who were either approaching or already ensconced in middle age, and attracted younger viewers curious about the past."

"Kids who were discovering their parents' records and old clothes in attics . . ."

"Films also conveniently tie most aspects of pop culture into one product, making them virtual catalogs of past fashions in numerous categories: clothes, hairstyles, cars, music, slang. And by the 1950s, critics and academics had begun treating cinema as an art form, making the older films illustrations of the medium's history rather than triggers for nostalgia. Younger viewers also relished their camp elements. A lot of the comedy from the 1950s to the 1970s consisted of parodies and caricatures of the movies from the 1920s to the 1940s. Carol Burnett practically built her career on such parodies. A few of the cognoscenti, like Scotty and me, found them campy and artful at one and the same time."

"Aren't 'camp' and 'art' generally considered mutually exclusive terms?"

"Erroneously," he said, "particularly for film."

"Why film especially?"

"As I said, they combine several different arts into one product: acting, music, direction, set design, costuming, and such. Individual elements in any given film might be poorly or artfully done. You could be dazzled by the costumes worn by a bad actor or have your heart broken by the music score for a lousy story. Winnowing the brilliant from the bullshit in a single film could easily consume an evening's worth of conversation."

"I see."

"The vogue for old movies also provided an opportunity for us to see those made before we were born: silents from the teens and 1920s with Chaplin, Keaton and Lloyd, Lon Chaney, Valentino and Gloria Swanson; and early sound films of the 1930s: screwball comedies with Carole Lombard and Cary Grant; the Busby Berkeley and Fred Astaire-Ginger Rogers musicals; Universal horror films—we loved Elsa Lanchester in *Bride of Frankenstein*—and the first Marx Brothers movies. But we were really in our element revisiting those from our adolescence: the 20th Century Fox musicals with Alice Faye, John Payne, and Betty Grable; the M.G.M. musicals with Judy Garland, Gene Kelly, and Jane Powell; Bette Davis and Joan Crawford melodramas, and the earliest film noirs. We recalled seeing them when they were first released, our minds roiling with ill-defined longings for Farley Granger, Montgomery Clift, and other matinee idols, and twenty years later, there we were, watching them again on a date with another man."

"Did you know then that some of those matinee idols were gay in real life?"

"There were rumors, especially in professional circles, some of which we managed to confirm. Speculating on who or who wasn't a member of the club was a nice, titillating pastime among friends and colleagues, but I found it quickly palled."

"Why?"

"Gossip is a fallow field of inquiry. I preferred discussing Laurence Olivier's Shakespearean performances to imagining who he might be sleeping with, because the subtler shades of meaning he brought out in the poetry had a direct effect on me, unlike his private pleasures, whatever they were."

"Did you have any interest in contemporary films?"

"Some," he said, "especially art cinema, which was nearing the end of its heyday by then. I'd been aware of Bergman, Fellini, Bunuel, and Kurosawa when their films were first shown in New York in the 1950s, and we saw others from the 1930s and 1940s by Marcel Carne and Jean Cocteau. But they never inspired the same affection as the old Hollywood products. Of course, we viewed the Hollywood films differently, in the light of our life experiences since we first saw them, especially our professional training."

"You were better able to distinguish the brilliant from the bullshit?"

"Yes. Have you seen many classic films?"

"My fair share."

"Did you, by any chance, take a film history course for easy credit in college?"

"Yes."

"Then you know how the studios lavished money on sets, especially for musicals. The action played out against stylized backgrounds that were often separate, or separable, artworks, crafted by gifted designers."

"Like the Venice set in *Top Hat*."

"Exactly," he said, "built entirely on a soundstage, without a shred of realism, and all the more pleasing for it. Watching those films as adults, I'd study the actors, and he'd pore over the sets. I admired line readings by Katherine Hepburn or Spencer Tracy, and he'd point out details that gave a room or building its unique and often memorable look. He had a theory that people repeatedly watched certain movies for the sets as much as for the story and characters. They revisited Rick's café in *Casablanca* the same way they returned to favorite places in life. He claimed even the best films would have had less impact with less appealing backgrounds, just as they would if other people had played the leads."

I uncrossed my ankles and rearranged my shoulders against the cupboard as images from favorite films flitted through my mind. "He may have been onto something."

"Our discussions also revealed the extent of Scotty's talents. The demands *Marmoset* placed on him barely scratched the surface."

"How so?"

"I mentioned *Splendid Transients,* the play he tackled after *Marmoset?*"

"Yes."

"*Transients* was a comedy of manners laid in an elegant hotel in an undisclosed European capital circa 1900. The play unfolded in a single set, the hotel lobby, which its producer had a budget to outfit in detail. Scotty spent weeks in libraries and second-hand bookstores searching for information about turn-of-the-century European hotels and their lobbies. I'd read the play and glanced over his research materials, and every night, after chasing around the *Marmoset* stage, I'd return to find another sketch on his drafting table, different from the one before. Each seemed an ideal combination of authentic detail adapted to the requirements of the play's action, but he'd toss them aside, saying 'wrong' or 'no good' and start on another the next day. Finally, he arrived at one that not only melded historical accuracy with stage mechanics but was as individual as the characters in the story. I was even more impressed because I had no idea how he'd done it."

"An aesthete like you?"

He shrugged. "My appreciation for visual art, like music, is entirely that of an informed spectator."

"The art lover as opposed to the artist?"

He nodded. "The night he showed me his final sketch, I expressed my bewilderment. He said: 'I've no idea how you do it, either.' I said: 'Do what?' He said: 'Be a different person onstage.' I said: 'That's nothing,' and I realized how much I took the craft of acting for granted. He kissed me and said: 'Neither is this for me.' There you have the first phase of our relationship, the one that established our dynamic."

"Mutual admiration?"

"Leavened by mutual mystery. Our professional and personal interests in the arts established a common ground yet with an extra, unintelligible quality that maintained our fascination with each other. He'd explain how he created sets, and I'd instruct him in acting, and we succeeded up to a point. I acquired a keener sense of the pictorial, and he became more attuned to the complexities of character and dramatic tension; in art and in life. Ultimately, though, how he turned what he saw into sets baffled me, and how I transformed written words into stage personas baffled him. Enjoying what we shared and striving to solve the enigma of each other's skills, plus the great sex, ratified our alliance. Six months after *Marmoset* closed, I moved in with him and stayed for seven years."

"What happened after that?" I said.

"It ended."

"How?"

"Badly," he said and glanced at the pastry mold clock. "I'll finish next time you come. You should get ready for your date with David, and I have mine with *Grandview Park*." He leaned on the cane and stood.

"I'll hold you to it." I lifted my near-numb buttocks from the counter. "Where's your sweater?"

"You don't have to take it to the cleaners."

"It's no big deal. Where'd you leave it?"

"In the bathroom, on the clothes hamper."

I walked through his Spartan bedroom to the bathroom. The sweater lay atop a plastic clothes hamper. As I picked it up, it unfolded, revealing a dark red splotch along the front. I folded it again, draped it over my arm, and returned to the living room.

"I'll be back with the sweater and groceries next week."

"Thanks, and in return for the Scotty story, you'll tell me about meeting David's parents."

"Deal."

"You see now what I meant about art enhancing one's ability to think about the world. Imagine the difficulty you'd have had describing how you feel about David without Coleridge's wings."

"Right again, you flinty old coot."

He laughed gleefully.

Back in my car, I cast the sweater on the passenger seat and drove around the corner to a cleaner's I had noticed on my first trip to the Roxbury Apartments: a little box squeezed between a comic book store and a Chinese restaurant, with the optimistic name Wonder Wash Dry Cleaners in orange plastic letters on a white plastic rectangle over the door. Beside the door, a wide plate glass window, clouded by steam, exposed a rail hung with clothes in garment bags. Inside, a college-age girl with long brown hair dampened and flattened by the humid air presided over the counter.

"It'll come out like new," she said after a cursory glance at the stain.

Next, I headed to the Argonaut.

David looked up from his computer as the door opened. An encouraging mixture of surprise and delight transformed his face when he spotted me.

"I thought we were meeting at Brewer's," he said, "not that I'd refuse more workplace wooing."

A middle-aged man twenty feet away turned from the pages of a book bound in faded green cloth to glance at us.

"I need your expertise again," I said.

"Another treasure hunt? You must've just left Robert."

"Yeah. And since I'm here, we can have dinner at Brahmin's Banquet."

"Cool. What are you looking for?"

"A play from 1966 called *Serve Me the Honorable Marmoset*."

He burst into disbelieving laughter. "You amaze me."

"Something I hope never changes. That's why I didn't call. I had to see your expression."

"Had to?" he said instantly flirtatious.

"It was practically compulsory, though it's the last time today I'll defer to your princely privileges."

"Thanks. Are you serious about the title, or did you make it up?"

"It's a play Robert appeared in. I'm guessing you don't have it on hand."

"I doubt anybody does." He entered the title into his computer. "Let's see what happens."

I waited while he bent toward the screen, examining the results.

"Nothing," he said. "What's the author's name?"

"He didn't say. I'll ask him next time."

"It probably wouldn't matter. If a title like *Serve Me the Honorable Marmoset* doesn't pop up the second I hit enter, the author's name won't help. I'll keep my eyes open, though."

"Thanks. What about dinner?"

He leaned nearer and lowered his voice. "I'll close as soon as this guy leaves. He's been wandering around for an hour without a sign of buying. He may be addicted to the smell of old paper. Don't laugh. I've caught more people than you'd care to know about sniffing open books. Are you still up for going to my sister's?"

"I've cleared my schedule, not that it was unduly cluttered."

"Great. We have to leave before seven to make it for lunch."

"I know. Don't remind me."

"I was thinking it might be easier if you spent the night at my place, and we left from there."

"How about I go home, pack a bag, you get take-out from the Banquet, and I meet you there?"

"Great. What do you want?"

"The chicken Tandoori was good."

"Again?"

"I'd rather not strain my palette before the big day. What kind of wine does your sister like?"

"Why?"

"I have to bring a hostess gift."

"Merlot's her favorite, but I'm sure she's not expecting anything."

"What about flowers?"

"What about them?"

"I can't decide between wine and flowers. What kind would she like?"

"Any would be welcome."

"Which would be better, flowers or wine?"

"Surprise us," he said, on the brink of exasperation.

"Okay, see you in a bit."

We exchanged a quick kiss, and I hurried from the store.

Walking downstairs to my car, I remembered what Robert said and wondered if the overconfidence I found both attractive and amusing about David had pressured me into a premature meeting with his family.

"He's the baby and probably used to getting his way," I thought, negotiating the late afternoon traffic. "You can't let him being an ideal playmate override your better judgment."

A long, wide turn brought the sun out from behind a skyscraper. I lowered the visor and replied to my own objections.

"And what if your better judgment is simply a less pejorative term for fear?"

Attempting to understand Jacobson's decisions had renewed my appreciation for the complexity of human motives, at least as far as arriving at their ultimate source. Mine proved even more resistant to analysis than his; besides, I had committed to the trip.

I stilled my thoughts by turning on the radio, and drove home in the company of a twenty minute block of pieces by Satie, picking up my hostess gift on the way.

5.

David jostled me awake at quarter to six on Saturday and waited for me to recover enough wherewithal to sit up before saying, "Bad news."

"What?"

"I forgot to get coffee last time I went shopping."

"Great."

"We can stop at Brewer's if you want."

"It's not a want; it's a need."

David prepared an omelet that I ate without tasting. Afterward, I drowsily donned the blue linen shirt, beige linen pants, and grey canvas shoes I had packed and stood squinting at his bedroom mirror, again struggling to contain my academic dishevelment within presentable bounds, while he—washed, dressed, and ready to leave in what I considered preternatural speed—stood by the front door, keys in hand, announcing the time every few minutes with the strained impatience of a retriever on a short leash.

"It's after six-thirty."

"How much after?"

"Four minutes."

Thinking that, at six-thirty-four on every other morning of my existence, I had rolled over and resumed sleeping, I left off my primping, grabbed my hostess gifts and followed him out to his car. Unable to choose, I settled on a medium-priced Merlot for his sister and flowers for his mother. I considered impressing them with a selection of genetically engineered specimens from

Fantasy Floral, but on visiting their website I found their stock far beyond my price range. I settled for a bouquet from a florist around the corner from my apartment, combining common asters, birds of paradise, stargazer lilies and hibiscus, offset by some Queen Anne's lace, yellow yarrow, and assorted greenery, swaddled in pale purple tissue paper.

As promised, David stopped for me to grab the largest available dark roast from Brewer's sleepy first shift of baristas. Fifteen minutes later, we barreled down a lightly traveled rural turnpike, the closed car distilling the scents of his mother's flowers, our colognes, and my coffee into a soporific vapor relieved only by the crisp breeze of the air conditioner. Following my lead, David drove in silence. Unlike me, he gazed out the windshield with a complacent grin, basking in the bright morning as if siphoning renewed energy from the sunshine and cloudless blue sky. I shrank from both, thanks to my protracted awakening and the trial by fire awaiting me at our destination. I stared at the dashboard, sipped my dark roast in a manner combining my thirst for the coffee with an equally strong desire to prevent any stray drops from marring my clothes, and every so often turned to check whether a sharp turn or quick brake had disturbed the items on the back seat.

Twenty minutes passed this way before my neurons felt sufficiently caffeinated for me to speak coherently. "What are they like?"

"Who?"

Our voices sounded unreal, and our words almost senseless after the long silence. "Your parents and your sister's family."

"They're great. Why?"

"How formal should I be?"

"Plying them with goodies will break the ice. Stick to baseline politeness after that."

I drank more coffee, cool but still fully charged. "How do I look?"

"Adorable."

"Am I too dressed up?"

"No, not that there's much you can do about it now unless you'd rather make a grand entrance in your underwear."

I gazed at the sunlit trees. He reached for the air conditioner control.

"Don't turn it down," I said, more vehemently than intended.

"Aren't you cold?"

"I don't want to get there all sweaty."

"You'd prefer freeze-dried?"

"I want to make a good impression. And if it's too hot, the flowers might wilt."

His hand dropped to my leg. "You and the flowers will be fine."

"None of that, now."

The hand crept up my thigh. "Maybe we should have a quickie by the side of the road . . . you know, to relax you."

"I told you I don't want to get there all sweaty."

He returned his hand to the steering wheel. "Okay," he said, "just don't expect to proposition me on the way back."

"I'm sorry I'm on edge."

"Don't be. They know I'd never go out with anyone who wasn't worthy of me."

"Wasn't worthy. . ." I turned, noted his grin, and altered my response to a tart: "Oh, shut up."

He complied for another ten minutes, during which I held fast to his confidence in me. "If I'm not allowed to touch the air conditioner," he said, "how about the radio? Some music might soothe you."

"Try it," I said.

He turned on the radio, and for the next half hour, several currently popular songs suffused the car.

Eventually, I stopped listening and started wondering. "Do you think these songs will mean anything to us twenty years from now?"

"You sure know how to change a subject," he said.

"It's a new driving game called *non-sequiturs*." I sipped my bitter, cold dark roast dregs. "Answer the question."

"How should I know if they'll mean anything to us twenty years from now? And why should you care?"

"Robert told me he bonded with one of his boyfriends over pop songs from their youth."

"Every generation has its songs, I suppose."

"I know, but these seem to exist solely as background for driving, dancing, or filling ear buds for joggers. I can't imagine anyone hearing anything more in them, now or in the future."

"You just don't care for contemporary music."

"True."

"And he's an old guy. He probably has a severe case of nostalgia."

"I'm sure nostalgia plays into it, but it's not necessarily the whole reason. I listen to Mozart, Beethoven, and other composers because I like how their music sounds, not because I'm nostalgic for the eighteenth and nineteenth centuries. And I'm sure Robert's appreciation of Shakespeare doesn't signify a wish to return to the socio-economic conditions of Elizabethan England. Just because he was alive when his favorite songs were written doesn't mean they lack qualities capable of transcending time."

"Point taken," he said and turned to the classical station, at that moment playing the opening chords of Liszt's *Hungarian Rhapsody*.

"Too dramatic," I said. "Turn it off."

He shut the radio and watched the road, grinning again.

I surveyed the distant mountains, their peaks shining in the sun. "This is the first time I've been around here," I said.

"Beautiful, isn't it? And great for hiking." He described camping in the hills with his dad and, later, with his high school and college friends.

I recalled Robert's claim to orthodox urbanity. "You must miss it living in the city," I said.

"A bit, but I have my weekends at Lake Bellow. And Brad's been talking about us taking Mark and Adrian camping."

"What about your sister?"

"She's a domestic pastoralist, according to Brad."

"A what?"

"She prefers the outdoors nearer the house: gardening, swimming, sunbathing."

"Oh."

He glanced at me. "You and I should go hiking sometime."

"One ordeal at a time, please."

"You might like it."

"I'd like it with you, probably."

"Imagine having sex up there." He pointed to a slanting mountain range with pale blue tops.

"Something you've done or only imagined?"

"Done," he said, with offhand pride, "a couple of times. I'll save the details for the return trip."

"Tease."

He smirked.

The challenge to supersede his earlier mountain romps distracted me until we turned off the highway into a small town called Denton. Ten minutes outside Denton, we turned off the main road onto a gravel driveway. The drive wound for a hundred yards between rows of trees interspersed by flowering rhododendron, skirted a lawn dotted with flower patches in bloom, and ended at a garage shaped like a small barn, with pansies and nasturtiums bordering its sides. A compact silver car stood before the closed garage door.

"Mom and Dad are here," he said.

A flagstone path cut across the lawn from the driveway, halting at three crescent brick steps leading to the front door of a two-story cottage. An eclectic group of ceramic flowerpots, overflowing with similarly eclectic groups of flowers, lined the steps. Open lawns on either side of the house afforded unobstructed views of the lake. Thick clumps of trees and shrubs on the far sides of the lawns screened the property from its neighbors before ending ten feet shy of the lake shore. As we ground to a halt behind his parent's car, a dog barked, and the collie from David's photos galloped from around the back of the house to the driver's side door and stood, wagging.

"Here we go," David said and opened his door.

A blast of humid air, tempered by a tangy, flower-scented breeze, entered the car, followed by Chop, who planked his paws on David's thigh and reached up to lick his face. I turned to the back seat, grasped the flower stems and bottleneck in my left hand, eased them around, and lurched out my door. Chop, spying a stranger, abandoned David and ran over to bark and wag at me. David trailed behind and bent down to pat him.

"It's okay, Chop. That's my friend Paul."

Chop wagged and looked from one to the other of us. Two shrill voices called, "Uncle Davy! Uncle Davy!"

We looked over as the boys from David's photos streaked towards us along the route Chop had followed, Mark's black hair and Adrian's blonde shining more brilliantly in the sunlight than in the pictures, their deportment revealing still more than either the images or David's verbal descriptions.

Mark rushed ahead with frenzied force, focused solely on his goal. Adrian ran with fastidious precision as if trained to maximize the utility of every movement. When they reached David, still bent to pat Chop, Mark leaped and wrapped his arms around David's neck while Adrian grabbed him round the waist, both squealing joyously. David pressed them to his sides, freeing Chop to amble over and sniff my shins.

I lowered my empty hand. He sniffed and wagged. Reassured, I scratched his chin and said:

"Hi, Chop."

He pricked up his ears and tilted his head, startled to hear his name spoken by a stranger. Mark and Adrian, still glued to David, looked sharply at me as if uttering the dog's name had been a brazen presumption.

The front door opened. Brad and Marge descended the stairs and strode toward us, smiling. Marge walked, talked, and gestured energetically, her curvaceous figure enhanced by a white button-down shirt whose tails flared over her hips. Brad sauntered three steps behind her, wearing a loose brown tee shirt and jeans.

David escaped his nephews' clutches to greet them. The boys stood by him like sentries, watching me as they might a two-headed lizard found among the flowerpots, Mark suspicious and uncertain, Adrian with a zoologist's impartial stare, noting and weighing my every gesture, detail of appearance, and modulation of voice. Chop sat before them, his tail gently sweeping the grass.

Marge hugged and kissed David. Brad shook his hand. Then they turned to me, their interest less explicit than their sons' yet enough to further stoke my anxiety.

"You must be Paul," Marge said, glancing at the gifts.

"It's nice to meet you both." I disengaged the wine from the flowers and handed it to her. "This is for you."

"Thanks," she said. "Merlot, my favorite."

"The flowers are for Mom," David said.

She smiled with polite gratitude. "You didn't have to do this."

"I told him a quick shower and clean clothes would be enough," David said.

"It's my pleasure," I said, "since you were kind enough to invite me."

"You're more than welcome."

"I suppose I should introduce you, but he knows you from the pictures I showed him," David said. "Everybody, this is Paul."

I shook hands with Marge and Brad.

"Do you know us too?" Adrian asked. Mark glared at him, disapproving.

I strove to answer with casual confidence. "I think so. You're Adrian, and you're Mark, and the furry one's Chop."

Adrian giggled as if against his better judgment. Mark stubbornly resisted my humor.

"Your uncle showed me pictures of the last time he was here," I said, my casual confidence shriveling to trepidation. "Looks like you have lots of fun in the lake."

"Yeah, we do," Mark said, his belligerence indicating a determination to prevent anyone from intruding on the family traditions.

Marge rescued me from the quagmire I had inadvertently entered. "Let's go in where it's cooler."

"Good idea," David said. "He's been worried all morning about sweating through his linens."

We walked along the path to the door.

"How was the drive?" Brad asked David.

"Good. Not much traffic after we left the city."

"You have a wonderful garden," I said to Marge.

"Thanks," she said. "I love the English garden style, with everything mixed together."

The house felt comfortably dry and cool inside, less cold than the car. A hallway led directly from the front door to the back porch. A closet, coat rack, and umbrella stand stood just inside the front door on the left, after which a wide doorway opened on a kitchen stretching almost the entire length of the house. Directly opposite the hall closet, another doorway led to a dining room with a mahogany dining table surrounded by eight matching chairs and a corner cupboard displaying crystal glasses and china plates. A narrower doorway in the dining room and another further down hall led to a cozy, informal living room with a sofa, easy chairs, a fireplace, and the second-floor stairway.

Marge led us into the kitchen. A bay window, its sill lined by potted herbs, provided a view of the side lawn and the garage wall with its flowery border. An antique oak table and six chairs formed a breakfast area before the window. Their aged wood contrasted strikingly against the stainless steel appliances, tile walls, tile counters, and glass-fronted cupboards in the other functional half of the room. A hidden audio system played Mozart's *Magic Flute* overture.

An older man and woman waited in the kitchen. The man stood six feet five and had long gangling limbs like a basketball player, anachronistically combined with white hair, Basset-hound eyes, and bifocals. He had on grey slacks and a green plaid shirt open over a white tee shirt and bent over the table, arranging fruit in an antique porcelain bowl.

The woman, six inches shorter, had cream-colored slacks, a pink cotton blouse embroidered with rosebuds, and a salt-and-pepper pageboy cut that set off her features: large hazel eyes, gently sloping nose, and strong, high cheekbones tapering to a tiny chin. She stood at the counter, stirring lemonade in a bulbous, frosted glass pitcher. David grasped her shoulders and kissed her cheek.

"Okay, Mom, here's your pipeline to *Grandview Park*'s grand past."

She stopped stirring and approached me, leaving the spoon to pivot erratically in the swirling lemonade. Mark and Adrian stood just inside the doorframe, gauging their grandparents' reactions to me.

"Nice to meet you, Paul. I'm Delia, David's mother."

"Pleased to meet you, Mrs. Farmington," I said.

"Delia," she said. "This is my husband, Tom."

Tom loped around the table to shake my hand.

"Pleased to meet you both." I extended the flowers to Delia. "These are for you."

"They're beautiful. Thank you."

Marge brandished her bottle. "I got wine, Mom."

Delia glanced at her and back at me. "Somebody's done his research."

"As I'm sure David's told you."

"Indeed," Delia said. "I can't wait to hear about it."

Marge placed the wine on the counter and reached for the flowers. "Let me put those in water for you, Mom."

"Thank you, dear."

Marge located a fluted crystal vase in a cupboard and filled it at the sink. Chop sniffed my shin again. I scratched his ears. Mark and Adrian watched keenly.

"You like dogs?" Tom said.

"If they like me."

"Chop's the best," Delia said.

"I was interested to hear you're looking into Erich Jacobson's life," Marge said, arranging the flowers in the vase. "I loved his books as a kid."

Brad spoke over an open drawer from which he extracted a series of beige linen napkins that looked like swatches shorn from my pants.

"The ones with the talking halibut?"

"Herring," Marge said.

"David didn't tell me you were familiar with them," I said.

"She didn't tell me until a few days ago," David said. Chop, with a gentle leap, gripped David's waist with his paws. Without disrupting his answer, David sank cross-legged to the floor to play with him. "I was so focused on the *Grandview Park* angle I forgot about it."

"Didn't you read them, David?" Brad said.

"No." David rubbed the sides of Chop's neck while Chop swatted his arms with his paws. Mark and Adrian joined them on the floor, and in a few seconds, all became enmeshed in a series of reciprocal tickles, grabs, giggles, squeals, and barks.

"Why not?" Brad said, indifferent to the cacophony.

Tom explained. "We'd disposed of Marge's books by the time David came along. We bought him newer ones."

"Too bad newer doesn't always mean better," Marge said. "Harold was great. I remember the books all had the same dedication: *For the lost Lenore*. I always wondered why he chose a line from Edgar Allen Poe for kid's books."

"Everybody who's read them wonders that," I said.

"Maybe he had a hidden morbid streak," Brad said, counting out silverware.

"If he did, he hid it well," I said. "Everyone who knew him describes him as a pleasant, genial friend."

"I'm glad," Marge said. "I'd hate it if Harold's father turned out to be a creep."

"Think you'll learn the reason for the dedication?" Tom asked, his expression reminiscent of a burnt-out professor on the verge of retirement.

"I doubt it. Nobody named Lenore has appeared in any of the material I've seen so far. She'll probably turn out to be a Siamese cat or a Mynah bird. What I really want to know is why he switched from mysteries to children's books."

"He wrote mysteries, too?" Delia said.

I recited my speech on Jacobson's literary career and my involvement with it while Marge arranged the flowers, Delia pried ice cubes from a tray and dropped them in the lemonade, and Brad finished with the utensils. Mark, Adrian, and Chop continued roughhousing with David on the floor, my status as a guest, nominal stranger, and person of interest for the other adults not only excluding me from their exuberant play but convincing them to ignore me completely, except for Adrian, who now and again paused to glance up with his zoologist's eyes as if pondering the riddle of my existence.

Tom alone granted me his undivided attention, winning him my everlasting gratitude. I addressed my remarks to the pendant eyes peeping at me over his glasses, and when I finished, he said, "Are the detective novels any good?"

"They're okay, mainly relics of their era."

"Unlike the immortal Harold Herring?" Brad said.

Marge stuck the last hibiscus in the vase, stepped back to assess the overall effect of her styling, and disposed of the purple tissue paper. "I'll be interested in what you find out," she said.

"Me, too," Tom said.

"I only hope the end result's worth the effort."

Brad removed plates from a cupboard and piled them on the counter.

"Aren't you going to grill him about your soap stud, Mom?" David said, rubbing Chop's belly while Chop lay on his back across David's knees, causing Chop's left rear leg to paw the air and Mark and Adrian to laugh helplessly.

"David's heard all my Jacobson talk and then some," I said.

"Why don't we go into it over lunch?" Marge said. "Everything's ready."

"What's on the menu?" David said, leaning back on his ankles, allowing Chop's excitement to subside.

"Chicken salad with cranberries and pecans and buttermilk rolls," Marge said to the room in general but with a pointed glance at me.

"Sounds great," I said. "Especially after the sad little omelet I had for breakfast."

"That I cooked," David said defiantly.

Marge laughed. "He cooked? You're lucky you were able to make the trip."

"It wasn't any worse than what I've made for myself," I said.

Marge removed a serving platter from a cupboard and set it next to the stove. The music changed to Tchaikovsky's wonderful *Eugene Oniegin* waltz. David held Chop up on his hind legs and manipulated his front paws as if conducting the orchestra. Mark and Adrian again became helpless with laughter, Mark rolling on the floor, Adrian bobbing back and forth on his knees.

"You'll have to excuse us," Tom said. "The Farmingtons are a bit crazy. Ask Brad."

Marge peered into the oven, turned it off, and removed a baking sheet lined with buttermilk rolls, their tops golden brown.

"Fine with me," I said. "As they say, it's the ones who don't know they're crazy you have to watch out for. Can I help?"

"We've got too many hands on deck as it is," Marge said. "Dad, why don't you and David take Paul onto the porch? We'll be out in a second."

Tom unfurled his lanky body from behind the table and strolled to the door. "This way," he said.

David and Chop scrambled to their feet, followed by Mark and Adrian, looking disappointed that the play had ended yet happily primed for other diversions with their uncle. Appropriately, the music segued into Holst's *Jupiter the Bringer of Jollity.*

Halfway down the hall, Mark rushed to the living room doorframe, stopped, and turned back as Chop dashed past him into the room.

"Uncle Davy! Come see our new video game!"

"Another new game?" David said.

"Yeah!" Adrian said, fired by Mark's enthusiasm. "It's really cool!"

"Okay," David said and tuned to me. "This'll only take a little while."

"Sure," I said.

Mark regarded me stonily, resentful that my presence set limits to David's time with him and his brother.

Tom led me onto the porch. I recognized the screened-in walls, big wicker table, and chairs from David's photos. A square, wicker side table stood in the far corner, and a spindly, wrought-iron chandelier decorated with thin iron leaves hung overhead. The late morning sun gleamed over the lawn just beyond the screens, twinkled on the rippling water, and spotlighted the houses tucked amid the greenery on the opposite shore, along which various disturbances indicated swimmers. Birds, bugs, and the breeze churning the lake accentuated the deeper silence of forest and sky, unlike the incessant sounds of the city that seemed like a compulsive attempt to avoid silence at all costs. Tom sat at the table while I absorbed the view.

"A beautiful place," I said.

"Pictures don't do it justice, do they," he said, "especially on a phone."

"No, they don't."

"Do you swim, Paul?"

"Enough to stay afloat. My mom made me take lessons when I was young, but I didn't do much of it afterward. I'm sure Chop could beat me in a race."

"You'll have to bring a bathing suit next time."

"I'd like that."

Delia, in the hallway, called out "Lunch" to the game players in the living room and responded to the kids' disappointed moans with "Come on, you can play that later."

Delia arrived at the porch carrying her flowers, which she assigned to the corner table to prevent their blocking our view of each other around the big table. Mark and Adrian trooped in; their steps weighed down by frustration. Adrian climbed onto a chair between Delia and Tom and assumed another fastidious pose: spine straight, arms dangling at his sides, eyes on the door. Mark sat on Tom's other side, leaning back in his chair, his arms swinging in perfect non-synchronization, looking impatiently around the room but never at me. Chop pranced in at their heels and nestled on the floor, his nose to a screen.

David entered carrying plates, napkins, and utensils, placed them on the table, and returned to the kitchen. Marge arrived next, bearing a large ceramic bowl containing the salad, followed by David with the rolls on the serving tray and Brad with the lemonade and eight plastic tumblers stacked one inside another. David distributed the napkins and utensils, Brad poured the lemonade, and Marge scooped her salad onto the plates, added a roll, and handed them around.

"May I say, Paul," Delia began, "I think it's admirable of you to volunteer like you do."

"I don't know about admirable," I said. "It's a worthwhile way to spend my time and meet interesting people. One of my clients was among the first commercial jet pilots in the country."

"You never told me that," David said.

"He's new," I said. "I've only visited him twice. His house is full of old flying gear and pictures of him in the different uniforms they used during his career."

Delia lifted her lemonade to her lips. "How did he look in them?"

"Dashing enough to be in ads for the airline."

"David told us you said your actor friend doesn't have any personal items in his place," Tom said.

"True. There's only one picture from when he was in his early thirties."

Marge finished serving and sat behind her own plate. "Did he ever say why?"

"He thinks his career never amounted to much and doesn't want any reminders of it around."

Delia's forehead puckered behind the pageboy bangs. "How sad."

"Somehow, it never strikes me as sad when I'm there. I guess because it reflects his personality so well."

"What's his personality?" Marge said.

"He once described himself to me as a flinty old coot."

The adults laughed. Mark and Adrian looked at each other, bewildered and wary.

"How would you describe him?" Delia said.

"Smart," I said, "with a caustic wit."

"Does he have any friends or family?" Brad said.

"From what I understand, most of his close friends have passed away. Whatever distant relatives he might have are back east, where he grew up. But that's the case with most *Heart and Hands* clients. They're the reason it exists."

"What about hobbies or other interests?" Tom said.

"He reads a good deal. As a matter of fact, he often patronized the Argonaut after he moved out here."

"You mean I might have run into him there years ago without knowing it?" Delia said.

"Maybe," I said.

"Don't you think you'd have recognized him, Mom?" Marge said.

"Depends," Delia said. "When did he move out here?"

"Sometime in the early 1970s. I don't know exactly."

"About ten years after *Grandview Park*," Delia said, thoughtful. "He might have changed."

"Not really," I said. "I've seen footage of him from other shows and movies. He's recognizable at every age."

"How did you get tangled up watching a soap opera in the first place?" Brad said.

"My mother was a stay-at-home mom. She watched all the old daytime shows. *Grandview Park* was her favorite. She conned me into watching it with her after school, probably to keep me quiet and out of trouble."

"How long did you follow it?" Brad said.

"A good eight years," she said, "until I went to college."

"And you really liked it?" Tom said, his wonderment enriched by his professorial manner.

Delia pertly defended her younger self. "I loved it, but it was about more than the show. When you're a kid, sharing things with your parents makes you feel grown up. Watching *Grandview Park* seemed to put me on a par with her."

"And you remember Robert from then?" Marge said.

"Absolutely, though I only knew him as Grantland Hunnicutt."

Tom laughed. "What a moniker."

"He was a big deal for a while," Delia said. "The triangle with his brother and his sister-in-law was riveting."

"I guess women went for bad boys even then," Brad said.

Delia laughed. "Of course they did, and so did a lot of men. How do you think Marlon Brando got to be a big star? Grantland wasn't bad, though, just flawed. Mom used to say, 'Poor Grantland. He always takes the wrong turn.' I think she felt if she could only talk to him, she'd put him on the proper path."

"Most of his fans thought the same," I said. "He told me he received a thousand letters a week when his character got involved with black market penicillin."

Delia jerked upright, brows raised, bangs quivering. "I remember that. We were on the edge of our seats for months."

Tom peered over his glasses at Mark and Adrian and shrugged as if at a loss to explain their grandmother's eccentricities. They giggled. I also noticed that while Adrian had practically cleaned his plate, Mark had picked the cranberries from his chicken salad and stacked them in a fastidious little pile on the rim of his dish.

"How did it play out?" David said.

"His brother got him out of it, as usual, but not before the black marketers got to him. That was on a Friday. We spent the entire weekend afraid he was dead."

"Obviously, he wasn't," Tom said dryly.

"No, paralyzed. The only one he allowed to help him learn to walk again was his sister-in-law. That's the nearest they came to having an affair."

"What do you think grandma would think about Paul knowing him?" Marge said.

"She'd be delirious," Delia said.

"What would she think about his off-screen affairs?" David said.

"Startled," Delia said, "and maybe disappointed. Like many people then, she considered being gay an affliction, like epilepsy. Of course, you'd have changed her mind on that score, David."

David beamed.

"If you'd like to meet him," I said, "I'll ask if he's up for visitors."

Delia considered. "That might be fun. Thank you, Paul."

"You're welcome. I'm sure he'll be glad to know you liked what he did."

"What was he in after *Grandview Park*?" Delia said. "You mentioned movies and other TV shows, but I don't remember seeing him anywhere else."

"Theater was his first love. He did a lot of it in New York. The movies and TV stuff were mostly bits. You can find clips online, but he's rarely in anything for more than five minutes at a time."

"I assume that's the reason for his bitterness," Delia said.

"Mostly, I think," I said, avoiding the topic of his love life.

Mark consumed his abridged chicken salad in bored silence. Adrian, long since finished, looked around as if waiting for something to prevent the entire afternoon from being wasted. The moment Marge and Brad stood to collect the dishes, Adrian rounded on David. "Uncle Davy! Let's go outside!"

Mark immediately abandoned what remained of his salad. "Yeah! Let's go out!"

"What for?" David asked, offering a token show of hesitation.

"We can play Frisbee," Adrian said, pronouncing the word with joyful reverence while quivering on his chair like a coiled spring.

"Frisbee!" Mark repeated, already clambering off his chair. "Yeah!"

Chop, also familiar with the word, stood and stared at the boys, wagging.

"Shouldn't you wait a little after eating?" Delia said.

"No!" Mark said.

"Okay," David said, "but if you make me throw up, I'm coming back in."

Mark laughed uproariously. Adrian stared open-mouthed at the audacity of the idea.

"And you'll wash your own clothes," Marge said to David, increasing the boys' hilarity.

"See what I mean about insanity in the family?" Tom asked me.

"Will Paul play too?" Adrian said, tentatively pronouncing my name for the first time.

Mark shot Adrian a dirty look and regarded me with extreme doubt: about my ability to play, about the advisability of me playing, or both.

"I think he'd better not," David said. "He wore his best clothes for Grandma and Grandpa. He shouldn't get them dirty."

"Oh," Adrian said.

His and Mark's subsequent silent stare indicated relief combined with contempt for my ostentation. A wave of self-pity crashed over me as I wondered if, Popcorn Tag notwithstanding, I had grown too adult to relate to anyone under thirty.

Brad returned for the half-empty chicken salad bowl.

"Dad!" Adrian said. "Come play Frisbee!"

"I'll be out after your mom and I load the dishwasher."

Brad spirited the bowl away. Mark and Adrian followed him out and ran upstairs for their Frisbee.

"Do you mind?" David asked me.

"No," I said. "I'd like to take a closer look at the lake if that's okay."

"I'll walk down with you," Tom said. "I can give you all the gossip about the neighbors. Dee?"

Delia leaned back in her chair, drowsy and content. "I'd rather digest my lunch and admire my flowers."

Tom and I strode across the lawn to the lake. The view of the shoreline on either side expanded where the flora bordering Marge and Brad's property ended. Hints of lawns and a few small docking areas attested to other cottages, similar to those opposite us, screened by the trees.

"I've always liked being near water," I said.

"Most people do."

The kids laughing behind us on the lawn mingled with the water lapping at our feet.

"Do you swim?" I said.

"Only when it's very hot. The water up here stays cold, and at my age, you feel it more."

I reached down and touched the water. It felt about sixty degrees. "It must be nice floating around out there, staring at the sky."

"You'll have to come back and find out, not that I'm authorized to issue invitations on my children's behalf. Are you enjoying your research?"

"Pretty much. Of course, it helps if you have a taste for minutiae."

"Like what?"

"Like the cost of living statistics from eighty years ago."

He chuckled. "I imagine it must be solitary work."

"Mostly."

"Are there exceptions?"

"The curators at the archives are usually pleasant. And I've gotten in touch with descendants of people who knew or worked with Jacobson when he lived here, looking for old letters or diaries."

"How's that gone?"

"Good, on the whole. I've gathered a lot of material."

"What about the people?"

"They've been cooperative, with one exception." I related my encounter with the greedy rodent, who had since become not only a symbol for every obstacle to my work but a reliable figure to amuse whoever asked about it. He smoothed over a number of awkward moments at Rene's party.

"I never knew a researcher's life could be that fraught," Tom said.

"Which is why being alone with a stack of dusty old papers isn't always a bad thing."

"Dad!" David called.

We turned to spot the Frisbee, which had veered off course, soaring straight for Tom's head. Tom lifted his hand, caught the Frisbee, and without missing a beat, swung his long arm like a scythe to fling it back to them.

"Nice to know I retain adequate hand-eye coordination," he said.

"More than adequate, I'd say."

A modest grin modified his hang-dog face. "Working at a semi-sedentary job like a bookshop, I tried to be active in my free time. When David was young, he and I went hiking all around here."

"I know. He told me about it on the ride up. He invited me to go with him sometime."

"Are you?"

"I'm mulling it over."

"You'll be in good hands. He knows everything you'd want to about hiking."

"I'm sure he does. I'm just not sure how compatible I am with the countryside."

"You seem comfortable now."

"Sure, in a house with air conditioning, plumbing, and a gourmet cook."

He laughed. "You'd probably love it once you started."

"Maybe," I said.

A water skier sped by, the roar of the motorboat silencing us during her passage.

"I'm glad David's met someone like you," he said over the fading echo of the boat.

"Like me?"

"Yes. Polite, sensible . . ."

"Am I that transparent?"

"I'm sure you have hidden depths, but I'd be shocked to find you'd done anything untoward."

"I don't think I have. Are David's friends often untoward?"

"No . . . it's just that, well, we were worried about him for a while."

"Why?"

He stared across the water. "He never had much direction; rather, he changed directions quickly. When he was a teenager, he'd get interested in a subject for about a month and drop it for something else. Once, he went from photography to animal husbandry to meteorology in a single summer. Nothing inspired any prolonged effort. That's why we were surprised when he wanted to take over the family business. He'd never shown much interest in it before. We expected him to find another enthusiasm after a short time."

"He told me it's like a second home."

Tom smiled ruefully. "I'm not surprised. Dee returned to work after David finished grade school. Rather than go home to an empty house after school, he'd come to the store and wait for her to pick him up on her way home. I'd get back two hours later, after closing. He'd spend his time reading and helping me out. I'm surprised he didn't get sick of it long ago, with his mercurial nature."

"He said he expects to end up an old man showing tourists curious relics called books."

"That's another thing. How long can a store like the Argonaut hold out against technology? I'm glad he's buying and selling online. He might be able to switch to another product if and when books become obsolete."

"I get your concerns," I said. "But though we've only recently met, I find him refreshingly stable compared to the party animals you often encounter."

"He never lapsed into that lifestyle, thankfully. Maybe he's maturing."

"Whatever he's doing, I like being around him," I said.

"Good. I'm sorry if I sound overprotective. That's what happens when you have children in middle age. You start out worrying whether you'll live long enough to raise them, and it escalates from there. Do you want children, Paul?"

The question threw me. "Someday," I said. "One of the advantages of being gay is you don't have to think about kids until you're really ready."

"Just don't wait till you're pushing fifty."

"If Mark and Adrian are indicative, I may need to hone my parenting skills a bit. They don't seem to know what to make of me."

"Kids often take a while to warm up to new people. And with so many of us here, you haven't had a chance to get to know anyone particularly well."

"I hope I do . . . get the chance, I mean."

Chop trotted between us to the water and drank. Tom watched him fondly. "Poor guy, you must be hot in the sun with all that fur."

A happy shriek returned our attention to the lawn. Brad and Mark reclined on the grass, watching David turn in place, holding Adrian by the hands. Adrian skimmed the air like a kite caught in a circular current, hair dancing, legs akimbo, his fastidiousness lost in the joy of being airborne.

Delia and Marge watched from the porch, their faces clear enough through the screen for me to observe their amusement.

The revolutions slowed until Adrian's feet touched the ground, and he wobbled a few paces like a newborn fawn. Chop trotted over to Brad and Mark. They petted him, and he nestled in the grass at their feet, head up, alert and panting. Again I envied David for his extended family.

"If you've had enough of the view," Tom said, "how about organizing a card game until the playdate's over?"

"Great," I said.

David began swinging Mark around. Chop stared at them, head tilted. Tom and I veered around the flying feet to the porch, where Marge and Delia sat sipping the last of the lemonade.

"The kids are having a high old time," Delia said.

"All four of them," Tom said.

"I'm sure Paul would've made it five if he'd known," Delia said. "You should've specified casual dress."

"David knows we're informal," Marge said. "He could have mentioned it."

Tom relieved my embarrassment. "How about playing cards until dinner?"

Marge and Delia agreed enthusiastically. Tom disappeared into the house for the cards.

"Speaking of dinner, what's it going to be?" Delia asked.

"Vegetable lasagna and green salad," Marge said. "I put the lasagna together last night. It only has to bake for a half hour." She turned to me. "I hope you'll like it."

"I can't imagine not liking it."

Tom returned, and we gathered around the table for draw poker.

"We don't have any chips, so it'll have to be for fun," Marge said.

Tom shuffled the cards. "When I was young, we used matchsticks," he said.

Marge stood. "We don't have matches, either, however . . ."

She entered the house and returned with a can of Suffolk's mixed nuts, a brand founded in 1884. The Suffolk's mascot, a cartoon squirrel named Spiffy, introduced in 1912, grinned at us from the label.

"You want to play for nuts?" Tom said.

"Eating them after will give us some profit," she said, prying the can open, "unlike matchsticks."

We established a scale of value, ranking the peanuts, filberts, cashews, and Brazil nuts lowest to highest and began playing.

"Did you enjoy your walk?" Marge said, fanning out her cards.

"Yes, thanks," I said. "It's a beautiful place."

"I hope my husband didn't distract you too much," Delia said. "I could see him bending your ear from here."

"No. It's a relief to talk to someone about anything other than Erich Jacobson."

"I'm pretty sure that's the first time anyone described Dad as a relief," Marge said. "He's more often considered blunt."

Tom stared at his cards and said, "I can be charismatic when there's sufficient reason to draw on such a precious resource."

"I'm honored by your largesse," I said.

Marge and Delia laughed.

"You must possess an almost supernatural appeal to win him over that fast," Marge said, her eyes gleaming impishly.

Tom replied while still staring at his cards. "He's a damn sight more personable than Cretin Corey, at any rate."

Delia turned and said, "Tom," transforming his name into a reprimand carrying the crack of a willow switch.

I rearranged my cards, suppressing the obvious question.

"What's the difference?" Tom said to Delia and looked at me over the tops of his glasses. "Corey and David dated a while back. He was seven years older than David and had a proprietary attitude toward him that was sickening to behold."

"He wasn't that bad, Dad," Marge said.

"Oh?" Tom replied. "Remember what he said about your rose hip jelly?"

Marge shrugged off the incident, but it obviously still stung.

Delia intervened. "My husband has a way of approaching life the way critics approach events in a novel."

"If more people took the same approach, they'd get into less trouble," Tom said. "And I'm past caring about being blunt."

"At least I'm on the better side of your bluntness," I said.

"There's another point in your favor," Tom said, transposing two of the cards in his hand, "your wit. Corey was oily when he thought he was being witty."

"I can be blunt, too, when necessary," Delia said, offering him a more threatening version of Adrian's unblinking stare.

Tom heeded the warning and resumed planning his bet, his tongue rolling inside his cheeks.

Delia shifted her attention to me. "Please don't tell David we mentioned him. Let him tell you in his own time if he wants."

"Sure," I said.

Delia, Marge, and I sought the shelter of small talk for the rest of the game. Apart from his bets, Tom preserved a dignified silence.

Marge had accumulated an impressive hoard of cashews and Brazils by the time Brad, David, and the kids returned from the lawn, breathless and starved.

"What time's dinner?" Brad said.

David grabbed a handful of Marge's cashews and started flicking them into his mouth.

"May as well be now," Marge said, "since my fortune's being devoured faster than I accumulated it." She left to preheat the oven.

"You boys should wash before dinner," Delia said.

"Yeah," Brad said, "we must be pretty ripe."

I noted the familiar scent of David's musk filtering through his *October Mist*. "I didn't bring a change of clothes," David said.

"I left some the last time we stayed over," Tom said. "Take them."

"You could have mine," Brad said, "but I'm a size smaller."

"No problem. I'll use Dad's."

"You should've known you'd be dragged into outdoor games," Delia said.

"I was too busy calming this guy's anxiety." David looked at me. "How are you getting along?"

I gestured to the meager remnants of my initial stake. "Pretty good, except for a slight case of diminished nuts."

Brad, Delia, and Tom chuckled. David smiled approvingly.

Marge poked her head around the doorway to announce: "I'm going to toss the salad. You keep playing if you want," and disappeared again.

Brad, David, and Mark clambered upstairs to wash. Adrian hesitated, studying the cards and nuts as if wondering whether our game had been more fun than theirs, after which he walked with slow, precise steps from the porch into the living room and up the stairs. Delia, Tom, and I switched to rummy, turning our nuts back into appetizers.

The game ended after Brad and the boys returned, and Brad and Marge began setting the table. David arrived once the plates had been laid. He had on a pair of grey seersucker pants three inches too long for him, the extra cuffs rolled up over his ankles, and a similarly outsized shirt with the sleeves bunched up past his elbows. He posed in the doorway, and said:

"Looks like I shrank in the shower."

The boys laughed shrilly.

"I like it," I said. "It makes my ensemble seem twice as good."

Mark and Adrian ceased laughing as if replying in kind to one of David's jokes constituted another serious breach of etiquette.

Brad carried in the salad and the open Merlot, followed by Marge with a steaming casserole containing her lasagna. She had opted for a red sauce, which paired nicely with the Merlot, earning me added praise for providing it. Marge served.

Praising the dinner opened up a discussion of Marge's early attempts at cooking prior to entering culinary school: macaroni and cheese that burnt so badly they had to throw away the baking dish; crab salad that resulted in food poisoning; five stovetop fires, one requiring intervention from the fire department; and leaving the sugar out of a chocolate mousse. Marge silently rebutted these testimonials with a delectable fruit salad for dessert, combining red, green, and black grapes; strawberries; papaya, pineapple, and mango chunks; orange segments and fresh shredded mint leaves.

As we gobbled the fruit, dusk dimmed the lake and horizon to a pale purple. Brad switched on the overhead light. David scraped a last spoonful from his dish, leaned back in his chair, and said to me, "We should think about getting back."

Adrian looked up from his dish, brow furrowed. Mark cried out, "No!"

"Sorry guys," David said, "but we're only here for the day, and it takes me four hours to drive home."

"Read to us first," Mark said.

Adrian's brow cleared, and he chimed in with a commanding "Yeah!"

"Do you mind?" David asked me.

Mark glowered, resenting the veto power allotted to me. Adrian watched and waited, anxious for my reply.

"I won't be the villain in this piece," I said.

David grinned and said to them, "Okay, but let's make it quick."

The boys each grabbed him by a hand and dragged him to the living room.

"They always wrangle a story out of him when he's here," Delia said.

"I know. He told me."

We stood to carry our dirty dishes to the kitchen.

"And for your information," Tom said, "you're the least villainous young man I've ever met."

Passing the living room, I glimpsed David and his nephews on the sofa, within an oval of amber light cast by an antique brass floor lamp behind them. Mark leaned against David's left arm, legs scrunched up under him. Adrian leaned against David's right, legs dangling over the edge of the sofa, hands limp in his lap. Each bent his face to the book in David's hands while he recounted the efforts of a monkey to build a tree house.

Listening to David mimic the voice of the monkey imploring his elephant friend to lift lumber into the tree, I imagined being both a child hearing the story and an adult reading it. The blissful concentration on Mark's and Adrian's faces led me to wonder whether, contrary to my claim about not missing much as a child with my father gone and my mother working, something had been missing. At the same time, the vivacity with which David enacted the story roused a longing more imperative than the imprecise 'someday' with which I had answered Tom's question about children.

The potential for satisfying that longing foundered quickly against the evidence, apparent earlier, of my inability to relate to anyone under thirty. I recalled what Robert said about allowing his paternal instincts to atrophy in the face of social and legal taboos against his becoming a father and wondered if, for different reasons, I had condemned mine to the same fate.

Unable to grapple with these new and unsettling ideas at that moment, I turned away from the living room and followed the others into the kitchen. I handed my plate and utensils to Brad, who loaded them in the dishwasher while Marge tidied up the counters. Delia, Tom, and I gathered around the kitchen table, out of their way. Chop wandered in and lay down next to us.

"I'm glad you could come," Delia said.

"Me, too," I said, again seeking comfort in small talk. "Let me know if you want me to introduce you to Robert."

"I will," she said. "Talking about *Grandview Park* brought up many wonderful memories."

"I'm glad."

"I hope we'll see you again," Tom said.

"So do I."

"Are you any less anxious than when you arrived?" he said.

"Yes, thanks," I said, "probably because the food was as agreeable as the people."

"Flatterer," Marge said from the sink. "You'll be back."

David joined us, followed by Mark and Adrian. Mark clutched the storybook to his chest, chewing the corner of his mouth. Adrian stared, his eyes revealing without hindrance the desolation his brother struggled to conceal.

"Okay," David said. "I think we're ready."

He hugged and kissed his parents and sister, shook hands with Brad, knelt to hug his nephews, and patted Chop.

"Next time, I'll stay over and read you stories until you fall asleep, I promise."

"Okay," Mark said as if agreeing to something too far in the future to perceive. Adrian simply nodded.

We exited amid a swarm of thank-yous and goodbyes.

As the car reached the main road, I slouched down as far as my seat belt allowed, staring at the stars beginning to appear like pinholes in the dusk, my mind blank. David looked at me.

"Adrenaline withdrawal?"

"I guess," I said, "along with the wine."

"You brought both on yourself. I told you there was nothing to worry about."

"They seemed to like me."

"They liked you."

"Your dad at least made it clear."

"When?"

"When we were standing by the lake. According to him, I'm intelligent, stable, and pretty much a catch."

"You are . . . all those things."

"He also told me about your fickleness."

"My what?"

"I heard about you going from photography to animal husbandry to meteorology one summer."

He sighed. The tale had apparently been related as often as Marge's youthful cooking catastrophes. "I was thirteen. Besides, I told you I never had much ambition. Things interested me for a little while, and then I'd get bored and go on to something else."

"Are you that way with people?"

His eyes darted to me and back to the road. I had been as blunt as Tom, and like him, refused to recant it. "Not with the ones I like," he said at last, in a way leaving little doubt he included me in his charmed circle.

Reassured, I allowed the mysterious Cretin Corey to drift into the night like the phantom in a Gothic novel, something by Wilkie Collins, perhaps. "I hated taking you away from your nephews."

"You didn't. I need sleep to function in the store tomorrow."

"I had the impression they wanted to cast me adrift on the lake like Captain Bligh, never to be heard from again."

"Captain Bligh was heard from again."

"You know what I mean."

"They're just trying to figure out how you fit into things."

"I've been doing that since high school."

"Haven't we all?" He switched the radio on, still tuned to the classical station. A passionless pianist desiccated Beethoven's *Appassionata Sonata*. "Were you serious about introducing my mom to Robert?" he said.

"Sure, if she wants. I figured it'd be a kick for her, and he might like to know at least one person thinks fondly of his work as Grantland."

He nodded and drove in silence. The streetlights turned on. The sonata ended, and Dvorak's *Five Bagatelles* began. I yawned.

"Want to come back to my place?" he said.

"I'm not up for any further excitement tonight."

"We can set the alarm a half hour early and get tomorrow off to a good start."

I yawned again. "Anything you want, Davy."

His shoulders sagged. "I knew that'd happen."

An hour outside town, we stopped at a roadside gas station-convenience store to buy ground coffee. The sky had turned overcast, and by the time we arrived in the city, drops beaded the windshield.

Snug beneath his plum duvet, we fell asleep to a light, pattering rain that, for me, summoned dreams of Lake Bellow.

6.

The rain persisted for the next four days, a steady, monotonous drizzle erupting in infrequent downpours that had pedestrians scurrying for cover. The gloom enhanced the archive's characteristic claustrophobia, as if it had been shifted to an underground locale to protect it from the weather. The previous Friday, I had completed Castle's box six and started on box seven. Monday and Tuesday, I plowed through the last three boxes. The memos concerning Jacobson between Castle and his superiors became increasingly combative until, around eleven on Tuesday morning, I reached a terse note announcing Paramount's decision to drop their option on both *Midnight Sun Murder* and Jacobson.

I celebrated the last of Castle with lunch at Sheaves, which over the weekend had added a logo to its sign and window, a rebus clearly intended to explain the shop's name to customers once and for all: two wheat sheaves on their sides, one over the other, with lettuce leaves and tomato slices in between.

Inside, the lanky, long-haired brunette who waited on me sported a small plastic rectangle pinned to his shirt, bearing two more horizontal wheat sheaves with the name 'BEN' in between. Glancing around, I found the other employees similarly branded.

"Has the new logo curtailed the questions?" I asked him.

"Not really."

He handed me my turkey and Swiss and concentrated on wiping down the counter with a limp yellow towel as if he found the topic of the rebus too demoralizing for discussion.

As I ate, I reviewed the recently copied items to my phone, which rounded out my understanding of Jacobson's association with Paramount and Castle yet still left me without insights into his personal and creative lives. I returned to UCLA at one, and Hilda directed me to material belonging to Gil Waterman, a producer at M.G.M. who had been among the handful of industry executives Jacobson approached after the Paramount deal collapsed. Unlike the pragmatic Castle, Waterman peppered his letters and memos with gossip about studio personnel that, too often and for too long, diverted me from my main purpose.

Leaving the archive on Monday and Tuesday afternoons, I delivered to my *H&H* clients, all of whom offered me especial gratitude for running their errands in the rain. The weather also predisposed them to talk longer than usual. I returned home at five-thirty or six to review what little I had learned from Waterman and wait for David, who showed up at six-thirty with take-out and stayed the night, compensating for my stalled research and the rain. Tuesday night, after describing my day, he asked, "How much of Waterman's stuff is there?"

"Six boxes."

"You should be done with him a lot sooner, then."

"Maybe," I said. "I knew when Jacobson worked for Castle, so I could pinpoint the boxes to focus on. I don't know when he had contact with Waterman. It might have been anywhere between 1938 and when he went back to Denmark in 1946."

"Meaning you might have to go through all six boxes before you find anything."

"If then," I said. "Whatever documents Waterman may have had concerning his encounter with Jacobson might have been destroyed or for some other reason never made it into his archive. The only advantage is that his stuff is more entertaining. He's always repeating the latest rumors about people in the industry."

"Really? If you find anything good . . ."

"Don't worry. I'll let you know."

Wednesday morning, while again indulging in the guilty pleasures of Waterman's scandal-mongering, my phone rang.

"Hello, Mr. Heywood? This is Veronica Quinn, Rodney Quinn's mother."

The name immediately recalled the delicate horticulturalist from Rene Arlington's party.

"Hello," I said. "I'm glad to hear from you."

"Rodney says you might be interested in some letters of my mother's. I doubt they're very important, but you're welcome to look them over."

"I'd appreciate it. I'm free this afternoon, if you are."

"I'm recently retired. Free time is my chief asset."

Veronica Quinn lived fifteen minutes from UCLA in a four-room apartment stocked with nearly every bio-tampered bloom I had browsed on the Fantasy Floral website.

"Rodney always brings me the first of his new breeds to survive. I'm hopeless with plants, so he stops in every few days to tend them."

A pot on a small table just inside the door, holding a group of tightly clustered daffodils, their blooms sky blue with denim blue centers, particularly struck me.

"Aren't they gorgeous? His boss was so impressed she named them after him. They're called Blue Rodneys."

She led me into a cramped living room with a dozen framed photos of her son at different ages peeking out between the mutant plants, lending it the unsettling atmosphere of an alien funeral parlor. She offered me a chair, which I accepted, and a drink, which I declined.

"I'll have one," she said, pouring a glass of gin from a tea cart stocked with bottles and glasses.

"Rodney told me your mother had a friend who was a patient of Dr. Jacobson."

"Yes. Her name was Mona Jackson." Veronica sat in a chair angled to my right, beside a small antique writing desk with a green-glazed pot of fuchsia bachelor's buttons whose synthetically distended petals flowed downward like a fountain sculpted from tiny silk panels. "She and my mother were childhood friends. Mona had a hard time coping with the war. That's why she started seeing Jacobson. She and my mom knew people in the service, some of whom were killed. Everybody did then, but Mona took it especially hard."

"And she wrote letters to your mother about it?"

"Five," she said and sipped her drink.

"If Mona and your mother both grew up in L.A., why were they writing to each other?"

"They weren't here during the war. My mother joined the WACs, and they sent her to work in San Francisco."

"Oh. Do you have the letters on hand?"

Veronica leaned over, opened the top left drawer of the writing desk, extracted five beige envelopes with dark brown spots, and handed them over. "My mother didn't save many letters. She held onto these because she'd read Jacobson's mysteries and was impressed that Mona was his patient."

"Luckily for me," I said.

I opened the first envelope and started reading. Veronica sipped her drink and watched me, interest, speculation, and amusement appearing successively in her watery eyes like goldfish circling a bowl of gin.

The first three letters commented on Jacobson's style as a therapist, which again offered nothing related to the Harold books but provided a rare inside look at his practice, a not-insignificant detail for a biographical sketch. The fourth, dated September 8, 1943, and the fifth, from December 9, 1943, complained of Jacobson's being abstracted and abrupt, more fragments of circumstantial evidence supporting my belief that something occurred in his life then, though what and whether it influenced his writing remained maddeningly obscure.

"May I scan these to my phone?" I asked after finishing.

Veronica blinked as if dispelling a daydream. "Go ahead if you think they're worth it."

"The last two are extremely suggestive."

"Is that good?"

"All I do at present is follow up on suggestions. Do you know if Mona has any family in the area who might know more about her interactions with Jacobson?"

"Her son has a construction company here. You can find him online, though I've no idea if she told him much if anything."

"What about other friends she might've written to?"

"I'm pretty sure they're dead, but I can give you their names if you want."

"I might be able to follow up with their family members. It's worth the chance."

As Veronica jotted down a list of her mom's and Mona Jackson's mutual friends, Angela Winslow messaged me.

Can you pick up Danielle Cray's blood pressure meds? She forgot she needed them until this morning. If you're busy, I'll get someone else.

Danielle, another of my first clients, began her career in 1958 as a cellist with the L.A. Philharmonic under the name Daniel Cray before undergoing gender reassignment surgery in 1973.

No, I can do it. Tell her I'll be there around four.

"Anything serious?" Veronica asked after I pocketed my phone.

"Just about some volunteer work I do."

"Oh. Here's your list. I hope this has been useful to you."

"It has been. Thanks."

Danielle's apartment bore little resemblance to Lena's or Robert's. It combined classic mid-century modern furniture, which she bought when new, with souvenirs of her career: her cello, framed programs from concerts at which she had soloed, pictures of the orchestra through the years, and autographed photos of famous musicians: violinist Isaac Stern, conductor Felix Slatkin, and her hero, cellist Pablo Casals.

"I'm sorry I didn't realize I needed these before," she said. "I didn't take you from anything important, did I?"

"No, just following a lead for my research."

"How's that going?"

I again browsed the items on her walls while describing the bread-crumbs Oliver Castle and Veronica Quinn had strewn across my path. "Of all the people I deliver to, yours is my favorite apartment," I said.

"Thanks. But I'm sure that's due to your taste for the past and classical music . . . though I still can't forgive your ambivalence toward Bach. He was the first master of the standardized scale in Western music, after all."

"That's the thing," I said. "Some of his works sound too much like a mechanical exercise, like factory-testing the newly tempered keyboard. For me, art should be about more than the capabilities and limitations of its medium."

"You're too romantic."

"Not long ago, I was accused of not being romantic enough," I said. "Do you ever find it strange seeing yourself as Daniel in the old photos?"

"No. Some people try to erase who they were before transitioning, but Daniel's life was pretty good, except for the gender identity issue."

"I have another client who was an actor. He doesn't have anything personal in his place except for a single framed headshot."

"Did he have much of a career?"

I summarized Robert's TV and film work.

"I recognize some of the films," Danielle said, "but I don't remember them very well. I never watched much TV. I was more of a theater person."

"He did theater, too," I said, rattling off more titles.

The phone in my pocket vibrated. I removed it and glanced at the screen.

"Anything important?"

"David," I said. "I'll call him when I leave."

"Which should be now," she said. "I'm grateful for your attentions, Paul, but I've taken up enough of your time. We can have a longer chat next week when you bring the groceries."

"Sure."

I dialed David as I trotted down the front steps of Danielle's apartment building under an oblong glass canopy from which the rain ricocheted like BB shots.

"Sorry I didn't answer," I said. "I've had a busy afternoon."

"Enjoying Waterman's gossip?"

"I had to pick up meds for a client and went to see Rodney Quinn's mother."

"Who?"

"Rodney Quinn," I said, "my lead from Rene's party."

"Oh, yeah. How'd that go?"

"At the moment, it's more promising than anything I've gotten from either Castle or Waterman. I'll give you the details later."

"Okay. Instead of braving the rain, why not come to my place, and we'll get take-out?"

"Great."

"What do you feel like having? I was thinking Chinese."

"Fine. You know what I like."

"The most flaccid flavors on the menu," he said.

"Are we going to debate my tender palate again?"

"I've given up on that. The matter of flowers, on the other hand . . ."

"You should've seen Veronica's apartment," I laughed. "It's full of Rodney's weird plants."

"At least all I have to contend with are common-or-garden roses."

"What do you mean?"

"They came this morning. I get why you lavished flowers on my mom, but I'm securely hooked."

"I didn't send you roses."

"Huh?"

"I didn't send them. Was there a card?"

"Yeah, but I didn't open it because I figured . . ."

"Maybe you should and find out who's vying with me for your affections."

"You mean you want to find out."

"Don't pretend you're not curious."

"Okay. Hold on."

I heard him shift the phone, followed by the crinkle of a small envelope torn open, and after that, complete silence. The suspense he hated prompted me to prompt him. "Well? Who's your second-string Romeo?"

"Let's talk about it in person," he said, completely serious for the first time since I met him. "Can you come to my place around six? I'll close the store at five."

"Is it that bad?"

"No, just . . . you can judge for yourself."

I drove home, left the contact list from Veronica Quinn on my desk, showered, and drove to his place slowly enough to cloak any sign of my unease.

David opened the door without a word and walked to his sofa. Entering, I noticed an absence of Chinese take-out and, on his coffee table, a clear, pot-bellied glass vase tied with a green and blue plaid ribbon, holding a lush bouquet of roses. He flopped onto the couch, legs splayed, body contracted, eyes staring blankly ahead like an errant adolescent enduring an interminable lecture. He grasped the little card from the flowers in his right hand, absently flicking its side with his thumb. As I approached, he held it up and out to me without lifting his eyes. I slipped it from his fingers and read:

David–May I please see you? It's important.–Corey

Enthralled for the last three days by Gil Waterman's gossip and, more recently, by Veronica Quinn's letters and my chat with Danielle, I had completely forgotten the name I first heard on Saturday afternoon. Unthinkingly I blurted out:

"Speak of the devil."

David looked at me. Surprise replaced the blank stare, and in another instant, horror replaced the surprise. "They told you about him?"

"Briefly," I said, hoping to mitigate the damage with nonchalance.

"Your dad mentioned you were seeing somebody named Corey a few years ago and that he was seven years older than you."

"Did he also mention that none of the family could stand him, and Dad referred to him as a cretin?" My inability to offer a judicious reply answered his question. He bent his head back and covered his face with his hands. "Oh my God."

Switching tactics, I appealed to our playful genie for aid, and offered an arch observation. "I thought you told me they knew you'd never go out with anyone who wasn't worthy of you."

He lowered his hands. Rather than respond in kind to my gentle sarcasm, the abstracted adolescent looked pathetically guilty. "I only said that because you were so worried about meeting everyone. I wanted to kid you out of it. My family does a lot of kidding."

"I noticed. It's fun, but I can see how it might be difficult if you just want to talk to somebody." His body contracted a little further. "I assume you want to tell me about him?"

"Where do I start?"

I assumed my voice recorder persona, for both our sakes. "What's his real name?"

"Corey Langdon. We saw each other for a while after I started running the store on my own."

"How long is a while?"

"Eight, nine months, somewhere in there," he said.

"Was it serious?"

"It could've been."

"Why wasn't it?"

He exhaled nervously,. "A lot of things."

"Look, if you don't want to go into it, I haven't any . . ."

"No, you should know. It's just—" he gazed between his knees to the floor "—some of it's humiliating."

This startled me even more than Corey's signature. I had a hard time imagining my overly overconfident playmate humiliated by anything. I perched on the coffee table beside the vase to lessen my resemblance to a righteous scold. "I promise I won't judge."

"You will," he said. "Everybody judges everything. They can't help it."

"Then I'll try to be as impartial as possible. In fact, I'm more inclined to leniency than not."

Our genie failed again. Rather than a grin, I received only a slight twitch of the lips, indicating mild mollification. "No matter how lenient you are, you'll see me differently after."

"Differently doesn't necessarily mean badly. Now tell me before the suspense compresses my brain to a tiny grey diamond."

The smile still refused to appear. "Corey's an investment counselor."

"Well, now," I said.

"I know. I wouldn't have thought I'd go out with an investment counselor, either. We met at one of Rene's parties."

"Nor would I expect to find an investment counselor there."

"He was a friend of a friend. I forget whose. We hit it off right away, mainly because we had the same sense of humor. We didn't stop laughing at one another's jokes for the first month. Then it leveled off to something nice and comfortable."

I granted him the right to sleep with others in the past, but I hated hearing he had ever been nice and comfortable with anyone else. "Did you live together?"

"No, thank God, though I thought it was heading there. The only problem was what you'd expect."

"That he was older?"

David shook his head. "That he was wealthier."

"I wondered . . ."

"He was a devoutly superstitious materialist who loved expensive restaurants and clothes and trips. I went along with it because I wanted to be with him."

"But it ended up causing problems?"

"He wanted to buy me stuff, too, which I hated. It felt gratuitous, as if being with each other wasn't enough or that he couldn't trust it. I know it's more or less a joke now that everybody is, or should be, willing to whore themselves out to whoever has money. But I couldn't stand it. It was the only thing we argued about . . . at first."

Tom's comment about Corey's proprietary arritude recurred to me. "Did you tell him what you learned from Marvell's?"

"Yeah. He said I was a fool and redoubled his efforts to convert me. But it only made me more uncomfortable." He stopped and swallowed dryly.

"What happened?" I said.

"I was still somewhat immature, starting to run the store without Dad's help."

"And you ran into trouble?"

He stood, removed his phone from his pocket, and hurriedly tapped the screen while pacing between the couch and the coffee table. "The short version is: I used my money to keep the Argonaut afloat."

"Why didn't you go to your dad?"

"I didn't want him thinking I couldn't handle things. But I fell behind on my rent. Corey covered it for two months. I paid him back, Paul, I swear. Look." He stopped pacing and thrust the phone beneath my nose. He had uploaded bank records showing two rent-sized amounts transferred to Corey Langdon over the course of five months.

"I believe you."

His eyes glistened with gratitude, painful to observe. He replaced the phone in his pocket and sat down again. "We were even in terms of money, but I was grateful to him. I still am. Just don't tell my parents. Even if you wind up hating me enough to kill me, please don't let them know I was Corey's whore for two months."

"Borrowing money doesn't make you a whore, especially when you pay it back."

"Then why do I feel like one?"

"Because you're too hard on yourself," I said. "I promise I won't tell them, if you promise not to tell them I told you they told me . . . oh God, you know what I mean."

"I know. I won't."

"And don't hold your breath waiting for me to hate you, much less enough to kill you. Is that what this is about? He's playing on your gratitude?"

David shook his head. "I'm pretty sure it has to do with our breakup."

"What about it?"

"I'll give you the short version again. He got addicted to internet porn."

"Oh," I said, once more adjusting to the unexpected. "Was he into it when you met?"

"I knew he watched it now and then, I assumed, when he was alone and horny. A few times, he had me watch with him. Then I realized he took it more seriously."

"What do you mean by seriously?"

"It was a field of study for him, the way stamps or old coins are for other people. He knew the performers and studios and even directors."

"What did you think?"

"I'm not a moralist, but I've always been ambivalent about it. I mean, it's so neatly divided into physical traits, scenarios, positions, and acts. Then there are the fetishes and the paraphernalia that has to be implemented so precisely. Basically, it's the mechanics of sex without the exuberance of Eros, the joy of being with another person."

"Did you tell him this?"

"I tried, but it was as futile as arguing with him about superstitious materialism. Eventually, the repetitiveness started to seem funny to me, like the mechanical figures in those old clocks that perform the same movements before striking the hour, and I began making jokes about it."

"That shouldn't have been a problem if you had the same sense of humor."

"It wasn't at first. But at some point, he stopped laughing and became consumed by it. And I mean consumed. He ignored work to watch in his office and spent upwards of a thousand dollars a month on it."

"What did you do?"

"I didn't know much about that kind of addiction, or any kind, for that matter. I tried talking him out of it. Actually, I tried kidding him out of it, like I did with you. I figured sooner or later he'd realize how silly it was, or he'd see the silliness I saw in it."

"But he didn't."

"He just went further into his head. That's what bothered me. He had a living, breathing person who cared about him and wanted to share his life, yet he preferred a private space filled with two-dimensional images of intimacy. A few times, I watched him watch it."

"How'd you manage that?"

"When I was at his place, he'd say he had to go online for work and then get lost for hours without realizing it. I knew what he was doing since he didn't bother turning down the sound. I didn't interrupt because I wanted to see how it affected him. He'd sit there, clicking and staring, never looking up from the screen, searching for something it didn't have to give, like a prospector digging in a barren mountain . . . not that I have any personal experience with prospectors."

"You never encountered any on your hikes?" He very nearly smiled then. "What did you do after that?"

"I stopped kidding and told him point blank what was happening. For one thing, he was risking his career. I thought sure the possibility of losing the money and prestige he worked so hard for would shock him out of it, but it didn't. Then I said it made me feel redundant. That meant even less to him. Finally, I gave him an ultimatum."

"How'd he react?"

David dropped his head into his hands, his limp hair streaming over his fingers. "He blew up. He said he wouldn't let me control him and called me every name in the book."

"Including whore?"

He nodded into his palms.

"Confronting an addict is like cornering a wild animal," I said. "You can't take what he said seriously."

"Somehow, it's harder to ignore when it comes from someone you really like."

"You mean love?"

He lifted his head. "I might've fallen for him. Later I realized the addiction wasn't really a separate issue from his wealth."

"How do you mean?"

"When we first broke up, I imagined he liked porn because he paid for it, which made it more of a possession. Once I gained some distance, I wondered if it was because he was also incapable of the joys of Eros, of really being with another person, from fear, mistrust, or whatever. And that's why he saw me as something to be owned, rather than someone to be loved."

"Then I'm glad you left him, not just because it made you available but because you had enough self-respect to get out while you could, despite being willing to consider yourself a whore."

"I guess."

"Have you seen him since?"

"He called the store a couple of times, but I wouldn't answer, and he stopped. At least he had the sense not to show up there. About two years ago, I heard through one of his friends he'd started drinking."

"Seems he's prone to addiction."

"If only I'd known that going in . . . oh, well."

"Why do you think he wants to see you?"

"I've no idea."

"Are you going to respond?"

"I don't know that, either. But if hearing my side of things—I mean really hearing it—can do him any good . . ."

"You're sure that'd be the only reason?"

He looked at me quizzically and then understood. "When he called me a whore everything changed. It showed he had a capacity and a willingness to hurt that I wouldn't have believed about him when we first met. I'd rather be alone than risk being a target for that again."

"What did you tell your family?"

"I said we broke up because we weren't hitting it off anymore. I didn't see any reason to burden them with the uglier details. Don't tell them, okay?"

Tom, Delia, and Marge's behavior on Saturday indicated they guessed or intuited there had been uglier details, a point I decided against pressing. "Okay." Another idea occurred to me, one I considered worth exploring. "Is this why you were uncomfortable with me meeting Rene and your other friends? You were afraid they'd mention Corey before you were ready to tell me about him?"

He nodded. "Though they know as little as my parents about what happened."

"Why?"

"I told you he wasn't part of our group when I met him. He wasn't any keener on joining it after we got together. We mostly hung around with his friends."

"He was isolating you from the people in your life?"

"Yeah, though I didn't notice it at the time."

"And you never discussed this with anybody, even after you broke up?"

"I told you, it was too humiliating."

"You've nothing to be humiliated about," I said. "Actually, you should be proud that you got out before it got worse."

He looked down, chewing the inside of his cheek. The longer silence signaled an end to the conversation but for one more question.

"Do you want me to stay?"

"I doubt I'd be worthwhile company tonight."

"You're always worthwhile company. But I get it if you'd rather be alone." I stood up from the coffee table, glancing at the roses to avoid knocking them over.

"I'll call you tomorrow," he said, the question phrased as a statement. "Sure."

I kissed him and tapped his forehead with mine, only rather than a prelude to intimacy it felt too much like me comforting him, and I realized that for the first time since we met, I had ceased receiving his undivided attention. I left without saying more.

Driving through the wet, depopulated dark, the Gothic shade that had been Cretin Corey became an all-too-real presence fretting our uncomplicated coupling. Back in my apartment, I looked up the names on Veronica Quinn's list, gathered contact information for their living relatives, composed and forwarded messages explaining my work and my reasons for approaching them, and crawled into bed.

However, rather than sleep, my internal voice recorder repeated the conversation with David on an endless loop, while I tossed and turned, searching vainly for the off button. I might still escape without much fuss rather than sort out the complexities introduced by Corey, but thanks to Samuel Taylor Coleridge by way of Robert, the ridiculous little wings that had sprouted in my imagination beat back every rash, or reasonable, or indeed any definite decision.

7.

The next morning, sluggish rather than refreshed, even after three mugs of dark roast, and dissatisfied with everything defining my life, I flouted my responsibilities to the Eldon Foundation and drove through the rain to the L.A. County Museum of Art.

Inside, the clarity of the bright, quiet rooms and the colors, shapes, and designs of the artworks refreshed my senses until, mimicking Isherwood's alter ego, I morphed from a voice recorder into a camera, or perhaps a photojournalist, drifting along as if on a jungle river, gazing at the flora and fauna inhabiting a shoreline of white walls. Here and there, I paused for a longer look at a particular piece, while on three occasions, other visitors, kids I pegged as art students, interrupted their inspections to flash me a grin. I returned the grins courteously, glad to find I still had options despite being unready to exercise them as yet.

A beep from my phone at quarter after eleven heralded a message from a Barbara Marcus claiming she had material on Erich Jacobson. I tried to recall if this had been one of the names on Veronica's list, failed, returned my number to her, and left the museum to talk more freely.

The rain had dwindled to a mist, allowing me to loiter beneath my umbrella just outside the main door. My phone rang.

"Hello . . . Ms. Marcus?"

"Yes. Mr. Heywood?"

"Yes," I said. "I'm pleased to speak with you."

"I am, too. My grandson found your post concerning Dr. Jacobson and brought it to my attention. My parents were quite close with him when he lived here."

"What were their names?"

"Carol and Jeff Quigley," she said.

This jogged my memory. "I've seen them mentioned in letters by Jacobson's other friends."

"I'm sure you have," she said.

"Do you have anything bearing on their relationship, I mean actual documents?"

"Yes," she said, "letters and my mother's diary. I think you'll want to see them."

"I'll be happy to take a look; grateful, too. But I should tell you upfront: I'm a poor scholar and not in a position to pay for anything." I had included this caveat in all research inquiries ever since the adventure of the greedy rodent.

"I understand. His Harold books have been a tradition in our family for two generations. I'll be glad to offer you any help I can. Shall I bring them to you, or would you like to come here?"

"I can meet you if it's more convenient."

"It would be. I live with my son and his family in Lemon Grove."

"Great. Just send me the address. When would you like me to come?"

"I have several appointments the next few weeks . . .'

"Text me whatever day and time are good for you, and I'll be there."

"Fine. I look forward to meeting you."

"Same here."

I hung up, glad for something to think about other than David and the Cretin. As I considered whether or not to return to the museum, Robert forwarded me his shopping list.

The rain spared me a crowd at the market. Checking out Robert's items, the kid manning the cash register increased my options by checking me out. Probably bored from the lack of business, I thought. If I believed in signs . . .

Ten minutes after leaving the market, I stopped at Wonder Wash Cleaners. True to the girl's word at the counter, Robert's sweater looked like new.

The clouds burst again as I parked at the Roxbury Apartments. I dashed along the walk and between the rhododendrons, juggling my open umbrella, the grocery bags, and his sweater, the latter shielded from the rain by Wonder Wash's plastic garment bag.

Robert opened the door in his grey cardigan. "Sorry to make you run around on a day like this, Paul."

The weather had altered his apartment. Previously, the afternoon sun invigorated the outdated colors and styles, as if encouraging them to defy present-day fashions. The rain dampened their insolence, leaving them tired and defeated.

"No problem. The market was practically deserted. Here's your sweater."

"Thank you."

Walking into the kitchen, I heard him remove the plastic.

"They did a good job," he said.

"I told you they would."

I placed his Hearth Fire in the breadbox and dried papaya and prunes on the counter.

He entered wearing the cleaned cardigan. "I feel like myself again. Thanks for going out of your way to clean it."

"*H&H* performs all errands within reason and legality. It's just that food and medication are the most common."

"I still appreciate it."

"You're welcome."

He sat at the kitchen table, watching me store his Velma's, bran flakes, and wild rice on their shelf. "How was the meeting with David's parents?"

"Good, on the whole." I lined his Gunter's shakes beside the cereals.

"What are they like?"

"Playfully affectionate. They kidded around and told stories about each other. His dad said they're a little crazy, but it's better than the formality some families assume, as if being together is just a duty."

"Are you playfully affectionate with your mother?"

I removed the Shale House, folded the bag, and opened the second. "Sort of, but it's not the same with two people. You need a larger audience to kid around to any effect."

"How did they treat you?"

"The same," I said, "of course, they were on their best behavior, as I was."

"I'm sure you at your worst are infinitely better than most people at their best."

"Thanks. His dad thinks I'm a good influence." I opened the refrigerator and arranged his salad ingredients in the crisper.

"How so?"

"I told you about David's lack of ambition."

"Yes."

I stacked his Bub's Tubs on the shelf above the crisper. "His dad said it worried him and was glad David found somebody stable like me."

"An important step. Winning over his family, especially one that close, should compound your attractiveness in David's eyes."

I set a package of ground turkey next to the yogurt and closed the refrigerator. "Apparently, I compare favorably to his other beaus, especially one named Corey. His dad referred to him as a cretin."

"Oh, dear," Robert said. "Is he definitely out of the picture?"

"He was. David never mentioned him, and his family was happy to consign him to the limbo of failed relationships."

"But . . . ?"

"He contacted David yesterday."

"Speak of the devil."

"My words exactly," I said and summarized the previous night's talk, leaving out the more uncomfortable moments.

Robert looked worried. "Do you believe David about not going back to him?"

"He said he wouldn't after what happened. He's no fool."

"Abusive relationships ensnare plenty of intelligent people. I've seen it happen."

"You mean Margaret and her husband?"

"Harlow," Robert said, nodding. "He never physically hurt her or their daughter, which I suppose made him more tolerable. But he could be verbally abusive to Mag, particularly when she confronted him about his drinking. I begged her to leave him, but she refused."

"Did she say why?"

"She thought it was better for Deb."

"Why would she think that?"

"This was when addiction and its effects on those around the addict weren't well recognized. People also considered it preferable for children to have both parents in their lives, no matter what the parents were like. Mag feared that without being at least partly responsible for Deb, Harlow would go into a tailspin. The only result was Mag endured many needlessly bad days, and Harlow died young from not getting the help he required."

"If you'd heard David last night, you'd know it's over. As far as he's concerned, it's just a sordid episode from his past. Everyone's allowed one or two of those."

Robert registered maidenly shock. "Even a goody two-shoes like you?"

The vague defiance of that morning crystallized into a desire to compete with his escapades. "I'm more of a goody one-shoe. A year after college, I had an affair with one of my former professors."

The enacted shock became genuine astonishment. "Did you now?"

"I'd always been attracted to him, and he'd just been through a bad breakup, so I went for it. We had a great time for a few months, but he felt too guilty, even though I wasn't his student anymore. And today, if I wanted, I could've had my choice of three art students at the museum and the supermarket checker."

He grunted. "Why don't you wave a porterhouse steak and some crepes Suzette under my nose and tantalize me into apoplexy?"

"I'm just saying . . ."

"I know what you're saying. You probably won't run into the students again, but I'd keep the checker in reserve."

Resenting the implication as well as the glibness of his advice, I inserted his boxes of Ice Floe lima beans and acorn squash into the freezer and changed the subject. "I talked with David's mom about you, too."

"Ah, yes, I was the pretext for the whole event. How'd that part go?"

"Good." I set a large bottle of Silken Sanitizer hand soap—to refill the smaller dispensers in his kitchen and bathroom—on the counter and folded the empty bag. "She watched *Grandview Park* as a girl with her mother and recalls Grantland vividly."

"How old is she?"

"Around seventy. I don't know exactly." I sat opposite him at the table.

"She'd have to be if she remembers my stint on the show. How old is David?"

"Thirty-two."

"Then David was a latecomer. . . or would that have been his father?"

"Delia had him in her mid-forties."

"A lovely name, Delia."

"She's nothing like the fans you described. She remembered the penicillin story when I mentioned it. She said you ended up paralyzed and nearly had an affair with your brother's wife while she helped you learn to walk."

Robert laughed. "I'd forgotten that. I spent four months in a bed and then in a wheelchair. I loved it. Everybody else had to worry about the blocking. You know what blocking is?"

"The moves actors make in a scene," I said. "They're choreographed so nobody bumps into the furniture or the other actors."

"Correct," he said. "Blocking was especially important for us since *Grandview* was broadcast live. I teased Mag and Gray about my being able to sit or lie down while they had to remember where to walk to avoid screwing up the camera angles. She retaliated by pinching and jabbing me whenever she adjusted my pillows or blankets. I got back at her by leaning going limp when she helped me up. On air, she had to coo over me and give me sweet, encouraging talks. After the scene ended and we broke for a commercial, I'd ask her for a glass of water or something, and she'd snap: 'Get up and get it yourself, you little bastard.'" Another laugh, pure and youthful, swept the room like a whirlwind and subsided.

"You took chances on live TV," I said.

"We were theater trained. You learn to adapt to every possible contingency for the stage because sooner or later, every possible contingency arises. Becoming a pro in any field is arduous, but once you do, you can have lots of fun. Does David's mother know about Gray and me?"

"Yes. It didn't faze her. David's sister asked what their grandmother would've thought if she'd found out."

"What did she say?"

"She said her mother considered being gay an affliction, like epilepsy."

"A common concept at the time."

"I offered to introduce Delia to you, pending your approval."

His brows tensed. "Why?"

"I think she'd enjoy your backstage stories as much as I do, probably more since she watched the show."

"I haven't had visitors in ages."

"What about me?"

"You're not exactly a social caller."

"It's felt more social than not. We've had great conversations."

"Consisting of me prattling on about my life."

"I've learned a lot."

"And for a reward, you're foisting unwarranted visitors on me," he said, sarcastic yet not manifestly opposed to the idea.

"You're under no obligation. I'll just tell her you're not up for company."

"And make me sound more pathetic than I am. When were you expecting this to happen?"

"It's up to you."

"Give me a week or two to adjust to the idea. I'll need refreshments."

"Soft drinks and mixed nuts would be fine."

"Mixed nuts?"

I described our repurposing the Suffolks.

"Turning cocktail nuts into poker chips," he said. "They do sound agreeably batty. Well, if it'll help you score points with David . . . will they all come, or just the mother?"

"The others aren't interested in *Grandview Park*. Most likely, only David would be with her."

"I'd like to meet him after all I've heard."

"Just promise to avoid the topic of ex-boyfriends."

"I'm not too old to appreciate the value of discretion."

"Think it over, then. We'll set a date when you're ready."

He nodded impatiently. "Now from here on, may we avoid the topic of visitors?"

"Sure. You owe me the rest about you and Scotty, anyway."

"Okay. Let's go into the living room. Would you mind making tea?"

"Sure."

"Choose whatever beverage you want, and bring some Velma's. The salad I had for lunch wasn't very filling."

The water heated while I prepared a mug, arranged the Velma's on a dessert plate, and poured my ginger ale. After filling his mug, I carried everything into the living room on a small tray which I set on the table next to his chair, beside his reading glasses and a volume of Edith Wharton's short stories, his place marked by an old pharmacy receipt. I grabbed my ginger ale and sat on the sofa. He thanked me, dipped a biscuit into his tea, and ate it with relish.

"Do you always dunk your Velma's?"

He nodded. "Steeped in the apple-cinnamon tea, the taste bears a remarkable resemblance to the apple pies my mother made when I was a boy. It's not as potent as Proust's madeleines, but it's comfortingly nostalgic. Where were we?"

"You'd moved in with Scotty and had seven years with him before it ended. You said it was like a marriage. Were you completely domesticated?"

"We lived together, we slept together, and were monogamous,," he said, sipping his tea. "Following my passion for Terry and the casual sex with Grayson, I welcomed domesticity with Scotty. Our tie was neither too tight nor too loose, but imperceptible . . . or perhaps instinctive might be more accurate."

"Was that the first time you lived with someone you loved?"

"Yes. People say it's a difficult adjustment, but we never had any problems apart from the usual clashing habits."

"Like what?"

"I washed dishes immediately after a meal while he preferred letting them soak a few hours or overnight. He folded his socks. I rolled mine until he demonstrated how much drawer space his method opened up. Things like that never led to any serious arguments, though. Our time during and after *Marmoset* threw a sort of membrane around us: a porous, transparent wall that excluded the rest of the world."

"Not unlike how you felt with Terry."

"Only more so," he said, his eyes losing focus as he stared further into the past. "Real life with Scotty was what I'd only imagined sharing with Terry. Scotty returned my affection, and rather than dreams, we had actual careers in creative fields. Talking, or more often grousing about actors and directors and producers, was part of our daily routine. And after venting our petty frustrations or celebrating our modest triumphs, we'd repair to the sofa or bed, to read, listen to music, or watch TV, ignoring everything but the comfort of being one another's refuge, as you described it."

"A stressful function to perform for seven years," I said.

"Not really. When Scotty and I were together, the world again made sense, and life had meaning. The first few months, I worked regularly in commercials, selling everything from insect repellent to soft drinks, which with the lines I had to speak, elicited endless jokes from our friends."

"What was Scotty doing?"

"Designing a set for a game show. I won't mention the name because, knowing you, you'll embark on an online hunt for former contestants."

"I promise I won't."

"It was called *Match the Mutt*."

"Come on," I said. "I bought *Serve Me the Honorable Marmoset*, but that has to be a joke."

"Look it up. It was based on the axiom that people and their pets often look alike. Pictures of people and dogs were projected on a large screen, and the contestants had to match the dog to its owner."

"Seriously?"

"Seriously. And it wasn't the silliest show on the air, either. It only lasted six months, as you might hope. But for a long time after, Scotty bitched that the contestants won more than he earned for designing the set."

"So you were doing commercials, and he was working on a show about people and their look-alike dogs. You call that an average life?"

"What happened between us was average. We battled for bathroom space in the morning, sometimes dueling it out with shampoo and shaving cream. If we resisted the temptation of morning sex, I cooked breakfast. If not, we had a bite on our way to work. I'd haunt the casting offices or spend hours in a TV studio hawking products while he sat in production meetings at the network. We'd meet back in the apartment at five-thirty or so and rehash the day, which for him at that time meant struggling to create a set that satisfied the network, director, and sponsor of *Mutt*. Do you know about sponsors in those days?"

"What about them?"

"Early TV shows were usually sponsored by a single product. This established a link between the show, its stars, and the product for audiences. Milton Berle's first show was sponsored by Texaco gasoline, and for a long time after, he and Texaco were welded together in people's minds. Game shows took this ballyhoo still further, splashing their sponsor's name, slogan, and product models on the backdrops, host's desk, and contestants' podiums. Look some up. You'll see what I mean."

"I will."

"Although, with filmed commercials, multiple sponsors for a single show became more common, some, like game shows, still had a primary sponsor whose sales pitch was delivered by the show's announcer in an area away from the main set."

"An area Scotty had to design for *Mutt*."

Robert nodded.

"Who was the sponsor?" I asked.

"Triple Star dog food. Their logo was a caricature of an epicurean Doberman with a top hat, bow tie, and monocle above the slogan 'Stellar Taste for Stellar Dogs.'"

"Did it have a name?" I asked, thinking of Spiffy Squirrel.

"Wagstaff," he said, "Wagstaff D. Pinscher. The sponsor—or the ad agency they hired—the director and network executives drove Scotty crazy for three weeks, bickering over where and how much the product, slogan, and pictures of Wagstaff should appear in the commercial area. The ordeal made him swear off pets. He promised to toss me out if I so much as brought home a guppy."

"I don't blame him. Did you ever want pets?"

"No. I like animals, but like children, they required more time than I was willing or able to devote to them, so he and I were in agreement on that point as well. Anyway, after he vented his spleen about Triple Star, I'd relate my adventures in the casting offices and the struggle to sound sincerely awestruck by the curative powers of a new headache tablet or the taste of an instant pudding. Depending on how tired we were, we'd go out to dinner, get take-out from one of the little places in our neighborhood or rely on my cooking skills."

"By way of Paolo's tutorials."

"Paolo, the gift that kept on giving. After dinner, we'd lay aside the inanities and pressures of our professions to remind ourselves why we entered them in the first place."

"How'd you do that?"

"By reconfirming the value of art and its value to us," he said.

"You make it sound like a religious ritual."

He smiled wanly. "Molehill Men commonly complain that art is a substitute religion. This, of course, is nonsense. Religion deals with the supernatural: a being or force that exists outside the physical world and controls it. The arts, for Scotty and me and those in our circle, had nothing to do with the supernatural. Since it derives from the senses and speaks to the brain, it's entirely of the physical world. Engaging in it is a form of mental exercise, no more supernatural than working out in a gym, though engagement does involve what might be termed rituals."

"What were the rituals for you and Scotty?"

"Attending the events I've already mentioned: concerts, ballets, plays, or a movie at one of the repertory theaters. When we were tired, we'd stay home, read, listen to the radio, or watch films on TV. Then we'd talk about it afterward. That really made me feel like I had with Terry, sharing the exhilaration of one's senses being heightened and one's faculties sharpened. When we felt romantic, we'd pull out his records and dance for a while." He nestled back in the recliner, smiling. "You can't imagine how nice it is to dance with the man you love in a darkening apartment after a long day. Try it with David sometime."

"Perhaps we should wait until the Cretin matter is cleared up," I said.

"Then again, it may help tip the balance in your favor."

"Is that a leftover plot device from *Grandview*?"

"Grantland had a few good ideas. Well, try it whenever you fall in love. Just make sure the music's truly romantic, with saxophones and strings laid

on thick. Scotty would rest his head against mine; I'd smell his hair and
cologne and imagine I was touring the Milky Way rather than skulking
around a cramped Manhattan living room."

"What songs did you dance to?"

"Oh, 'Stardust,' 'Always in My Heart,' 'Blue Moon,' 'Where or When' . . .
things we'd heard on the radio or that'd been featured in movies and shows
when we were kids before we understood what the lyrics meant."

"That was your everyday life, then?"

"The bare bones," he said. "We also had a healthy social life. Friends
came over or invited us to dinner parties, birthdays, and other get-togethers. Things changed a little after I was cast as the Fool in a modern dress
version of *King Lear*."

"Changed how?"

"We rehearsed *Lear* in the daytime, which left Scotty's and my routine
unchanged until opening night. This was the first time I'd performed Shakespeare since college, and it was gratifying to speak lines unconnected with
the shopping habits of the average TV viewer. I was also apprehensive since
it was the first time Scotty would see me in a play since *Marmoset*."

"Why'd that make you apprehensive?"

"I fell in love with Scotty in part thanks to his intolerance of mediocrity,
or in the case of *Marmoset,* unintended absurdity, and the witty way he expressed it. But he wasn't an insult comic sharpening his skills on whatever
crossed his path. His admiration for creativity meant he freely acknowledged when something reached or surpassed his standards. And because
he cared too much about what he admired, he could never offer false praise
with any conviction, even to me."

"How'd he react to *Lear*?"

"He sidled up to me backstage and said, 'You were great. In fact, the
whole show was superb. I can't even fault the sets.' Coleridge's wings flapped
so hard then I could barely stand. I'd been far more confident during rehearsals for *Lear* than for *Marmoset,* and the following day the show and
I received excellent reviews. But the only thing that really mattered was
Scotty's praise. That's when our mutual admiration solidified, and our relationship became like a marriage. Unfortunately, since I performed *Lear*
at night, except for matinees, our hours coincided less."

"Did that cause any problems?"

"No, it only necessitated another adjustment. Sometimes he'd wait up,
and we'd have a late supper before going to bed. He'd finished *Mutt,* and

his subsequent projects allowed him to work at home at his drafting table on things better suited to his ability. I'd wake up late in the morning, and in the afternoon, he'd take a break, and we'd spend some quality time before I left for the theater. I remember thinking then how I'd fulfilled the two desires I'd nursed since adolescence, to become a well-regarded actor and fall in love with another man."

"What happened after *Lear* closed?"

"More theater, commercials, and other random TV shots," he said. "Casting directors also began offering me parts in movies made in New York. This was the first flowering of independent cinema, following the demise of the Hollywood studio system and after the international New Wave directors demonstrated how to produce quality films on limited budgets, shot on the fly on location. I landed in a handful of small and not-so-small films done in the city. I'd mention titles, but you can find them online faster than I'd be able to remember them."

"They came up the first time I searched for you: *Starlings, City Beast, Sweet Wine, The Columbus Circle Affair, Cathy and Thomas* . . ."

He squirmed. "We needn't explore the entire list. The point is I was working fairly steadily on projects I liked—mostly—and not only was I proud of them, but Scotty was too. And if his pride in my work wasn't compliment enough, he sought my opinion on his. He'd ask me what I thought about his drawings at various stages of completion as if my insights could supplement his knowledge of set design."

"What'd you tell him?"

"I reacted to them as an actor. I told him where an element might prove awkward in performance or how another floor plan might make for easier blocking."

"Maybe that's the input he wanted."

"Perhaps," he said. "That was the best thing about our relationship: we trusted each other with our deepest vulnerabilities. When a play opened for which he designed the sets, I'd be next to him at the theater, calming his fears. When I opened in a play, he was in the audience, a trusted presence among the others, and when a film I appeared in premiered, he'd sit beside me, holding my hand. The same thing happened at social functions."

"Did you go to many?"

"Our fair share. Gray introduced me to the social strands weaving between the city's gay and creative communities, but it wasn't until after I'd established a presence in the theater and paired up with Scotty that my social life really took off. We never led the pack as an actor or set designer, but we had a few successes, and people liked us enough to invite us to functions alongside genuine luminaries."

"Like who?"

"Oh," he said, pausing with a dry biscuit between his fingers, "too many to recall. I met Leonard Bernstein, whom I admired. He told me he liked me in *Lear*. There was the poet Ada Grendel, who always wore the same green tweed cap she bought in 1933. She and I discussed poetry several times. She expressed admiration for Ira Gershwin, Johnny Mercer, Dorothy Fields, and others who wrote lyrics for the pop songs Scotty and I loved. I met Aaron Copeland, the composer, and the choreographer Angus Russell, who made a clumsy pass at me."

"I wouldn't expect a choreographer to do anything clumsily."

"He was drunk at the time. His new show had flopped, and he was lashing out in all directions. I also encountered Cassandra Angel."

"Who?"

"A socialite whose hobbies were collecting art, drinking bourbon, and falling into unrequited love with gay men." He dunked the deferred biscuit and ate it.

"Did she ever make a pass at you?"

"No, and to this day, I'm not sure whether to be grateful or offended. There was always some gathering where people like them—and us, I suppose—congregated to further their careers and personal lives, which back then often intertwined. Prior to the current worries about sexual harassment, co-workers often slept together, particularly in the arts. Scotty and I met on the job, as it were. But to return to my point, we were touchstones for each other in public, especially with strangers or people we barely knew. Intercepting the other's gaze, even from opposite ends of the room, proved an unerring barometer that registered when the other was bored or having fun or had gleaned some interesting gossip and couldn't wait to discuss it in private."

"Your life was more glamorous than you led me to suspect."

"We had a few glamorous moments, I suppose. Mostly it consisted of the routine I've outlined. I'd be out all day, rehearsing a play, filming a commercial or a bit in a film, and return to find him tinkering with a drawing at his drafting table. He'd enquire about my day, solicit an opinion on his sketch and we'd either go out to dinner or stay in. If I wasn't in a play or job hunting, I was home, cooking and cleaning while he sketched. Sunday mornings were my favorite."

"Why?"

"There's another old song called 'I Don't Want Him, You Can Have Him' . . ."

"An odd title to associate with one of your three loves, isn't it?" I said.

"Don't jump the gun, like the cowboy told the schoolmarm. The lyrics include a couplet that goes: 'Fetch the papers and when they've been read / Spend the balance of the day in bed.'"

"That's how you spent your Sundays?"

"When I wasn't doing a play," he said. "The Sunday *Times* then was a huge stack of papers. The least drowsy of us would fetch it from where they left it at the front door, brew coffee, fix breakfast and hop back into bed, where we'd spend the morning reading and discussing different articles. After that, we'd listen to the radio and resume whatever book each of us was on. I loved lying with his bird body against mine, sunshine pouring through the window, or hearing it rain or watching it snow, reading away the afternoon."

"You'd read for the entire afternoon?"

"Often," he said. "If Scotty and I considered the arts a vital aspect of life, we considered literature the most vital of the arts, as well as one of the most gratifying, a view we retained despite changing attitudes."

"How were they changing?"

"For one thing, the first generation to grow up with TV was maturing and exerting its influence."

"And you had a problem with them?"

"The problem wasn't with the generation per se but with TV, specifically, its drawbacks as a medium."

"What did you see as its drawbacks?"

"Mainly that it privileges sight and sound."

"So?"

"We've gone over how our brains arrive at abstract ideas via impressions of the world gathered from the five senses. Gathering and transforming impressions into ideas is only part of what our brains do. Humans, being mammals, have an equally instinctive need to communicate what they perceive and think. This is due to mammals being pack animals, surviving as part of a larger group."

"Because the survival strategy for groups involves trading information about threats and things that might prove beneficial."

"Yes. Less complex animals trade information with grunts, growls, and gestures. For humans, the supreme method of communication is language. Words communicate impressions and thoughts with greater precision, allowing for more precise responses to situations. This increases our species' chances for survival and enhances the value of survival for individuals."

"I understand how sharing information increases our chances for survival. How does it enhance its value?'

Robert cleared his throat and shifted in his chair. "We, or our brains, are too self-aware to be satisfied with merely finding food and shelter and avoiding harm. If artists require reasons for breaking the rules, people in general need reasons to survive, things to make existence a positive, satisfying experience."

"You don't think survival is a basic, inborn impulse?"

"Partly, perhaps, but any accurate observation of human behavior would reveal it isn't enough. How many people who are in all respects able to maintain organic life end up committing suicide or engaging in the protracted suicide of alcohol or drugs? Lacking a basic joy in being, a bare animal existence not only becomes meaningless but an insupportable burden. Trading information about what pleases us or makes us happy helps individuals cultivate that other yet equally essential motive for survival. Isn't this the reason for your efforts on behalf of Dr. Jacobson? Learning about him and his books wouldn't increase anyone's chances for survival, would it?"

"Probably not."

"But it likely will increase the pleasure of his books, giving his readers something to improve the quality of their lives. Another important point to make about language—or human language anyway—is that it relies on our capacity for empathy."

"What do you mean by empathy?"

"The ability to perceive and understand another's viewpoint," he said.

"You really think that's possible?"

"Obviously, we can't comprehend everything another person thinks and feels. But if we weren't able to comprehend sizeable amounts, there'd be no point in us talking right now. The entire human repertoire of arts, sciences, and technology is the result of people trading information, and refining their ideas. If we lacked the ability to perceive others' viewpoints, sharing information would be impossible. The ideas and impressions people have would remain isolated in the brain perceiving them."

"So empathy is imperfect but essential."

"Like everything in this world," he said. "Now, if human language represents an improvement over grunts and gestures, written words similarly improve on spoken language."

"Why?"

"As I'm sure you know, oral communication is susceptible to great errors across distances and generations, making it unreliable as a fund of information. Hieroglyphics were a sort of bridge between spoken and written language. They stabilized information by associating it with images of concrete objects, as in the Egyptian system, with its arrangements of animals, plants, tools, and the like. But while images of tangible objects easily convey the idea of what they portray, they're limited in their ability to signify ideas and emotions and other abstractions, precisely because they're images."

"Why does that matter?"

"If ideas and emotions derive from impressions gleaned by all five senses, images reduce or collapse those abstractions to copies of items perceived by just one sense: sight. Consider a hieroglyphic bird, for example. It may only indicate a bird. It may also refer to a region that's the habitat for that type of bird or a military or ecclesiastical group that uses the bird as a mascot. Then again, it may refer to being lighter than air, or flight, or the exhilaration felt when we gaze at a bird soaring overhead. The Rosetta stone allows us to decipher Egypt's hieroglyphics, but artifacts from other ancient societies are littered with images that resist clear interpretation because images are too imprecise, too readily associated with multiple meanings."

"I see."

"That's what makes the written word a triumph. Letters lack a direct connection to what the eye perceives. They're free-floating and may be combined in different and very specific ways to indicate more specific things. A species of bird, a geographical area, a military platoon, the act of flight, or a reflective mood are all made distinct thanks to the unique arrangement of letters we associate with each."

"Then yours and Scotty's quarrel with TV was that it relies on images rather than words?"

"Yes. Written words denote what our senses experience and the abstract ideas our minds develop from them. TV functions by stimulating just two of the five senses we use to construct our worldview: sight and sound."

"Marshall McLuhan thought the opposite. He said TV was the richer medium and that reading only stimulated the eyes."

Robert snorted and tossed his head like an agitated horse. "McLuhan was a fool. Scotty and I both thought so when we read his stuff. He was among a group of avatars that, in its early days, portrayed TV as another twentieth-century marvel. The more we thought about it, the more we began thinking of TV, and all audio-visual media, as just animated hieroglyphics, subject to the limitations imposed by representing ideas with concrete images."

"The same limitations as the hieroglyphic bird," I said.

He nodded. "A sunset in a film or TV show may illustrate the brevity of life or indicate an end to a satisfying day. Then again, it may mean both or neither. Rather than a way for artists to communicate an idea to their audience, the image of a sunset is an indefinite symbol to which the viewer may associate any number of meanings, usually taken from their personal reaction to sunsets rather than how that one sunset fits into that one story. This ambiguity is what makes film and TV criticism such a vast yet inconclusive field of pseudo-inquiry."

"More Rorschach tests . . ."

"The Rorschach as an academic parlor game. Words enable writers to pinpoint what a sunset means at a given point in a narrative to the characters involved. This allows for clearer, more specific understanding by the reader. One of the reasons I wanted to be an actor was for the privilege of speaking well-written, insightful words, rather than serving as an image symbol onto which viewers projected partially thought-out ideas and fantasies."

"Explaining your attitude to your soap opera career," I said.

"Quite so," he said and sipped his tea. "Words explicate; images imply. And for Scotty and me, and Terry and many others in our generation, the most gratifying dramatic art strives to explicate the human condition."

"The films you loved as a kid are also constructed of audio-visual images, and theatre is a matter of people watching what transpires on a stage."

"True, but we experienced theater, film, and concerts differently from how people experience TV."

"Because they were more ritualized?"

"If you wish to extend the metaphor, yes. In my youth, you went to the movies on average once or twice a week and to plays or concerts once or twice a month. The event lasted a few hours, after which you returned to life in the richer reality perceived by your brain and your five senses. There you spent the better part of your leisure hours reading, listening to the radio or to records. You also had friends over, or you visited them, to talk and sometimes to play cards or games like backgammon. The pastimes dominating life away from public cultural events exercised the intellect and the empathetic capacity for communication. Even when you attended a film, concert, or play, it was always more than mere spectatorship."

"What made it more?"

"The ritual of getting dressed and going to a venue, and knowing it was likely your one chance to see the film or play or hear the music, served as a framing device, a way of bracketing the event that focused your attention on it and heightened its effects. When it came to theater and concerts, you were also aware of the performers as living, breathing people exercising their talents before you in real-time. Then there were the audience members. Watching them enter or exit, jostling them to get to a seat, chatting with them in line for popcorn, or waiting with them for the show to begin demonstrated the varieties of human character, at least it did for me. I saw they lived and breathed and talked like me, yet had different traits and led different kinds of lives. I was always fascinated and awed by that, and in the end developed a basic respect for it."

"Which probably influenced your choice of profession."

"True. Acting, in part, enabled me to communicate my respect for human differences I observed in three-dimensional space. TV invaded that richer reality and, in effect, destroyed it."

"How?"

"A medium privileging sight and sound is problematic for several reasons. Sight and sound, as we've discussed, are only two of the five senses we employ to construct our worldview. Second, images, even audio-visual images, are a less precise means of communication. Third, privileging sight and sound means only audio-visual images that excite those two senses will be preferred by viewers. This is why, as has often been said, TV programming tends to be oriented around sex and violence, since these offer the most intense stimulation to the eyes and ears of viewers."

"Films exploited sex and violence from their beginnings."

"But watching movies was a sometimes thing, bracketed by periods of activities like listening to music or reading, which leads to the final objection Scotty and I had to TV—its pervasiveness."

"What do you mean by pervasiveness?"

"TV supplied hours of programming, one after another, while its presence in the home meant one didn't have to go out in order to enjoy it."

"Eliminating the framing devices that focus attention on other cultural experiences," I said.

"Indeed. Viewers could sit back and wallow in a near-continuous stimulation of eyes and ears without pausing to contemplate, much less criticize
what they viewed. The perpetual stimulation TV brought into homes also
tended to orient everyday life around that stimulation, seducing viewers
into abandoning the intellectually active pastimes that had formed a major
part of their leisure. Film, theater, and concert attendance decreased soon
after TV became widespread, reducing economic support for those arts
and eliminating the other benefits of going-out rituals. At home, rather
than read, play games or talk, people tended more and more to sit on their
couches or lie in bed, watching a parade of images whose purpose was to
excite the eyes and ears rather than communicate ideas."

"Don't characters on TV, in films and on stage use spoken words to
communicate ideas?"

"But in all those instances, the experience is passive. One watches and
listens, unable to make comments or pose questions that might clarify or
even alter the ideas under discussion. This disrupts the two-way exchanges
that facilitate information trade, not to mention the development of empathy necessary to comprehend another's point of view."

"There's no two-way exchange when you read a book, either, or watch
a play."

"But in those cases it wasn't as detrimental, since it was common to
discuss with others what you'd seen or read. For those interested in the arts,
they were a standard topic of conversation, and argument."

"Another framing device that subjected what the artist said to further
thought and consideration."

"The TV ritual is to sit and stare at a succession of talking heads talk
hour after hour, day after day. And since the attraction of TV is its appeal
to the eyes and ears, the validity of what talking heads say is second to their
status as audio-visual stimuli whose appeal and purpose is to engage the
senses rather than the minds of viewers. This is why the melodramatics of
soap operas are the typical form drama takes on TV. Audio-visual media is
also the perfect growth medium for Molehill Men. The pundits currently
infesting modern journalism bitch, insult, and exhort on topics from the
crucial to the trivial, creating hours of audio-visual images that excite the
eyes and ears, yet in terms of information, mean next to nothing. This was
what Scotty and I considered the most damaging aspect of TV and all audio-visual media: its viewers judge the value of what appears on it not on
the basis of intellectual appraisal but to the extent that it attracts the eyes

and ears. An ability to excite those two senses, rather than gratify a broader understanding, is the justification for the majority of what one's expressed in the medium."

"That's quite a generalization."

"But not untrue. Plenty of commentators and satirists remarked on the hypnotic and intellectually destructive power of TV before McLuhan composed his panygerics. You're accustomed to research. Look around. You'll find everything from essays and books to cartoons and even TV sketches from the 1950s onward targeting the changes in culture and thinking habits wrought by TV. But TV's appeal was too powerful. Huddled in their living rooms, shrinking their perceptions down to audio-visual images oriented around conflict that imply rather than explicate meaning, viewers gladly abandoned other forms of culture and, along with them, the opportunity to construct clearer ideas of the multi-sensory world around them. As Scotty once observed, over the course of a single generation, people learned to prefer pictures that dazzled the eye and numbed the brain."

"I love that."

"So did I. And once you understand how the nature of TV encourages intellectual passivity, you see more clearly how its content reinforces it."

"How?"

"Two ways," he said. "First, there's its status as a mass medium."

"Why's that a problem?"

"Continuous consumption of books, music, and drama creates a demand exceeding the human capacity to create interesting or innovative content. This forces mass media to rely on repetition. Whatever proves popular recurs until it congeals into genres: mystery, western, police procedural, legal drama, hospital drama, situation comedy, horror, sci-fi, action-adventure, and such. This reduces reality to a series of reiterated tropes that audiences approach with a foreknowledge of what will likely happen and what characters will likely say. Compare that to actual learning, which means satisfying curiosity about the unfamiliar. It's also the opposite of art. Rather than refresh your perceptions of the world, genres mire it within the confines of their conventions. Following an initial burst of creativity, with shows like *Studio One* that we've already talked about, TV became a clearing house for genre programs that repeat the same old clichés under different titles and with different actors, which viewers gladly consume so long as those programs sufficiently dazzle their eyes and ears."

"What's the other way content induces passivity?"

"At about the time TV became prominent, there was a relaxation of censorship in other media."

"You don't favor censorship, do you?"

"No, but its disappearance led to unforeseen consequences."

"Like what?"

"The argument against censorship is that artists have a right to explore every topic in the range of human experience. I agree. But there's a difference between exploring a topic and exploiting it. Does the name Heywood Broun ring a bell?"

"No. Sorry."

"He was a newspaper columnist in the 1920s and '30s. I read a quote attributed to him that I repeated to Scotty. It may be apocryphal, and thanks to my aging memory, I can only paraphrase it, but I believe it went: 'Obscenity is such a tiny country a single tour covers it completely.' The idea is that once you've learned all the dirty words and about all the different sex acts, the only thing left is to repeat them. The same applies to violence. And when it comes to art, narrative art especially, repetition leads to sterility. Unless you have something new or fresh to say about a subject, you're not creating an interesting work of art, at least for me."

"Although the end of censorship allowed access to a number of serious artworks: Joyce's *Ulysses,* Ginsberg's *Howl* . . ."

"Works that actually offered new and fresh approaches," he said. "If the fashion for avant-garde art encouraged too many aspiring artists to believe being avant-garde meant simply breaking rules, too many also believed exploring the human condition meant dumping as many previously taboo topics as possible into a work. Yet this shift dovetailed neatly with TV's eclipse of the written word since sex, violence, and their allied topics readily lend themselves to images that dazzle the eyes and numb the brain, mainly because they appeal not to the mind but to our basic, biological responses."

"Biological?"

"Erotic images excite the sexual urge, obviously. Violent images excite reactions to threats, such as fight-or-flight and the startle response. Horror films, for example, rely heavily on the startle response, with quick cuts to hideous monsters, mutilated corpses, or serial killers poised to attack. This is antithetical to the function of culture as Scotty and I understood and appreciated it."

"Antithetical how?"

"The narrative art Scotty and I admired employed events as springboards for an exploration of the moral and intellectual problems posed by human behavior. Erotic or violent images cue chemical changes that saturate the brain with adrenaline, dopamine, and other neuro-chemicals encouraging viewers to enjoy a response divorced from the mind's ability to contemplate the impact of the depicted events within temporal existence."

"What sort of impacts?"

"In terms of sexuality, it might be the development and progress of a relationship; its effects on those connected to the couple; an unwanted pregnancy, or the transmission of disease. As for violence, it's the moral questions raised by—and resulting from—inflicting harm. The reactions evoked by erotic or violent images not only lack the ideational content required to connect them to wider temporal sequences, those viewing them instead often have the illusion of stepping outside time altogether."

"Now you've really lost me. How do they step outside time?"

"Adherents of tantric sex regard the orgasm as a spiritual event similar to nirvana. Presumably, both provide a glimpse into a timeless spiritual realm, defined as such by its opposition to a physical realm subordinated to time. As with an orgasm, albeit to a lesser extent, the chemical euphoria accompanying the fight-or-flight or startle response focuses your attention entirely on the sensation for as long as it lasts. This creates an illusion of transcending time because the intensity of the chemical change leaves you momentarily unable to perceive, much less contemplate, time's passage."

"Then you're saying if narrative art helps train us to think in terms of temporal sequences, a series of sexual or violent images limits that thinking through an illusion of escaping time."

"The whole thing boils down to two opposing types of pleasure: the intellectual pleasure of following a temporal narrative, and the pleasure of chemical reactions that erase the perception of temporality."

"And since learning involves tracing the different sequences constituting a reality lived in time, preferring or privileging a euphoria that removes you from time leads to intellectual passivity or inactivity."

"As well as what Scotty and I termed moral passivity."

"Moral passivity?"

"Our responses to sex and violence aren't there merely for us to feel. They're a spur to action, much as the trade in information spurs us to actions that help us survive. And like communication, morality involves the exercise of empathy."

"What do the chemical responses to sex and violence have to do with empathy?"

"The response evoked by eroticism, in its general sense of longing for intimacy, urges us to establish bonds with others. The fight-or-flight and startle responses appear with the perception of threats, urging us to take appropriate action to minimize or avoid them. Empathizing with that response in others, even if we haven't directly perceived the threat, urges us to take the same defensive action."

"How?"

"If someone exhibits fear of something around a corner that we can't see, it puts us on guard against it, at least until we can ascertain the threat for ourselves. The same empathy also encourages us to take action for more than our safety alone."

"Why should it do that?"

"Animal packs are comprised of individuals. Therefore, the survival of the pack depends on preserving and reproducing individual lives, as it were banking them against threats beyond the individuals' and the pack's control."

"Such as what?"

"Plagues, earthquakes, or other catastrophes that threaten more than one member at a time. The best way for a pack to survive wholesale disasters is to preserve as many individual lives as possible. The empathy allowing us to communicate information also encourages us to bond with and value one another, and to act when we observe signs of distress in others, to render aid to individuals for the survival of the species."

"Logical, but rare in practice," I said. "Many animal packs, or individuals within the packs, attack and kill their own."

"Perhaps because being less complex animals, they lack the degree of empathy humans possess, the one that makes words and language possible. Also, like our brains' other abilities—from dancing to mathematics—empathy must be developed and exercised. And apart from individual variables, development depends on how much the surrounding culture values it. Despite present trends stressing evidence for the violent behaviors of our ancestors, evidence of empathy, like art, appears in the archaeological record: broken bones that healed because some other—or others—tended to the injured party. The point is that chemical responses to positive and negative events are preludes to practical action, actions intended to enable individuals—and the group—to survive and thrive."

"And failing to act on these chemical responses makes them completely passive experiences."

"Just as TV's talking heads disrupt the two-way communication required for intellectual activity, experiencing biological responses without a chance to act on them disrupts the mutuality necessary for empathic, moral activity. Watching others have sex or suffer and die is, for me, a profoundly uncomfortable experience since undergoing the chemical changes these images produce without being able to act on them makes me feel frustrated and powerless. What's the look for?"

"You reminded me of a book I came across during my film studies courses. It was by a scholar named Gaylyn Studlar, about the films Marlene Dietrich made with Josef von Sternberg. She approached them from a Freudian perspective, and her thesis was that their aesthetic is basically masochistic. She defined masochism in part as prolonged or perpetual deferment of pleasure, a constant postponement of satisfaction, and concluded that all spectatorship is in part masochistic. You're talking about the same deferment, finding pleasure in the ultimate frustration of impulse."

"I agree with her. Audio-visual media conditions audiences to the masochistic pleasure of being unable to act on their better nature, and instead find excitement in restraining their most characteristically human instincts and abilities, from literacy to compassion. Rather than ennoble our faculties, it stunts them and then asks us to enjoy that perpetual non-fulfillment."

"This also clarifies the difference between exploring a topic and exploiting it."

"Indeed. Exploration traces the consequences of events within larger temporal sequences. Exploitation induces a euphoric response removing viewers from the world of cause and effect, or at least blurs their perception of it. Following the end of censorship, the arts increasingly exploited sensations and sensationalism in the stricter sense of those terms. People paid for as much of it as showmen could supply, and as the film industry quickly learned, it proved a handy means for countering the deadening repetition of genre conventions."

"How'd they do that?"

"When television began eroding film attendance in the 1950s, film studios tried luring people back into theaters by tricking out the usual genres with gimmicks."

"Widescreen, 3-D, stereo sound . . ."

"Yes. After censorship ended, movies could also appeal to biology since, unlike the narrative tropes of genres, adrenaline and dopamine and the rest retain their potency despite repetition. Filmmakers enhanced genres with more explicit content, making war movies, police procedurals, and horror films bloodier and more action-packed and love stories more erotic. Scotty and I felt this explained why musicals disappeared by the end of the 1960s: they're the only genre whose conventions couldn't sensibly accommodate the addition of explicit material. It's also why I was ambivalent about the introduction of nudity in the theater, which was a hot topic in those days. I have nothing against the sight of the human body; in fact, I've often enjoyed it. It's just that our response to it disrupts the narrative flow on which most plays depend. But in a culture increasingly reliant on audio-visual images, spectatorship rapidly changed from a thoughtful observation of the human condition to the passive experience of chemical jolts derived from the sights and sounds of sex and, more sinisterly, of suffering and death. So while, as you said, many new and brilliant explorations of the human condition appeared after the end of censorship, bloodshed and copulation flowed in a much vaster torrent, aimed at audiences craving only chemical euphoria. This quickly reduced culture, especially popular culture, to a perpetual game of dare between audiences and artists."

"Dare?"

"Sure. Artists contrived ever more explicit representations of sex or violence, and audiences considered it a point of pride to accept the challenge to view them. They lined up to watch *Deep Throat* to show they could handle pornographic sex and flocked to *The Texas Chainsaw Massacre* to prove they could stomach watching another human being eviscerated before their eyes. Proving your ability to passively endure whatever images audio-visual culture threw at you became the purpose for consuming cultural products."

"Don't you think artists and audiences should push boundaries?"

"Pushing boundaries is one of many phrases used to justify the game of cultural dare. Pushing the envelope is another. They make it seem exciting and, more importantly, liberating. For Scotty and me, it's absurdly simple-minded."

"Why?"

"As with genres, it's too easily reduced to a formula. Every society lives within boundaries. If pushing boundaries is your cultural standard, to be an artist, you merely have to figure out where the boundaries lie in your society and deliberately cross them. The modern debate over political correctness is a case in point. Molehill Men characterize political correctness as a restraint on free speech and, by extension, creativity. But as people abandoned political correctness, rather than a Renaissance of creativity, all you had was a procession of third-rate stand-up comics building acts from a predictable checklist of people to offend, performed for audiences whose desire to prove their political incorrectness trained them to laugh regardless of the actual quality of the humor."

"What if your society embraces anarchy, which permits everything?"

"Then you question the value of anarchy."

"Naturally," I said.

"Sorry, Paul. Scotty and I considered our world too intricate and elusive for such easy approaches. But pushing boundaries and all the other tag lines proved easy justifications for the sensationalism preferred by the TV generation. Not surprisingly, the same generation pursued sensationalism in reality, too, embracing a hedonism named after the triumvirate of sex, drugs, and rock-and-roll."

"A lifestyle you and Scotty also disapproved of?"

"Only because it elevates the pleasures of the body over those of the mind. Still, we realized that what made hedonism alluring to the TV generation wasn't simply the medium that had shaped them since childhood."

"What else was there?"

"The same thing motivating the revived interest in post-World War I avant-garde art: confronting humanity's penchant for destruction. They'd grown up directly after the horrors of World War II, the atomic bomb, and in the middle of an escalating Cold War. This saddled them with the possibility of the world, and themselves, being snuffed out at any moment. Then, as young adults, many confronted a more immediate possibility of early death by being shipped off to the Vietnam War. Unsurprisingly, kids faced with such dubious futures abandoned the effort to think in terms of temporal sequences in favor of sensations that provided the illusion of escaping time. Not that this was a preference endemic to that generation."

"You think it's a recurrent pattern?"

"More than a pattern," he said. "It's a permanent condition for some. People so underprivileged they can expect nothing from the future often turn to pleasures that allow them to escape a time that can bring them nothing better. Likewise, those who are so over-privileged they don't have to worry about their futures also prefer escaping time since it, too, can bring them nothing new or better."

"Maybe you and Scotty were too much of a different generation to empathize with their position."

"We were occasionally accused of being out of date, despite being in

our late thirties. We sometimes wondered if we were until, during our discussions about the curious era in which we lived, we discovered something
that boosted our egos."

"What?"

"Both advocates and critics of the sex, drugs, and rock-and-roll culture
almost invariably portrayed it as a challenge or alternative to the consumer capitalism prevailing among older people. Scotty and I realized that
beneath this heavily touted antagonism, the new, hedonistic youth culture
and the older consumer capitalism rested on the same foundation."

"What would that be?"

"A belief in the value of mindless self-indulgence. Sex, drugs, and rock-
and-roll promote the chemical euphoria derived from physical sensations.
Consumer capitalism promotes the chemical euphoria derived from satisfying a desire for objects of industry. Both rank instant gratification above any
thoughtful reckoning with its consequences, or indeed any thinking at all."

"What do you see as consequences in those cases?"

"Irresponsible sexual behavior may lead to unwanted pregnancy or the
spread of venereal diseases, while drugs wreak havoc on the body and mind.
Chemicals used to manufacture consumer goods, like processed foods, undermine people's health, while pollutants emitted by factories erode the
environment. The staunch, often self-righteous disregard for consequences
among adherents of these supposedly opposite lifestyles explains why we
added the key qualifier 'mindless' to our formulation."

"A fascinating slant," I said.

"It also explains why those devoted to the hedonistic youth culture of
the 1960s switched their allegiance to consumer capitalism in the 1980s.
Received wisdom considers it a momentous political sea-change, but in reality, it was a slight shift from one form of mindless self-indulgence to another.
Hippies addicted to the euphoria induced by marijuana and promiscuity
became yuppies addicted to the euphoria of buying overpriced cars and
espresso makers. And since the pleasures of sex or drugs or buying luxury
items fade soon after, it leaves one always on the lookout for more of the
same, on a perpetual quest to recapture that brief yet intense escape from
time. Mindless self-indulgence thus devolves into repetition."

"Like mass media."

"Making mass media the characteristic cultural form of a self-indulgent
society, regardless of the nature of those indulgences or the ideologies jus-
tifying them," he said. "Ultimately, Scotty and I found these parallel shifts

to audio-visual media and the ethos of mindless self-indulgence changing culture into something that, rather than heighten the senses and ennoble the faculties, gluts the senses and stunts the faculties, ultimately resulting in what we termed a lower standard of adulthood."

The phrase struck me even more than "images that dazzle the eye and numb the brain." I asked, "What do you mean by a lower standard of adulthood?"

"Just that," he said. "Society prohibits people from engaging in activities like sex, drinking, smoking, driving, and others until they become adults. Theoretically, reaching a specific age means the individual has grown astute enough to handle them responsibly, an utterly ludicrous notion, as if a magic being descends from heaven on your eighteenth or twenty-first birthday, waves a wand, and grants you maturity."

"You don't expect me to believe your generation was above the usual prurient interests."

"Certainly not. I told you Terry and I discussed sex, and I sought out every scrap of information on the topic. I experimented with booze in high school and college, yet I only became a casual drinker. I never smoked since I'd heard it played havoc with the throat, and caring for my voice was important if I wanted to be an actor. The links to cancer and lung disease came later. And we had films, plays, books, and magazines that exploited biological responses, even if they weren't as explicit as they became after censorship. But for us, as for Haywood Broun, those indulgences represented small areas of a larger world, or better yet, tiny parts of a larger human experience, a handful among seemingly limitless possibilities. And for many, if not all in our generation, the only way to attain the maturity required to grapple with the possibilities of adult life was through learning."

"How does learning make you responsible?"

"I told you that when I was young, primary education encouraged us to think in terms of a reality formed of temporal sequences. This, in turn, taught us to view ourselves as an element in that reality and our actions among its larger sequences of events. Only by recognizing that your actions have an effect in the world you live in—and cultivating a habit of speculating on their possible effects—do you attain the responsibility necessary to deal with the privileges accompanying adulthood."

"But nobody can accurately predict the consequences of their actions as they play out in time. I mean, they set off a chain of events that conceivably extends well beyond one's lifespan."

"Being responsible means judging the effects of your actions to the best of your ability, however limited. For people like Scotty, Terry, and me, adulthood was a lifelong process of learning and acculturation that refined our ability to think about the world and our place in it, an ability that benefits both the individual and the species."

"How does it do both?"

"It improves the quality of life for individuals in the ways I mentioned, while only cultivated adults have a chance to create what our generation considered a civilized society."

"You've used the words 'civilized' and 'civilization' a lot. How do you define civilization?"

"Civilization is—or should be—a space shielding people from the threats of chaotic nature, providing the safety and leisure for them to develop their inborn abilities. When people prattle on about realizing their potential, they usually refer to something immediately and often visually perceived—athletes winning a competition, businesspeople displaying their wealth, politicians wielding power. Or else it's 'getting what you want,' which is just another term for mindless self-indulgence. The potentials Scotty and I considered most important were those we've discussed, the intellectual abilities that not only give you a deeper understanding of the world but a greater appreciation for and enjoyment of life, apart from whatever ephemeral pleasures and accomplishments come your way."

"And you felt the standard of adulthood associated with this notion of civilization was changing?"

"Unquestionably. As the self-indulgence preached by both consumer capitalism and sex, drugs, and rock-and-roll became the purpose of existence, more and more kids believed they attained maturity once they reached whatever age allowed them to drive, drink and have sex without interference from parents or the law. The idea is that since these behaviors are in legal theory restricted to adults, one becomes an adult simply by engaging in them, whether or not one is capable of pondering their consequences."

"Upending the rationale for the restrictions in the first place," I said.

"Yes. Instead of becoming a responsible adult in order to gain access to restricted pleasures, access to restricted pleasures became the universal sign of adulthood. This had a disastrous effect on the status of education, at least, as far we could see."

"How did you see it?"

"Once mindless self-indulgence became the purpose of existence, the purpose of education swung away from Renaissance to Utilitarian ideals. Instead of cultivating the faculties vital for maturity, individuals merely had to learn what they needed to perform whatever Utilitarian function earned the money to pay for their chosen indulgences. The brain, with its multiple abilities, narrowed to a pragmatic tool for solving whatever problems stand between individuals and their objects of desire. How can I get a well-paying job in a big building, what's the best car to buy, how can I lure him or her into bed . . ."

"All legitimate interests."

"But our brains are capable of so much more, and it seemed a waste not to at least attempt to use them for something other than securing pleasures that are valued mainly for their ability to deaden one's perception of the world and time."

"Hedonism isn't new, either. Philosophers have advocated hedonism for as long as there's been philosophy."

"But in order to elucidate that philosophy they must first become philosophers, which in turn requires learning. By priveleging hedonism over learning, they undermine the very process enabling them to articulate the idea in the first place, an irony if there ever was one."

"I suppose," I said.

"The same irony holds for philosophers opposing the exercise of empathy. They characterize empathy and the emotions associated with it as signs of weakness. But since empathy is essential for understanding language, without empathy, nobody would be able to grasp their ideas in the first place. This makes the very attempt to communicate their aversion to empathy an argument in favor of it."

He drank more tea. I waited for him to continue.

"McLuhan succumbed to a similar, fundamental hypocrisy. If he believed TV was a more complex and satisfying form of communication than written words, why did he write books? Anyway, since culture is a key part of the Renaissance approach to education, the demotion of education to a functional stepping stone to self-indulgence reduced culture to just another of those indulgences. Art as a reflection of the human condition fell from favor, and rather than follow the trajectory of human beings in time, drama deteriorated to flimsy strings on which to hang images whose attraction and purpose is to induce moments of euphoria, giving audiences the illusion of escaping the parameters of daily existence. And since, after the end of censorship, regulations limited access to explicit material in books, music, films, and, later, TV to people deemed adults by an arbitrary age marker, accessing such content became yet another false standard of adulthood. You reached adulthood when you were legally able to enjoy the masochistic pleasures of explicit sexual or violent material, just as you reached adulthood when you were legally able to enjoy the numbing pleasures of alcohol. Rather than develop a set of ennobled faculties, the prime indication of maturity became the legal right to access a set of illusory escapes from being. You can see, then, why Scotty and I took a dim view of the culture forming around TV and the TV generation, compared to a culture oriented around the other arts, especially literature."

"I'd say you bashed it pretty thoroughly."

"For all the good it did," he said. "There was no stopping the hegemony of audio-visual media, led by TV. People abandoned the habits that had been the basis of cultural life in our youth until, by the end of the 1960s, books, conversation, parlor games, and theater had dwindled to minority pursuits. We noticed that kids raised on TV in the 1950s found interpreting words on a page, for any extended period, an onerous task rather than a gateway to the joys and possibilities of civilization. And they judged the quality of films and TV shows by the number and intensity of biological reactions they produced. Spectatorship was replacing culture; the world narrowing from what the mind thought and felt about it to what might be seen and heard through a screen; and a population developing who were increasingly isolated in their homes, ignoring the active pursuit of knowledge for the near-continuous, passive reception of stimuli that blurred perceptions of the temporal world and their place in it."

"Huxley had the same idea in *Brave New World* about a population controlled by pleasure rather than coerced by pain."

He straightened up and sipped more tea. "Huxley, unlike McLuhan, was brilliant and prescient. Theodor Adorno voiced a similar suspicion concerning culture as a source of pleasure alone. Other critics, artists, philosophers, psychologists, and even filmmakers commented on the shift, as I've already mentioned. But the nature of audio-visual media also makes it practically immune to criticism."

"Why?"

"Understanding any critical argument requires the capacity for active thought that audio-visual media discourages. For instance, a 1968 film called *Medium Cool* portrayed a TV news cameraman's growing disaffection brought about by his constantly observing rather than participating in events around him. But how can a comment on the alienation induced by audio-visual media be truly effective when delivered by the medium inducing it? My old mentor Gore Vidal published essays regretting the absorption of literature into academia, which offered it as an object of study to pupils who preferred movies and TV to reading. And he mocked the elevation of movies to an art form, especially the auteur theory. But in a culture devoted to spectatorship, the influence of any thoughtful writing on any subject is limited, especially when it critiques spectatorship."

"You've drawn quite a picture."

"A caricature, you mean, composed of broad generalizations and simplifications. But like all caricatures, it highlights rather than falsifies what Scotty and I observed. Neither of us, for instance, objected to sexual or violent material if it advanced a larger, well-thought-out narrative."

"When it helps explore rather than exploit a subject," I said.

"And the euphoria brought about by sex, good food, or any of life's other physical pleasures improves the quality of existence. At least, I wouldn't have wanted to do without them. Problems arise only when they replace the more complex satisfactions that come from heightening our senses and ennobling our faculties."

"I get what you mean. But I'm still wondering what this has to do with Scotty's and your relationship."

"Our preference for art as intellectual stimulation enhanced our sense of being a refuge for one another. Some of our friends retained the discernment that our age group associated with a subtler, more thoughtful adult standard, yet too many others followed the fashion for sensationalism, in part—as you hinted—to avoid appearing outdated. Scotty and I felt we belonged to a vanishing breed, which was why those days we spent reading, listening to music, and talking about art were as intimate as the hours we spent dancing or in bed. It was how we made sense of a changing world and found continued meaning for our lives."

"The gay rights movement started around then, too, thanks to changing mores and interest in formerly taboo subjects. You must've been in New York for the Stonewall riots in 1969."

"I was, and I'm grateful for that, especially when I see how it's improved life for the kids who came after, like you and David. I simply have reservations about crediting those changes to the hedonistic culture gaining prominence at the same time. Molehill Men often characterize a concern for human rights as a matter of excessive emotion. Empathy, of course, plays a part, yet for me, it's an intellectual issue, a matter of applying abstract thought to human existence."

"Abstract thought?"

"The same we apply to ordinary objects—a table, for instance. We form a singular idea of a table, what it does, and how it differs from chairs and bureaus, despite individual tables having multiple sizes, shapes, and other details. Similarly, we note that all humans have desires, needs, and other traits that identify them as human despite their differences, which entitles them to basic respect and consideration, from each other and from the law."

"Something you realized while observing people in theaters and art galleries."

"In part," he said. "The racial, genetic, and religious theories advanced to restrict human rights by denying the humanity of their targets are, for me, merely excuses to avoid or resist one's capacity for empathy and abstract thought. I viewed the concern for human rights in the 1960s as an intelligent attempt to create a more civilized society, the very opposite of the concurrent push toward hedonism. As for the gay rights movement, you may imagine after what I said about my adolescence, I was thrilled and rather astonished by it, though my personal liberation occurred earlier."

"When . . . and how?"

"I told you how relieved I was as a teenager when I learned other men shared my attraction to men."

"Yes."

"Attending Columbia, I was just as excited to discover an entire gay social world, with traditions and conventions, wasn't only thriving in New York but had been in place for decades."

"Was it difficult to enter that subculture?"

"I hate the term 'subculture.' It sounds like something submerged, hidden from the dominant culture, which is the point I'm trying to make. It wasn't."

"Didn't you tell me that in your youth, gay culture was sharply delineated from straight culture?"

"Sharply delineated doesn't mean completely invisible. What I meant was that anything directly referring to homosexuality was limited, especially in pop culture. The everyday existence of gay people was a different matter, and it wasn't as difficult to locate or enter into as it had seemed in Braintree, mainly because I no longer had to conceal my interest from my parents. Being relatively freer in New York, I hung around places I'd heard gay men frequented, not just bars but cafes, theaters, and parks. Certain bookstores had a pronounced gay clientele, where, along with a few tricks, I also picked up some of the paperbacks I'd spotted on my trips to Boston. Amid their melodrama, I found fairly accurate and useful depictions of gay life and sociability that helped me get to know other gay people. Much of this, of course, remained a mystery to straight society, or perhaps I should say those only comfortable within the confines of straight society. As time went on, I met men of all ages and in all professions who'd accepted their sexuality and enjoyed friendships with straight people who accepted and valued them."

"Do you remember any?'

"I remember one quite vividly: Warren Craig. He was twenty-eight when we met. He'd been in the army during the last year of the war, drafted at age eighteen. Shrapnel in the leg got him discharged just before the war ended and kept him from being shipped to the Korean War in the early 1950s. Yet it gave him a sweet, loping gait like a cowboy, though I naturally associated him with the photos of soldiers in *Life* I mooned over a few years previously. He told me a number of bars in the city catering to the military during the war had surreptitiously functioned as rendezvous for gay servicemen."

"Did he point you toward the cafes and bookstores and other gathering places?"

Robert nodded. "He also belonged to the Mattachine Society, which, as you probably know, was the first gay rights organization, and he subscribed to *One*."

"The first gay magazine," I said. *One* began as an offshoot of the Mattachine Society and continued publication until 1967. I had read about it in college but never expected to stand one degree away from an actual subscriber.

"I read a number of issues in his apartment. He taught me to decode the signals gay men used when discretion was required and gave me tips to avoid entrapment by the police. Most importantly, he demonstrated how to live as a gay man without it defining or limiting me. He worked in a brokerage firm and had straight friends who were aware of his sexuality. There was one married couple whom he often accompanied to shows and baseball games. Naturally, my mind harked back to Coward's *Design for Living*, but he assured me there was nothing sexual in it. He and I slept together on and off for three months."

"He wasn't one of your loves?"

"I was too young and too busy with college to engage in any romantic reveries. The experience with Terry was also too fresh. And Warren knew well enough where I was in life to risk forming an attachment to me. I think he just liked aiding a novice, for which I'll bless him forever."

"Of course, in a city like New York, it was probably easier to find gay people and for them to find acceptance, at least among the better educated and more sophisticated of the straight world."

"True enough, but even though homosexuality was severely limited in the straight world's pop culture, it wasn't entirely absent, either. There were mentions in newspapers and magazines, albeit in connection with criminal cases mostly, which was only to be expected since being gay was still a crime then. Even before I was born, there were cross-dressing entertainers in vaudeville, like Julian Eltinge, who were quite popular, drag balls and drag nightclub revues in the major cities that became quite fashionable among straight audiences in the late 1920s and into the early 1930s. A handful of blues and jazz records from the same time dealt fairly explicitly with the subject; Scotty had found a few of them, on 78 records, of course, while rummaging in the second-hand stores in New York. A familiar punch line for burlesque sketches had the comic exiting the stage in the company of an effeminate gay man after striking out with one of the beautiful showgirls, not surprisingly since burlesque theatres were a hunting ground for gay men seeking straight men looking to release their sexual tension. As we discussed, gay characters had begun appearing in novels, and a slew of gay actors popped up in films, like Franklin Pangborn and Clifton Webb, whose mannerisms were unmistakable to anyone with any insight into human sexuality, though they never openly discussed being gay and played their personas for comedy. Jack Benny, one of the nation's most popular comedians, had a strongly effeminate public persona and cracked jokes about dressing in drag. Then there was Rock Hudson's ruse in *Pillow Talk* when he plays at being gay to get close to Doris Day's character. These references wouldn't have had much effect or, indeed, any purpose if their meaning had gone over the average person's head, making it safe to assume there was more acknowledgment if not sophistication, about homosexuality among the general public even before Kinsey's report and other developments shone a brighter, clearer light on it. To us, Stonewall was less about thrusting gay culture onto a completely naïve straight culture than about decriminalizing homosexuality and challenging stereotypes."

"Crucial steps, nevertheless."

"To be sure," he said, "yet not as wholesale as making the utterly invisible visible. Scotty and I supported the movement, though. He participated in the early marches."

"You didn't?"

"The matter was more complicated for me."

"Why?"

"Because of my work. My career would've been seriously harmed or destroyed if I'd acknowledged my sexuality."

"There were some visible gay actors around then . . . Charles Nelson Reilly and Paul Lynde . . ."

"Who followed the Clifton Webb–Franklin Pangborn tradition of not discussing their sexuality and playing it for comedy. A serious actor breaking into films in the late 1960s still would've had a hard time finding work if he admitted to being gay. Sal Mineo, who established a career on TV and in films during the 1950s, lost his leading man status after he came out in the 1960s. My career was as meaningful and essential a part of me as my sexuality. Rather than risk losing it, I maintained the discretion I'd adopted at the start."

"Friends and colleagues knew, though."

"Sure, but for practical purposes, it remained an open secret, which I guess shows how well I'd adapted to the limitations placed on me after that initial, exuberant entrance into gay society."

"Maybe you adapted too well and stopped seeing them as limitations."

"Perhaps," he said. "People in the gay community, and letters in the pages of *One* decried the unfair laws and police harassment and the like, yet it had the feeling of the old saying 'everybody complains about the weather, but nobody does anything about it.' The restrictions seemed too widespread and too deeply entrenched to change anytime soon, so you went about your life as best you could. Scotty, being a behind-the-scenes talent and less liable to scrutiny, had less to lose by being active in the movement."

"Did this create any conflict between you?"

"No, he understood. We understood pretty much everything about each other."

"What finally drove you apart?"

He paused, hiding his discomfort with a sip of tea. "Last time you were here, we discussed siblings. Scotty had a sibling, a twin sister named Sandy."

"Scotty and Sandy?"

"Their real names were Scott and Sandra, of course. I doubt their parents realized how the diminutives would sound, at least after third grade. They were very close."

"Twins usually are."

"In their case, circumstances conspired to make them even more so."

"How?"

My phone beeped. Robert withheld his answer as I read a message from Angela Winslow instructing me to call her. I also noticed the time.

"Damn," I said.

"Anything wrong?"

"It's five-thirty. You missed *Grandview Park*."

"It didn't promise to be a particularly worthwhile episode. Someone sent you a message to tell you the time?"

"No, it's my supervisor at *H&H*. She wants me to call her. I figured out the time myself."

"I knew you were bright the day we met."

"I should get going. Anything else I can do before I go?"

"Would you mind leaving some vegetable soup in a pot on the stove? Put it on medium-low. I'm a bit worn out."

"You talked a lot. Shall I put the rest of your biscuits away?"

"They'll be dessert."

"Promise you'll take the proper precautions with your sweater before tackling the soup."

He grinned. "I'll be careful."

Inside the kitchen, I placed my empty tumbler in the dishwasher, opened a Cal's Cardio vegetable soup, set it simmering in a pot, and returned to the living room. Robert sat with the Wharton stories unopened on his lap, holding his reading glasses by the left earpiece.

"See you in a few days," I said.

"Okay. And as always, thanks for everything."

"You're welcome."

I grabbed my umbrella and opened the front door. Robert donned his glasses and lowered his eyes to the book.

Downstairs, standing by the lobby door waiting for another downpour to abate, I phoned Angela.

"Lena Crenshaw had a fall yesterday," she said.

"How bad?"

"Enough to convince her to move to an assisted living facility. She's in Fowler Memorial Hospital."

"I'll be making one less delivery, then."

"Unless you want me to assign you someone else," she said. "That's why I called. Is your plate too full?"

"No, I can handle it."

"Good. I'll give you the info in a few days."

"Would I be violating any regulations if I visited her in the hospital?"

"No. I'm sure she'd be happy to see you. Talk to you soon."

I pocketed my phone and leaned against the doorframe, watching the rain. Lena first alerted me to the stories my clients retained and the enjoyment we both might derive from their telling, by treating me to a string of outrageous anecdotes in response to an innocent inquiry about her nursing career. Once, I called her my Scheherazade, though I had to explain this referred to the inexhaustible tale-spinner from the *One Thousand and One Nights*.

Thinking of my first Scheherazade led me back to what the Scheherazade in the blue cardigan had left me pondering. He offered few original observations, yet I let him continue out of a burgeoning affection toward him and curiosity about how those observations formed his particular worldview. I had long been aware of the gap between individual lives and the generalizations of social history, yet Robert illustrated that gap more vividly than anyone I had ever encountered. His take on culture and the brain, on the other hand, had been rather startling, and I wondered if I might locate the studies he vaguely alluded to or others supporting his contentions; at the very least, his claims about erotic imagery tallied with what David told me of Corey's addiction. Finally, although I doubted whether the world made much sense, thinking of David in the light of what Robert said about his and Scotty's union prompted a review of the things lending my life meaning.

Ten minutes later, without a lull in sight, I sprinted to my car, extracted a handful of tissues from the glove compartment, blotted my face and hair, and phoned David.

"Hi," I said.

"Hey. Where are you calling from? I can barely hear you."

Large, heavy drops pounded my car like hail. "Outside Robert's," I said. "It's pouring again."

"You're not driving, are you?"

"No. Feel any better today?"

"Some, now that the shock of hearing from Corey's worn off."

"Did you call him?"

"I think it's better to wait," he said, "for me to get used to the idea and to keep him from thinking I'm in any hurry to respond."

"Want to come over tonight?"

"Yes," he said, audibly relieved. "I'm past wanting to be alone."

"I'll order pizza."

"Great."

"I've got a surprise for you."

"Nothing weird, I hope."

"A little unusual perhaps, but a consent form won't be necessary."

"What time should I get there?"

"I'm running late. How about seven?"

"I'll grab a couple of coffees from Brewer's."

"Great."

The rain impeded the drive to my apartment. I showered, changed, and divided the next hour between scouring the internet for a handful of studies exploring the links between art and the brain, some of which meshed with Robert's musings, and downloading popular songs of the 1940s, including those Robert had named: "Blue Moon," "Stardust," "Always in My Heart," and "Where or When." I compiled forty minutes' worth, mainly instrumentals heavily reliant on strings and saxophones.

Fifteen minutes before seven, I ordered a large cheese pizza with onions, peppers, mushrooms, and a salad. David arrived early, wearing a light brown jacket, and his hair as wet as it had been in the pictures of him swimming in Lake Bellow. He carried two coffees on a cardboard tray. He handed a cup to me, placed his on the table, and removed his jacket, unleashing a cloud of recently applied *October Mist*. Underneath, he wore a button-down shirt with blue and white pinstripes and solid white cuffs and collar, the cuffs and collar unbuttoned.

"What's with the fancy shirt?" I said.

"A pipe burst in the laundry room in my building, and I didn't have time to get to a Laundromat. I had to resort to my formal wear."

"No tie?"

"I didn't want you swooning. I need a towel." He disappeared into the bathroom and, in a few seconds, strolled back, rubbing his hair with a dark green bath towel that draped his head like a cowl.

"How was your day?" I said.

"Good. I filled a lot of online orders. The rain limited the in-person customers, except for a few students." He slipped the towel off, revealing a spiky crown of damp cowlicks.

"I like your hair like that," I said.

He grazed the cowlicks with his palm. "I probably look . . ." he said and stopped.

I supplied the appropriate description. "Like the cutest puppy in the world just saw a ghost."

He blushed and laughed. "Shut up." Flattening the licks with his fingers, he returned the towel to the bathroom.

Dinner arrived as he reappeared, hair more or less in place. I set the pizza and the box with the salad on the table. He followed me to the kitchen. We gathered forks, salad plates, and napkins, our harmonious passage between drawers and cupboards reminding me of Marge and Brad prepping for lunch the day we visited. I kissed him.

"What's that for?"

"I like having the cutest puppy in the world in my apartment."

"He likes being here."

We set the table, and he opened the pizza box.

"My favorite," he said.

"Research trains you to remember details."

We chose our slices, scooped portions of salad onto our plates, and doused them with dressing from little covered cups tucked in the box.

"I'm thinking about hiring some part-time help," he said. "With the online sales taking off, I figure if someone else tends the store, I can focus on them."

"Someone like a handsome college student?"

He looked up, a string of mozzarella dangling from his lower lip. "Jealous?" he asked and swept the mozzarella into his mouth with his tongue.

"Maybe."

The smile crinkled. "Cool."

"Cool?"

"Nobody's ever been jealous of me before. I'm flattered."

I wondered if Corey had ever been jealous of him but swallowed the question with a sip of coffee. David, thoughts elsewhere, slipped off his shoe and stroked my calf with his foot. "Let's not get crazy at the dinner table," I said.

"Prude." He stabbed his salad, his foot resting against mine. "How was your day?"

"Good. I made some deliveries."

"And had another long talk with Robert. If anybody should be jealous, it's me."

"Even if I had granddaddy issues, his health would preclude my acting on them. I also had a call about one of my other clients." I discussed Lena Crenshaw, and then Gil Waterman's letters for the rest of the meal.

Afterward, David helped me clear the table. Returning from the kitchen, he said, "Where's the surprise you promised me? If you're all about details, you should remember I hate suspense."

I started my playlist and, at the first lush notes of "Stardust," faced him, my hands outstretched.

"What's this?" he said.

"Since you're all dressed up, and we've no place to go, may I have this dance?"

He grinned and grasped my hands. I drew him close, and we swayed to the music. Near the end of the third selection, an instrumental version of Jerome Kern's "Lovely to Look At," he said, "Where'd you get this idea?"

"Remember I told you Robert bonded with one of his boyfriends over songs from their youth? He said they'd dance to them in their apartment after a long day. What do you think?"

"Not bad." He touched his forehead to mine. "Actually, I kind of like it."

"Have you ever heard any of these songs before?"

"No."

"Lovely to Look At" ended and we attuned our steps to Duke Ellington's sensual "Prelude to a Kiss."

"Then nostalgia has nothing to do with your appreciation?"

He grinned, grudgingly conceding the point.

"Nothing," he said.

He shifted his head until his temple rested against mine, and for the next three minutes, I drank in the scent of his rain-washed hair, his *October Mist,* and the musk drifting up from his open collar.

8.

The rain ended overnight. The next morning the sun spread an ivory aura around the marble-clad façade of Fowler Memorial Hospital.

The door to room 414 opened at my approach. A woman with tightly curled brown hair and an orange satin jacket walked out and almost into me.

"Oh, I'm sorry." She stopped short, blinked, and tilted her head. "I'll bet you're Paul."

"I am."

She held out her hand. "I'm Lena's niece, Heather. She's told me a lot about you."

"She's told me about you, too." According to Lena, ten years ago, Heather had defied their older family members' proscription against contacting her.

"I'm grateful for everything you've done," Heather said. "It's hard for me to see her as often as I'd like with work and all. She has some friends left, but they've got their health problems . . ."

"I know," I said. "It's been my pleasure. How is she?"

"Her hip's broken, but her mood needs more attention. You know what they say about doctors and nurses making the worst patients."

"I've heard."

"Are those what I think they are?" She indicated a big pink coffee mug filled with chocolate-covered espresso beans, wrapped in cellophane and tied with a pink ribbon, that I held in my hand.

"Direct from Brewer's," I said.

"She's talked about hardly anything else since she first had them. She'll be happy to see you."

"I'd like to visit her in her new facility if that's okay."

"It'd be great. Now I really have to get back to work. I'm glad to meet you."

"Same here."

Lena brightened when I entered. "Paul," she said, her firm, rough-edged voice unaffected by either injury or mood, "great to see you."

She brightened still more when she learned I met Heather in the hall and entered into raptures over the espresso beans.

"I couldn't let you go without them," I said.

The nurse in the room warned her against consuming too many. "We want to keep your blood pressure under control," he said.

As he turned to leave, she narrowed her eyes at his back, and the moment the door closed behind him, she dug out a handful and devoured them like peanuts.

"Maybe you should be careful," I said.

"I know my body better than they do. If I could pig out on them at home with no problem, there's no reason to hold back now."

"But without me coming every week, you won't get them as often."

"Yeah, I suppose so," she said and closed up the cellophane.

"Heather reminded me doctors and nurses make the worst patients," I said.

"Because we know too much to be pacified by excuses and doubletalk," she said. "The people around here are so incompetent I don't know how I lasted the night. Things weren't like this when I started nursing."

Lena enumerated the glaring differences between hospitals then and now, winding up her diatribe with, "Enough of that. Let's hear something gayer. How's the research? How's David?" I related the cheeriest news on both fronts, which pleased her. "Don't forget to invite me to the wedding."

"We're nowhere near that."

"Don't drag your heels. Who knows how much time I've got left? Once you're in assisted living, it's all downhill."

"I'll do my best. Would it be okay if I stopped in at your new place now and again, if just to keep you from going downhill?"

"I'd love it . . . as long as you bring the magic beans."

I heard the cellophane crackle again as the door to 414 closed behind me.

The remainder of the morning and into the afternoon, I searched Gil Waterman's box three without results. Replies to messages sent to people connected with Mona Jackson trickled in, some expressing interest in my project but none able to elaborate on what Mona wrote in Veronica Quinn's letters.

David showed up at my place at seven with take-out and listened to me grouse. "You have to be patient," he said.

"I've been. If I don't find something soon, I'm moving on to Leonard Edelman's stuff, and the hell with Waterman."

"Who's Leonard Edelman?"

"A Warner Brothers producer Jacobson courted," I said. "How was your day?"

"Busy. All the bookworms came up out of the ground after the rain."

Following dinner, he screened *The 5,000 Fingers of Dr. T*, a favorite film of his that he felt might interest me since it had been penned by another children's author, Dr. Seuss. Halfway through, he said, "You look like you're ready to jump out of your skin."

"I am. It's not the movie. I'd love it any other time. I just keep thinking about Veronica Quinn's list. I was sure I'd get something good out of it."

"Because you had a reason to be sure, or because you wanted to be?"

"I'm in no mood for nitpicking."

"You've got other sources of information," he said, beginning to massage my shoulders. "What about his relatives and friends in Denmark?"

"I've posted a request directed at people there, but so far, no luck. I may have to go over and search their archives if the Eldon people agree to it."

"You sound discouraged." The swirling fingers drew me backward.

"More frustrated than discouraged." I reclined against his chest. "I knew what I wanted wouldn't jump out the moment I started looking for it. What I didn't expect was to be led down so many dead ends. And sometimes it takes a while to realize they're dead ends. What if I'm wrong and I'm doing all this for nothing?"

He kissed the nape of my neck. "It hasn't all been for nothing."

"I know. But testing this theory has been a goal of mine for a long time."

"People often reach goals they didn't start out for. Maybe you're worried because you can't stand the possibility of being proved wrong."

"Who can?"

"Whether you can stand it or not, you might have to face it."

"What Mona Jackson said about his being a little off in their sessions keeps going through my mind. And the date of her letters matches up with those of his where he talks about complications."

"It still might not mean anything. Mona wasn't a trained observer. She could've exaggerated a little absent-mindedness on his part. And it's always possible that whatever happened, big or small . . ."

"Nothing survives to say exactly what it was. And if it did, it still might not have anything to do with Harold. I've worried about all this from the beginning."

"I'm sure you have. But when someone else says it . . ."

"It's a whole lot worse. But I can't give up until I've done everything I can to find out."

"That's one of the things I like best about you, your tenacity."

"You don't get to be a champion Popcorn Tagger without it."

"How about another dance, champ?"

"Seriously?"

"Why not, now you've rejected poor old Dr. T?"

We stood, and I started the playlist. The languid melodies eased my uneasy mind until at last, I thought of nothing but the strings and saxophones and my nearness to David's alluring mix of suppleness and sweetness. Contrary to my expectations, Robert—or Grantland—had been spot-on about dancing.

"This really is amazing, isn't it?" I asked after "Where or When" ended.

"Very," he said. "I don't even miss the rain beating on the windows."

The next two days, I rifled Waterman's boxes four and five without success. The third morning, shortly after eleven, I found a brief memo at the top of box six describing Waterman's meeting with Jacobson, addressed to another executive at M.G.M. Shorn of his masculine bitchiness, a rarity among his papers, it read simply:

> *Saw the head doctor you told me about. Sent him packing after five minutes. If his work's anything like him, it's no wonder Paramount dumped him. Castle must be an idiot to think there was a script there. Do me a favor and be more selective in the future.*

I returned box six to its shelf and fled the archive, bypassing Sheaves to lift my spirits with an overpriced lunch of broiled scallops and salad Provencal at a sidewalk café packed with people wearing designer sunglasses. I considered another stroll through the L.A. County museum or a downtown art gallery for further distraction when Robert messaged me requesting a bottle of aspirin. Twenty minutes later, I knocked at his door.

"Sorry to call you back so soon," he said, allowing me in. "I didn't notice I was running low until this morning. Taking meds becomes such a habit you come to regard the bottles as endless founts of pills. But I need them for my heart regimen."

"No problem."

"You needn't have rushed."

Entering the living room, I found the perennial cup of tea on the table by his chair, next to a soup bowl with a puddle of Cal's Cardio lentil soup at the bottom and a spoon resting against the edge.

"I'm at a loose end anyway," I said. "Shall I bring this to the kitchen for you?"

"Don't trouble yourself."

"I don't mind."

I carted the bowl and spoon to the kitchen, placed them and the empty soup pot in the dishwasher alongside his few breakfast dishes, dropped the empty Cal's Cardo can in the garbage, wiped a few spills off the counter, and returned to the living room just as he downed an aspirin with a gulp of tea.

"What has you at a loose end?" he asked after swallowing.

I sat in my usual spot on the sofa to explain about Waterman and recite the memo, preserved like the others on my phone. "Can you believe it?" I said, the indignation held in check during lunch, flowing freely. "How could he not see what he had in front of him? What a moron . . . what an asshole . . ."

Robert laughed. "The majority of creative talents would say the last two epithets are the first two qualifications for a studio executive."

"Still . . ."

"You can't expect everyone to like Jacobson as much as you do. And you knew beforehand he never got anywhere with his script."

"Which means the more I investigate, the likelier it is I'll find more garbage like this," I said.

"Probably. Those of us in the industry learned to deal with people in power that lacked taste and insight. I'm sure being an analyst made him even more proof against it. Besides, you're looking for clues to his later writing. Focus on that, and don't fret about the rest."

"If only I could find them," I said. "Just one, solid hint would be heartening."

"I can't help you there." He looked at me speculatively.

"What?"

"Paul," he said, with the pronounced gentleness of one broaching a sensitive subject, "what would you do if you uncovered something truly damning?"

"How do you mean?"

"What if Jacobson did something immoral or illegal, or both?"

"I don't know," I said. "I never imagined it would be."

"As you said the other day, everyone's allowed a sordid episode or two. A great many have episodes that are more than sordid. What if his 'complications' could damage his reputation . . . seriously damage it?"

"I'd have to face it. I'd be disappointed, but I couldn't change it."

"Would you still write your monograph?"

"Sure. It's my reason for being here."

"I get the feeling it's more like your reason for being, period."

"What makes you say that?"

"Were I an analyst, I'd suggest you see Jacobson as a substitute father figure, and you undertook your project to make him that for others. People should be acknowledged for their accomplishments, but it's dangerous to idolize, mainly for the idolaters."

"I don't idolize him. I'm sure he was flawed, maybe seriously. But it's a big jump from being flawed to being a monster."

"Jumping points separated by a broad grey area."

"I know. How I react would depend on what I find out about him, and we could sit here for hours inventing faults or even crimes without getting anywhere."

"True," he said, "speculation is usually unprofitable. I just want to be sure you know the difference between admiring and idealizing and that you aren't investing too much in him."

"I've got other investments going."

"The blush and coquettish smile indicate thoughts of David. Are things still going well with him?"

"Very," I said, glad to table the Jacobson question.

"Any further mention of the cretin?"

"Not since the roses appeared. It's up to him to mention Corey to me if he wants. I took your advice, though."

"What advice?"

"About dancing with your boyfriend in a darkening apartment. I created a playlist and sprang it on him the other night."

He smiled. "How'd it go?"

"I see why it was an important part of your life with Scotty."

"Romance is a good deal more than realists crack it up to be."

"Knowing more about what held you and Scotty together also made me more curious about what drove you apart."

The smile weakened. "We never did get there, did we?"

"Not after the long detour through your cultural theories."

"Which were also a big part of what held us together," he said.

"Would you mind finishing? I'm still at a loose end until dinner with David."

"Dinner with David," he mused, "a great title for a romantic comedy."

"How about the story?"

"Why not?" he sighed. "I've nothing better to do, either. Where did I leave off?"

"You said Scotty had a twin sister named Sandy, and for some reason, they were closer than twins usually are."

"Yes, well, they had a weekly dinner to which I was invited after Scotty and I got together."

"Was that the only time they saw each other?"

"No, there were the typical chance encounters around town and phone calls. The dinners started after Sandy got married. With what I heard then and what Scotty told me in private, I pieced together the story of their early lives, or at least enough to understand how they became who they were."

He nestled back in the recliner and continued. "Their parents were well off, though not rich by New York standards. Like my parents, they had high regard for the arts. They exposed Scotty and Sandy to literature, music, fine art, theater . . ."

"Awakening an interest in the arts similar to yours."

He nodded. "Living in Manhattan, they also had greater resources to draw on to cultivate their tastes. They were closer to Terry than me in that way, infinitely more sophisticated at an earlier age."

"And on their way to a higher standard of adulthood."

"More or less."

"I gathered from what you said Terry's parents weren't especially well off."

"They weren't. It's just that living in New York placed him within reach of more cultural outlets than me. I wouldn't have been surprised to learn Terry had crossed paths with Scotty and Sandy in the same book or record shops or theater lobbies. I know you were joking about their aiming for a higher standard of adulthood, but that's what they were doing. Like me— like all children—they spent their formative years struggling to comprehend the world around them. Education and immersion in the arts, especially literature, aided their quest and gave them an ever-expanding vocabulary to articulate what they'd learned, first between themselves and later on with others. This developed the insightfulness I first noticed during the *Marmoset* rehearsals."

"You believe articulation develops insight?"

"Not solely, but it helps. You have to be aware of what you think before you can find words to express it. And being more aware of what you think prompts you to think more—that is, to approach everything more thoughtfully."

"I see."

"Later on, in adolescence, they relied on this ability more than they or anyone else could've foreseen."

"Why? What happened?"

"Their mother struggled with high blood pressure since giving birth. She died of a stroke when they were fifteen. Two years later, their father succumbed to a heart attack, though Scotty and Sandy maintained cardiac arrest was just the official term for a broken heart."

"They were alone at a fairly young age, then."

"And in an awkward position vis-à-vis their extended family."

"Why?"

"Their father left enough to support them. But to ensure the inheritance went first and foremost for their education, his will placed it in trust. More precisely, it was split between two trusts he and his wife had established for them at birth, which they couldn't access until they turned thirty."

"And since they were orphaned at eighteen, someone else administered them."

"Their father's sister, their aunt Marion, who was married to a man named Ted. Scotty likened them to an avaricious pair from a Dickens novel transposed to an elegant mid-century Manhattan apartment."

"They had designs on the trusts?" I asked, lapsing into Dickensian phraseology.

"No. They simply refused to approve expenses beyond tuition and bare necessities, leaving Scotty and Sandy in reduced though not dire circumstances and in a permanent state of antagonism toward their guardians."

"Did they have any other relatives, someone to intercede for them with Marion?"

"There were uncles and aunts and cousins. They sympathized with Scotty and Sandy's plight as orphans but sided with Marion and Ted about the trusts and, in general, treated the twins with an unease bordering on contempt."

"Why?"

"Scotty said in their world, wealth is passed from generation to generation like genes. Individuals exist to transmit family money from one to another, increasing it whenever possible but never detracting from it."

"Obviously, you came from a different world."

"Fortunately," he said. "My parents taught me respect for money but they weren't wealthy enough to fetishize it."

"How did this fetish affect the family's attitude to the twins?"

"Lacking parental guidance, Scotty and Sandy seemed perpetually on the brink of breaking the sacred cycle, which was why Marion kept them on a tight budget. She, Ted, and the other relatives also pounced on any word or act that hinted at a possible deviation from financial decorum."

"If they were eighteen, they must've gone directly into college. They had to enjoy some freedom there, even without a disposable income."

"A freedom that often lapsed into loneliness, according to Scotty."

"Why?"

"He said that while some of their peers had twins and others had lost a parent or even two, being both twins and orphans placed them just far enough beyond the norm to appear freakish."

"What about friends?"

"A few from childhood carried over into maturity, but for the most part, they had to wait until they graduated to come into their own socially. Meanwhile, between the family's conditional affection and their peers' limited acceptance, it more often than not felt like him and Sandy against the world."

"Strengthening their bond," I said.

"And their dependence on the habits of mind they'd developed in childhood."

"Like what?"

"Experiences with family and peers underscored the need to appraise people and their motives, to distinguish genuine friends from others less kindly disposed to them."

"Isn't that true for everyone?"

"Yes, but most people rely on their parents to develop those skills. Scotty and Sandy plunged into the social rapids, barely able to swim. Their familiarity with the arts, particularly literature and theater, helped buoy them."

"How?"

"It offered prototypes. People and events in novels and plays became shorthand for those they encountered in real life."

"Like comparing their aunt and uncle to Dickens characters," I said.

"Nor were they above mining pop culture for references. They referred to their antagonistic college classmates by nicknames culled from characters in the old *Our Gang* films. Are you familiar with them?"

"Enough to know what you're talking about," I said.

"They reappeared on TV, rechristened *The Little Rascals.* Scotty and I watched occasionally, and he'd tell me about the kids they'd turned into the characters' unwitting namesakes. Anyway, the tactic eventually became a feedback loop, and from relying on art to frame their experiences in the world, they judged art on the basis of how incisively it portrayed the world they'd experienced."

"If they were both so enamored of the arts, why was Scotty the only one to pursue it professionally?"

"I'm not sure. Sandy may have felt she lacked the necessary talent or was too afraid to try. Then again, her marriage may have prevented her."

"Who did she marry?"

"A surgeon named Harrison Gallo. He was ten years her senior. They met a few months before she graduated college through a girlfriend of hers who graduated the year before."

"Some peers managed to penetrate their hermeticism, then?"

"A few, yes. Gallo was quite successful and well-to-do."

"The family must have been pleased."

"Scotty described their reaction as smug ecstasy. Marrying Gallo ensconced Sandy in a reputable upper-middle-class Manhattan home, leaving Marion with little to worry about apart from managing Sandy's trust. When they divorced five years later, Sandy won a hefty alimony that left her free of Marion until she turned thirty, and the trust reverted to her."

"Why did they divorce?"

"Unfaithfulness on his part."

"And you suspect he kept her from a career in the arts?"

"I doubt it was that cut and dried. She wasn't only younger than Gallo; she was at an age where one is still working out one's destiny."

"And he might've manipulated that to his advantage?"

"Possibly. On the other hand, when I met Sandy, she was content being a wealthy divorcee, and from things she said in passing, I deduced she'd been just as content being the wealthy doctor's wife. Like many affluent New Yorkers, during her marriage, her involvement in the arts was as an informed audience member: she patronized the symphony, ballet, opera, and such, a role that again seemed to suit her better than any other."

"How did Scotty fare after college?"

"Less well. As you might expect, the family held firm to the social division between art and artists, respecting art while considering artists a species of servants whose purpose was to amuse them. Scotty studying graphic art with a view to working in theater constituted a serious breach of both financial and social etiquette. Marion was livid."

"Would his parents have thought the same, do you think?"

"We never discussed it, but I gathered from various comments he believed they'd have been more supportive, though I suspected this was just wishful thinking. His dislike for Marion and Ted encouraged him to deify his parents. He also never mentioned being gay to the family, though they probably had an inkling or two. That and his career choice placed him well outside the upper-middle-class ideal Sandy attained."

"How'd he imagine his parents would've reacted to his sexuality?"

"He never speculated, even in passing. But by that very omission, I assumed he knew they'd have been appalled. Marion forbade him access to the trust to support his ambition, so after college, he lived like any other indigent artist, accepting menial jobs while searching for theatrical work."

"Of course, he'd lived on a tight budget in college," I said, "and the eventuality of gaining his trust at thirty probably made it easier."

"Sandy sometimes slipped him money, too, unbeknownst to Gallo or Marion. He landed his first job as a set designer at an independent TV station in the city. This opened the door to more design work in both TV and theater. The family expected him to crash and burn after a few years and accept a more conventional job with a higher salary, but he managed to earn a regular if modest living at what he loved before reaching thirty."

"He was more fortunate than the average aspiring artist."

"He also had talent on his side. Yet he never lost sight of his good fortune despite his sardonic bent."

"If I've calculated correctly, you met him after he turned thirty."

"Yes, and I know why you brought it up."

"I didn't. . ."

"Don't dissemble. You're wondering if his being a trust fund baby fac-tored into his appeal for me. It's a fair question. He was certainly wealthier than me and had a nicer apartment, though he could have afforded a big-ger one in a better location. He and Sandy had learned to spot male gold diggers early on. He'd never have given me the time of day if I'd been one."

"Why didn't he go for a better apartment?"

"He preferred being near the theater district and his work, though it was still a solidly middle-class neighborhood."

"What was it like?"

"A spacious combined living and dining room, a serviceable kitchen, and a bedroom that was snug rather than small, off of which was an ex-tra room with a window where he had his drafting table. The workroom preserved the slapdash environment of a destitute artist: sketching para-phernalia everywhere and walls papered with what he considered his best sketches. The bedroom and main rooms were more neatly arrayed, as a backdrop for a small collection of paintings and sculptures, including an early Lichtenstein."

"Sounds nice," I said.

"It was heaven after the trap I took when Grayson and I parted ways. But though Scotty was wealthier than me, I was in a sound enough financial position."

"With residuals from your commercials pouring in," I said.

"Which nearly compensated for their returning to haunt me the nights we watched TV. Combined with my theater work and infrequent film roles, they allowed me to pay half the rent and all my expenses the entire time we lived together."

"Between the family fetish and his years scraping by, what was his at-titude to money?"

"Indifference, I'd say."

"Of course, most people who're indifferent to money have it in the first place."

"True, but we shared David's attitude to the things money buys. They had to be meaningful rather than costly. Scotty retained many of the frugal habits he developed before his career took off, not from greed but because they were comfortable."

"He found poverty comfortable?"

"I didn't say poverty. I said frugality. He worked at the same cheap drafting table he bought directly out of college because its familiarity facilitated his work. He wore old shirts, worn sweaters, and well-broken-in pants while he sketched. Except for rare formal occasions, he dressed the same way in public. His hair was perennially askew, too, as if tousled by a breeze. Sandy often chided him for his slovenliness, though it was just another of what seemed hundreds of private jokes between them. I viewed it as another manifestation of his sardonic indifference to the rest of the world, like the grin with the crooked tooth. Aunt Marion and the rest of the family were less tolerant."

"Maybe that's why he did it, to yank their chains."

"I'm sure he loved annoying them, but his primary concern was comfort. He also went to parties to reconnect with friends rather than to see and be seen. Art was his one major expense, and then he only bought what he liked, not what advertised his wealth or might increase in value later. Apart from a more secure existence, money for us meant better seats at plays and concerts and meals at better restaurants. But if we had to choose between staying home reading a good book and going out to dinner, we'd stay home and read."

"Or dance."

"Or dance," he said.

"Something Grayson never understood about you."

"Never. I always felt Gray would've been happier had he learned to appreciate quiet evenings at home."

"How did Sandy react to your relationship with her brother? I assume she knew he was gay."

"After a fashion. Like I said, Scotty became quite open after Stonewall, though he didn't force issues with the family. He knew what they thought and preferred avoiding needless conflict."

"Did he see them often after his thirtieth birthday?"

"No. Mostly at holidays—very few of them—and at funerals. Sandy, I think, accepted her brother's sexuality but didn't care to dwell on the details."

"Why do you say that?"

"She was always pleasant to me, complimented me on how I looked, and asked about my career. But she stiffened at any sign of affection between Scotty and me or the mention of domestic matters like picking up laundry or forgetting to buy milk—the minor details of united life straight couples discuss or argue over in public without a qualm. Perhaps it was jealousy. I shared the one thing with Scotty she couldn't, which would've annoyed her even if I'd been a woman. I think she was jealous of him in general, anyway."

"What do you mean, 'in general?'"

"It goes back to her not pursuing a career in the arts. Whatever prevented her, I think she'd have liked it. And I think she envied Scotty not only for doing it but for being relatively successful at it. She'd listen to him describe his newest projects with a kind of wistful, mesmerised look in her eyes."

"Maybe she was just proud of him."

"Oh, she was, definitely. But there was yearning in it, too, a desire for something beyond her reach. She probably supported him during his lean years for the same reason. Later I thought she may have been living vicariously through him and his career."

"Did they look a lot alike?"

"At times," he said.

"Only at times?"

"Their divergent lifestyles obscured their natal similarities. On the day of their usual dinner, Scotty would go from his drafting table to the restaurant without changing clothes. A few times, the maitre d' refused to admit him, which he found hilarious."

"How did Sandy dress?"

"In the standard uniform of a wealthy divorcee, at least for that period: designer clothes, jewelry, and furs, all bright and shining and carelessly flaunted. She had his thin blonde hair, too, though hers was meticulously coiffed and protected from the least puff of wind by an elegant silk scarf. Seated across from each other, they looked like they'd come from opposite sides of the tracks . . . until they started talking."

He leaned back with a gruff, happy purr.

"You should have heard those conversations. They covered everything under the sun: current events; books, music, theater; childhood reminiscences; gossip about family, friends, and acquaintances, including old schoolmates. That's when I learned how much they'd relied on one another's viewpoints after their parents died because it was still very much a habit when I knew them."

"For example?"

"Well, when the advertising agency representing Triple Star dog food was tormenting Scotty over his designs for *Match the Mutt*, it turned out Sandy had met the agency executive assigned to the show at several parties. She dubbed him 'a hedgehog with blunted quills,' and Scotty said from then on he knew exactly how to deal with him. Another time Sandy started dating a man named Dillard, who was high up in a brokerage firm. Scotty called him 'a frustrated Richard the Third' and said his pretension to deviousness was the only thing preventing him from being a total dullard. She dropped him after that, and two months later, they arrested him for fraud."

"You're kidding."

"Look up the trial records. Of course, Dillard was an extreme example, which is why it sticks in my mind. But you get the idea. They trusted one another's insights implicitly, all the more so because, as far as I saw, they were rarely wrong."

"Did you discuss your cultural theories with her?"

"Some. She agreed with the salient points but, for the most part, found it amusing, like you."

"Well. . ." I shrugged guiltily and changed the subject. "Did they ever argue?"

"There were minor disagreements, nothing worse. Mostly, their shared outlook covered all the joys and absurdities of life, which their erudition enabled them to render in the brightest, wittiest words at their command."

"A heady atmosphere."

"But splendid," he said. "And the more they talked, the more alike they grew, as if their ideas altered their features from the inside out, turning them into such precise mirror images that rather than a pair from opposite sides of the tracks, they became quite clearly twins. The same thing happened on the phone. If I arrived home in the middle of one of their chats, who he was talking to would've been apparent even if I hadn't heard what he said or how he said it."

"Why?"

"The longer he talked, the more like itself his face became—as if a camera were pulling his features into sharper focus—because it was becoming more like hers."

"You said she might have been jealous of you. Were you ever jealous of her?"

"No, for two reasons. First, I more than held my own in their company. My experiences with Terry, Warren, and Gray taught me a little about appraising people, while my exposure to the arts taught me to articulate my ideas with a similarly extensive vocabulary. Meeting them on their own terms this way encouraged her to move past jealousy—and Scotty's and my sexuality—to see me as a kindred spirit, the same kindred spirit I found in her brother."

"What's the second reason?"

"As I said, I shared things with him she couldn't. They had their bond as twins, and their childhood memories, neither of which would change. But those things belonged to the past, or so I imagined. Scotty's and my sexual attraction, and our mutual respect, both as people and as creative professionals, formed the foundation of a relationship built in the present that I believed would last well into the future." He picked up his mug, only rather than sip the tea, he stared into it.

"You were wrong, though," I said.

"Yes."

"Sandy split you up?"

He spoke without looking at me as if replying to the mug. "Not intentionally. She never would've done that to him."

An ominous inflection weighted the word 'that.'

"What happened?"

He drank and shifted in his chair. "You may or may not know that New York was suffering an epidemic of violent crime in the 1960s and 1970s."

"I know. I researched the period in college for a dissertation on the impact of high crime rates on urban gay mating habits."

"I daresay you received high marks."

"My professor was satisfied."

"Good. Just don't tell me your findings. I'd hate to have to contradict you at this late date."

I laughed. "Okay. Still, it must have been terrifying."

"It was. Robberies, rapes, and murders were as familiar as the taxis and tourist traps. Those of us with enough incomes at our disposal managed to keep much of it at bay. The building where we lived beefed up their security, and Scotty installed a high tech burglar alarm to protect us and his art collection. We also avoided certain streets and neighborhoods and took taxis more often. We were also lucky, I guess."

"What happened?"

"Late one night in November 1973, the phone woke us. I was deep in one of those slumbers that, on being deprived of it, seemed more desirable than anything in the waking world. I felt Scotty roll out of bed and heard him shuffle into the living room. This was back when phones were tethered to a single spot in a room. Ours dwelt on an end table by the sofa. From the edge of oblivion, I heard him lift the receiver and mumble: 'Hello.' After a brief pause, he said, 'What?' His quiet, intense disbelief banished my drowsiness. I sat up and glanced at the clock on our bedside table. It was two a.m. I looked through the doorway. He stood beside the sofa, the receiver at his ear, staring as if a portal to hell had opened in the far corner of the room. He said 'Yes' and 'Okay' several times, and after 'I'll be right there,' he dropped the receiver onto the cradle, ran into the bedroom, and started dressing. I said: 'What's wrong?' He said: 'Sandy's in the emergency room.' I said: 'What happened?' He said: 'She was mugged near her building. They grabbed her purse but weren't happy till they beat the hell out of her. She has internal injuries. They may have to operate.' I said: 'How bad is it?' He said: 'They didn't tell me. I'll let you know when I find out.' He got into his coat wearing a blank, rigid expression I'd never seen on him before . . . or on anyone else for that matter."

"I'm not blaming her, but if you were in the habit of taking precautions, why was she out at two a.m.?'

"She wasn't. The attack happened at ten-thirty. She was unconscious before the police arrived, and since her identification was in her purse, they didn't know who she was or who to call. She didn't regain consciousness until one forty-five, and then barely enough to tell them her name and what'd happened to her."

"You said 'they' beat her. There was more than one?"

"Three teenagers, according to what she said in the emergency room. I offered to accompany him to the hospital, but the next day I had the final dress rehearsal for a play called *A Tinker's Dam* and . . ."

"What?" I said, too startled to refrain from interrupting.

"An unfortunate title since it opened the door for critics to claim the play wasn't worth its name. It depicted life in an eighteenth-century Welsh village. The rehearsal was important because we were opening the following night. Scotty told me to stay and go back to sleep. I made him promise to call me if anything happened."

"Did you sleep?"

"Off and on. I figured a few shallow catnaps were better than nothing, given what the following day would probably be like, worrying about him and Sandy and *Tinker*. The next morning he phoned before I left for the theater. He said: 'She's stable, but her liver and kidneys are damaged. They're still deciding whether to operate.' His even tone seemed encouraging. I told everybody at the theater about it and to let me know if I had any calls. My mind was only partly on the play when rehearsals started, but as time passed and I heard nothing, I assumed her condition hadn't changed, or at least hadn't worsened, and I devoted more attention to the work."

He sipped his tea and continued.

"We finished late. I picked up a pint of chowder from an Irish pub around the corner from our building. I remember gripping the bag around the container to warm my hands as I walked home. The apartment was dark and quiet, in the absolute way that follows an early November dusk. I turned on the lights. Scotty was on the sofa, staring at the window. I left my chowder on the little table we kept just inside the door for our keys, mail, and things, ran over, and sat beside him. He didn't speak, or turn his head, or acknowledge me in any way. I said: 'What are you doing here? How's Sandy?' He said: 'She's gone.' His flat, factual voice struck me as brutally as the news it conveyed. I said: 'What?' He said: 'She had a stroke on the operating table,' still looking at the window, as if he were addressing someone on the ledge outside."

Robert sighed and rubbed his chin.

"I liked Sandy, her humor and her vivacity, and I certainly knew what she meant to him. After seven years of mutual support, I was more than prepared to be his refuge as he dealt with the worst loss he'd suffered since his parents. I put my arm around him and rested my head against his shoulder, my usual gesture of comfort with him. Only rather than lean against me in turn, as he always did, he remained exactly as I'd found him, as if his body had frozen to the couch."

"That must have been awful."

"It got worse. He kept saying 'A stroke, like mama' in that awful flat voice, like a child struggling to understand the punch line to a joke. I sat up and rubbed his back, waiting for his grief to erupt."

"Did it?"

"No. Five minutes later, the phone rang. He ignored it, leaving me to answer. A woman, anguished and imperious, said: 'Is Scott there? This is his Aunt Marion.' I covered the mouthpiece and whispered: 'It's your Aunt Marion.' He shook his head. I said: 'What should I tell her?' I'd never spoken to her before, and while her anguish evoked pity, the imperiousness was intimidating. He flicked his shoulders and said: 'Whatever.' I mustered my improvisational skills and said: 'I'm sorry. He took a sleeping pill. He's fast asleep. I'll have him call you when he gets up.' A sob disrupted her initial attempt to respond. She said: 'His sister Sandra died today.' I wondered why she imagined the person in his apartment wouldn't already know. I said: 'He told me. I'm sorry for your loss.' She said: 'Thank you,' as if acknowledging the services of a waiter or doorman. Then she added: 'Their parents died some years ago. We're the only family he has left.' This, of course, was a dig at our relationship, which she managed despite her sorrow."

"She must've been a real piece of work."

Robert assented with an eye roll. "The phone rang all evening, first his relatives, then our friends. I repeated the sleeping pill story and wrote down names for him to call the following day. In between, I encouraged him to eat or drink. He only shook his head as if the shadows passing before the windows in the opposite building held all the interest of which he was capable. Around twelve, I said: 'You should try and sleep. You'll have to call all these people tomorrow.' He nodded and said: 'I suppose so,' in the weary, annoyed voice of one accepting a trivial yet necessary chore. He shuffled to the bathroom, showered, shaved, and slipped into bed. I followed and embraced him, but it was like holding a statue."

"Didn't he ever mourn her?"

"I don't know."

"How can you not know?"

"The next morning, I woke to hear him talking on the phone. The bedroom door was open. I sat up and watched him. He sat cross-legged on the sofa, the phone on his lap. He said: 'It surprised the doctors, too. She must've inherited mom's hypertension. I'll be doing that this afternoon. I'll let you know the details later.' He sounded like a junior executive describing plans to entertain a boring out-of-town client. He hung up, crossed a name off the list I had drawn up for him last night and looked up, straight at me. He said: 'I was about to wake you. You'll be late for the theater.' I said: 'What do you mean?' He chuckled as if at an unaccountable absent-mindedness on my part. He said: '*Tinker* opens tonight if you recall.' I said: 'The understudy can go on.' He said: 'Why?' with such genuine surprise I couldn't reply. Finally, I said: 'You must have a million things to take care of. I figured I'd stay and help.' He said: 'I'll be fine. You can't miss an opening.' I said: 'Are you sure?' He said: 'Absolutely' with a reassuring smile that, under the circumstances, chilled me to the marrow. I said: 'Will you be there?' He said: 'This'll probably take all day. You don't mind, do you?' I said: 'Of course not.' He said 'Thanks' and resumed dialing. I got up, took my shower, dressed, and breakfasted to the eerie sounds of his peremptory conversations before heading out."

"Did you really perform that night?"

"What else could I do? He made it clear he didn't want my sympathy or support. What made it worse was he didn't seem resentful or angry about it, which would at least have been plausible. People suffering intense grief often lash out rather than seek comfort. He not only wasn't seeking comfort, he didn't seem to understand why I offered it."

"Was he in denial?"

Robert pursed his lips and shook his head. "Everything he said indicated he was fully aware of her death. The attitude just didn't match the words. I was glad to escape to the street, where everything was as I'd remembered it. I was even happier to enter the theater and a milieu I understood, and engage in something over which I had more control. I told them about Sandy dying and described Scotty's behavior. They said he was likely in shock. Brian Martin, our lead, told me his aunt acted the same way after his uncle died. He said: 'She was serene until the morning of the funeral. Then she smashed all their good china. Scott will probably do something like that.' The possibility reassured me even though I dreaded the actual onslaught. Despite it being my first opening night Scotty had missed in seven years, I managed a creditable performance. The audience reaction was good, too. But rather than join the cast party afterward, I headed straight home."

"How was he?"

"He was working at his drafting table, his eyes as clear and focused as they always were while sketching. I was close enough to touch him before he heard me. He looked up and said: 'How'd it go?' I said: 'Good. The audience seemed to like it.' He said: 'You didn't go to the cast party?' I said: 'I was too tired. How did it go for you?' He said: 'I called everybody, and the church and a caterer and reserved a banquet hall for after. I'll consult the minister tomorrow about the ceremony.' I said: 'Is there anything I can do?' He said: 'No, it's all set. You should get some rest.' Nothing, not even a catch in his voice, betrayed any sadness, much less the devastation he had to be experiencing. I showered and got into bed. Rather than sleep, I listened to his pencil scratch the drawing paper for another hour. When he finally joined me, he kissed me goodnight and lay beside me, not touching me, not even moving, until he dozed off."

"What did you do?"

"Waited for the delayed reaction. How could he lose someone that close and not explode? The next morning I woke late again. He was relaxing at the dining table, sipping coffee and reading the papers like he had the morning after every opening night for seven years. He said: 'You got good reviews.' I sat, poured my coffee, and he handed me the paper. I read the review; a glowing one that bolstered my confidence in *Tinker's* run. Scanning the other pages, I found Sandy's murder related in a brief, graphic article that reduced her to another of the city's elevated crime statistics. Since he hadn't mentioned it, I didn't either. He prepared fried eggs and toast for two, worked on his sketches until lunchtime, and after that, left to meet the minister. He returned for dinner. I asked him what they talked about. He said: 'Music, Biblical texts . . . the usual things. Tomorrow I select a menu at the banquet hall.' I offered to accompany him, but he fended me off with my commitment to the play. For the next two days, he sketched in the morning; after lunch, he ran errands for the funeral or that dealt with her estate; and came back at dinnertime, after which I left for the theater. When I returned, he was either at his drafting table or in bed. I showered, slid under the covers, and we fell asleep as if a glass partition separated us."

"What was the funeral like?"

"Somewhat farcical. I worried about his choices, considering that he refused to include me in them and was in such an unfathomable mental state. But the church looked lovely, banked with autumn flowers, while Sandy's favorite music played in the background. She had an elegant mahogany coffin, and the minister delivered a dignified eulogy."

"What was farcical about it?"

"The two parts of Scotty's life colliding," he said. "Our friends from the gay and theatrical communities turned out *en masse* for his sake. The family and Sandy's friends treated them like something between poor relations and a leper colony. Later, the two factions decamped to opposite ends of the banquet hall while Scotty passed back and forth or was approached by brave reconnoiterers from the other side. This was the only time I ever laid eyes on Marion and Ted."

"What were they like?"

"I'll never forget their grand entrance and stately stroll down the church aisle. He looked like Charon, the figure in Greek mythology who ferries the souls of the dead over the river Styx. She looked like the ferryboat."

"She was overweight?"

"No, imposing," he said. "She loomed large over everyone and everything around her, walking as if her nose were a prow cutting a swath through choppy waters. It matched the voice I'd heard on the phone."

"How did Scotty act?"

"Quiet and composed during the service; at the banquet hall like the host of the dull business dinner it seemed he'd been arranging on the phone. People hugged him, yet he accepted the gesture without really responding.

He also seemed oblivious to the hostile undercurrents around him. When one of the family or Sandy's friends made a remark about the unsavory elements present, he just explained who they were, never defended them, or responded in kind like he usually did. Nothing, neither grief, anger, resentment, nor any other emotion, broke through his staunch, indifferent politeness."

I thought of the death mask David assumed for Rene's party. Robert continued.

"A few from the family asked me if he was drinking or on drugs, imply- ing I'd lured him into a den of iniquity where we reveled in every imagin- able vice. I told them he'd been like that since Sandy's death. I doubt they believed me, not that I blamed them. I hardly believed it, either."

"What happened after the funeral?"

"Two days later, he cleaned out her apartment alone. I had a matinee that day and returned to a dozen cardboard boxes stacked against the bed- room and workroom walls. He donated her clothes to charity, except for her silk scarves. He also kept some of her paintings and antiques. The other furnishings he split between an auction house and a second-hand dealer."

"What was in the boxes?"

"Jewelry, books, records—many of which Scotty already had in his col- lection—a million trinkets, souvenir programs from concerts and plays—in- cluding all those for which Scotty had designed sets. In short, it was all the little things people collect without realizing how much they've accumulat- ed . . . and what remained of their parents' effects."

"What do you mean 'remained?'"

"After their father died, Marion liquidated the contents of the apartment to pad the trusts. Their father's will granted her a free hand to do it, but it persisted as one of the many sore points between her and them."

"I'm not surprised."

"To be fair, Marion did allow Sandy their mother's jewelry, and Scot- ty got his father's cufflinks, tie clips, signet ring, and watch, all gold with small, precious stones. It indicates how much they adored their parents that neither sold nor hocked a single piece no matter how hard up they were for money, in college, or afterward, in Scotty's case. Sandy also kept more of the little things that weren't valuable enough to sell: photos, her and Scotty's baby shoes, a jade compact, a half-empty bottle of their father's cologne, a dented chrome cigarette case, porcelain figurines and an array of other oddities."

"He must have inherited her money, too."

"He did, though she left a sizeable chunk to her pet arts organizations. Anyway, I peeked into a few boxes at what looked to me a jumble of high-end garage sale stock and said: 'What're you going to do with this?' He said: 'I'll sort it out later. I'm too tired.' That was the first time he associated any personal condition with her death. I imagined, or hoped, he was finally confronting it and braced for more. But it never came."

"Why not?"

Robert placed a thumbnail against his front teeth and shrugged. "Following the funeral, we resumed our everyday lives. Days he'd sketch at his drafting table or head to a theatrical office to consult with producers or to a theater to oversee the construction of his sets. If he had a TV job, he'd be in a studio or at a production office for meetings. Afterward, we'd have a quiet dinner, and I'd leave to perform in *Tinker*. Everything stayed the same, but was completely different."

"Different how?"

"The qualities I loved in him, his intelligence and wit, disappeared. Worse, rather than share the refuge we created for one another, we simply went through the motions as if we were fulfilling some Pavlovian preconditioning. Sunday mornings, we'd lie in bed reading the newspapers. He'd listen while I talked about different articles, and agree or disagree without elaboration. We read as often as before, only now he never commented on the content or quality of the writing. Sometimes we'd watch an old movie on TV or go to a repertory theater. I'd remark on the set designs, and in place of his former astute analyses, he'd simply say, 'Yes, it's quite good' or 'No, that's a definite failure.' The same thing happened at the concerts or plays I convinced him to attend. We danced a few times, but I had to choose the records, and he moved with little affinity to the music or to me. Sex was the same. I initiated each encounter, and while he never objected, he never returned my affection, let alone my passion. His work also became routine. He stopped consulting me about his assignments and drew one or two sketches rather than the former lithograph series, obeying the orders of producers and directors without aspiring to any finer quality."

"How was he with friends?"

"The same. I had to coax him to accept invitations people extended after they felt enough time had passed since the funeral. Whether it was a small dinner or large party, he hung back, only speaking when spoken to, without cracking jokes or offering takes on the topics under discussion. The barometer also failed. When I caught his eye, he'd grin blandly, without any indication of how he felt at the moment. Mag and a few others quizzed me about it, but I had no explanation."

"Maybe he was in shock like they said at the theater."

"Probably at first, but over time I realized it was more. For six months, I clung to the belief he'd have some sort of breakdown, recover, and things would return to normal. When that didn't happen, I tried forcing it."

"Force it how?"

"I mentioned the changes I'd noticed in him and suggested a psychiatrist might help with his grief, but he didn't seem to understand and brushed the idea aside. Then I tried breaking him down by profaning Sandy's memory."

"A drastic choice," I said. "Risky, too."

"I would have endured the most violent reaction if it meant restoring him to his former self."

"I take it the reaction was anything but violent."

"He just stared at me like I was crazy. And the whole six months, I kept bumping into those damned boxes. When I asked when he'd sort it out, he'd say: 'Soon.' The longer I waited to recover our former dynamic, the more futile life with him felt. Finally, I knew I had to end the relationship, or more accurately, escape it."

"When did you decide that?"

"*Tinker* ran for another four months. A few weeks after it closed, my agent got a call from Nathan Grant."

"He directed you in *Cathy and Thomas*," I said.

"Yes. Nate was in L.A. preparing to direct a pilot for a TV series, *The Balancers,* about four young, attractive cops operating outside the rules. There were many such programs at the time. *Balancers* even had a faux Lalo Schifrin theme tune. He wanted me for a small but pivotal role, a drug lord whose identity was revealed in the final ten minutes, in time for the heroes to riddle him with bullets. My task was to invest the villain with enough nastiness for viewers to condone the heroes' unlawful tactics. I liked and respected Nate, but I hated leaving Scotty. I knew it meant the end for us, like graduating high school had been for me and Terry. I told Scotty about the offer. He said, 'Sounds good.' I said: 'It won't be for long. You don't mind my going?' He said: 'No. Why?' I went, filmed *Balancers,* and before it wrapped, I received offers for more TV work. My agent encouraged me to grab them. If I landed a regular series, I'd have a steady salary, and with a series' seasonal filming schedule, I'd also have the option to return to do more theater. By then, I'd acquired a sterling reputation in New York, and commuting between coasts was easier than it had been even ten years ago."

"Your career was more important than repairing your relationship?"

"Both parties have to repair a relationship. Scotty made no effort either to repair or even maintain ours, which was why it felt futile. Here, the futility disappeared. I dealt with people whose behavior was comprehensible, even if I didn't always approve of it. The wings still fluttered when I heard him on the phone, but his unresponsiveness drained the interest from everything I told him: about places I visited, the aging film stars from our childhood whom I met, the good and—mainly—lousy scripts being offered to me. Eventually I had to admit that, despite still being in love with him, I was happier here, working and living alone."

"That must've been difficult."

"Difficult, but a relief. And I tried reaching him one last time. When I phoned to tell him I wanted to stay and explained about commuting between coasts, he said: 'They must really like you.' I said: 'I like it, too. Why not come out with me? You'd love the scenery, especially the desert. I'm sure you could get TV work, and there's professional theatre, too. You need a change.' He said: 'I can't,' as if the reason were self-evident. I said: 'Why?' He said: 'I can't leave her,' and I understood from the way he said 'her' he meant Sandy."

"Wow."

"I remember standing with the phone in my hand, staring at the sunlight outside my window, shivering like he had when he first heard about Sandy's attack. He was as willing to let me go as I was to let him go, albeit for different reasons."

"I wonder why," I said. "I mean, I've found you to be intelligent and caring, and you were obviously good-looking. What more did he want?"

He replied to my compliments with a brief, indulgent grin. "Oh, it wasn't about the charms I might or might not possess. The problem was I had mistakenly believed his and my relationship could surpass his with Sandy. He and I had the sex and the creative professions in common. But what I imagined truly connected us, the love of art and wit, had been cultivated in tandem with her, first as part of a happy childhood and later on to weather a tumultuous young adulthood. They were each other's refuge long before I came along. Despite a similar temperament, instead of a kindred spirit, a true equal, I was and always would have been an outsider, condemned to observe their private world rather than join in, no matter how graciously or sincerely they welcomed me."

"You make them sound like the siblings in Cocteau's *Les Enfants Terribles*."

"You are a well-read young man."

"I thought you'd be impressed."

"Their bond lacked the incestuous frisson of Cocteau's pair, probably due to Scotty being gay. But it had the same exclusivity. When Sandy died, there was nobody left for him to observe the world with in quite the same way as he had with her."

"And so the world ceased to interest him enough to respond to it."

"Either with disdain, curiosity, or love," he said, "including me. There was nothing more I could do. I accepted every role I was offered, rented an apartment, and flew back for my belongings."

"What was your last meeting like?"

"Awful," Robert said, his body writhing in the chair. "He sketched at his drafting table while I packed. Gathering everything to ship here revived the better memories of our domesticity. When the movers lugged the boxes away, I rested my suitcases by the front door, walked to his workroom, and said: 'I'm ready.' He looked up and said: 'Okay.' I said: 'Goodbye' and embraced him. He returned my hug like a puppet and said: 'Bye.' I searched again for the bright, sardonic spark that attracted me at the *Marmoset* rehearsals and said: 'I love you, Scotty.' He said, 'I love you, too, Robert.' There was a hollowness in these declarations that they never had before. Our notions of love had acquired two very different, incompatible meanings. I said: 'Will you be okay?' He nodded and said: 'Sure.' I kissed his brow and started for the door. Reaching the living room, I turned for a final look. He was bent over the table, drawing contentedly, the boxes from Sandy's place against the walls around him. I knew then that as long as he was near her—or what remained of her—he would be okay. And I left."

"You never saw him again?"

"No. Mag and a few others kept tabs on him for me. From all accounts, apart from his work, he became a recluse. As my New York friends died or our connections loosened, thanks to the distance between us, I stopped hearing about him. And before you ask, I prefer he stay in the past, like Terry. Even if he's alive and in possession of his faculties, our relationship could never be what it was before. Contacting him would most likely end up being as painful as when I left him forty years ago."

"I won't interfere."

He sighed and straightened up. "I'm sorry if I sounded harsh. I don't mind recounting my past as long as we keep a clear distinction between past and present. The only good thing left to me of the people I loved is the memory of how it felt to love them. If I learned they'd died, I'd have to mourn their loss all over again. If they're alive and I got to know them as they are today, I might decide it was just as well our relationships fizzled. Either way, the nice romantic bubbles they inhabit in my brain would burst, and I'd have nothing."

My phone beeped. I glanced at the screen.

"David," I said.

"Answer him."

Robert watched while we traded messages.

Dinner at my apt tonight? David wrote.

Sure. Seven o'clock?

Yeah. Eggplant parm from the pizza place?

Great. See you then.

"Short, but sweet, I hope," Robert said as I pocketed my phone.

"He wants to have dinner at his apartment. I'd better get going. Are you okay?"

"Certainly," he said. "All that was long ago. The wounds are scars. And I can always pick out a nice lighthearted farce to read in bed tonight."

"See you soon, then."

I reached the trellises when he called after me. "Paul?"

"Yes?"

"Bring David's mother the next time you come, if that's not too soon."

"I'll check and let you know. And only if you promise not to get anywhere near the subject of Cretin Corey."

"After my successful invitation to the dance, I wouldn't disrupt your progress with David for the world."

"Thanks."

Back home, I showered, shaved, dressed, and, impelled by a perhaps impertinent curiosity, searched online for Scott Christopher, set designer. A brief *New York Times* obituary from four years ago said Scott had died of lung cancer and been buried beside his parents and sister. The obit listed a dozen stage credits but neither next of kin nor a surviving partner. Following Sandy's lead, he divided his estate among several groups supporting the arts and arts education.

An hour later, I discovered the roses had vanished from David's apartment, and a bag with our eggplant parmesans and the ubiquitous salad sat on his kitchen counter. As we ate, he talked about interviewing potential employees for the Argonaut and listened to my descriptions of Waterman's disheartening memo and the unscheduled visit with Robert.

"He said if your mom wants to talk to him about *Grandview Park,* invite her for next week."

"Cool."

"I told him you'd probably come with her."

"How'd he react?"

"He's curious to meet you. And you should meet him. I'm sure he'll be even more entertaining with two other people in the room. Then you'll know why I spend so much time there."

"I'll phone her after dinner and see when she's free."

"He seemed open to the idea no matter the day."

Following dinner, he sat on the couch to phone Delia. I cleared the table, tossed out the empty food containers, and rejoined him at the conclusion of their talk.

"Okay, Mom, I'll tell him. Love you too." He laid his phone on the coffee table. "She's set for next week."

"Great. I'll call Robert tomorrow and set a day."

"Now," he said, "shall we dance?"

He stood, but before I extracted my phone to start our playlist, he tapped his phone and began another, opening with Cole Porter's "You'd Be So Nice to Come Home To."

"Where'd you get the songs?" I asked after a few measures.

"I looked them up in my downtime at the store. I also asked my parents about the ones they remembered, though I didn't say why I wanted them."

"You and your parents have good taste."

He leaned his forehead against mine. "We like you, don't we?"

Ten minutes later, the list segued into a song Robert mentioned several weeks ago: "Wait Till You See Him" by Rodgers and Hart. Listening, I recognized in Hart's lyric the picture of David I had sketched for Robert that day.

"How about making this our song?" I asked.

"You have good taste, too," he said.

9.

David slid his car into a parking spot at the Roxbury Apartments. Delia, staring out the front passenger side window, examined the orange stucco walls. I watched her from the back seat, Robert's bag of groceries beside me.

"Here's where he lives?" she said. "I didn't think there were any buildings like this still standing."

"Pretty archaic," David said

"It has every modern convenience," I said, mimicking an eager real estate agent, "electricity, indoor plumbing . . ."

Delia laughed. "Paul's right. We shouldn't disparage."

We headed between the rhododendrons, across the shabby-elegant lobby into the elevator. Delia studied me during the ride to the fourth floor.

"You look anxious, Paul."

Robert's ability to avoid the Corey issue seemed less sure upon entering his domain. "Sorry, it's just that you and Robert have comprised separate parts of my life until now. I feel like a scientist experimenting with two unknown elements."

"An ordinary scientist or a mad one?" David asked.

"What do you think?" I replied.

"Mad," he said, looking at Delia, "undoubtedly mad."

"I doubt there'll be any ill effects," she said, grinning.

I hoped not.

The elevator stopped. We clambered into the fourth-floor hallway, and I led them to Robert's apartment. David knocked.

Robert opened the door in his usual blue cardigan, augmented for the occasion by beige slacks, a crisp white dress shirt, and a silk tie with black and purple stripes. He had carefully combed his sparse hair and applied a stronger aftershave, all of which lent him a dignity his cane and crooked posture failed to diminish. His eyes darted from one to the other of us.

"Hello, Paul. Please come in." He shuffled to one side. We entered, and I stood, holding the grocery bag, until he closed the door before introducing his guests.

"Nice to meet you," he said, shaking their hands in turn. "Paul's told me a good deal about you."

"We've heard a lot about you, too," David said.

"I'll put the perishables away," I said.

Hurrying to the kitchen, I heard:

"Please sit down."

"Thank you."

I stuffed his Ice Floe frozen vegetables into the freezer, his salad ingredients, Bub's Tubs, and some chicken cutlets into the refrigerator, left the non-perishables in the bag on the counter, and rejoined them, sliding beside Delia on the sofa. David sat on her other side.

Robert had laid the coffee table with three glasses; a bottle of Shale House; a pitcher of water; a little crystal bowl with ice cubes and a spoon; paper napkins, and two dessert plates, one displaying some Velma's biscuits arranged in an overlapping pattern like chrysanthemum petals, the other with an equally well-constructed pyramid of dried papaya. He sat in his recliner facing the sofa, as when he and I talked.

"If you'd care for a snack or drink, that's the best I can offer. It's been a long while since I've entertained, and my food supply is restricted by my health. I'm not very mobile, either, so I'll deputize Paul to serve if he doesn't mind."

"Sure," I said.

The three of us opted for ginger ale. As I spooned ice cubes into the glasses, Robert said, "I was pleased to hear you run the Argonaut. That was a favorite place of mine when I first moved to L.A. Forty percent of the books on my shelves are from there."

I poured the ginger ale.

"I'm glad you found it useful," Delia said. "I only wish I'd known you were a customer. We'd have met long before now."

"Yes," Robert said and addressed David. "I'm sorry if I've taken you away from your work."

I handed the glasses around.

"No problem. I just hired somebody to take care of the store while I fill online orders. It also allows me to play hooky for visits."

"A student, I assume?" Robert said.

"A business major named Margot," I said, checking his instinct to play the protective parent.

Robert nodded, and we sipped our ginger ale. Delia noticed the picture on his writing desk.

"May I have a closer look at that?" she asked.

David followed her gaze. Robert partially turned in his recliner to glance at the photo.

"Certainly. Would you mind getting it, Paul?"

"Sure."

Delia propped the picture on her lap. David leaned over, peering, his absence of expression conspicuous beside his mother's delight.

"This is exactly how you looked on *Grandview Park*," she said. "You've barely changed."

"You're very kind."

"I mean it. If I'd seen you on the street, I'd have recognized you. It may have taken me a second or two to remember why, but I'd have gotten it eventually."

Robert laughed.

"You'd also be in a very select group. There probably aren't more than twenty in the world who remember Grantland Hunnicutt."

"I'm sure there's more than that. When David said he knew somebody who knew an actor from *Grandview*, I was only mildly interested. I mean, hundreds of actors passed through there over the years. When he said you were Grantland, a slew of memories I didn't realize I had came tumbling out."

"Perhaps they were forgotten for a reason," he said.

She shook her head.

"I'd forgotten them because I had nothing to remind me. Did Paul tell you my mother and I watched every day?"

"He did."

"Whether we were on the best terms or arguing, we always had common ground in *Grandview Park*."

"Did you argue much with Grandma?" David said.

"Not more than the average mother and daughter. We had a few spectacular tiffs, like when I monopolized the car after learning to drive . . . and Parker Morgan . . ."

David arched his eyebrows. "Who's Parker Morgan?"

"I dated him for a while. Grandma disapproved."

"Was he a bad boy?" David said teasingly.

"Only by proxy."

"What's that mean?" David said.

"Parker's parents were divorced."

"So?"

"Your grandmother's generation considered divorce a scandal and a possible sign of moral degeneracy the children might inherit. Parker was nice but prone to sullenness, thanks to his parents' split. Grandma believed the sullenness confirmed her suspicions about inherited flaws. I used to sneak out to see him."

David stared. "Really?"

"Really," Delia said, reveling in the effect of her revelation. "And he was the second boy I ever kissed, too. I don't hear you confiding in me about the first boys you kissed."

David blushed brick red, to Robert's and my amusement.

"Rather unusual to recall the second boy you ever kissed," Robert said.

"Oh, I have vivid memories of the first, Freddy Harkness. He was the center on our high school basketball team. I'd completely forgotten about Parker until I heard the name, Grantland Hunnicutt. Parker was one of the bigger issues Mom and I put aside for your show."

"And you truly believe our foolish melodramatics strengthened your parent-child relationship?" he said, his doubtful tone recalling a clip I uncovered from the penultimate episode of a courtroom drama called *Approach the Bench* that aired on NBC from 1973 to 1976, in which he appeared as a zealous district attorney, examining witnesses with the finesse and latent hostility of an Ivy League pit bull.

"Yes," Delia said, undaunted by his skepticism. "It reminded us we had more in common than not. And it didn't seem foolish . . . or not much, anyway. We liked those people and cared about what happened to them, no matter how improbable. That was the attraction. It wasn't what they said or did that mattered. We simply enjoyed spending an hour each day in their company."

"Unfortunately, other viewers developed less balanced attachments to them," he said.

"I suppose the danger of confusing fantasy and reality inheres in every medium. Most people, I hope, enjoy stories for what they are."

"I'm afraid my judgment was warped by my fan mail."

Delia laughed. "Paul mentioned your letters."

"Were they that crazy?" David said.

"More than you can imagine. Grantland received death threats; advice to consult a psychiatrist; marriage proposals; warnings about other characters; nude photos; requests for nude photos; food that I prayed had been fresh when it began its journey through the mail; locks of hair; and other objects I shudder to recall. They often made me think the entire world was insane."

"Probably because the sane viewers never felt compelled to write in," Delia said.

"Like you and your mother," Robert said.

"Not that we didn't have our crazy moments."

"And the show really meant something to you?"

"Maybe not as much as a great novel or play," she said, "but something. And I think of it now with genuine fondness."

"I'm glad."

"Okay," David said, "when do we get the dirt about you and your co-star?"

Delia swatted his knee.

"Hey," David said, "I never saw the show. I came for the backstage melodrama."

"Quite right," Robert said, "it was more interesting, at least to me." He looked at Delia. "Were you startled to learn Grantland was gay in real life?"

"Not really." She sipped her ginger ale. "I never thought about it, so I didn't have any illusions to shatter."

"My parents are blasé about people's sexuality since I came out," David said.

Delia cocked her head at him. "Don't give yourself airs. Your father and I didn't live under a rock. We knew plenty of gay people, from every walk of life, in college and through our work. Most of them were very happy, too. In fact, we realized you were gay long before you told us."

"Really?" David said, dumbfounded.

"Yes, so don't think you broadened our horizons. If anything, our already broad horizons made your coming out a good deal easier."

"This is more fun than I expected," I said, glancing at Robert. He smiled back at me.

"Thanks a lot," David said.

Delia resumed answering Robert's original question. "You were a part of my life for so long I couldn't help being intrigued by yours, though. Learning what really went on with that famous love triangle was marvelous."

"Good," Robert said. "We felt the same way. Our deception balanced out the hysteria of the fan mail."

"Did you really sneak gay references into your scenes?" David said.

"Oh yes." Robert recounted the tales he told me about their games with the audience and his misbehavior during Grantland's paralysis.

"Then you were good friends with the actress playing Judith?" Delia said after we stopped laughing.

"Very much . . . until she died."

"When was that?"

"Five years ago."

"I'm sorry to hear it. I was in awe of her as a teenager. Judith was so beautiful, and a wonderful combination of intelligence and compassion."

"Mag was the same," Robert said. "In fact, her personality shaped Judith more than the writers did."

"I loved how she handled Grantland, encouraging yet intolerant of his nonsense. Female characters back then tended to be either sex kittens or housewives. Judith was always level-headed, always quietly in control of every situation. She was probably my first role model."

"Mag would've loved that. Usually, her mail was split between ordering Judith to cut Grantland out of her life and urging her to give in to his advances."

"What about the guy you were sleeping with?" David said.

"I never knew you were such a gossip, David," Delia said.

"He told Paul about it. I figured it was fair game."

"It is," Robert said, "as long as you aren't expecting any intimate details. It was very casual and lasted my entire time on the show."

"The brother's name was Brice, wasn't it?" Delia said. Robert nodded. "What was his real name?"

"Grayson."

"Almost as pretentious as Brice," David said, for a moment sounding like his father.

"Soaps are founded on pretension," Robert said, "like all fantasies."

"He was so handsome," Delia said. "We had a soft spot for Grantland, but Brice was the one girls imagined in their wedding photos, probably because he personified the ideal man advertisements exploited in those days. Not that you weren't attractive . . ."

Robert waved away her reassurances. "I accepted Gray as my superior in looks long ago. He turned heads wherever we went, and only a few belonged to *Grandview Park* fans. That's why our relationship was casual. Nobody could've roped him into monogamy, least of all me, with the chances he had to capitalize on his fame and beauty. Loving him would've been too frustrating. Thankfully, I preserved enough objectivity to find his adventures amusing. Sometimes I felt a little sorry for him."

"Why sorry?" Delia said.

"Acting was an art for me, and *Grandview* a way to survive while seeking better roles in plays. For Gray, it was a way to enrich his ego and his bank account. But there were benefits to his philistine goals. His charms made him the perfect guest for cocktail and dinner parties. Moving in with him made me his permanent plus one, and allowed me to become acquainted with some fascinating people."

"Like who?" David said.

"The first party he took me to, I met Flora Dowd, the costume designer. She created a dress for a play in 1964, a popular comedy called *Gentlewomen's Code*, that was later mass marketed as the Dowd Gown, an unusual fate for a theatrical costume."

Delia brightened. "I had one of those. It was yellow tulle, with a single strap around the neck, and a wide flare at the bottom."

"That's the one. She made tons of money from it but preferred to remain in the theater. This was before celebrity clothing lines became big moneymakers. Later on, I met Tennessee Williams. He'd been a hero of mine since I read *The Glass Menagerie* as a teenager. He almost cast me in a play, but it fell through, something I count among the bigger disappointments of my life."

"You never told me that," I said.

"It was the kind of promise people make after they've had a few drinks, and I was young enough and star-struck enough to believe it. I also met Carl Wolfram."

"Who?" David said.

"He produced avant-garde plays across Europe in the years following World War I. He emigrated to the U.S. in 1934."

"How old was he when you met him?" Delia asked.

"As old as the century, about sixty-one or two, handsome in a distinguished older man sort of way, but reduced to living off his reputation. He'd talk about Max Reinhardt and Serge Diaghilev and Jean Cocteau and others from the 1920s, people who, for me, were more mythic than human. It was like hearing someone say they'd dined with Zeus or Apollo. He'd entrance us for hours with his store of anecdotes until his lover spirited him home."

"Who was his lover?" David said.

"A middle-aged stockbroker, if I remember correctly . . . or perhaps he just looked like a middle-aged stockbroker. Then I met Garbo."

Delia gaped. "You knew Garbo?"

"Who?" David asked.

"Greta Garbo," Delia said, "probably the most famous movie star ever, at least for your grandmother's generation. She retired at her peak in the early 1940s and lived in seclusion for the rest of her life. There's a mythic figure. I can't believe you knew her."

Robert lifted his hand. "I didn't know her. I met her once, through Cecil Beaton, the photographer. She was mythic in my eyes, too, yet our encounter proved disappointing."

"Why?" Delia said.

"She was quite shy, and Beaton warned me she refused to discuss her career, so we spent the whole time talking about antiques. It's nice to say I met her, but . . ."

"You wanted more than advice on antiques," I said.

"You're getting to know me too well, Paul. It's true. I was focused on the arts and wanted to learn from everyone associated with them. If Gray appealed to them for his looks and personality, I appealed to them because I respected their work and the craft involved in it. Garbo aside, if I'd been able to record some of the conversations I had, I could've compiled one hell of a book. The writers alone would have provided sufficient material."

"Such as . . .?" I asked, like David and Delia, carried away by his rapid-fire name-dropping.

"Well, I met Frank O'Hara, the poet, shortly before his death in 1966. And I had a passing friendship with Gretchen Ives, the playwright. She stopped writing in 1955, but her plays were constantly revived. *The Hawthorne Tree* was a staple for professional and amateur groups alike."

"About the soldier returning from World War I," Delia said.

Robert nodded. "He's lost a leg, and he and his fiancée have to rebuild their relationship. I played it in college. It's a lovely piece of writing."

"Where does the hawthorn tree come in?" David said.

"The soldier's parents had a hawthorn tree in their front yard where the lovers met during their courtship," Robert said.

"What was Gretchen like?" Delia said.

"An unlikely combination of shyness and showoff. Her bright platinum hair drew people like a beacon at parties, and she'd spend hours relating stories and tossing off *bon mots*. We wondered why she never channeled her verbal skills into more writing, but she said she liked entertaining better, which to me indicated she disliked the solitude necessary for a writer. On the other hand, when someone proposed she do a one-woman show, she said she could only scintillate with no more than ten or twelve people around. As she got older, her shyness won out, and she disappeared from the social scene. She spent her final years in a cottage on the Long Island shore, subsisting on seafood and Geritol. I also met Fiona Vale, the novelist . . ."

"Who wrote *Cornflower Blue*?" Delia said.

"Yes."

"I loved that book. I read it when I was sixteen. There was another great female role model."

"What's it about?" I said.

"A woman named Cornflower trying to salvage her family farm during the Dust Bowl days of the Depression," she said. "Her father's died of typhoid, and her mother's an alcoholic."

"What happens?" David asked.

"She hires a young man named Zeb, ten years her junior, to help around the place, and they fall in love. The climax comes when the mother, in a drunken rage, attacks Zeb with a pitchfork."

Stunned by this twist, I asked, "How does it end?"

"The mother's carted off to a sanatorium, and Cornflower and Zeb face another uncertain growing season."

"Pretty downbeat," David said.

"It was set in a downbeat era," Delia said. "The descriptions of farm life were exquisite, though. Cornflower was only happy among the seasonal rhythms of growth and change. When Zeb arrived, you weren't sure if he wanted to be there or was just looking to take advantage of the family. But he soon developed a similar devotion to the land. The passages comparing Zeb's falling for Cornflower with him learning to tend the farm were beautiful."

"If Fiona were here," Robert said, "you'd receive a signed first edition tomorrow morning."

"Was she that generous or just susceptible to flattery?" David said.

"Generous to people who understood her work," Robert said. "I found creative people, especially writers, established strong defenses once they attained a measure of fame. They were besieged by social climbers eager to feed off their notoriety but who couldn't care less about what they did to acquire it in the first place. If you genuinely appreciated their work, they'd open up to you. I'm sure that's changed since fame has surpassed art as the main goal nowadays."

"Probably," Delia said.

"Fiona was fascinating. She was slight, with hair like straw. She wore thick black glasses and tweed skirts and liked to fade into the background. But she was full of stories about her youth in Nebraska in the early 1900s, working at her parents' general store and staying at her grandparents' farm. She loved crawling into the hay loft with a stack of books from their local library. She said from then on she always associated the smell of books with the smell of old wood in the barn."

David locked eyes with me at the mention of the smell of books. Robert continued.

"She also had an astonishing collection of medieval amulets that she started on her first trip to England in 1924. Her tales about dickering with the British antique dealers were priceless. She even earned her pilot's license but abandoned flying after Amelia Earhart disappeared. Too bad she never wrote an autobiography."

"You've got enough stories for one," Delia said, "even without transcripts."

"Titled *Memoirs of a Gate Crasher,* perhaps?" Robert laughed. "No, I was always farther in the background than Fiona. Who'd be interested?"

"I've been," Delia said, "and I know Paul has."

"Me too," David said.

"Thanks, but all I possess are a few random scraps not worth the trouble to record. Pry into anyone's past, and you'll find an evening or two worth of anecdotes. I'm a trifle luckier given whom I rubbed shoulders with, but it wasn't enough to offer fresh insights into their lives or work."

"Did you continue rubbing shoulders after you left Grayson and the show?" David said.

"Oh yes. Thanks to my interest in their work, I had my own appeal as a guest for the folks I met through Gray. I also started seeing a set designer who joined his social connections to mine."

Robert repeated the stories he told me about Leonard Bernstein, Ada Grendel, Aaron Copeland, Angus Russell, and Cassandra Angel.

"Paul told us you concentrated on theater after leaving *Grandview*," Delia said.

"As much as possible, and I did a few commercials."

"Didn't you do one for a men's cologne?" Delia said.

"Desert Island," Robert said, wrinkling his nose, "a vile brew smelling of cedar, sandalwood, and formaldehyde. They put me in a long, fake beard and tattered clothes on a burlap island with a palm tree in the middle. It was like the Looney Tunes version of Robinson Crusoe. A bottle of Desert Island washed ashore, I dabbed it on, and instantly a scantily clad native girl—or rather a busty New York model portraying the ad agency's fantasy of a scantily clad native girl—minced over and embraced me."

"I remember," Delia said. "What about the plays?"

"As I've told Paul, I only played leads in revivals or off-Broadway shows. I was a supporting and bit player in some full-scale Broadway productions, few successful."

"What leads did you play?" David said.

"Henry Higgins in a *Pygmalion* revival; Othello and Julius Caesar and Macbeth; an evening of short plays by Ionesco and Beckett; and a modern dress version of *Peer Gynt* that had Peer living on Long Island, with excerpts from Grieg's music adapted for a jazz trio. I was Tony in *You Can't Take it with You*, and I even had a crack at Willy Loman."

"My husband and I made several trips to New York in the late 1960s. I wish I'd caught you on stage."

"If you had, you might have happier memories of my acting than Grantland left you with."

"What about your memories?" Delia said. "What do you recall most about your theater work?"

"The fun of crafting shows and the pleasure of presenting them to audiences," he promptly replied.

"Were their reactions generally favorable?"

"Generally. Critics tended to like me, as did the minuscule audiences who showed up at the minuscule theaters we usually played. Every now and again, I felt I'd performed particularly well, and I became the artist I believe actors can be. I also had the pleasure of having Walter Kerr or

Brooks Atkinson corroborate my belief in their reviews when such things were enshrined in newsprint. Those moments were very satisfying."

"Yet you're modest to the point of disdain about your career," Delia said.

"I suppose I was greedy. I wanted it to consist entirely of those moments played for larger audiences. I wanted to be an artist all the time, not just now and again."

"Do you regret staying with it rather than doing something else?" Delia said.

Robert thought.

"No. If it never amounted to much, or as much as I thought it should, it would've been worse living a different life yet wondering what might've happened had I followed my inclinations, both personal and professional. That's how I know, despite everything, I made the correct choice. The only thing I ever wanted was to be an actor, and I'm glad I was one. I never wonder what might've happened had I followed a different path since I honestly can't imagine anything else being better."

"I told you what your work on *Grandview* meant to my mother and me. I'm sure there were others for whom your efforts there and elsewhere meant as much."

Robert smiled. "I'd like to think so."

"I don't see why you shouldn't," she said. "Perhaps, rather than failing as an actor, you just never met the people you really influenced."

"Perhaps," he said, pondering the suggestion.

David finished his ginger ale, the shrunken ice cubes jangling as they slid down the upturned glass. I noted the restiveness in his movements.

"We'd better go," I said, my words dragging Robert from his reverie. "Delia has a long drive."

Everyone stood.

"Can we help you clean up?" David said.

"No," Robert said. "I'll manage."

"I left the rest of your groceries on the counter," I said. "I can put them away while David picks up."

"I'm fine. See you next week, Paul?"

"Absolutely."

Delia extended her hand. "It was wonderful meeting you. I loved hearing about *Grandview* and everything else."

"My pleasure," Robert said, shaking her hand, and then David's. "I'm glad Paul has you for friends."

We left the apartment, rode the elevator to the lobby, and walked to the car without speaking. Once the car doors shut and we fixed our seatbelts, I asked, "What did you think?"

Delia answered first. "He's more complex than I expected."

"Complex?"

"I imagined something closer to the young schemer I used to see on TV. A lot's happened to him since then. I'm sure we only heard a fraction."

"You can't expect a detailed confession in a few hours," David said, backing out of the parking spot. "He seemed a bit maudlin to me."

"He has regrets," Delia said, "and too much time to think about them. He never had a long-term partner?"

David swerved across the lot and onto the road.

"No," I said.

"That's the great bulwark against age," she said, "someone who's weathered your successes and failures and prevents you from taking either too seriously. I feel sorry for him not having that. It's good you let him talk to you, Paul. Reliving his past probably helps him put it in perspective."

Ten minutes later, David pulled up to my apartment building. Delia left her car at his place; after dropping her off there, he had to head across town to close the Argonaut.

"Six-thirty at Brewer's?" he said while I unbuckled my seatbelt.

"Sure."

Walking along the front of Brewer's at six-thirty, I spotted David at a table by the window, staring at the upper floors of the buildings across the street. I tapped the glass. He looked down and smiled. Inside, I found fewer customers than usual, with only sixty percent of the tables occupied and the line at the counter three deep. I bought a latte and walked to the window, enjoying the anomalous calm. David turned his coffee cup around on the tabletop, gazing at it pensively, not unlike how he had been the night we discussed Corey.

"Hey," I said.

"Hey."

I sat down. "How did Margot fare soloing at the Argonaut?"

"Good. I think she'll work out."

His reticence puzzled me. "But . . . ?"

"But what?" he said, with poorly feigned ingenuousness.

"Something's bothering you. Is it Margot or Robert?"

"Robert, I guess . . ." His voice trailed off, and his eyes sought sanctuary in other parts of the room.

"What about him?"

"He got me thinking. Here's a guy who always knew what he wanted to do and did it. But he still ended up alone with regrets. I told you I never had any purpose and only started running the Argonaut because it was familiar."

"You also told me you led a life of quiet contentment."

"I did …I do . . . it's just . . . this is the first time I ever thought that despite being content, there's a possibility I could end up like him, alone and regretful."

I breathed deeply. "Okay, first of all, in the unlikely event there's nobody else around when you're Robert's age, Mark and Adrian would never allow you to be alone."

The pensiveness weakened. "Probably," he said.

"Undoubtedly. Second, Robert's regrets are fairly specific. He never fulfilled his ambitions, at least the way he wanted. Do you have a secret desire awaiting fulfillment?"

"No. But there's always a chance things will happen I'll wish I'd handled better, an opportunity I missed or bungled."

"Nobody controls everything that happens to them; at least, that's what you said when you lectured me on the myth of adulthood. Much of what Robert regrets resulted from events beyond his control. I'd give you examples, but I'd be betraying his trust."

"Okay."

"I doubt you can ever be entirely free of regrets, either. Everyone wishes they'd handled something differently. Anyone who says otherwise is either lying or looking back with blinders. And like everything that's too good to be true, blinders come with a price."

"What price?"

"They make your existence easier by limiting your perceptions. But limiting your perceptions also limits your existence. Robert also said that despite the disappointments, he didn't regret his major life choices. I guess that means we should do what makes us glad to be alive so that when we're his age, we'll be glad we were alive."

"Not a very original idea."

"There aren't many original ideas left, which isn't an original idea, either. Originality and validity aren't synonymous, anyway."

"Is that how you see your research project? The attempt alone makes you happy, no matter how it ends up?"

I met the challenge in his voice. "Yes. I've run up against brick wall after brick wall, but I can't imagine not having tried. And I'm still not done, so we can't declare it a failure yet."

He nodded and continued twirling his cup.

"Something else worrying you?"

"I'm a little disappointed."

"About the visit? I thought it went well. Your mom seemed pleased."

"She was. The thing is, I never imagined my parents knew I was gay before I told them."

"What's wrong with that? You should be grateful they reacted so well."

"I am, believe me. But I always felt my coming out changed them a little. They were older than my friends' parents, and I assumed their attitudes to sex were more old-fashioned. I thought I'd broadened their horizons, as she put it. I was always proud of that. Now it turns out I didn't have any effect on them at all."

"No effect? Isn't it enough you make the people around you happy?"

"What makes you think I do that?"

"I've seen how they are with you, especially your nephews."

"We do seem to get along," he said, "which reminds me, Marge and Brad want to know if you'd like to spend the weekend."

"This weekend?"

"Unless you're too busy with research," he said. "The kids are bugging her to ask me back, and she said to include you in the invitation. My parents will probably put in an appearance, too. What do you say?"

"I'd love it."

"Cool."

He stared at his cup again.

"Anything else?" I said.

He turned the cup a couple of times, and the volatile subject I considered safely contained erupted.

"I called Corey."

"When?"

"Today, half an hour before my mom was supposed to be at my place. I figured if we were still talking when she got there, it'd be a good excuse to hang up."

"How was it?"

"Strange. He sounded . . . chastened."

"What did he want to talk to you about?"

"He wouldn't tell me on the phone. He wants to see me in person."

"What'd you say?"

"Contacting him in the first place pretty much committed me. We're having dinner next Wednesday."

"Where?"

"He suggested his apartment. I held out for a restaurant. If he's tempted to revert to his old abusiveness, having other people around will stop him. He always maintained an immaculate public persona."

"A hypocrite and an addict."

"I guess the two go together. Do you think we could put him aside and have fun this weekend?"

"Is that wise," I asked, "or even possible?"

"What's the alternative? I thought it'd be over and done with after I phoned him. Now we can't do anything except go around in circles until Wednesday. Unless you're not up to trying . . . They'll be disappointed, though."

"I can't risk that. Apart from Robert, your dad's my staunchest ally in these parts. I've also been looking forward to swimming in Lake Bellow for too long."

"Cool. Only rein in your impulse for hostess gifts."

"I'll buy one little bottle of Merlot and call it a day."

He sipped his coffee, gazed into the cup again, and asked, "Do I make you happy?"

I thought it best if he carried the truth to his dinner with Corey. "Yes." He lifted his eyes. I added: "Except when you sabotage my efforts to be the perfect houseguest."

He grinned. "Okay, then."

10.

Saturday morning, my phone rang. I glanced at the screen and answered.
"Hi, mom."

"Happy birthday, Paul."

"Thanks."

"Did you get my present?"

A brown cardboard box containing two smaller gift-wrapped boxes had arrived at my apartment on Friday. The gift-wrapped boxes each contained a dress shirt, one maize yellow, the other salmon pink, both with short sleeves.

"They came yesterday. I love them."

"Do you think they'll fit?"

"I'm wearing one now."

"Which one?"

"The yellow," I said. "They're perfect for this climate."

"I thought they'd be. I wish I was there."

"Me too."

"I hope you'll at least be going out with David tonight. Does he know it's your birthday?"

"No." I sipped from the mug of coffee David fetched for me ten minutes earlier after we woke to the smell of it brewing. "I didn't want him feeling obligated."

"I wish you weren't so reticent, Paul. Sometimes I wonder if it's my fault for kicking your father out."

"What's that got to do with it?"

"With me taking care of everything else, I couldn't give you the attention you deserved. You brought yourself up alone, reading and watching TV. If you'd had two parents that were more involved in your life, you might be more open."

"I'm a regular chatterbox with my clients."

"That's another thing. You were always more interested in older people. If you had better parents, you might've spent more time with kids your age."

"You were a great parent. And I've learned a lot from my clients."

"You'd learn more by learning to enjoy yourself."

"I'll try, Mom."

"Then you wouldn't be alone on your birthday."

Her voice quivered. I quickly reassured her. "I won't be alone. David's sister asked us up to her place for the weekend. I sent you pictures, remember?"

"Oh, yes," she said, the quiver subsiding after a stifled sniffle. "It's such a pretty place. When are you going?"

"We got here last night. We'll have two days of swimming and games and great food. I told you his sister was a caterer."

"It'll almost be like a party, then, won't it?"

"A house party rather than a birthday party."

Sipping my coffee again, I looked out the second-floor guest room window, with its privileged view of the front lawn. Directly below, Mark and Adrian played fetch with Chop. Beyond them, the lake, mirror flat in the early morning, reflected the sky, opposite shore, and far hills.

"They're great people," I said. "You should meet them."

"I'd like to, but you know me and flying. Give me time to think about it."

"I will. I should go, mom. We're late for breakfast."

"Okay, dear. Happy birthday again. Call me when you get a chance."

David entered from the bathroom, glistening from his shower, a towel around his waist.

"I will," I said. "Love you."

"Love you too."

We hung up.

"Who are you loving on the phone?"

"My mom."

"Oh," he said, sauntering toward me.

I warded him off with an outstretched hand. "Hold on, drippy. You'll get my new shirt wet. You should've thought of that before I dressed."

He unfurled the towel and slung it over his shoulder. "You know what you're missing. And who brings new shirts to a weekend on a lake?"

"Someone who's still on probation with his boyfriend's family and needs to make a good impression."

"They like you as much as I do. You just want to show off your taste in clothes."

The old overconfidence had returned, even more appealing after glimpsing the insecurities it masked. Our surroundings and his family, blissfully ignorant of his coming encounter with the Cretin, undoubtedly aided the masquerade, inspiring me to participate in it with greater skill than I imagined possible.

He finished drying and began dressing.

"Are we late for breakfast?" I said.

"Probably. I'm sure Marge kept something warm for us."

"I'm okay with cold cereal."

"Tell her that, and your probation will be extended another six months."

We found Marge and Brad in the kitchen. Marge sat at the oak table, funneling peppercorns into a stainless steel mill. Brad loaded the dishwasher with their breakfast dishes. The invisible audio system played the sprightly "Spring" movement from Vivaldi's *The Four Seasons*.

"Sorry we're late," David said.

"You had a long drive last night," Marge said, removing her peppercorns and mill to the counter. "Just don't let it happen again. How was the coffee, Paul?"

"Heaven. I'm nothing till I've had at least one cup in the morning."

"David told us. Want a refill?"

"Please."

I extended my empty mug like Oliver Twist pleading for more gruel.

Marge carried the mug to the coffee maker while Brad laid place mats, napkins, and silverware before us.

"We could've set the table," I said.

"Relax," Brad said. "You helped enough last time."

Marge served us plates of French toast smothered with apples and walnuts sautéed in butter, after which she brought our coffee.

"This is like a bed and breakfast," I said.

"You're dressed for one," Brad said, removing Marge's now empty pans from the stove to the dishwasher. "You may want to rethink your wardrobe if you're playing croquet with us."

"We're playing croquet?"

"Mark and Adrian love it," David said.

"We encourage outdoor activities," Marge said. She finished filling the mill and hid it away in a cupboard. "What's the point of living in a spot like this if they spend all their time staring at video games?"

"We'll probably take a dip in the lake to cool off before lunch, too," Brad said. "Did you bring your bathing suit?"

"It was the first thing I packed."

"Good."

"He's gorgeous in it, too," David said.

I swiped his ankle with my foot. He smiled his crinkliest smile.

The porch door opened and closed. Mark, Adrian, and Chop galloped through the house to the kitchen. Chop wandered to his water bowl and drank. Mark leaned with his elbows on the table and his head on his hands. Adrian stood a step away, his arms by his sides. Both watched us eat, Mark impatient with our pace, Adrian as if collecting notes for a later excursus.

"Morning, Uncle Davy," Mark said.

"Morning, guys. Been having fun outside?"

"Yeah. Morning, Paul."

"Good morning."

The two had been markedly more welcoming to me when we arrived the previous night, obeying a parental directive, I assumed.

"How come you didn't eat with us?" Mark asked.

"We had a long drive," David said. "Your mom and dad let us sleep a while longer."

"Oh."

Adrian's studious gaze focused more intently and quizzically on me. "Are you going to wear that for croquet?" he said.

"No. I didn't know we were playing before I put in on. I think your uncle wanted to surprise me."

Mark laughed rather inordinately at this. Adrian glared at him, brows compressed in disapproval.

"Think you'll want more?" Marge said.

We declined. She added our dishes to the dishwasher, poured in the soap powder, and turned it on, placing its steady, quiet hum beneath our conversation and the first movement of Grieg's *Piano Concerto*.

"When will grandma and grandpa be here?" Adrian said.

"For lunch," Marge said.

"Oh."

"How about helping me set up the game?" Brad said to them.

Mark and Adrian followed Brad to the garage, from which they emerged with a worn, wooden croquet set and proceeded along the side of the house to the rear lawn.

"I'm surprised your yard's big enough for croquet," I said.

"If you use gentle strokes," Marge said. "Otherwise, your ball could end up in the lake."

"A consummation devoutly to be avoided," David said.

Upstairs I changed into a green tee shirt and blue shorts that doubled as a bathing suit, spread sunblock over my face, arms, and legs, and descended to the backyard. Thanks to a near-continuous breeze from the lake, the sunshine felt gentler, less merciless than in the city. I donned my sunglasses and entered the playing field.

"Have you played croquet before?" David said.

"A little late to ask, isn't it? I did a few times as a kid. You may need to coach me on the rules."

Accustomed to being the outlier when his humans played croquet, Chop retreated to the shade beneath an azalea and watched us distribute the mallets and balls. Mark and Adrian attacked the game with more enthusiasm than ability, in deference to which the rest of us curbed our skills. This, for me, felt as leaden as ignoring the return of Cretin Corey, a view David either intuited or shared since, fifteen minutes after we started, he knocked my ball three feet off course. A play I considered unnecessarily harsh, under the circumstances, and looked over at him. The same unspoken challenge that had propelled our night of Popcorn Tag issued from his cerulean eyes and crinkly smirk. I responded without hesitation, or even thinking. I aimed my ball back at his, propelling it farther than he had mine, inaugurating a more compelling, secondary competition to knock one another's balls farthest from the playing field, which we pursued with an escalating series of tit-for-tat maneuvers like those in the old Laurel and Hardy movies I had watched in my film studies courses, embellished with mock threats, insults, and catcalls like those that had seasoned Popcorn Tag, albeit sanitized for Mark and Adrian's benefit.

Following a moment of stupefaction, one by one, like a group of fireworks attached to a single fuse, Marge, Brad, Mark and Adrian adopted our secondary game, knocking their opponents' balls farther and farther afield, and contrived ever more outrageous distractions to unnerve the player about to shoot. Brad turned cartwheels, Mark rode his mallet around like a stick horse, Marge threatened to prepare a dinner of grubs and other garden creatures if she lost, dismissing the object of the original game, except for Adrian, whose fastidious poise enabled him to switch from strategy to frivolity with impressive ease. I glanced at David, expecting to share a moment of smug triumph at how quickly they had succumbed to the influence of our playful genie. He observed their antics as if nothing unusual had occurred. And, recalling their behavior on my first visit, I realized that, rather than being conjured by Popcorn Tag, our genie had instead been a long-standing familiar of theirs, its influence more likely spreading from them to me through David.

The damage to my ego, not unlike the damage he sustained after mentioning his coming out while at Robert's place, proved shorter-lived. Evoking the others' laughter felt nearly as gratifying as evoking his, and I anticipated their antics with an eagerness that diminished all else to a few randomly observed markers of the day's progress: bathers from other houses around the lake splashing in the shallows, their shouts and laughter mixing with ours over the water, motorboats buzzing by, and an enormous blue heron that flew overhead, disturbing Chop's serene sleep, though not enough for him to abandon his spot in the shade. Most significantly, from my point of view, by the middle of the first game Mark and Adrian began joking with me as freely as with their parents and uncle until, independent of any urging from Brad and Marge, my status as a suspect intruder vanished with the general decorum.

Adrian, to nobody's surprise but Mark's, won the first game after knocking his brother's ball under the azalea, inches away from Chop, costing Mark four strokes and Chop the comfort of his retreat. The five losers demanded a rematch, which Chop watched from a place near the scrub bordering the yard. An hour later, Adrian basked in a second victory, and Mark clamored for a third game.

Marge consulted her watch. "It's almost eleven. I'd better start lunch."

Brad turned to his sons as she set off for the porch. "We may as well clear the lawn," he said.

Mark, thirsting for revenge, and Adrian, confident of another win, responded with a protracted, distressed "aw," that matched my unexpected, yet silent, disappointment.

"We want some time in the lake before we eat, don't we?" David said

His authority as a beloved uncle, combined with the appeal of a late morning swim, convinced the boys. We plucked the hoops and balls from the lawn and fit them with the mallets into the wooden rack, at the same time revisiting the games' high points, or the points we each considered the highest.

"It was so cool when Mom faked Dad out," Mark said.

"And when Dad made Uncle Davey hit the hoop instead of his ball," Adrian said.

"He surprised me, that's all," David said. "I didn't know he could make those kinds of sounds . . . with his mouth, anyway."

"I picked it up from Mark," Brad said.

Mark giggled, flattered.

"You weren't any more surprised than me when Adrian started his ostrich impression," I said. "It never occurred to me that croquet balls were about the size of ostrich eggs."

"I saw them online," Adrian said.

"What about when Paul made Uncle Davey laugh so hard he got hiccups and couldn't shoot?" Brad said.

"And he hiccupped all through Paul's turn," Adrian said.

"Hiccups like a drunken seal's," I said.

"Under what circumstances does a seal get drunk?" Brad said.

"When he meets a couple of sailors on leave and they take him bar hopping," I said, reducing the boys to screaming laughter. "Anyway, I did all right, even with the hiccupping."

"Wait till next time," David said.

The equipment had barely been collected, and our post-mortem concluded when Marge emerged from the porch wearing a one-piece purple bathing suit with a pink plastic gardenia affixed to the décolletage, and several beach towels slung over her arm. The sight of her dispatched Mark and Adrian inside for their bathing suits, followed by David. Brad returned the croquet set to the garage.

"Aren't you getting your suit?" Marge asked me, laying the towels in the grass by the shore.

"I have it on," I said, and indicat my shorts.

"Sneak," she said. "Shall we get the jump on them?"

"Sure."

Marge strode into the water. I peeled off my sweaty tee shirt and followed.

The first step barely submerged my arch, touching off a wave of goose bumps that flowed up and over my scalp. I shivered.

"You should be used to cold water, being from the northeast," she said, watching me with the grin that so resembled her brother's.

"I wasn't much of a swimmer there, either. And I've been soaking up the L.A. heat for months."

I forged ahead, behind Marge. As the water crept over my calves, it began feeling less harsh and more like a protective cover, a species of shade offering a more substantial alternative to the sunlight than its mere absence. The goose bumps ebbed, the shuddering ceased and, after the water reached my knees, I managed to walk on without hesitation.

Marge, already in up to her plastic gardenia, turned around. "How are you doing?"

"Pretty good," I said.

"Great. Come on."

She dove down and swam a dozen yards. My less athletic strokes plowed a wobbly furrow behind her. The water washed away the remainder of the morning's heat and sweat and relieved the greater pressures of gravity, leaving me cool, limber, and light. I caught up to Marge, and we bobbed in place. The sky, daubed with a few innocuous clouds, looked majestically large, dwarfing the houses along the shore.

"I can't thank you enough for inviting me."

"You're welcome. Thank you for bringing Mom to visit your friend. She had a ball."

"I'm glad. I think it did him some good, too."

"Mom says he had quite a life."

"He has. I've never met anyone like him before."

"Davy was impressed, too. Would he consider an invitation to dinner if you and my parents came?"

I wondered if her years of catering had left Marge a compulsive host.

"He barely gets around his apartment with his arthritis. I doubt he could tolerate the ride up here. I'll ask, though."

"Good. It's a shame about his arthritis."

Shouts from the lawn disrupted us. Mark, David, and Chop careened across the lawn and into the water, splashing wildly, followed by Adrian, traveling at his more sedate pace. Brad emerged from around the side of the house, rolling a large inflated inner tube I assumed had been in the garage. He and the tube entered the water and lingered close to shore with Mark, Adrian, and Chop. David dove under and, in a few moments, emerged beside Marge and me. He shook the water from his hair and wiped his eyes.

"The lake's great today," he said.

"Especially after four hours of croquet," Marge said.

"Was it only four hours?" he said, the words drenched in sarcasm.

"You're a good swimmer," I said.

"Thanks," he said. "When's lunch?"

"Whenever Mom and Dad get here," Marge said. "There's a choice of cold salads ready in the fridge. We can swim till our skin wrinkles if we want."

David turned to me.

"Then you'll see what I'll look like when I'm dad's age."

Marge laughed and splashed him. He splashed back, and for several seconds the water churned about us, attracting Mark and Adrian.

"Uncle Davy! Come see how good we swim!" Mark cried, his voice smaller and shriller across the water.

"I'll relieve Brad," Marge said and struck off for shore.

David drifted closer to me.

"Having a good time?"

"Amazing," I said.

"As long as you aren't just dating me for the swimming privileges."

"I'm content with a coffee from Brewer's and an after-dinner dance."

"So am I."

His hand drifted to my bathing suit.

"Save that for later, you horny little merman," I said.

He laughed and squeezed my thigh.

"Uncle Davy!" Mark called again. "Look!"

The boys sat opposite each other on the inner tube, bouncing it up and down like a seesaw.

"Your presence and approval are urgently requested," I said.

"Uncle Davy!"

"I'd better go before everyone on the lake starts calling me Uncle Davy."

He tweaked my leg and shot through the water.

Brad seized the opportunity to leave the kids with Marge and David and embark on a longer lap. I began a leisurely drift toward the shore. As our paths crossed, he said, "You seem to be having more fun this time around."

"I am."

"Good. I know it's difficult meeting a lot of new people at once, especially with this group. They can be overwhelming at first."

"The voice of experience," I said.

"Exactly," he said, grinning. "I didn't know what to make of them at first. Then I learned you just have to go along with them. Otherwise, they'll flatten you like a steamroller. Later, you're glad you went along."

"I was beginning to think that, too. It's nice having it confirmed."

Screams of laughter, and barks from Chop, erupted from the group nearer shore. I turned in time to watch David slip backward off the inner tube.

"How are things with you and David, if I'm not too inquisitive?"

"Fantastic. And for the record, you are inquisitive, but not too."

He laughed. "Sorry. David means a lot to us, especially the kids. Sometimes, like now, it's as if he's their age. But when he talks to them as an uncle, tells them to go to bed or . . ."

"Or it's time to pick up the croquet set?"

"Yeah," he said. "You saw it. They listen without a fuss. That's why if anything happens to Marge and me, he'll be their guardian."

"He never told me."

"It'll probably never come to that, but it eases our minds knowing he's there for them. Has he told you anything about Corey?"

"A little," I lied.

"He's gone out with a few people since, but you're the first he's introduced to us. I'm not trying to put any pressure on you or scare you off. It's just that, like I said, he's important to us."

My quip about being on probation with them had been nearer the mark than I imagined.

"We're getting to be important to each other," I said, "and you'll have to find something a good deal more terrifying than Mark and Adrian to scare me off."

"Have you ever considered having children?"

"I have," I said, flashing back to my first conversation with Tom, "but I'd like to wait until I'm settled."

"Settled down as in married, or after your project's done?"

"Both, I hope. I also hope I'm still young enough to enjoy a few more unsettled years."

Joyous squeals directed our attention to shore.

"Grandma! Grandpa!"

Delia and Tom walked around the side of the house, wearing linen slacks, sandals, and light summer shirts—Tom's a solid mint green, Delia's decked with gold seashells on a cream background. The kids and Chop sloshed from the water to greet them. Delia and Tom bent to kiss their grandchildren and pat Chop, after which the boys led them by hand to the water's edge. Marge started for shore.

"No, no," Tom said, "go on with your swim."

Mark and Adrian plunged back in. Delia and Tom removed their sandals, rolled up their slacks, and waded in up to their calves. Chop hovered beside them, wagging his wet tail. Brad and I swam over. Delia listened to the kids' play-by-play account of our croquet games. Tom talked to David about the Argonaut's new shop assistant.

"I'm glad she's working out," Tom said and waved to me. "Hello, Paul."

"Hi."

Delia glanced over, waved, and resumed listening to Adrian describe how he had bested Mark, who sullenly twisted his lips.

"Having a nice time?" Tom said to me.

"Great."

"He did well at croquet," Brad said. "He claims he hasn't played since childhood, but I have my doubts."

"You'll have to admit I'm as bad a swimmer as I said."

"Agreed."

"What time is it, dad?" David said.

Tom consulted his watch.

"Ten minutes after one."

"No wonder I'm hungry."

"His hints are always so subtle," I said.

David flicked water at me.

A promise of more swimming in the afternoon convinced Mark and Adrian to abandon the lake for food. Brad hauled the inner tube onto the grass. Delia and Tom started over the lawn to the house, pausing at the porch door to slip back into their sandals. The kids ran after, their towels, draped over their shoulders, flapping like capes. Marge, Brad, David, and I lingered on shore, applying our towels more diligently. David dried his head before his torso, leaving his hair in total disarray.

"There he is again," I said.

"Who?"

"The frightened puppy I like so much."

He snapped his towel at me and ran his fingers through his hair. I grabbed my tee shirt, accompanied him to our room, and changed back into my yellow shirt for lunch.

Marge and Brad carried bowls of lobster salad, three bean salad, and green salad to the porch table for us to mix and match. We ate, talked, and glanced at the lake, its perimeter now infested with swimmers and its midsection crisscrossed by boats. David and Tom discussed the store's increasing online trade.

"I'd ask how you've been, Paul," Delia said, "but I assume nothing's changed in the three days since I've seen you."

"Only that I have one less delivery for a while."

"Something happen to Robert?"

"No, another client, a former nurse. She fell and broke a hip. She's going to an assisted living facility."

"Too bad," Marge said.

"That's what I like most about *Heart and Hands*. We help our clients maintain a semblance of independence. And though they don't get out much, it also allows them the comfort of familiar surroundings."

"Did you talk to her like you do with Robert?" Brad said.

"Not as much, but enough. She told me a lot about her nursing days, none of it appropriate for mealtime."

Following lunch Marge and Brad declined my offer to help clear the table. Delia and Tom quizzed me further about *H&H* while Mark and Adrian turned their attention to the promised afternoon swim. Marge and Brad forestalled the inevitable for nearly an hour, at the end of which the kids began tugging David's sleeves.

"Come back in the water Uncle Davy!"

David looked at me.

"Do you mind?"

"No. I'll stay here. I'm breaking in this shirt no matter what."

Mark glanced at me with only mild disapproval.

David and the boys changed into fresh bathing suits and, carrying fresh towels, left for the lake. Marge surveyed the rest of us.

"How about more poker?"

"Are we playing for nuts again?" Tom said.

"Hold that thought," I said before anyone else had a chance to reply. "I'll be right back."

I ran up to the guest room, removed a small square gift-wrapped box from my bag, returned to the porch, and handed it to Marge. Brad had already begun shuffling the cards.

"What's this?"

"Open it. I was hoping to do this when David wasn't around. When he finds out I gave you something on top of the Merlot, I'll never hear the end of it."

Marge unwrapped the box, revealing an inexpensive set of poker chips in a wooden rack. Judging by their response, I advanced several steps nearer the end of my probation.

"I like it even better than the wine," Marge said.

"It'll last longer, anyway," Brad said.

We played for the next two hours. Despite providing the chips, I again had the worst luck at the table. The biggest loss occurred when I bet three jacks against Marge's full house.

"Starting Monday, I'm practicing an hour a day online," I said, unable to prevent the statement from sounding petulant.

"Maybe you should stick to croquet," Marge said, stacking her chips.

"What are the nurse's stories you couldn't tell us before?" Tom asked me.

"My husband has what used to be called a morbid curiosity," Delia said.

"These should pretty well satisfy it," I said and for the next four hands, I related Lena's tales concerning her first days on the job, featuring a defective colostomy bag, an amputated leg, and excesses of blood and vomit in varying circumstances. Unfortunately, lacking her gruff, matter-of-fact delivery, they lost much of their outrageous humor and sounded merely scatological.

"I see why you kept these from us at lunch," Delia said afterward. "My appetite may be gone for days."

"I'll coax it back, mom," Marge said, standing.

"What are we having?" Tom said.

"Chicken Marsala. If you hear any pounding, it's me flattening the chicken breasts."

Brad dealt. During the first round of betting, a series of dull, methodical thumps reached us from the kitchen, like someone attempting to hammer putty to a wall. Delia inherited Marge's winning streak, accumulating piles of chips over the next seven hands. A scent of chicken and mushrooms sautéing in Marsala drifted out to us, followed soon by Marge, who stood in the doorway and assayed the table.

"You're doing well, Mom," she said and looked at Brad. "Better reel in the lake monsters. They'll just have time to change for dinner."

Brad dropped his cards and stood with a small grunt combining resignation with disgust. "My hands have been as bad as Paul's anyway."

"And that's no mean feat," I said.

Brad strolled to the water and returned in time for the next hand. "It's getting overcast."

We looked out. The sun, nearing the western horizon, shone clearly, yet a bank of large clouds with grey underbellies loomed above the houses across the lake.

"Think it'll rain?" Tom said.

"It's not supposed to," Brad said, fanning out his cards, "but you can never tell around here."

Mark and Adrian, towels again draped over their shoulders, tramped through the porch and up the stairs. David entered, rubbing the side of his head with his towel.

"I think I'm growing scales." He glanced at the table and paused. "Where'd you get poker chips?"

"Paul gave them to us," Brad said, frowning over his hand.

David gaped at me. "Another hostess gift?"

I shrugged. "They needed poker chips."

He shook his head and started for the stairs. "Monday morning, I'm finding you a support group for compulsive gift-givers."

Tom won the hand before Marge reappeared.

"We'd better set the table," she said to Brad.

"Can I help?" I said.

"Sit tight," Brad said. "We've got it."

Tom gathered the cards. Delia and I sorted the chips, returned them to their rack, and she carried them to the living room. Mark and Adrian appeared, dried and dressed, and sat at the table. Brad laid placemats and silverware. David returned in time to fetch plates, after which Marge and Brad carted in four serving dishes, which apart from the chicken held wild rice, green beans almandine, and fruit salad.

"I hope this is to your liking, Paul," Marge said, sitting.

"It looks fantastic."

Brad sat between me and Marge. David sat opposite me, and we passed around the serving dishes.

During dinner, the clouds massed overhead, blotting out the sunset. A rain shower began, marked by leaves twitching on the surrounding flora and random pitting over the lake.

"Should we move inside?" I said warily regarding the screens separating us from the rain.

"We're safe if the wind doesn't pick up," Brad said.

The rain introduced a musty scent into the warm air. As daylight failed, Marge switched on the overhead lamp, casting a soft glow over the table and adding a twinkle to the Marsala sauce and fruit salad.

Marge turned to me after we finished. "I hope you left room for dessert."

"Wasn't the fruit salad dessert?"

She stood and collected the dirty plates. "Tonight it was a side, something tart to offset the Marsala."

Brad gathered the serving dishes.

"Can I help?" I asked again.

"We've got it," Marge said.

Brad and Marge left for the kitchen. Tom studied the dim, rainy view. "I wish it'd stop. I hate driving in the rain."

"As long as it clears by tomorrow," David said.

"Why?" Tom said. "It'll keep you from growing scales."

"If I wanted to stay indoors, I'd stay in town."

Brad returned with eight dessert plates and forks. As he laid the plates, the light on the porch began flickering, which I attributed to a dying bulb in the overhead lamp. Looking up, I found the bulbs glowing steadily. The next moment Marge lowered a large, round cake spiked with a circle of lit candles before me, and everyone sang "Happy Birthday." I gaped.

"Blow out the candles!" Mark prompted after the singing.

Adrian echoed his brother. "Yeah! Blow them out!"

I extinguished the candles with a single breath. receiving a clamor of approval from the kids. David watched, smug.

"How did you know?" I asked him.

"I looked at your driver's license."

"The oldest trick in the book," I said.

"Why didn't you tell me?"

"I didn't want to make a big deal out of it."

Marge handed me a long, serrated knife. "The birthday boy cuts the cake."

"Wait." I reached for my phone. "Would someone take a picture for my mom? She called this morning to say happy birthday and was worried I'd be alone."

Brad held out his hand. "I'll do it."

He stood back from the table, snapped the picture, and returned the phone to me. I forwarded the photo.

"You should ask her out here," Delia said. "We'd like to meet her."

"I have, but she's squeamish about flying. She needs a week or two to summon her resolve."

Marge watched me cut the first slice and slide it onto a plate. Satisfied with my skills, she returned to the kitchen to fetch a pot of coffee and six cups. I plated slices and handed them round as she poured and distributed the coffee. When Mark turned to hand a plate to David, I stopped him.

"Your uncle gets his last for being such a sneak," I said, unconsciously borrowing Marge's term.

Mark snickered, recognizing the bantering tone from croquet. Adrian smiled quietly.

"Hold on," I said, pausing with the knife halfway through the next slice. "Is that why you thought it was so funny this morning when I said he wanted to surprise me?"

Both nodded and laughed out loud. I turned to Marge.

"And that's why you wouldn't let me help clear the table."

"I was terrified you'd find the cake in the refrigerator."

"You're certainly a well-oiled machine when it comes to surprising people."

Mark and Adrian gloried in the deception, and we proceeded with the serious task of consuming the cake, two layers of chocolate fudge covered in vanilla frosting, with a half inch of cherry preserves in the center.

"Delicious," I said.

"Thanks," Marge said.

My phone beeped. I removed it from my pocket and summarized the massage.

"Mom's happy about the party. She's playing bingo. The cake impressed the people at her table."

"At least she knows you're not alone," Delia said.

"She's probably drinking a diet cola, daubing her bingo card, and wiping her eyes. She sent me this shirt and another I have upstairs. The other's salmon-colored."

"So that's why you brought them," David said.

"It suits you," Delia said.

"Can we get our presents now?" Adrian asked.

"Presents too?" I said.

"A few tokens," Marge said, "nothing much."

Mark flew to the dining room; Adrian strolled behind him. When they returned, each carried a flat, gift-wrapped box, the one in Mark's hands topped by a loose piece of paper, folded in half. They handed them over and stood by me, waiting.

"Mark and Adrian made the card," Brad said.

"Really?" I slipped the folded paper from the boxes, imagining my probation with them depended a great deal on the next few minutes. "Thank you."

The front had 'Happy Birthday Paul' written in large, uneven crayon letters, each a different color. Inside, eight stick figures and a dog stood on a green lawn with a blue lake in the background and a big yellow sun overhead. The stick figures boasted enough distinguishing marks to indicate the image had been inspired by my first visit.

"You did all this?" I said.

They nodded. Adrian began identifying the figures.

"This is grandma, that's grandpa . . ."

I joined in, my ready recognition increasing their pride in their accomplishment.

"Do you like it?" Mark said.

"It's great. I've got to send a picture to my mom." I grabbed my phone, snapped the front of the card, opened it, snapped the inside, and forwarded the photos. "Thank you both."

Mark indicated the box he had handed me. "Open this one."

The box felt quite light. Inside, beneath folds of tissue paper, lay a pale blue tee shirt fronted by a vintage advertisement for Suffolk's mixed nuts, featuring a very early version of Spiffy the squirrel hovering above their slogan: 'Suffolk's - The Spiffier Nuts.' I burst into laughter.

"You weren't the only one taken with our nutty poker game," Tom said.

"I love it."

"Do you think it'll fit?" Marge said.

I held the shirt against my chest. "It's perfect. Thank you."

"This one now," Adrian said.

The second box felt too heavy for clothing. David watched me unwrap it, his lips twitching with the effort to contain an irradiating self-satisfaction.

Inside, under yet more tissue paper, I found a stack of papers, edges worn by age, fixed together by brass brads, topped by a thicker, green page. Scribbles from a pen with blue ink marred the cover, between which I clearly read, stamped in thick black letters: "*Serve Me the Honorable Marmoset*–a play by Calvin Marquis." I looked at David. A satisfied smirk illuminated his face.

"Where did you find this?" I said.

"Dad helped me. When I told him what you were looking for, he suggested I try the rare manuscript dealers."

Tom explained. "I knew that even if the play hadn't been published, if it'd been performed, there had to be copies for the actors and director. I figured one might've landed with a dealer. I've done business with quite a few over the years, so we were able to cast a wide net."

"And lo and behold," David said, "one in New York had it in a stack of scripts he got from a director who died ten years ago."

"You shouldn't have gone to the trouble," I said, bothered by the term rare manuscript, "or the expense."

"There wasn't much of either," David said. "I sent out a few emails, and the price was only a few bucks more than the shipping fee. It's such an obscure title the guy never thought he'd unload it."

"Still . . . thank you."

Tom looked at David. "You were right. He's bowled over."

Mark peered into the box, distinctly unimpressed by its contents. "What's that?"

"A book that a friend of mine told me about. Your uncle found it for me."

"Oh," he said as if wondering whether a book constituted an appropriate birthday gift.

"I know it doesn't seem like much, but I can't wait to read it."

"Do you like it better than the card?" Adrian said.

"Nothing's better than the card."

The pair grinned.

Chop, perhaps following their lead, placed his front paws on my thigh and lifted his head to sniff inside the box.

"I wonder what scents he's getting," Tom said.

"We probably wouldn't want to know," Brad said, his medical credentials lending heft to the dire implications of his reply.

"Hey," I said. "I'm bringing this home with me."

My phone beeped. I read the message to the kids. "My mom says it's the best birthday card she's ever seen."

"She doesn't know who's in it," Adrian said, his fastidious mind pinpointing the one flaw in her praise.

"Sure she does. She saw all of you in the first picture I sent. And it's such a good drawing. I'm sure it was easy for her to figure out who was who."

Adrian thought a moment and grinned, satisfied.

"Does anyone want more cake?" Marge said.

We pleaded satiety, and she carried it back to the kitchen. Brad collected the dirty plates and silverware and followed her. I placed my card in the box with the shirt, closed both boxes, and shifted them to the side table.

Tom swallowed the last of his coffee and turned to Delia. "We should think about getting home."

"So soon?" David said.

"We have a ninety-minute drive, and it's almost eight-thirty."

"I didn't realize it was that late," David said. He looked at Mark and Adrian. "As soon as you say bye to grandma and grandpa, get ready for bed, and we'll have a story."

They agreed, patently reluctant to let the evening end, even for the sacred ritual of story time with David.

Marge retuned as Tom and Delia stood. "You're leaving?"

"We have a ways to go, and I don't like driving in the rain."

We followed them to the door. Delia included me in her hugs and kisses. Tom shook my hand.

"Happy birthday again."

"Thanks . . . for everything."

When their car left the yard, David shooed the kids upstairs to wash and don their pajamas and choose a book, a feat accomplished in record time, according to their parents. They sat on the sofa in much the same positions they assumed on my first visit, and David began reading. Chop stretched out on the rug before them. Marge, Brad, and I returned to the porch, eerily hushed with only the rain pattering outside.

"You didn't have to go to all this trouble," I said.

"We weren't about to let your birthday pass unacknowledged," Brad said.

"I appreciate it, as does my mom. I really liked the cake."

"Thanks," Marge said.

"Is cooking difficult?"

"No, once you learn a few basic techniques."

Brad laughed. "I've found the few basic techniques utterly defeating."

"Why do you ask?" Marge said.

"I've been thinking about learning to cook, at least enough to make some simple meals rather than rely on take-out or pre-made stuff from the market."

"I'll show you some easy tricks tomorrow if you want."

"That'd be great. Thanks."

We stopped talking, looked at the lights across the blackened lake, and listened to the rain until David and the kids reappeared.

"Time for goodnights," David said.

I thanked Mark and Adrian again for my card. They coerced David into tucking them in, and after five minutes upstairs, he returned to the porch, a half glass of Merlot in his hand.

"How come you're not having any?" he asked Marge.

"The cake filled me up," she said.

"It's your fault for making it so rich."

"Fine," she said, "for your birthday, I'll have the bakery set aside a day-old angel cake."

We listened to the rain a minute more, sunk in a torpor I attributed to our morning's activities and the heavy dinner.

"How's the research coming, Paul?" Marge said.

"Yeah," Brad said, "any more on Frankie Flounder?"

"Kevin Kipper," David said.

"Harold Herring," Marge and I corrected in unison.

"I have an appointment Monday with a woman whose parents were friends with Jacobson. She says she has some material on him. Other than that, I've had to be content with piecing together the portrait of a man exiled by war, struggling to acclimate to an unfamiliar place. It's not a big stretch to see traces of that in the Harold books, issues of alienation and loneliness, of—"

"—of being a fish out of water?" David said.

"A phrase I solemnly swear will never appear anywhere in my monograph."

Brad and Marge laughed drowsily. A twinkle on the lake caught my eye. Above, a three-quarters moon shone through a rent in the clouds.

"It's stopped raining," I said.

Marge, Brad, and David glanced out. David tilted the wine glass to his lips.

"Should be another sunny day tomorrow," Marge said and yawned.

"Want to turn in?" Brad asked her.

"We may as well. The boys will be up early with these two here."

David and I followed them upstairs, tiptoeing to avoid waking Mark and Adrian. We whispered goodnights on the second-floor landing and separated into our rooms. Inside the guest room, I placed my presents on a chair near the bed, after which David caught me in his arms.

"Having a nice weekend?" he said.

I wondered if any thoughts of Corey compromised the desire he focused on me. I held to our agreed-upon affectation rather than ruin the moment.

"Why did you do all this?" I said.

"I have a reputation to maintain."

"What reputation?"

"For making the people around me happy."

He kissed me.

"I think I've made progress with your nephews," I said. "They didn't seem as eager to cast me adrift."

He laughed. "They were all about the party after we told them you didn't have any friends or family out here, and without us, you'd be alone on your birthday."

"Ah," I said, "emotional blackmail. I wondered . . ."

"Don't be so cynical. Kids take birthdays very seriously. And you did well by them, making a fuss over their card."

"It was sweet. And maybe it'll help efface my miserable first impression."

"Awkward, maybe," he said, "not miserable."

"It seemed miserable in light of our second date at Brewer's."

"What do you mean?"

"When you told me how after playing video games and reading to your nephews, it was good to have an adult conversation, and I said I probably needed a good play day to keep me from becoming too adult. After I came here, I was afraid it might be too late."

"Too late for what?"

"Robert told me that because being gay and being a father were pretty much mutually exclusive when he was young, he allowed that part of himself to atrophy. The first time I was here, I thought maybe the same thing happened to me without my intending or even noticing it. Then I wondered if I want to keep the Harold books alive because I'm trying to keep that part of me alive, the child who didn't have much of a childhood."

He smiled his crinkly smile. "I think that part's very much alive. You just keep it under wraps, like a lot of other things about you."

"I've been told."

"Whether you wanted it to or not, it showed during croquet and at the party. The kids both noticed."

"How do you know?"

"Just now, when I was reading to them, they said you were a lot more fun than last time. That's why I didn't want you to worry about meeting every-body then. You get very formal when you're unsure of yourself or others."

"Formality's how I handle strangers. It's what I do on interviews."

"You're not here to interview us. You're here to share part of our lives, and to do that, you have to hold yourself a little closer."

As if illustrating his point, he gradually held me closer during our dis-cussion until he spoke his final sentence with his lips against my neck.

"If I'm in the habit of keeping people at a distance, why'd you go out with me?"

"First, you were the cutest thing that'd sashayed into the Argonaut for a while."

"I never knew I sashayed."

"Just enough to catch the eye of an old sashay fancier like me. Second, by the time you finished telling me about *H&H*, your research and Robert, I was pretty sure a great guy lurked behind all that propriety."

During his explanation, he kissed a path up my neck and along my jaw line. When he reached my earlobe, I dragged him into the shower to muffle the sounds of our spending everything I had instructed him to save for later.

Afterward, yawning, clean and content, he slipped beneath the covers on his side of the bed. I picked the *Marmoset* script from its box and lay nearer the table by my side, which had a small lamp with a ceramic starfish base.

"You're going to read it now?" he said.

"A few pages. I hate not knowing what it's like."

He laughed and turned onto his side, away from the lamplight. I reached page thirty-three when he stirred and stumbled from the bed to the bathroom.

"I shouldn't have had that last glass of wine."

He returned, slid under the covers, and leaned his head against my shoulder.

"Is it as bad as Robert said?"

"Worse. I can't wait to tell him you found it."

"You should get some sleep. The kids will be up early."

"Yeah."

I closed the script, noting the name Peter Cohen on the inside front cover, placed it on the bedside table, doused the starfish lamp, and rolled into David's arms.

11.

B arbara Marcus, her son Mike, his wife Joyce, and their son Tim shared a raised ranch house in Lemon Grove, a quiet community forty-five minutes outside town. Mike had left for work and Tim for school when I arrived at nine on Monday morning. Joyce, tall and in her mid-forties, with violet-black hair, conducted me to a spare room that had been turned into a mini-apartment for Barbara.

Joyce knocked and said, "Your visitor's here, Mom."

Barbara opened the door. She looked near Delia's age but had wavier, greyer hair and a fuller figure. She wore grey slacks, a white blouse with a ruffle down the front, and three thin gold chains around her neck, their lower loops submerged in the ruffle. Behind her, I noted a compact living room with a sofa, two chairs, and a coffee table. A pair of plastic boxes with blue lids and milky bodies, each a few inches larger than the tubs in which busboys stack dishes, stood on the coffee table. Barbara extended her hand.

"Pleased to meet you, Mr. Heywood."

"Call me Paul. I appreciate you contacting me."

"I was surprised to hear anyone's interested in Erich Jacobson. Sit down."

Barbara and Joyce sat on the couch. I faced them in one of the chairs, reversing my usual position at Robert's.

"Before we begin," I said, reaching for my phone, "will you allow me to record our conversation?"

"Yes."

I turned on the voice recorder, laid the phone on one of the blue lids, and after she repeated her permission to record, said:

"Mrs. Marcus, you told me on the phone your parents knew Dr. Jacobson when he lived in Los Angeles, and you have letters and a diary that mention him."

"Yes."

"And I have your permission to examine them?"

She gestured toward the boxes. "Everything's there. I've copied it all. You can take the copies or the originals, whichever you prefer."

"You didn't have to take the trouble. I usually scan everything to my phone."

"As you can see, there's quite a bit of material. I thought it'd be easier for both of us."

"It will be for me, thanks. I'll take the copies. Can you tell me how your parents came to know Dr. Jacobson?"

"They met at a cocktail party before the war. Psychoanalysts were still unusual in those days. and being from another country as well as a published author involved in the movie industry, he had the exotic appeal that makes for desirable guests. At least, that's how my mother described him in her diary. He and my parents hit it off and were inseparable for a while."

"Did they have any contact after he returned to Denmark?"

"He corresponded with my mother. My father had passed away by then."

"I'm sorry."

"Thank you. May I ask you a question?"

"Absolutely," I said.

"I'm not quite clear what this research is for. Are you writing a biography of Dr. Jacobson?"

"Not exactly," I said. "'I'm preparing a monograph chronicling his years in Los Angeles, though it may serve as a resource for later biographers."

"Why are you interested in that particular period?"

"You told me over the phone that you're familiar with his Harold Herring books. Did you know that before he wrote them, he published three mystery novels?"

"Yes. They're why he came to California in the first place, according to what my mother wrote."

"There's never been a clear explanation for his decision to switch from detective novels to children's books. I believe studying his life here may provide clues."

"Have you found any . . . clues, I mean?"

"Not yet, but it's been interesting and informative nonetheless."

"Why?"

"He was an unusual man—involved in the film industry during its glory days and working at a controversial trade, as I'm sure you know psychoanalysis was then. That's why I asked if your parents had any contact with him after he went back home, in case he gave them any reasons for inventing Harold."

Barbara stared at her lap. Joyce placed a hand on her arm. "You don't have to do this, Mom," she said.

"No, it's better I talk about it. It can't matter now. Just as long as you, Mike, and Tim are okay with it."

"Whatever you decide is fine with us."

Barbara smiled at her and looked back at me, apparently summoning her courage. I waited, mystified.

"You've come to the right place for your information."

"What do you mean?"

"I'm Erich Jacobson's daughter."

The two waited while my brain stopped and restarted.

"But," I said, for want of anything better, "he never had any children, at least, no documented ones."

Barbara tapped the box nearest her. "All the necessary documentation is here."

I swallowed and said, "Can you summarize it . . . slowly?"

"It's quite simple. As I said, my parents met Dr. Jacobson before World War II. Erich and my father were too old to fight. Erich continued with his practice. My father quit his job to become a foreman in an airplane factory."

"What did he do before?"

"He was a mid-level executive at an accounting firm in L.A. called Stevens and Butler."

"How did your mother feel about the change?"

"She was all for it. The factory job filled a more pressing need, and the number of young men being inducted into the armed forces created a labor shortage at home so that even people in ordinary positions were earning higher salaries than before. The job paid less than Stevens and Butler, but it didn't impose any hardships, especially since my mother also had a war job in charge of supplies at Fowler Memorial Hospital."

"They were pretty busy."

"Like everyone in those days. Do you know what a 'swing shift' is?"

"Factories operated twenty-four hours a day to meet the military's demands," I said. "The overnight hours were called the swing shift."

"My father was assigned the swing shift, while my mother had regular hours. He slept while she worked; she slept while he worked. They only saw each other two hours or so a day."

"And she was lonely," I said.

"Evenings especially," Barbara said. "Erich started coming by for drinks and conversation after leaving his office. A few months later, they began an intermittent affair."

"Intermittent?"

"According to the diary, their physical encounters were few and far between. But they persisted until February of 1944 when my mother learned she was pregnant."

"Did Jacobson know he was the father?"

"Not then. My mother knew, of course. She debated telling him for a long time. Illegitimate children were a scandal in those days. Erich was also eager to return home after the war. She hated the idea of tying him down with a child as much as she resisted the idea of moving to Denmark. What finally determined her to keep it a secret was that a month after learning about her pregnancy, my father—or the man who raised me—was in a car accident that left him a paraplegic."

Barbara stopped.

"Do you want a drink, mom?" Joyce said.

"No. This is the first time I've told it all out loud. I never realized it'd be so draining."

"Take your time," I said.

"My father couldn't work at the plant any longer, and a friend of his who had a clothing company with a minor government contract offered him a job in the payroll department behind a desk. The department was on the ground floor; luckily, since back then, nobody thought to make buildings wheelchair accessible. The work paid well, but to him, it lacked the prestige of building planes. According to my mother, his only interest in life after that was being a father. She couldn't rob him of it."

"Of course."

"Please understand, my mother never stopped loving him. She was just lonely with him away nights."

PARTS OF ROBERT   259

"Such an arrangement would strain any marriage," I said. "What happened next?"

"I was born in October 1944. Erich stayed for a while after the war, helping his patients transfer to other analysts. He left in 1946. My parents and I were quite happy until my father died in 1951."

"How did he die?"

"Complications from the accident. A bone fragment entered his heart. After, my mother decided Erich deserved to know the truth. She wrote him explaining she wasn't after money or anything, but simply wanted him to know her daughter was his."

"What did he reply?"

"The letter's there, the first of four they exchanged about it. He was overjoyed to find he had a child and heartbroken over my father's death. He agreed with her about concealing my paternity but regretted not being able to get to know me. Travel was a lot more difficult then, especially right after the war. He'd also married Ingrid and hoped to father his own children, but as you probably know, that never happened. So he and my mother decided to leave things as they were."

"Did they correspond after that?"

"My mother sent reports about me every now and then, and he responded. This went on until Erich died." Barbara sighed and folded her hands. "You're wondering why he switched to children's books. You'll understand when I tell you my middle name is Leonora."

An unprofessional croak preceded my response. "The lost Lenore."

Barbara nodded. "The summer of 1953, a package arrived containing the English translation of his first Harold book. The other three arrived upon publication over the next five years. A note accompanying the first explained that he wrote them to compensate for his inability to act as my real father." She swallowed hard and squeezed her hands until the knuckles whitened. "Basically, they're his love letters to me."

Barbara stopped again. I struggled to process the revelation and, at the same time, form follow-up questions.

"How long have you known?"

"Fifteen years. We found the diary and letters while cleaning out my mother's house after she died. I assume she kept them because she wanted me to know the truth but lacked the courage to tell me directly. I imagine she was too ashamed to discuss the affair yet too proud of my connection to the books to leave me in the dark. And by then, the books had gone out of print. I never expected anyone to show any interest."

"I'm floored," I said.

"My only question is: what will you do with the information now that you have it?"

"Well, it confirms my suspicions about his L.A. years. As such, it'll be central to my monograph. I realize it must be different for you."

Barbara pressed her palms atop her thighs. "I came to terms with it a while ago. I ask because I'm concerned about exposing my mother to judgments from people who aren't interested in literary history."

"I'll relate the story as straightforwardly as you have and only in connection with Jacobson's motives for writing the Harold books. I can't promise someone else won't be interested in exploiting it afterward. It's the sort of tale popular culture thrives on. The important thing, from my perspective, is that it tells us why the Harold books exist. You should also consider donating your mother's papers to a reputable archive. They'll be of tremendous value to any scholars who follow me."

"I'd wondered if a school or library might want them."

"I've spent lots of time in the university archives here. I could tell them what you have and let you know. It's important they're properly preserved. And if you're okay with it, I'll include a prominent acknowledgment in my monograph."

"I'd like that. I still find it hard to believe anyone's interested in this."

"Everyone who loves the Harold books will be, which includes me. They were an important part of my childhood."

"I suppose what they mean to others outweighs the circumstances under which they were written," she said.

"I think so. I think most people will think so, too. But I've taken enough of your time. Unless there's something else, I'd like to begin studying this material."

Joyce, Barbara, and I stood. Barbara indicated the box on which my phone lay.

"These are the copies. I've arranged everything in order by date."

I shut the voice recorder, tucked the phone in my pocket, and lifted the box.

"You've gone above and beyond in every way," I said.

"You as well. You've been a lot kinder than I expected."

"You're the kind one, entrusting me with this. May I call you if I have any more questions?"

"Sure."

"You'll hear from me about the archives; and my monograph if and when it's published."

"I look forward to it."

Barbara and I shook hands. Joyce escorted me to the front door, offering her own gratitude for how the encounter played out. I walked into the afternoon heat, opened my car door, slid the box across the driver's seat to the passenger side, leaped behind the wheel, and sped back to town.

Traffic, increased by a minor accident involving a cement truck, prevented me from reaching the city until eleven-thirty. Despite my raging curiosity, rather than head home, I pulled into the nearest fast food place, ordered a salad and bottled water from the drive-through window, and settled in a shaded parking spot. I swallowed half the water and three bites of salad before phoning David.

"Hey there," he said in his flirtiest manner.

"Are you busy?"

"Just sorting orders. Margot's doing the rest."

"Can you come directly to my apartment tonight?"

The manner became flirtier. "Why so urgent? Did you have aphrodisiacs for lunch?"

"My lunch is a grisly little salad that's probably been decomposing in its plastic coffin since seven this morning. Something amazing happened."

"What?"

"It's too complicated to go into. I have a stack of papers to read. It'll probably take me until you arrive."

"Shall I bring dinner from the Banquet?"

"That'd be great."

"I'll be there around six-thirty, okay?"

"I can't wait," I said.

"Me either."

We hung up. I choked down the salad and drove home.

Once in my apartment, I flopped onto the sofa with the box and delved into its contents, beginning with the copy of Carol Quigley's diary, neatly encased in a brown school binder.

The elegant, flowing script with which Carol chronicled her moral and emotional crises from 1942 to 1952 survived the crude copying method Barbara or her children had employed. The entries began with accounts of her and her husband Jeff's lives up to and including their meeting Jacobson on August 20, 1938. The next four years, they formed a gregarious trio that attended parties, dined out, and shared trips along the California coast from Catalina to San Francisco, with longer journeys to places like the Grand Canyon and the newly emergent Las Vegas, their pleasure in one another's company shadowed only by the mounting conflict in Europe.

Carol, like most people, reacted with grim resignation to the U.S. entering the war in December 1941, a mood augmented by discontent after she and Jeff embarked on their war work in March 1942. The solitude and boredom resulting from their work schedules weighed on her, and she felt only gratitude for Jacobson's first visit on the night of May 6. Two months later, she admitted her physical attraction to him. Their first kiss, initiated by her on June 7, occasioned four long, soul-searching pages. Loneliness finally overcame guilt on July 22, and for the following nineteen months, she and Jacobson slept together approximately every two weeks, during which she described her bliss and shame with devastating, relentless precision.

Two ecstatic pages poured from her pen on February 29, 1944 when a doctor's appointment revealed her pregnancy, followed by inner turmoil after a quick calculation disclosed the baby's paternity. The turmoil mounted to despair after March 4, when a tire on Jeff's car blew, and his vehicle spun into a ditch, leaving him paralyzed. His doctors predicted a long, homebound recovery, motivating Carol and Erich to end their affair on March 20, the night before Jeff returned from the hospital. Six three-page entries, from March 13 to April 4, chronicled the thinking that led to her decision to conceal Barbara's paternity by lying about how far along the pregnancy was. Jacobson continued visiting them to avoid suspicion should he unaccountably disappear from his friends' lives, particularly after such a traumatic accident. Carol's references to him diminished to a few obligatory mentions until he left for Denmark in 1946, whereupon he disappeared entirely from the diary.

He reappeared after Jeff's death on September 12, 1951, when for two weeks, Carol anguished over whether or not to inform him about Barbara. She summarized the letter she wrote him on January 7, 1952, and the one he wrote back, in which he thanked her for revealing the truth and agreed on the wisdom of preserving the secret. She never referenced the subject again, except for brief comments when each of the Harold books arrived for Barbara, which Carol termed 'nice little gifts,' as if acknowledging tokens from a distant uncle rather than highly original remembrances from her child's biological father.

I closed the diary and started on the letters. Carol preserved only those Jacobson wrote her, leaving me to guess by implication what hers contained.

The first expressed his astonishment and happiness about Barbara, assured Carol she had acted in everyone's best interests by concealing the truth and agreed to maintain the pose, at the same time begging for regular news of them and requesting her to contact him if they needed anything. The remaining letters replied to Carol's reports about Barbara starting school, her minor illnesses, first dates, graduating college, and marrying. They ended with his reaction to Barbara's pregnancy, dated April 24, 1981, less than two months before he died on June 10. The stash also included the four notes he enclosed with the Harold books, the first confirming Barbara's claim about his motives for writing them.

A brisk double knock roused me from my absorption in Carol's life. I glanced at the clock, which to my surprise, read quarter to seven. I sprang to the door and opened it.

David stood on the threshold. A plastic bag dangled from his fingers, wafting an aroma of Tandoori chicken around him like smoke from a church censer. He kissed me and headed for my tiny dining table.

"I'm sorry I'm late. There was a high demand for take-out tonight."

The instant the bag hit the table, I flung my arms around his waist and swung him around nine or ten times, laughing triumphantly. He stared down at me, indulgent and wondering.

"Are you still excited about what happened today, or should I call 911?"

I returned his feet to the floor and gripped his arms. "This is beyond my wildest dreams."

"I have an awful feeling you aren't referring to me or the food. What's up?"

I pointed to the pages littering my couch. "Those."

"The papers you told me about?"

"Oh, David, not papers. They're everything I've hoped for and more."

"Tell me while we eat. I'm starving."

We settled at the table, and apart from a few questions about Barbara and Carol, he chewed and listened while I rambled.

"I have the whole story, including the secret of the lost Lenore."

"Marge will be happy to hear that. In fact, the whole thing would make a great movie."

"That's what Barbara's afraid of."

"Why?"

"She doesn't want her mother exploited. I promised I'd focus on Jacobson's work, which is what I intended, anyway." I ate some rice. "It's strange. Conventional wisdom held that Jacobson wrote the Harold books to compensate for not being a father. I started out thinking it was something else, only to discover the conventional wisdom was basically correct. The only difference is he actually was a father."

"Maybe that could be your approach, how people were both close to yet still far from the truth."

"Possibly," I said.

"So, do I get the juicy details now, or will I have to wait for your monograph?"

I leaned back, squinting at him. "You know, your mom was right. You're a gossip. You'd have gotten along great with Gil Waterman."

He blushed. "Shut up."

Following dinner, I cleared a space for him on the couch and walked him through Carol's diary and letters.

"What's even more amazing," I said, "is a lot of what Carol mentions shows up in the Harold books."

"You never told me Harold had an affair with a married herring. I'll have to read that one."

"Not the affair, muckraker," I said. "Harold's best friends are two star-fish: Cora and Jake. They're always moving from place to place on the ocean floor, and whenever Harold has a difficult problem, he goes to discuss it with them. These visits resemble the trips Carol and Jeff took with Jacobson, at least those described in Carol's diary. There's a part in *Herring Overboard* where he finds Cora and Jake offshore at an unnamed port city. It's clearly the memory of a trip Jacobson and the Quigleys took to San Diego."

David lowered his head, not far enough to conceal a silent laugh. "So Carol and Jeff Quigley became Cora and Jake Starfish?"

I ignored his bemusement. "Jacobson doesn't admit it anywhere that I know of, but the parallels are clear. There may be others I haven't noticed yet. I'll have to reread the Harold books while it's all fresh in my mind."

He looked at me again, his urge to laugh under control. "I'll bet the analyst never dreamed he'd be so thoroughly analyzed."

"Probably not, but I think he'd appreciate the effort."

I reassembled the papers and returned them to the box. He watched, still smiling.

"What?" I said, prepared to dispute further ridicule.

"Enthusiasm suits you," he said, "even more than your birthday shirts."

Thereafter, we set aside Carol Quigley's affair to advance ours.

12.

The next day, Tuesday, apart from fixing a bagel and two mugs of dark roast at eight, and a grilled cheese sandwich at one-thirty, I spent all my time in my apartment cross-referencing Carol's and Harold's particulars. Soon I found that, perhaps typically for a Freudian, more and more of the people, places, and events central to Jacobson's L.A. life had been transposed or conflated into the characters, settings, and episodes of Harold's universe.

Professor Harding, dean of Harold's herring school, with his comic yet benevolent pedantry, fit Carol's description of Dr. Peter Cork, the analyst Jacobson partnered with after leaving Paramount. Oliver Castle, who had nursed along the adaptation of Jacobson's final mystery for two years, found his counterpart in Casper Oyster, an enthusiastic, ultimately ineffectual shellfish whose endless supply of failed schemes frequently inspired Harold to more practical action. Inveterate gossip Gil Waterman became Ivor Waterspout, a whale whose constant chatter about characters not present rivaled Casper's scheming and, like those schemes, often supplied Harold with information crucial for solving a pressing problem. Anxiety-ridden Mona Jackson had a key role in *Herring Overboard* as Julie Jellyfish, a chronic worrier whose fears irked the other ocean dwellers but which, in the end, alerted Harold to a faulty motor that enabled him to rescue a crowded luxury liner. Ingrid Jacobson's illustrations, undoubtedly at her husband's urging, similarly drew on Southern California's geography: the Coral Tower, a structure central to the section of sea Harold and his friends inhabit, resembles the Los Angeles City Hall, while the underwater ravine into which Cindy Sardine's daughter wanders follows the general outline of the San Andreas Fault. Finally, the references to Southern California's beaches in Jacobson's published letters suggested his passion for the Pacific shoreline accounted for his choice of characters and setting, even more so since he addressed the Harold books to a daughter growing up in the area.

The search for connections stopped at seven-thirty when David showed up with dinner, during which I monopolized the conversation with my findings.

The search resumed Wednesday morning, even before I finished my dark roast. Vintage 1940's maps of L.A., its environs, and of places Jacobson had traveled to with the Quigleys, joined Carol's papers, the volume of Jacobson's published letters, the Harold books, and those of my research materials that mentioned Jacobson's movements—which like the maps I printed out for easier reference—covered my sofa, dining table, computer desk and most of the floor. Except for a can of tomato soup at two, the day escaped me while I compared the topography in the Harold books with environments linked to Jacobson, my exultation increasing with each new parallel I identified.

The day's yield had climbed to twenty when, at nine-thirty that night, I received a text from David.

Can you come over? I need to see you.

I had forgotten about the dinner with Corey. I wrote back: *Be right there.*

I drove to his apartment, uneasily adjusting to the heat, traffic, and piercing lights. Forty-eight hours straddling Jacobson's and Harold's worlds had left the one I inhabited overwhelmingly drab, even dispiriting.

David opened his door without a word and wandered to the window, which admitted the only light in the room. He stood very still, body language unreadable. The little light from the panes landed on an impassive face. I closed the door and watched him for a moment before speaking.

"How'd it go?"

He walked to the sofa and sat down as if unable to remain upright. I turned on the lights. He tilted his head until it rested on the back of the sofa and looked at me, his eyes weighted with unshed tears. I sat beside him, close enough to observe yet far enough not to crowd him.

"The minute I saw him, I knew it'd be awful," he said, his voice, like his eyes, conspicuously dry.

"Why?"

"You know he's seven years older than me, and we only broke up three years ago."

"Yes."

"He looks twenty years older now."

"Really?"

He nodded loosely, like a marionette.

"Pale, gaunt," he said and exhaled. "It was like sitting down with Dorian Gray's portrait."

"Why'd he want to see you?"

"To make amends."

"Then he's been through rehab."

"He claims he hasn't used porn or alcohol for a year. He said he knew what he'd put me through, that he knew while it was happening, but he didn't care. Then he said that of all the people he had to make amends to, I'm the one whose forgiveness meant the most to him."

"You think he meant it?"

He nodded again, with more assurance. "Yes. When you got to know him, you could tell when he was lying. That's why it was easy for me to figure out about the porn. He's incapable of a plausible cover story."

"Did you forgive him?"

"Of course," he said, surprised I doubted it. "What he's gone through cost him a lot more than it did me, more than he'd probably admit."

"Why do you say that?"

"The way he looked, how he carried himself. I told you he sounded chastened on the phone. In person, he was almost broken."

"Is he still an investment counselor?"

"He said he was. I'm glad he hung onto that, at least. He really liked his work."

"And all he wanted was forgiveness?"

David looked at the coffee table. "He asked if I was seeing anyone. He said it like we were old friends catching up, but I knew he was fishing."

"What did you tell him?"

"That I was. He asked if it was serious. I said I didn't know, but I wanted to find out. Actually, I said I was looking forward to finding out. His jaw clenched a little then. He asked about the store and said he was glad I was doing well."

"How did you leave things?"

"I told him no matter what, he and I'd always be exes. He promised he wouldn't contact me again." He drew his knees up almost to the fetal position, leaned toward me, and rested his head on my shoulder. "I just wish I knew if I did the right thing."

I reached my arm around him. "What makes you think you didn't?"

"It seemed like he was looking for some kind of happiness to carry him through, to keep him going. What if what we had was the only thing he could think of, the only real thing around for him to reach for?"

"You can't be responsible for his recovery. If he's gone through the process, he knows that, too."

"The problem was he needed to be in control. Then he ended up being controlled by his addictions. Apart from that, he could be a lot of fun and really sweet."

"I wouldn't expect you to be attracted to a total train wreck."

"The good qualities were there tonight. I'd hate it if he lost them again."

Robert's comment about abusive dynamics became clearer to me.

"Unless you're willing to hold his hand the rest of his life, the best you can do is wish him well."

"I know. I did wish him well when I left. He still looked like he wanted more."

I inhaled and asked, "Would it have been different if I weren't around?"

He pivoted his head "no" against my shoulder.

"Hopefully," he said, "he learned to control his temper in rehab. But I won't be the one to test him." He sat up, hair again adorably spiked. "The thing is, I was so angry with how he treated me at the breakup I took off instead of standing up to him. On my way there tonight, I realized I'd been angry for the last three years." He closed his eyes and sighed. "When I saw him, I knew he got whatever he deserved, probably more."

"And the anger dissipated."

"Yes," he said, the recent sigh ushering a convincing tranquility into his voice. "If he needed to see me to ask my forgiveness, I needed to see him to exorcise the anger."

"That's why you had to go."

"If we rely on twenty-twenty hindsight."

"The important thing is you've finished your unfinished business." I smoothed his hair. "I can't believe I forgot about tonight when you were at my place yesterday. All I did was jabber on about Jacobson. You must think I'm . . ."

"No. I wasn't going to load you down with my baggage when you were so cute and excited. And at that moment, all I wanted was to be excited with you."

"I never felt better about being inconsiderate."

He smiled. "You know, you're the only one I can talk to about tonight. None of my friends know how bad it got between him and me."

"Why didn't you tell them?"

"Shame," he said as if ashamed of being ashamed.

"Or fear you might actually be the things he called you?"

"Maybe," he said, the equivocation as usual serving as a de facto admission. "Of course, my parents would think I'm an idiot for meeting him again, even without knowing the rest."

"I also don't go out with anyone unworthy of me, meaning whores and idiots and everything in between."

"Did you really think I'd go back to him if I hadn't gotten mixed up with you?"

Our playfulness bobbed to the surface in the lightly sarcastic phrase "mixed up," to my relief.

"I hoped not," I said, "but I had to be sure."

"I may be easygoing, but I'm not a glutton for punishment."

"No, but you're used to making the people around you happy, and I think you're bothered when it doesn't happen. That's probably why you couldn't discuss it with anyone else. You hated admitting failure more than you worried about being what he called you. You'll just have to accept your princely charms aren't infallible."

"Is that what Harold Herring would say?"

"And drive the lesson home with a sound tail slap."

"Good thing your tail isn't that flexible."

"Only because I've spent most of my time lately sitting behind a desk," I said.

"You're not only the one person I can talk to about this," he said, "you're the one person I can imagine making me laugh about it. Thanks for not turning it into more of an issue than it needed to be."

"I may not make everyone around me happy, but I have my moments."

Looking at him, I felt I had regained, if not all, then the better part of his attention. I also noticed his exhaustion.

"You should get some sleep," I said. "Will I see you tomorrow?"

"If you can walk away from the Quigley papers."

"I'd better if I don't want to lose touch with the outside world entirely."
I kissed him and stood to leave.

"Paul?"

"Yes?"

"Do me a favor. Don't call him cretin again. I let my dad do it because
he's my dad, and there's no stopping him. But between us . . ."

"If he must be mentioned, he'll be plain old Corey."

"Thanks."

Thinking of David and Corey at dinner reminded me I had eaten nothing
since my soup at two. I stopped for a vegan burger and salad at a small fast-
food place on my way home. Its nearly deserted interior offered a comfortable
place to eat and mull over what had just happened. I concluded that David's
sympathy for Corey had been the only reaction to expect from someone with
the capacity for love I first intuited in him, yet involving only as much compassion as required. I arrived home at eleven and by eleven-fifteen had dropped
into a blessed, dreamless sleep that lasted until seven-thirty the next morning.

Following a cool shower, a pot of dark roast, and a bowl of bran flakes
with milk that had recently turned sour, I resumed hunting for links between
Jacobson's life and books, my late meeting with David on the periphery of
my otherwise narrowly focused thoughts.

Robert forwarded me his grocery list and medication pickup at noon.
I wolfed down a chicken salad sandwich and a bag of cheddar corn chips,
within the disordered paper nest on my sofa, and left for the pharmacy, the
market, and the Roxbury Apartments.

Robert opened his door, greeting me with a brisk "Happy Thursday,
Paul," and stood aside.

"Hi." I passed by him and between the trellises. "I've got what you
wanted."

"I know. Unfortunately, I'm too old to use it."

He closed the door, followed me to the kitchen, and eased onto a chair
at the table while I opened the first bag.

"Your Bub's were on sale—twenty little tubs for ten bucks."

"Splendid. And at my age, twenty is the maximum commitment I dare
to make." He watched me place his Hearth Fire in the breadbox and dried
papaya on the counter. "You're conspicuously buoyant again. Anything you
can discuss with an old codger?"

"I've found what I was looking for," I said, slipped his Velma's onto their
shelf, and recounted my interview with Barbara.

"So," he said after I finished, "rather than a dry academic study, you have the scandalous tale of an illicit wartime affair."

"Essentially. But as I promised Barbara, I'll ignore the scandal to focus on how it impacted and enriched his writing."

"Strange," he said, watching a box of Field Treasure wheat squares assume their place beside the Velma's, "scratch the surface of any life, and you find elements of soap opera. I suppose that's why art has devolved into what it is today: a bunch of jaded exhibitionists exposing their bodies and personal lives to crowds of jaded voyeurs."

I began arranging his seven Gunter's shakes beside the Field Treasure. "Don't novels and plays expose the personal lives of their characters?"

"Yes, though some do take a different tack. The best use characters to illuminate the variety of human experiences for an audience sophisticated enough to understand the value of pondering those experiences."

"What's the difference between sophisticated and jaded?"

"Sophisticated means appreciating everything the world has to offer. Jaded means no longer being able to appreciate much of anything. The saddest cases lack the capacity for appreciation in the first place."

"The Oscar Wilde influence grows clearer each time we talk."

"I considered that a compliment in my youth, and I consider it a compliment in my decrepitude. Let me have those, please."

I handed him a cardboard canister of Vineyard Pride raisins that had just emerged from the bag. He tore the outer plastic band from around the lid, removed the plastic seal beneath the lid, and began snacking, his gluttonous pleasure comparable to Lena Crenshaw attacking her espresso beans. I stacked eight Cal's Cardio soups in their cupboard, set his Shale House ginger ale on the counter, folded the empty bag, and doubled back to his first comment.

"Luis Bunuel said in his memoir that dying was like leaving in the middle of a serial. Perhaps the human condition is just one big soap opera."

"Only because humans seem incapable of making anything better of it," he said. "But I won't downplay your achievement. You've managed to uncover your pet writer's hidden secret."

"His only one, I hope." I transferred his produce from the second bag to the crisper.

"I hope so, too, for your sake. What did you mean by it enriching his writing?"

"Carol's papers also revealed how much of the Harold books drew on his life in L.A.," I said and described my prized parallels.

"Your work will be complex as well as scandalous. But if it enhances the enjoyment of his writing for others, I suppose it's worth the taint of melodrama."

"I agree."

A five-pound package of ground turkey entered the fridge.

"How did David's dinner with the cretin go?"

"You remembered," I said.

"Why shouldn't I?"

"I didn't until it was over."

"You've more to occupy your mind than me, lucky boy. What happened?"

I summarized the previous evening's conversation while crowding the top shelf of the refrigerator with his twenty Bub's Tubs.

"And you're satisfied that David's through with him?"

"Yes."

"I'd keep watch for while, just in case. A savior complex can be difficult to shake off."

"Sympathy doesn't automatically translate into a savior complex. I'm pretty sure he saw the dinner as a favor. Corey wanted absolution. David gave it to him, not that there was any reason for him to withhold it."

"And now that he's done his duty, everything will go back to normal."

"I think so. Things weren't very different before the dinner. You should've seen him at his sister's place.'

"When were you there?"

"This past weekend. It was in the works before he made the plan with Corey. He made me promise not to let on to his family about it. After last night I'm sure he'll be his usual self again."

"Or else he's one of the greatest actors not attending auditions."

I paused with a bottle of Chef's Special raspberry vinaigrette in my hand.

"Paul," he said, nipping my reply in the bud with a smoothness and swiftness that probably helped him upstage many of his fellow actors, "I don't say this lightly, and I say it only because I'm fond of you. Don't rush into anything unless you're sure."

"I won't. And I'm not that fragile, either."

"We all become fragile when we fall in love."

I set the Chef's Special beside the Bub's tubs, chagrined at his doubting David and, by association, my judgment. I also nearly laughed imagining David's reaction if I told him Robert recommended I place him on probation.

"How'd the weekend go otherwise?" Robert said, wisely changing the subject. "Does his family still adore you?"

"More than ever, I'd say. They gave me a surprise birthday party."

This news, at least, mellowed him.

"Happy belated birthday. When was it?"

"Saturday. My mom sent me two shirts." I tugged my salmon pink collar. "This is one."

"Very becoming."

"David's family gave me a tee shirt with an old ad for Suffolk's nuts on the front."

"In honor of the poker game," he said.

"David's gift was fun, too."

"What was it?"

"A copy of *Serve Me the Honorable Marmoset*," I said.

His eyes widened. "You're kidding. I didn't know it'd ever been published."

"It wasn't. He got it from a rare manuscript dealer in New York who had it in a collection of scripts." I placed his Shell Stream and Tropic Morn on the bottom shelf beside a clear glass baking dish, covered in foil, containing two leftover baked chicken cutlets.

"Have you read it?" he said.

"Yes. You were right. It's terrible."

"Do you know whose collection it came from?"

I closed the refrigerator and turned back to the counter. "The name Peter Cohen is written on the inside cover."

"Peter Cohen," he said, inhaling as if filtering memories from the air, "a sturdy twenty-two-year-old with a rugged face prettified by two thumbprint dimples. I'm generally attracted to slenderer builds, but he was the first in the company I imagined sleeping with. This was before I noticed Scotty."

"Did you? Sleep with him, I mean?"

"No. Peter was straight."

I folded the empty bag and sat opposite him. "How was he as an actor?"

"Moderately talented. He was among the most committed to the play. Remember the milkman in act two, who climbs in and out a window about nine times?"

"Yes."

"Peter played him. He had the white uniform milkmen wore then and the wire basket they used for carrying bottles. He was quite dashing in the uniform. If he'd been playing a romantic lead, he'd have been a sensation. The milkman was a comic variation on a Greek chorus, as you probably noticed. Peter had to climb through a window, deliver meaningless comments on the meaningless action and climb out again."

"And he couldn't do it?"

"The problem wasn't whether he could do it, but how he did it. Despite looking like an Olympic athlete, he was one of the worst klutzes ever born. Scotty had devised a simple, abstract window from a few wooden crates. Peter hit at least two with an elbow or knee at every performance. Then, he'd stagger across the stage, struggling to regain his balance while the milk bottles rattled like bells on a runaway sleigh."

"He should've switched parts."

"The director didn't ask him to. He felt Peter's clumsiness added to the character, which pleased Peter to no end. Afterward, I was never sure whether his stumbling was intentional or not. Three days after the opening, on his final exit, he tripped and landed sprawling on the floor. The bottles broke, gashing his arm, and his knee swelled up like a blowfish. He crawled off, and somebody bound his wounds with bandages from a first aid kit that looked as if it'd been languishing backstage since the death of vaudeville. He probably should've gotten the arm stitched."

"Why didn't he?"

"He had the third act to do. We were a small company with no understudies. The milkman from act two morphed into a ballerina in the third if you remember. The lines depended on her assuming the accurate positions. Peter limped across the stage, wincing with every entrechat, which detracted considerably from the intended effect."

"What was the audience's reaction?"

"Hysteria. Everyone else assumed they were laughing with the play rather than at it. I, on the other hand, was well aware of what it meant."

"Apparently, he continued acting, if he left behind a collection of scripts."

"He switched to directing after his next two plays, a smart move not only because directing required less dexterity. He was a far more able director. He had a string of hits through the 1980s. Still, whenever I ran into him or heard his name, I recalled the slapstick milkman from *Marmoset*."

"I could bring the script next time I come if you'd like."

He flinched. "I wouldn't. It'd remind me too much of those first days with Scotty."

"And Scotty being the reason for your aversion to mementos . . ."

"What makes you say that?"

"You broke up because he couldn't let go of his sister. The things he brought home from her apartment symbolized that, so . . ."

"You'll have to be more careful with your assumptions when you analyze Jacobson's influences."

"What else is there?"

"I've described two of the three times I fell in love. My attitudes to the past, my past, are bound up with the third."

"Do you feel like going into it?"

"Why not? I owe you the final third of my triumvirate anyway."

I prepared our usual refreshments and followed him into the living room.

"The eighteen months after I left Scotty and came here were miserable. I was in an unfamiliar if beautiful environment, but still too used to seeing the world with him to appreciate it. Without his perspective, mine was diminished."

"As his was after Sandy died."

"Exactly. The beaches, deserts, exotic plants, and new people felt less real, or at least less than they would've been with him. My apartment was worse. The books, clothes, and photos I'd brought with me smelled like our apartment, our colognes, and the New York atmosphere. To avoid it, I'd drive around around, gazing halfheartedly at the scenery, exploring the tourist traps, and parking at the beach to watch the waves and the beach boys. When that became untenable, I'd return to my apartment and try to read or curl up in bed and try to sleep."

"How'd you cope?"

"I dove into work. Following *Balancers*, Nathan Grant gave me a supporting role in an independent film, *Riverbank Rundown*, about rural bootleggers in the 1920s, during prohibition. It was one of many *Bonnie and Clyde* clones made at the time. I also instructed my agent to book me for every available commercial. Once, I was a farmer obsessed with growing the perfect peas for Arctic Wonder frozen foods."

"I found that one online. The dialogue was inane."

"Now you know why I insist on Ice Floe vegetables. They were Arctic Wonder's main rival, and I still want Arctic Wonder to suffer. After *Balancers* aired, I had more TV offers, mainly small roles in dramas and sitcoms. I played cops, lawyers, doctors, executives, next-door neighbors, salesmen, and family friends. Sitcoms were the easiest. The bit players usually walked in, delivered a gag, and left. Directors loved you if you could do it without any mistakes to slow production."

"Another benefit of your theatrical training."

"And if it happened to be a successful show, there were residuals if the reruns went into syndication. I also had fun driving viewers crazy. After showing up in so many shows, people began recognizing me, but they were never sure why."

"How come?"

"This was before shows were launched into perpetuity on completion. They appeared onscreen at their appointed time and disappeared. You couldn't go through them with a fine-toothed comb the way people do now. My appearances were always brief, and I hopped from series to series. I was never associated with one title the way the leads and supporting players are. People would approach me and say, 'I know you from somewhere' and guess everything from their cousin Audrey's wedding to a police flyer. Sometimes they'd say, 'Aren't you the guy from that show?' but they could never remember which one they associated me with. Perplexing the vidiots was an unexpected yet welcome fringe benefit."

"What about the movies?"

"Sometimes I scored a hefty supporting part, but never in an important film, and for me, the TV things were never important. I earned a nice living, but the nature of the work haunted me as much as losing Scotty."

"Why?"

"It was meaningless," Robert said. "The scripts were almost always exactly alike. The sitcoms were either family comedies, workplace comedies, or a combination of the two. You walked into a living room and told jokes about family life or into a workplace and told jokes about the featured profession. The dramas usually revolved around angry cops hunting criminals, angry lawyers seeking justice, or angry doctors fighting to save a patient, things that rarely, if ever, occur in reality. I began my career believing art should comment on the human condition and ended up helping popular culture draw a soothing curtain of fantasy over it. After failing in my love for Scotty, I was failing in my purpose as an actor."

"Maybe you were too hard on yourself."

"Maybe. I'd also passed forty, which I think played into it."

"You were suffering a mid-life crisis?"

"I suppose. I had enough past to taunt me with the good and bad I'd done and enough future for me to believe I might change, to do or be what

I'd always wanted but hadn't been as yet. I wasted whole afternoons sitting in my car, staring at the Pacific Ocean, thinking over what had happened with Scotty and my career, only to conclude all that'd come of it was me sitting alone in my car staring at the Pacific Ocean."

"Didn't you have a social life?"

"Oh, sure. Nathan introduced me to lots of industry people, and I met many in the old-guard Hollywood gay set, like George Cukor. There were parties, but they consisted mostly of small talk and schmoozing people for jobs. When I got too lonely, it was easy enough to pick somebody up. I was still reasonably attractive in my early forties. But that was only a physical release. Nothing promised to improve the future I anticipated."

He paused and laughed.

"I'm forgetting Howard Brock."

"I wouldn't want you to do that."

"I would. He was a shoe salesman in an upscale men's store, Petersen's. He had thin, arching eyebrows, bright blue eyes, and a cleft chin. I might've fallen for him if it hadn't been for one insufferable habit."

"What?"

"He sucked his teeth at meals."

"I've met people who do that. It's gross."

"Howard was the world's champion. He'd chew, suck and swallow from the first bite. Even after the meal, he'd go on sucking his teeth for what seemed like hours. We'd be reading the papers after breakfast or watching TV after dinner, and every so often, his lips would twitch as if he were about to smile, but instead, he'd make a sharp slurping sound that drove me up the wall and across the ceiling. The hours following a meal are usually relaxing, yet every time I saw his lips twitch, I had to dig my fingernails into my palm to keep from screaming. I timed him once. He sucked and slurped off and on for thirty minutes."

"You should've had some toothpicks around."

"I did. They only augmented the sequence to probe, suck, and slurp. I stuck it out for three months because, in other ways, he was great, but the more I heard of his teeth, the more I wanted to punch him in the mouth. One day I realized it was exactly the kind of thing Scotty and I would've laughed about after hearing somebody doing it at a party, so it was goodbye, Howard."

"What about acting? Didn't you tell me you intended to do theater out here and maybe go back to New York for roles?"

"I went back five times for leads in three short-lived off-Broadway shows, and minor parts in two major productions: a modern dress version of *Agamemnon* and a musical called *Stop Motion*. The work was great, but returning to the city proved harder than I expected. I'd be looking for a place to have dinner, thinking about rehearsals or a performance, and without warning, I'd be on a street or near a restaurant where Scotty and I often went. I'd run into acquaintances who'd ask me about L.A. and say they'd spotted me in a movie or on TV, but their manner indicated they now considered me an outsider. Some asked if I'd heard from Scotty. Others told me without my asking that he was the same as he'd been after Sandy's death, reclusive apart from his work. I hated admitting it, but despite my love for New York and its theater, returning seemed increasingly like a futile attempt to reconstruct the first half of my life rather than a viable way to build the second."

"What about theater out here?"

"It was sparser and less prestigious, but it was my only option, so I dove into it as I dove into TV and films. Actually, it wasn't my only option. I traveled with the road companies of *Fiddler on the Roof* and *Camelot*, but I found it too exhausting. It was better being based here, earning money in crappy mass-media productions, and doing whatever plays I could. That's when I met Jeremy Griffith."

"Your third love?"

He nodded. "We were cast in a production of *Long Day's Journey into Night* mounted by the California Crescent Theatre, a long-defunct group. I played the father, which at forty-three required some extra makeup. Jeremy played the elder son."

"How old was he?"

"Twenty-two."

"Goodness," I said, returning the maidenly shock with which he greeted the news of the tryst with my ex-professor.

"I know, from this vantage point, it's a clear case of a mid-life-crisis affair. But it was more at the time. Part of the blame rests with O'Neill."

"How can a dead author be culpable, even partly?"

"People who leave things behind after they die are always culpable for the effect they have on others. I loved O'Neill since high school. *Journey* was my favorite of his plays, not a particularly original preference, but there you are. I'd acted in two others in New York, but for the first time, I had a chance to play the lead in the work I respected the most. Even though it was for a small theater and few people would see it, I wanted to be able to say I'd done O'Neill justice at least once."

"Which was probably more important given how you felt about your other work."

"Making it also something of a mid-life-crisis affair," he said. "We had a good director, a young man named Vernon Dalrymple, but for some reason, he worried more about re-creating the Connecticut of O'Neill's youth, getting the details of costumes and setting right. I'd read the play many times, teasing out the characters' complexities and their relationships with each other until they were more like my family than the people I'd left behind in Braintree. I dreamt for years about applying my ideas to an actual production, and I wasn't about to miss what might be my only chance."

"How'd Dalrymple react?"

"I'm not sure he realized the extent to which I interfered. I had by then dealt with every imaginable type of director. I knew how to handle him. I also knew the play and O'Neill's life. I offered suggestions deferentially yet authoritatively, which the alchemy of his ego transformed into his inspirations. Others in the cast soon caught on, but since they liked how the play was shaping up, they allowed my deception to play out. That's how Jeremy and I connected. He was struggling with his role; only rather than approach Dalrymple, he asked my advice after rehearsals. He'd dropped out of college and hadn't been in many plays. *Journey* was his first attempt at a complex classic."

"Were you attracted to him from the beginning?"

"If you mean did I appreciate his appearance, absolutely. He was tall and gangly, with shiny black hair, a sharp, aquiline nose, and glistening dark eyes, like a young hawk. But I reacted against his age. He talked mostly about movies and TV shows, and I pegged him as a typical member of the audio-visual generation. When he questioned me me about his character and our scenes, I realized he genuinely wanted the play to work and was relieved to dispense my advice without the subterfuges I employed with Dalrymple. We'd meet for coffee after rehearsals, and he'd quiz me about gestures and inflections and O'Neill's occasionally arcane language. Sometimes we analyzed the scenes line by line. The whole time he watched me with those hawk eyes, hanging on every word."

"And you liked the attention."

He slumped back in the recliner. "Oh, Paul, it was more than attention. I'd been drifting from one idiotic role to another, believing everything I'd done, the experience I'd accumulated, all my reading and thinking about theater, had been meaningless. Here was a young man craving the knowledge I struggled so long to acquire. If I'd failed to make the best use of it, it might serve him better. We formed a bond during rehearsals, but at that point, I considered him nothing more than a protégé. Protégé was often a euphemism in an era that relied on euphemisms, but it was sincerely how I saw him."

"What happened with the play?"

"Those who saw it liked it. The few critics that reviewed us singled me out for special praise. But I didn't need it. I knew I'd done the best job of my life. Millions witnessed my mediocre moneymaking appearances on film and TV while only a couple of hundred at best saw my finest work, yet even that failed to diminish the sense of achievement. For the three months we performed *Journey,* I believed, for one of only a handful of times, that I'd actually fulfilled my potential."

"How'd Jeremy do?"

"Better than any mentor had a right to expect. Our scenes had an intensity I attributed to our private collaboration, while his positive mentions in the reviews not only validated his ability and my instruction but were important items for his slim resume. We kept meeting for coffee after each performance to complain about sluggish audiences or identify shaky line readings. He never stopped thanking me for my assistance. I thought if he only knew how much it meant to me."

"When did you realize you were falling for him?"

He sipped his tea. "After the run ended, he entered the Crescent's next production, *Once in a Lifetime* by Kaufman and Hart. He played George, one of the three leads."

"You weren't in it?"

"I had several commercials and some sitcom bits booked. The recycled humor of the sitcoms was a letdown after *Journey*, but while I expected that, I didn't expect to miss my talks with Jeremy. I wondered how he was doing. I assumed that Kaufman and Hart, being light comedy writers, presented fewer difficulties for him. One night, after I got home from filming an episode of *Brandywine and Cuddles* . . ."

"What the hell's that?"

"You never disinterred *Brandywine* from your graveyard of bad television? It was the worst sitcom ever produced. It lasted four weeks. And if you're wondering whether my appearance helped kill it, I'll only be too glad to take the credit."

"I don't make unsubstantiated accusations."

"Meaning you'll review the online evidence later?"

"As soon as I clear up the Quigley case. What happened when you got back from filming?"

"I put on some music, brewed some coffee, and was recuperating from the idiocies I'd uttered when my doorbell rang. Jeremy was there, a script in his hands and a strained expression on his face. His first words were to beg me for help. He was having serious trouble with their director."

"Dalrymple?"

"No, he'd moved on to another production in San Francisco. Jeremy was at a loss about how to play George. The new guy merely pointed out Jeremy's errors in ways that, rather than help, only made Jeremy feel inept. He began to cry, telling me about it. I poured him a cup of coffee, calmed him down, and promised to work with him. The problem was obvious to me."

"What was it?"

"The play describes George as naive and guileless. This also described Jeremy, to a degree. Actors, in my experience, often have the most trouble with characters nearest their own."

"Why do you think that is?"

"It's easier being objective about other people and their traits, which means it's easier to mimic them in performance."

"How'd you help him?"

"A simple application of reverse psychology, or a tactic close to it," he said. "I told him he was having trouble because he was an intelligent young man trying to play his direct opposite. This made him think about George as a separate persona to study. We read over the play, and I told him how I saw George and asked him what he thought until we arrived at an approach he felt comfortable with; one that, unbeknownst to him, invested George with Jeremy's youthful naiveté. This went on until one in the morning. Before leaving, he said, 'Can I come back if I have any more questions?' I said, 'Sure.' I hated seeing my protégé in such distress and relished being his mentor again. I also liked going behind the back of his dense director."

"I assume he returned."

"The rehearsals lasted another two weeks. He showed up every night. I'd have coffee ready, and we'd run lines and concoct bits of business. He improved quickly, as with *Journey*, which eased the tensions with his director. One night, after we exhausted the possibilities of the act three climax, he glanced at my walls, covered with photos from plays I'd done in New York. He said: 'You've been acting for a while.' I said: 'Twenty years.' Since this constituted the bulk of his existence, he reacted as if I'd claimed to be a survivor from the Mesozoic era. He wandered from picture to picture, asking 'What's this from?' or 'Who's that?' I talked about the plays and people involved, and he listened with the same attention as when we fleshed out his characters. Thereafter, our coaching sessions invariably strayed to discussions of my early career. I allowed him to leaf through my scrapbooks and displayed props and wardrobe pieces I'd spirited away from assorted productions. His curiosity transformed them from reminders of my past to vessels of information brimming with interest in the present. My standing as an acting guru increased, as did my status as a person. Probably I was seeking to repair the vanity that had been marred by Scotty's indifference, but I reveled in Jeremy's regarding me as a fount of wisdom or, at the very least, of the practical knowledge he wanted. And in many cases, it's a short step from wanting knowledge to wanting the individual providing it, as you probably know from the fling with your professor."

"Ex-professor," I said, my face warming. "Did you know Jeremy was gay from the beginning?"

"No. Despite increased visibility, discretion remained the preferred strategy for many in the early 1970s, especially aspiring actors. He might also have been worried about my reaction had I been straight."

"Didn't the company share anything about their personal lives when you were doing *Journey*?"

"A little. Our leading lady was married. She often talked about her husband and kids. The young man playing the other son had been acting since his early teens; he, Dalrymple, and I mostly discussed our professional lives. Jeremy was thoughtful and diffident, which might have indicated a discrete young gay man or a shy young straight man, or the self-consciousness of a less experienced performer. I was too busy with my character to think about it much. His visits during the *Lifetime* rehearsals made me more aware of his attractiveness, which increased with his commitment to performing and his interest in my life. I wondered about his sexuality, though at that point, only to define the bounds of our acquaintanceship. Luckily, one of my artifacts opened the door to the subject."

"The love triangle photo from *Grandview Park*?"

He nodded. "The sole souvenir I kept from my soap opera days, thanks to my fondness for Gray and Mag and our private jokes. When it turned up in my scrapbook, I told him the story as I did you."

"How did he react?"

"He laughed and asked about other gay people I'd worked with or known, most at that time still living in secrecy to protect their careers. He nearly fainted when I told him I knew for certain Tab Hunter was gay."

"What was the big deal about Tab Hunter?"

"He had the honor to be Jeremy's first crush after he caught *Damn Yankees* on TV one night. We'd about exhausted the subject, and I sensed a change in topic—you know, the moments when conversation devolves from rapid dialogue to muttered monosyllables—when he said, 'I'm that way too.' I said, 'I thought you might be,' without pressing the point. He smiled shyly, and I wondered how many others, if any, he'd come out to before me. Nonetheless, we'd acknowledged another correlation to link us as surely as our interest in acting. The admission also exposed his early life to view."

"How?"

"He asked me about coming to terms with my sexuality. I told him what I've told you, especially about Terry and Warren. He asked if my parents knew. I told him I considered it prudent not to mention it to them, and they never questioned me. I assumed they never thought about my sex life and probably imagined I hadn't married because I never met the right girl, a common evasion for my generation. He was quiet after I finished, said, 'I wish it were like that with me,' and at my urging, described his childhood. He'd grown up in a lower-middle-class home and spent his free time going to the movies, watching TV, and reading comic books. He also enjoyed recreating what he saw and read, altering scenes according to the whims of his imagination, not unlike me as a child. He thought little about himself and, prior to puberty, nothing about sexuality, much less homosexuality, until his father rather brutally pointed both out to him."

"How'd he do that?"

"According to Jeremy, his father was a typical armchair adventurer."

"A what?"

"Someone who worked long hours at a job he hated and spent his free time living vicariously through the exploits of cops, private eyes, and soldiers in movies and on TV. This was before comic book superheroes became entertainment for adults. He disliked or didn't understand anything else, including his son. Usually, he limited his disapproval to a silent glare whenever he found Jeremy imitating scenes from comedies or musicals.

One day, when Jeremy was ten, he and his parents were out driving, and some kids threw a stone that hit the rear fender. His father swung the car to a stop at the curb and watched the kids scurry away between some houses. He resumed driving and said, to nobody in particular, 'I'd have got out and said something if I had a son instead of a Tom-girl.' Jeremy realized then there was something different about him, something his father disapproved of that would prevent them from ever developing a true relationship."

"Brutal indeed," I said, unable to express my indignation any better.

"But sadly, not untypical. I'm sure, like most straight male armchair adventurers, he counted on leavening his middle age with fresh fantasies of his studly adolescent son screwing a bevy of nubile young girls. Relinquishing that comfort probably increased his aversion."

"Reminds me of what you said Scotty's family's attitude was to him."

"It's a common if rarely examined belief that rather than developing unique identities and following unique destinies, children exist to gratify the needs and vanities of their parents, or as in Scotty's case, other representatives of the generation before them."

"What about Jeremy's mother?"

"He said she'd run interference with his father but never offered any reassurance or comfort. She probably disapproved of him, too, and her maternal instinct was limited to not amplifying his father's attacks. Either way, an insurmountable wall separated him from them, the resulting solitude driving him further into a fantasy life. Puberty revealed what his parents had already perceived, while the fear they instilled in him because of it cautioned him to hide his attraction to boys at school and in his neighborhood. When he graduated high school, his parents threw him out. He found work and a place to live and, after a year, saved enough for drama classes at a community college. His teacher advised him to try modeling for extra money, and he began appearing in print ads for local businesses, which led to work in local TV commercials. Then he started trying out for local theater groups, which landed him with California Crescent. He had encounters with other young men on occasion and, a few times, traded his favors for work. But the shame instilled by his parents, and the fear of other people's reactions, prevented him from fully exploring his sexuality. Now, he turned to me for advice on how to live with his desires, just as he turned to me for ideas about performing. I was flattered he considered me a suitable guide on that score too."

"How long after he told you he was gay did you become intimate?"

"A week," he said. "The opening of *Once in a Lifetime* was approaching, and he grew proportionately nervous. We set aside sexuality to review our work on the play up to the night before."

"How'd it turn out?"

"Unevenly, which I expected after what I heard about the director. But for a small theater, it was passable. Jeremy displayed excellent comic timing. His character garnered laughs and sympathy, and he exuded the appeal that gains and maintains an audience's attention. He received the loudest applause at the curtain calls. The rest of the cast, and even the director were impressed."

"You must've been proud."

"My coaching accounted for only part of his success. His innate ability was first, followed by the contrast of our mutual creation against the lackluster production in which it appeared. I attended the opening and saw him after. He thanked me for my help. The next day he arrived at my apartment with the local newspapers. The reviewers concurred with his peers and the audience. He thanked me more fulsomely, and when words failed, he lunged forward and hugged me. I returned his hug, and for a while, he leaned against me, his head on my shoulder. I liked how it felt and stroked his hair. He lifted his head, studied me with those bright onyx eyes, and kissed me. Touching his lips, I realized that every night for two weeks, when he rang my bell, I'd felt those tell-tale wings fluttering. The ardor of his kiss convinced me that after all the time we spent discussing the play and our lives, he belonged in my apartment, belonged with me. When the kiss ended, I picked him up and carried him to the bedroom."

"Were you really in love with him, do you think?"

Robert smiled. "You sound skeptical."

"I don't mean to. It's just—"

"I know. May-December pairings are tricky. They involve multiple possible motives: on May's side, gold-digging or the search for a substitute parent; on December's side, a desire to recover one's youth. All I knew was I had a gorgeous, smart, talented young man in my arms, estranged from his parents and struggling to establish a place in the world. Making love to him was my way of demonstrating that everything about him was wonderful to me, that it mattered. And I believed his making love to me demonstrated that I mattered, too."

Robert lifted the mug from the table beside him, only rather than raise it to his lips, he rested it in the palm of his other hand. "I don't know how you define love," he said, "but for me, it's two people who matter to each other."

"It's as good a definition as I've heard."

"At least it's more precise than little wings fluttering inside you." He sipped his tea and glanced at the clock. "I've rambled again. Do you mind if we continue this the next time you're here?"

"Sure. Can I get you anything?"

"I'm fine. Don't let my stories distract you from your studies."

"I'm also good at compartmentalizing. I'll see you next week."

"Thanks, Paul. Give David my regards."

"I will. Call me if you need anything."

"I will."

Back in my car, I phoned David, who agreed to dinner at my place at seven.

True to my boast about compartmentalizing, from four-thirty on, I set my talk with Robert aside to outline my monograph, provisionally titled *Transition: Erich Jacobson in Los Angeles 1936–1946*. I set the table at five minutes to seven. Ten minutes later, David arrived with Chinese food.

"Am I interrupting?"

"Yes, and about time."

He placed the bag on the table and sorted the containers of food.

"How was your night?" I asked.

"Better than I expected," he said. "Finishing unfinished business is draining but satisfying. Are you still poring over the Quigley papers?"

"Actually, I'm outlining the monograph."

"You've done researching?"

"I'm still making connections between the Harold books and Jacobson's life, and there's more archival material to explore. But what Barbara gave me clarified the main issue. The rest will probably just fill in more background."

"How do you know? Maybe there's another bombshell awaiting you."

"I couldn't stand another one," I said, tucking into my crab Rangoon.

"How's the food?"

"Great. I was starving."

"When do you think you'll finish the monograph?"

"I'll start on the first draft while I'm concluding the research. If I'm lucky, and Barbara's bombshell is the only one I have to deal with, I could be done in four or five months."

"I have time then," he said and inhaled an unusually long lo mien noodle.

"For what?"

"To read the Harold books."

"Why?"

"To prep for yours."

"You don't have to read mine."

"Yes, I do. I want to know what you've been talking about and why you like it so much. It's the only big thing I don't know about you." He paused, grasped a steamed dumpling, and regarded me speculatively. "Unless there's a bombshell or two hiding in your arsenal."

Recalling what Robert said about people mattering to each other, I leaned over and kissed him. "You're even better than your nephews think you are. And for the record, there are no bombshells in my arsenal . . . unless you toss another at me, in which case I'll invent a doozy to retaliate."

His crinkly smile broke out behind the upraised dumpling.

"Kiss my arsenal," he said.

13.

The following Wednesday, I spent the morning working on my first draft with one eye on the television. Twenty minutes to noon, Robert phoned to say his health insurance had forced a change in the pharmacy handling his medication.

"You'll be picking it up at Med Mart now. Do you know where it is?"

"Yes. A couple of my other clients get theirs from there."

"I'm sorry if I disturbed your work. I know texts are the preferred mode of communication, but with the arthritis in my fingers, it's easier to dial the phone than type lengthy explanations."

"No problem. I'll be there in another two hours or so. I guess you won't be visiting *Grandview Park* today."

"Why not?"

"Haven't you turned on your TV?"

"No. Why?"

"There's been a school shooting. All the networks are covering it."

"Was anyone killed?"

"Three students, a teacher, and the gunman, from what they've reported so far," I said. "Such a tragedy."

Robert grunted. "Sadly, school shootings are the perfect emblem for a society that values violence over education."

Exhausted by the intricacies of Jacobson's creative process and the demoralizing news reports, I abandoned my TV and computer for the bright sun of early afternoon, the fluorescent lighting of the supermarket, and the drive-up window at Med Mart. I arrived at Robert's by quarter past two. Passing through the living room, I found his TV off and an old, leather-bound copy of Shakespeare's sonnets open on the table by his chair.

Inside the kitchen, he watched me place his Hearth Fire in the breadbox and his papaya and prunes on the counter.

"How's the research going?"

"I'm drafting the monograph."

"So soon?"

"Thanks to Barbara, I've got a story rather than speculations. I only need to shape it into a coherent narrative and fill it out with whatever details are left in the archives."

I slid a box of Field Treasure wild rice into its cupboard.

"What'll you do after it's finished? Go back east?"

"It's too soon to think about." A box of Velma's and a canister of Hearth Fire bread crumbs followed his Field Treasure onto the shelf. "Contrary to expectations, I've been constructing a pretty nice life here."

"Meaning David?"

"And my *H&H* work." I arranged his chocolate Gunter's in the cupboard and closed the door.

"If you mean you're developing an attachment to me, I'm flattered, but I wouldn't want it factoring into any major decisions. If anyone keeps you here, it should be David."

"He may." I stacked five cans of Fine Flake tuna in the second cupboard.

"I'm happy for you both."

"Good to hear your experiences haven't soured you on love." I stood his Shale House on the counter and folded the bag.

"I'd be pretty wretched if I resented anyone's happiness, especially yours. Love isn't restricted to other human beings, anyway. Despite what some people say about the word's overuse, anything that enhances your existence is susceptible to being sincerely loved: places, food, even the weather. Much of what I love is on my bookshelves."

I opened the second bag. "I noticed you're reading Shakespeare."

"It seemed a day for profundity."

"The sonnets are also about love." I placed his salad ingredients in the crisper.

"And their faint air of homosexual desire makes them doubly appealing to me, an interpretation I emphasized to introduce Jeremy to Shakespeare."

I stacked his Bub's Tubs by a bowl of leftover canned apricots.

"Were you refreshing your memory because you knew I'd ask for the rest of the story about him?"

I placed a half pound of chicken cutlets on the shelf below the Bub's Tubs, closed the refrigerator door, and stacked five boxes of Ice Floe in the freezer.

"I may have been refreshing my memory for the pleasure of it. But I'll provide the conclusion if you wish. I haven't yet refused you access to my checkered past."

I folded the second bag and laid it on the counter. "By the way, another client of mine saw you in *Long Day's Journey into Night*."

"Really?"

"She was an avid theatergoer. That's how it came up. She was talking about different productions she'd seen. She mentioned California Crescent, and I asked her about it. She said it was incredible."

"What did she do for a living?"

"She was a cellist with the L.A. Philharmonic."

"Then she has more than a modicum of taste."

"At least as much as you," I said.

"Then I'm even more grateful for her praise. Funny . . . no matter how far beyond their freshness date, compliments never grow stale."

Following our established ritual, I brewed his apple-cinnamon tea, poured out my Shale House, and joined him in the living room.

"Where did I leave off?" he asked.

"You were saying making love to Jeremy convinced you that you mattered to each other."

"Oh yes . . . though at the time I merely thought of it as falling in love. Jeremy wasn't a virgin, but ours was his first real relationship, and he entered into it with all the enthusiasm you might expect. In the weeks following our sleeping together, we were, like most new couples, practically inseparable. We made love in the morning before leaving for whatever projects we had on deck for survival, usually commercials for me and modeling assignments for him. When I got home, we had dinner, after which he left for the theater, and we made love again on his return."

"You must've been exhausted."

He bristled. "I wasn't that old, and there wasn't any sight more alluring than him naked beside me. After about a month, the passion leveled off to once a day or every two days, and we talked instead."

"What about?"

"Work, mostly. He'd describe the evening's performance and his concerns about line readings or stage business that fell flat, and I'd mine my experience for examples to illustrate whatever advice I had for him. This led to another million questions about what New York had been like when I was his age. Although it felt like only two or three years ago, it sounded like eons when I recounted it. I talked about doing early TV and the people I'd met, including Scotty. Then, like a dutiful spouse, he'd ask about my day. Watching him laugh at my assessments of the scripts I had to perform was as satisfying as watching him in bed."

I recalled the satisfaction I derived from the laughter I wangled from David. "You had a lot in common despite the age difference."

"Although, aside from sex, it was still very much a mentor-protégé relationship. Following *Once in a Lifetime,* he found intermittent roles in plays and TV commercials, and I continued coaching him. The extent of my technical knowledge about different media surprised me. I advised him about producers, directors, and agents and used the little power wielded by a supporting player to get him bits on TV shows. At the same time, I introduced him to my favorite plays and authors."

"I assume from his background he wasn't familiar with many."

"I was shocked when he admitted he'd never heard of O'Neill or Kaufman and Hart before he acted them. I gave him free rein of my library, and he'd stretch out on my couch, his hawk eyes fixed on a book propped on his chest, oblivious to the sounds of my cooking or cleaning. He struggled with Shakespeare's archaic language, and the highly stylized, like Wilde's. Once he cleared that hurdle, they captivated him. Afterward, we'd discuss what he'd read. He'd suggest different ways of playing various characters and scenes, some quite insightful. After years of studying Moliere, Aristophanes, Racine, Pirandello, and others, revisiting their work with Jeremy refreshed my perception of it, making it almost as exciting as when I first encountered it. And more often than not, we concluded our discussions by making love, the physical contact punctuating our exchange of ideas."

"Not unlike how it was with Terry and Scotty."

"True."

"You must have been happy."

"And not just about being in love again. Perhaps it's ego talking, but our first year together, his acting improved, not only creatively, but professionally."

"What's the difference?"

"The first five or six plays he did after *Lifetime,* he turned to me for help as before. Then he began analyzing characters and scripts alone and suggested blocking and line readings to his directors without consulting me."

"Did it bother you that he stopped asking for your advice?"

"He didn't stop entirely. The approach changed. Rather than wait for my input, he'd present me with an idea or observation fully formed and say, 'What do you think?' and I'd critique it. Later, he mentioned his ideas only after he'd discussed them with his director. One night he described a radical suggestion he'd made during rehearsals for *A Doll's House,* and I noted the change. The assurance disappeared, and the novice returned. He said: 'I'm sorry. You know I want to know what you think.' I said: 'Don't apologize. It shows you're becoming a real actor.' The sex that night was unbelievable."

"Forgive my asking, but given the nature of your relationship and the difference in your ages, what did you imagine would happen between the two of you?"

"I was too much in love to care. I only wanted to revel in the extraordinary fact of this beautiful young man looking to me for affection and guidance. In return, I wanted to share with him all the things that had heightened my senses and ennobled my faculties; that had buoyed me after losing Terry and Scotty and compensated for wasting my time on *Grandview* and the other heap of shit I did to survive. Giving him something with the power to help weather the ups and downs of existence and improve the overall quality of his daily life, as the arts had for me, was the greatest proof of my affection I could imagine."

He stopped and smiled.

"What?" I said.

"I've just realized that telling you about these people, I've talked more about our initial meetings and ultimate partings. The years in between, when we were in love and happy, don't lend themselves to narration."

"Why's that?"

"Probably because that kind of happiness consists of repeated, almost circular patterns rather than linear events. You fall for someone, learn about their tastes and habits, they learn about yours, and you adapt to them to create a combined life, like who showers first or which brand of toothpaste to buy. Conflicts arise, but you resolve them because you believe that, ultimately, being with that person is better than being without them. Linear events thread through the relationship, like lost hotel reservations or your attempts to unblock a drain, stories you tell at parties. But they're incidental to the basic reality of being together day after day. If you try analyzing the relationship for outsiders, after describing how the person made you feel, the best you can do is summarize the patterns you formed and tell your listener to multiply them by however many years the relationship lasted."

"What happened with Jeremy?"

"You've already guessed. The entire time we lived together, I barely noticed the difference in our ages, except when I mentored him, and then it was wonderful opening his eyes to the joy of literature and the craft of acting. I never imagined it presaged disaster until the night it did."

"How?"

"He was getting more and more roles, in plays, TV and in films, parts like mine, clichéd bits with clichéd dialogue a ventriloquist's dummy could deliver convincingly. Though I had less input than before, I imagined we were preparing him for a better and longer career. The turning point came when a New York producer, Hugh Greenberg, offered to star him as Nicky in a modern dress version of Noel Coward's *The Vortex*. Do you know it?"

"No, sorry."

"I'm not surprised. Its fame has dwindled, but it was Coward's first big success. The story concerns a vain, middle-aged woman chasing younger men and her neglected, drug-addicted son."

"Nicky's the son?"

"Yes."

"When was it written?"

"Around 1923. I can't remember exactly."

"Daring subjects for the time," I said.

"Which accounted for its success and Hugh's interest in a revival. The modern drug culture had taken hold by then, and Hugh wanted to alter the setting from an upper-class household in 1920s Britain to an upper-class household in 1970s Southern California. He wanted to mount it here first, smooth out the production and transfer it to New York. He caught Jeremy in the Crescent's version of *Barefoot in the Park* and decided on him for Nicky."

"He must have been thrilled."

"He was, for a week or two."

"Why only a week or two?"

"I realized what Hugh's offer might mean. If Jeremy played it well enough to go to New York, he'd gain a foothold in the theater there. He had doubts, but I assured him he had the talent, and I offered to go east with him if he wanted. He was ready to accept when he had another offer for a supporting role in a film called *Galaxy Troop*."

"Never heard of it."

"I'd be disappointed if you had. It was one among dozens of science fiction epics producers scrambled to make after *Star Wars* became a hit. Like the others, it gathered various clichés from old Westerns and war movies and shot them into space. Jeremy, however, considered it the better opportunity."

"Why?"

"Exactly what I wanted to know," he said. "I'd been schooling him in acting for three years, introduced him to the classics, and coached him in playing a few. From the way he listened and studied the texts, I believed I'd awakened him to their beauty and depth. I imagined I'd not only refined his talent but his taste."

"But you didn't?"

"There was something about him I hadn't noticed or that he concealed from me. When he told me he wanted to do *Galaxy Troop,* I was appalled and asked why. He said: 'It's a sci-fi movie. They're really hot now and make tons of money.' I told him *The Vortex* was a big opportunity. He asked for what. I said: 'To further your career.' He said: 'A big movie will do more for me than an old play.' I said: 'The script stinks.' He said: 'So what? More people will see me in it, and it could lead to more.' I said: 'More what?' He said: 'More movies.' I said: 'Is that all you want, to be in movies?' He said: 'I'll be a hell of a lot more famous in movies than if I went to New York. Who'd know me there other than a few snobs? If not movies, maybe I could be a regular on a TV show. There's money there too.' I said: 'You just want to be rich and famous, then?' He said: 'That's what being an actor's about, isn't it? And it'd really stick it to my mom and dad.' His eyes gleamed on these last words, not with intelligence but with the deadly malice of a hawk sighting its prey. I reminded him of our discussions about the craft of acting and the mechanics of quality plays. He said: 'Look, I'm grateful for what you've done. But today theater's just a way to get noticed so you can get into movies or TV.' I said: 'You'd be wasting your talent.' He became combative at that and said: 'It's my talent to waste, isn't it?' As the conversation escalated to an argument, the gap in our ages broke open like the San Andreas Fault."

"What did your ages have to do with it? Sounds like a difference in perspective."

"Perspectives due entirely to our ages. Jeremy represented my first pro-

longed contact with someone who had grown up with TV. His initial difficulties interpreting words on a page should have alerted me."

"Alerted you to what?"

"That he considered movies and TV the gold standard. I thought I'd
awakened him to the value of art that observes and comments on the human condition and to the pleasure of exercising the intelligence required to
develop comparable performances."

"But you hadn't," I said.

"The aptitude he displayed concealed the fact that continuous consumption of audio-visual images from an early age had built up an immunity to
the things I valued. His comment about sticking it to his mother and father
made it clear. He wanted the easily inflated self-worth obtained by appearing in mass-produced images, regardless of content, in order to compensate
for his lack of familial approval. The rest—learning about theater, reading
plays, gaining insight into characters—was merely a means to attain that
other, and to my mind lesser, end."

"Did you say this to him?"

Robert nodded grimly. "When he said it was his talent to waste, I
thought of the hours I'd spent placing my past experience at his service,
out of respect for his innate ability and for love of the person I considered
him to be. He was wasting that as well, and the more cavalier he became
about it, the more resentful I became. He shrugged off my resentment like
someone shaking off a few drops of rain and said: 'Oh Jesus, Bob'—he always called me Bob—'nobody cares about that old-time shit today.' I said:
'Then why'd you listen? So I'd coach you?' He said: 'Pretty much.' I said:
'Why not just ask for acting lessons? Why lie in my bed for three years if it
meant nothing to you?' He tilted his chin and said: 'You needed me in your
bed, and I felt sorry for you. And it was easier and cheaper than paying for
lessons.' I remembered what he once told me about sleeping with people
to get modeling jobs. In one quick, agonizing moment, I went from mattering to someone who mattered to me, to being a stepping stone in what
amounted to a plan for exacting revenge on his parents for disowning him."

"What did you do?"

"I'm sorry to say I made it worse."

"How?"

"I stared at him and said: 'Congratulations. You just became your father.' Given how much he despised his father, I knew pointing out any
similarities in their behavior would hit him harder than a physical blow. I

shoud've stayed true to my position as mentor and kept a cooler head, but in the heat of that moment I only wanted to retaliate."

"How'd he react?"

"His eyes held mine for a second, but the arrogance quickly faltered, and his chin trembled. Then he grabbed his things and left. I never saw him again."

"What happened to him? Did he continue acting?"

"For a while," Robert said. "*Galaxy Troop* turned out as I predicted: a fiasco. He appeared in a few exploitation films and on TV. He even went to New York to try theater. Sometime in the mid-1980s, a friend of mine told me he'd moved in with an older doctor in Sacramento."

"You never fell in love after that?"

"No. What he said broke something inside me."

"What?"

"My self-confidence, I suppose. I'd already been brooding over my failures with Scotty and as an actor. Jeremy represented another failure on both counts. His rejection also showed I was clinging to things, and an entire way of being that others, especially younger people, considered ridiculous. That's what broke in me—my sense of relevance, of having something worthwhile to contribute to the present. Instead, I was a pathetic, contemptible anachronism. From then on, when I met new people, professionally or socially, I could never believe they might find me interesting, much less attractive. I even doubted the sincerity of my oldest friends.

"Later on, I realized that with Jeremy, I'd succumbed to the *Pygmalion–Vertigo* syndrome of trying to remake someone according to my specifications without reckoning with the durability of their innate identity. I wanted to recreate what I'd had with Scotty and Terry, and for that, I needed someone who shared my appreciation for the arts. This further undermined my confidence by making me doubt my judgment. How could I trust my instincts again when they'd let me down so spectacularly?"

Now I understood his concerns about David, but I decided not to pursue the subject.

"That's when I set about exorcising my past," he said. "If who I was and what I could offer no longer had any value, neither did the tokens of my past, the past that had made me who I was."

"Couldn't you still enjoy your past for its own sake?" I said. "From what I've heard, you had many happy moments."

"I felt the same after my fury abated. But I also realized I'd fallen into the same trap as Scotty, clinging to his family treasures as if they could substitute for Sandy's and his parents' presence. What my life and career had been, and most importantly, what it meant, remained entirely within me. The pictures, reviews, props, and costume pieces couldn't substitute for the events they represented, nor could they lend the recollection of them any greater value. The past had passed away, and the only sensible thing was to dispose of the corpse. A week after Jeremy left, I tore everything from the walls, shelves, and drawers and destroyed them in one tremendous orgy of rage."

"Like the plastic ivy on your trellises."

"Like the plastic ivy."

"Do you ever regret it?"

"No, although I'm sure a professional snoop like you is gnashing his teeth over it. At the time, I imagined it'd be as wrenching as losing Jeremy, Scotty, and Terry, but I was in the mood for self-immolation. I suppose it was the closest I ever came to suicide. After, I felt relieved. I never noticed how burdensome it was, dragging around the detritus from days gone by. The best of those days I could recall at will. The rest fell into oblivion, where they belonged."

"Reminds me of what David said about letting go of the anger he'd carried around after breaking up with Corey."

"Maybe you're right to trust him, then. There's nothing more invigorating than a clean slate."

"You kept one picture," I said, glancing at the desk behind him.

"Only because it's how I like to remember myself. It's a tonic after shaving or accidentally confronting my reflection in a mirror. Tossing the rest taught me a crucial lesson not only about clinging to the past but about memory. Accuracy isn't the point of memory. It's a side issue unless you're building a criminal case. Memory preserves how things affect us because it's what motivates our subsequent actions."

"How so?"

"Remembering the pain of a knife cut reminds me to take care with knives in the future. Remembering how ridiculous I felt being in *Grandview Park* and *Marmoset* and how good I felt being in *Journey* and other plays guided my subsequent career choices when economically feasible. Holding onto the photos, props, and costumes from those productions to remind me of their lessons was as absurd as holding onto the offending knife to warn me to be careful with knives in general."

"What about the people you worked with, and others you'd known? Didn't you want reminders of them?"

He smiled and shook his head. "The same applies to people. We never really recall their faces or bodies. We remember their spirits, amorphous shapes associated with how we felt when we were with them, what we learned from it, and how what we learned carried us into the subsequent phases of our lives. That's why I didn't regret tossing out photos of friends and lovers. The geography of their faces and bodies has little connection to how they influenced me and certainly can't restore any of it to me today."

"True," I said, thinking of people from my past while he sipped his tea.

"Though sometimes at night, before falling asleep, their features appear to me for a few seconds with almost photographic clarity, like those silent film fragments movie buffs collect: a few pristine images between ragged ends of crumbling nitrate. I'll see Terry's smooth skin aglow in his room on a sunny afternoon, Scotty's sardonic grin, or Jeremy's inquisitive eyes with a precision that startles me. Sometimes I remember with such force that I almost weep over my inability to grasp the fragments and consummate the old loves. The same happens with friends and colleagues. I'll recall the sympathy I shared with Mag and want to phone her for a split second before realizing she's dead. But that's the curse of memory. I'm glad there aren't any photos or other ephemera around to make it worse."

"Do you think the people you remember feel the same about you . . . the live ones, I mean?"

"I'm not bitter enough to wish them my fate. I hope they've found something better to occupy their final years. When all's said and done, I'm grateful to them for helping me become who I am, and I'd be happy if they recalled me with comparable gratitude."

"Are you grateful to the people who hurt you as well?"

"Absolutely. Those experiences also indicate a life lived, one encompassing both good and bad. If the good rarely met my expectations, the bad never impeded my ability to continue existing, or undermined the satisfactions I found in it. Are you familiar with Tennyson?"

"The poet?"

"Who else?"

"I know the name but haven't read much of him."

"There's a line in his poem about Ulysses that goes: 'I am a part of all that I have met.' I've thought about that since Delia's visit. I'd never met her or her mother, yet I became a part of their lives by acting in something that drew them together even in times of conflict. The entire time I acted—onstage, on TV, or in movies—I became, for those moments, a part of the lives of whoever watched and listened. The majority undoubtedly forgot me immediately after. But as Delia pointed out, it's also likely I influenced some for the better. Perhaps I embodied a character familiar to them or elucidated an idea on behalf of a playwright that resonated with them. Hopefully, I had a similar influence on those I loved, those I liked, and those that only briefly crossed my path. The older I get, the more I aware I become of the temporal sequences in which we live and how much truth is in the cliché about who we are and what we do spreading from us to the people we encounter to the people they encounter. The opposite is also true."

"What opposite?"

"If we can claim, with Tennyson's Ulysses, that we are a part of all that we have met, all that we have met are a part of us, too. God or natural selection or whatever endowed us with the ability to communicate our ideas, emotions, and perspectives."

"Making it inevitable that we become parts of each other," I said.

"Yes. Terry's interest in writing and theater encouraged me to cultivate my creativity. Warren's comfort with his sexuality made it easier to live with mine. Mag taught me about friendship. Gray, by being almost my complete opposite, confirmed my dedication to the things that were important to me. Scotty and I challenged each other to think about whatever touched us, except perhaps his sorrow. Jeremy exposed the fallacy of clinging to the past. Even you, Paul, remind me that intelligent, literate, good people still exist, which adds considerable sweetness to my bittersweet old age. Friends, lovers, colleagues, neighbors, and people on the street, exercised my ability to perceive, think, feel, and act in different ways, just by interacting with me, thus contributing to an ever-expanding sense of my identity and the world in which I existed. I am who I am, and I lived a gratifying life because all that I have met became a part of me."

He stopped and chuckled.

"What?" I said.

"I was just thinking how this was a far more common phenomenon in my youth. Today, people not only fail to become part of each other, they actively resist it."

"How?"

"We've discussed the connection between empathy and learning."

"Learning requires one to develop an ability to understand others, and then allowing others and what they communicate to become part of you."

"Practically every technology introduced during my lifetime has discouraged both empathy and learning. Instead, they've reduced the function of the brain to wallowing in a perpetual supply of pleasures that isolate individuals not only from one another but from the general flow of time."

"You honestly believe that?"

"I'm afraid so. Thirty years after TV transformed our cultural rituals into passive, isolated spectatorship, cable, and satellite TV multiplied the number of channels available to viewers and extended the broadcast day to 24 hours. Then, to attract viewers, channels began specializing in content. Networks devoted to 24-hour news, 24-hour porn, 24-hour cooking, 24-hour shopping, 24-hour sci-fi, 24-hour religion, 24-hour politics, 24-hour sports and so on, sprouted up like mushrooms."

"Doesn't that just make the diversity of subjects associated with Renaissance Man more readily available?" I asked.

"You'd think it would," he said. "But for the average viewer, it imposes more of the limitations of Utilitarian Man. The aim of the educational program associated with Renaissance Man, and the culture deriving from it, isn't simply for individuals to become versed in various aspects of the world. It's about learning to derive greater satisfaction from existence by creating a larger, more complex whole from those parts."

"A diverse whole mirroring the diverse abilities of the brain," I said.

"Yes. Specialized media, on the other hand, promotes the limiting of brain function typical of Utilitarian Man's view of existence. Being perpetually available, as well as narrowly focused, specialized media not only fails to relate its parts to a whole, but it makes its parts wholes unto themselves, like genres."

"I'm not sure I understand what you mean."

"Remember what Heywood Broun said about obscenity?"

"It's such a tiny country that a single tour covers it completely."

"TV, in its infancy, was characterized as a fount of information and a window on the world. Specialized media fragmented the world, dividing it into dozens of kingdoms for viewers to inhabit, hour after hour, day after day, kingdoms whose borders determine their notions of reality."

"You really believe the absorption is that complete?"

"Perhaps not. But how often have you heard people reduce life to trite metaphors derived from sports, warfare, engineering, gardening . . .?"

"Too many," I said.

"If specialized media advanced TVs erosion of the arts by promoting the single-mindedness of Utilitarian Man in viewers, the same limited content also eroded the arts from the craetive side, by confining actors, directors, and writers to repeating the established tropes of a given media outlet. Partly as a reaction to unchanging content and partly as a result of the renewed faith in superstitious materialism brought about by political changes in the same era, from the 1980s onward, audiences shifted their focus from cultural to technological achievements. How ingeniously artists communicated a perspective on the human condition had less value than how clearly a certain brand of TV screen reproduced a car crash or how clearly a certain brand of speaker reproduced a guitar solo. The minutiae of audio-visual stimuli rather than ideas became the point of interest."

"A trend that continued with computers and the internet," I said.

"In ways Scotty and I, at our most cynical, never foresaw," he said. "If we had, we might have entered a suicide pact. Digitization expanded specialization to a nearly-infinite number of kingdoms—porn, politics, religion, video games, news, fashion, food, gossip, shopping, conspiracy theories, and more—each fractured into its narrowest possible subdivisions and available without respite. Computers also extend isolation and passivity by performing basic intellectual operations for users. They correct spelling and grammar and solve math problems, and indeed take over all the fundamental building blocks of human thought my generation was encouraged to develop in grade school. Computers also provide instant access to information, answering every possible question at every moment of the day or night."

"Shouldn't access to information promote rather than hinder intellectual activity?"

"You'd think so, and it's certainly welcome in emergencies. But when I was a kid, if you wanted to know something, say the date of Lincoln's Gettysburg Address, you opened a history book or encyclopedia and found the date within a larger text concerning the event. The advantage of this was, after zeroing in on the date, you more often than not continued reading about the circumstances leading up to and away from it."

"Training you to think in terms of temporal sequences."

"Yes. Today, if you consult a computer about the date of the Gettysburg Address, the date alone appears, abstracted from other information concerning it and apart from the larger historical context in which it occurred. This discourages intellectual growth and, by extension, morality."

"How does it affect morality?"

"Relying on knowledge stored in devices frees users to spend yet more time in the kingdoms oriented to their personal pleasures, pleasures that more often than not offer an illusory escape from time. Also, perceiving only disconnected bits of information trains them to view the world as discrete fragments, isolated from each other as well as in time. The two combined encourages them to regard themselves as similarly demarcated from our world's temporal sequences—the exact opposite of cultural education—diminishing any incentive to ponder either the motives or consequences of their actions—those same motives and consequences being the basic topics of narrative art. Devices then enable users to work from home and have necessities delivered to their doors, thus augmenting their intellectual isolation with physical isolation. After eliminating both the need for human contact and to learn about the world, technology delivers the *coup de grace* by extracting users from the world itself, maintaining them in the large or small shoeboxes they call home, from which they observe the rest through a screen. This physical and mental isolation then serves as an ideal breeding ground for the self-indulgence of narcissism."

"How does narcissism enter into it?"

"Visual media always appeals to narcissists. Ever since humans learned to create images in stone and pigment, rulers, aristocrats, and their ilk have tried to make their images permanent, in the hope, undoubtedly, that a part of them would evade death to continue receiving the obsequies proffered by those they ruled. When I was young, long after still photography became common and people began making home movies, a stock character was the photography nut that bored people for hours with snapshots and films they'd taken of themselves, their families and friends, imagining every trivial event acquired significance through the miracle of being caught on film—an early example of visual credulousness TV later exploited."

"What do you mean by 'visual credulousness?'"

"We've talked about how visual culture creates an unspoken belief that only those things, people, and ideas that give rise to the most exciting audio-visual imagery have any validity. Stimulus to eyes and ears replaces considered thought as the final arbiter; that's why the number and intensity of biological stimuli became the standard by which people began judging the quality of cultural products. And it's why, when the second TV generation matured in the 1980s, the notion that 'image is everything' became a popular aphorism. Today, the internet allows users to enter the medium via blogs, video posts, and the like to pursue the spurious legitimacy attached to being an audio-visual hieroglyphic. The bulk of online content consists of trivial moments from the lives of the famous, infamous, and obscure, that for both those posting them and those viewing them, possess importance simply because they appear on billions of screens and are viewed by billions of people."

He sipped his tea and continued.

"The opportunity to gratify one's narcissism by entering into the medium encourages every exhibitionist and Molehill Man to post ramblings on any given subject, their rants again acquiring significance due to their reproduction on a screen. And since the disdain for education espoused by Utilitarian Man, along with audio-visual media encouraging intelectual passivity and moral sterility, more and more people are drawn to the charismatic images and words of preachers and pundits to supply answers to questions they're too unlearned to arrive at on their own. The internet allows anyone cherishing a belief in the value of whatever ideas flit through their heads to enjoy an illusory confirmation of that value through the number of approving viewers they attract, while observers who find the ideas credible thanks to their dramatic or visually exciting presentation, form a symbiotic relationship to their presenter, a cultic dynamic between what we might term active and passive narcissists."

"How do you define active and passive narcissism?"

"Active narcissists, believing in their essential superiority, unleash their ideas and images on the world with the press of a button. Passive narcissists read or view the posts and become convinced of the active's self-assessment without submitting it to any critical evaluation. Indeed, because actives attract passives by proclaiming what passives already think or believe, passives resist applying critical thought to it. Passives derive a sense of superiority by agreeing with the superior self-image of actives, while actives derive confirmation of the same superiority from the number of passives supporting them. Given the decline in general education over the last fifty-odd years, there are more than enough passives to scaffold the ego of every active that comes along."

"A dynamic as old as the species, probably," I said.

"We've fallen into the habit of framing it in terms of alphas and betas, terms used by natural scientists to describe interactions among less complex pack animals. Applying these terms to people detracts from or ignores qualities unique to human beings, foremost among which is our capacity for culture. In the present case, it whitewashes the tensions between our capacity for empathy and our tendency to narcissism, narcissism meaning a self-regard limiting one's ability to contemplate a viewpoint other than one's own. Modern media cultivates the symbiosis between active and passive narcissists to an extent never before possible. Passives wallow for hours in audio-visual images oriented to their beliefs and pleasures, while actives bask in the dispersion of their audio-visual images onto billions of legitimizing screens, both without regard to consequences, since the neurochemicals released by these thrills conveniently blunts their perception of time."

"Don't you think you're exaggerating the extent of visual credulousness a little? Some people resist the snares of audio-visual media."

"Like you and David, I know. And many raised in the literate culture prior to TV remarked on all this long before now. Elia Kazan, in his 1957 film *A Face in the Crowd,* and Paddy Chayefsky, in his 1976 film *Network,* broached the topic of passive credulity. But again, the effect of their criticisms was neutralized because they were delivered through the same audio-visual media they criticized. And by another ironic twist, resistance to audio-visual media often helps rather than hinders many skeptics from withdrawing into a narcissistic kingdom."

"How?"

"The backlash against modern media has created a reactionary habit of applying blanket doubt to whatever appears in it, which too easily becomes another strategy for limiting one's perceptions. If the news or a website confronts someone with an event or discovery or some other information that challenges or contradicts their beliefs, they avoid it by attributing it to another deception by an inherently deceptive media. Rather than a liberating rebellion, skepticism reinforces the narrow borders within which skeptical rebels exist. But whether embracing modern audio-visual media or opposing it, the consequences are the same."

"And they are . . .?"

He shifted in the recliner and cleared his throat.

"There's an old story about a monarch who wished to hear the original, primitive language spoken by humans. He had two infants—a boy and a girl—taken to his palace and maintained in strict isolation. Attendants provided for their material needs but were forbidden to talk to them. The idea was that, being isolated from outside influences, the infants would spontaneously speak the original, primal human language. Instead, the lack of verbal interaction caused the infants to wither and die before reaching the age to talk. This is a fable, of course, yet many studies show that lack of contact leads to health problems in infants."

"What's that got to do with modern technology?"

"The similarity is glaring, I should think. As people rely on devices to gather and store information, abandon the empathy essential for learning, and live outside time in a private world comprised of what they think and feel reflected on a screen as in a mirror, the less they develop the mental habits forming the foundation of culture and, to me, lend genuine pleasure to existence. This lack, in turn, diminishes satisfaction in life and increases hostility."

"Why should it increase hostility?"

"People lacking satisfaction in life are often hostile. Conditions of isolated narcissism also mean the unfamiliar registers as a threat to the stability of the narcissist's kingdom rather than as an opportunity to learn. And since the unfamiliar constitutes the bulk of the outside world, this fear has the potential to develop into overriding paranoia. Rather than become parts of each other, people fall into the opposite habit of defending their little kingdoms from invasion, a defense generally consisting of what I call the three D's: derision, denial, and destruction."

"How do you define those?"

"They're pretty self-explanatory. Derision means holding a person, thing, or idea up to ridicule, usually with insult humor, as if contempt invalidated its status as a part of the outside world. Denial means pretending it doesn't exist, as if one might invalidate it by ignoring it. Destruction, naturally, means physical annihilation. The unifying theme of these strategies is a desire on the part of narcissists to remake the world in their own image rather than confront it on its own terms and adapt to it. These, and the mental laziness behind them, motivate all the bullying and general nastiness plaguing the internet until you arrive at a character like the kid who shot up the school today."

"What about him? I thought you weren't watching TV."

"I had it on for a half hour after you phoned. Turns out he was obsessed with an action-adventure film called *Iron Backbone* about a muscle-bound vigilante who, rather than solve problems by thinking them through, picks up a gun and starts blowing people's heads off. Of course, it's only natural that in audio-visual culture, violence emerges as the preferred method of problem-solving."

"Why is that natural?"

"Violence, or the fantasy that physical force is sufficient to deal with the complex problems humans face, makes for more vivid audio-visual images than people thinking or explaining ideas, so violence is considered the more legitimate, productive behavior. The same thing happens with sex and other self-indulgences: the biological responses to their imagery codify them as the greatest possible pleasures for viewers. From the summary of *Iron Backbone* and the clips they showed on the news, it's typical of this kind of thing, what Scotty and I called 'straight camp.'"

"What do you mean by that?" I asked, feeling overwhelmed by the sheer number of private terms he had already thrown at me, let alone the challenge to remember their definitions.

"Camp is notoriously difficult to define. For Scotty and me, it meant exaggerating experiences or emotions out of proportion to reality. Musicals and melodramas are prime examples. Musicals exaggerate positive emotions, such as love and bliss, while melodramas exaggerate negative emotions like hate and envy, far out of proportion to how the average person experiences them. Straight culture also identifies musicals and melodramas as camp not only because gay men elevated them to that status but because their heightened emotions are considered feminine and therefore readily associated with gay men. What most straights fail to note is that the cultural products associated with them are also rife with attitudes and viewpoints exaggerated out of proportion to reality. Foremost is the belief that physical strength rather than thought is the ideal or preferred solution to issues. According to this definition, Joan Crawford and John Wayne are equally camp figures because each built their careers on reiterating such exaggerations. The only difference is that Crawford ended up ridiculed for exaggerating what's associated with femininity and gay men, while Wayne is still venerated for doing the same for attitudes associated with masculinity and straight men."

"Of course, the value judgments applied to both set of traits are as arbitrary as their links to specific genders."

"Yet most people accept the arbitrary assessment without a second thought since they're usually portrayed through images, and again, images imply rather than explicate. A careful exploration of what humans are, and our history as a species, would make it less easy to discard our emotional range or believe in the ability of violence to decide issues. But in a visual culture, people react to what exciting images imply rather than respond to what considered reflection teaches."

"Then what you're saying is a bias toward traditionally masculine behavior along with a bias toward visual perception leads to an entrenchment
of straight camp in an audio-visual culture."

"Along with intellectual passivity and loss of empathy, which further
support the idealization of violence. Another thing is, as visual media over-
took the written word in the 1960s, the gay influence on pop and high culture grew more visible. Susan Sontag's 'Notes on Camp' brought the camp
sensibility to wider notice; the gay fan base for stars like Judy Garland and
Bette Davis was more openly discussed; the interest in old movies we talked
about inspired a number of memoirs and biographies that outed gays who
helped create them; while the gay rights movement aggressively pointed out
the influence of gay artists in all media."

"To counteract the vilification of gender and sexual nonconformists by
demonstrating their positive contributions to society," I said.

"A necessary corrective," he said, "but Scotty and I noted that as audiences grew more aware of the gay camp elements in early twentieth-century
popular culture, straight camp elements became more prevalent in the latter
half of the century. This was likely, if not entirely, due to a fretful backlash
against the gay rights movement, while the end of censorship allowed for
more explicit images of sex and violence. As post-literate culture became
established in the 1970s and 1980s, audio-visual media tended to collapse
popular culture into hetero sex and violence, embodied not by actors whose
purpose was to portray a range of human experiences but by figureheads
whose bodies were rigorously sculpted into idealized straight camp gender
traits—musculature in men and hips and busts in women—images audiences accepted uncritically because, again, such exaggerations make the
strongest visual impact. Even pop music concerts became one-half music
and one-half the pyrotechnics associated with action-adventure films and
video games."

"Perhaps you're just annoyed that acting styles changed during that time
and you envied their success."

"Things were changing, and they certainly annoyed the hell out of me.
There was no envy, though; only dismay at the overturn of the standards
I'd grown up with and still believed in."

"What standards?"

"As I've told you, when I was young, culture was the outgrowth of a
society that valued literacy and general education, which meant that being
a good artist in any field required a familiarity not only with techniques but

with the history of your art form, as well as other art forms: polymaths were fairly common in those days. For an actor, it meant knowing the literature of the theater, its great plays, and its great roles. Art was a vocation presupposing a degree of learning that had for its purpose, like all the arts, to build on culture's legacy of commenting on the human condition."

"There were still plenty who were only in it for the money or fame, even then."

"Unquestionably," he said, "but most of those left little if any mark in the cultural record. Whatever place they might still claim is in the history of culture as a business rather than an art. Even so, in a society valuing education, some degree of intelligence was required for success. One reason many older films retain their appeal is that they were written by people who, despite being limited by standards of mass production, had been educated in literary traditions and wrote their scripts for audiences who read books and magazine articles. Even lowly burlesque comics like Abbott and Costello with their *Who's on First* routine, or the illogical logic used by George Burns and Gracie Allen in vaudeville and other media, explored the same limits, potentials, and ambiguities of language as Modernists like Gertrude Stein and James Joyce."

"You really think that's a legitimate comparison?"

"Sure, and there was reciprocal appreciation. Many of the literati admired popular comics like Chaplin and the Marx Brothers. T. S. Eliot was a Groucho fan. James Joyce's writing is a phonetic transcription of the same ethnic dialect that was the bread-and-butter of many a vaudeville comic. Beckett conceived *Waiting for Godot* in terms of a music hall or vaudeville sketch, and the actor who first played it in America was Bert Lahr, a burlesque comic of the old school. Beckett also chose Buster Keaton to star in his one and only foray into film. As I said, one had to winnow the brilliant from the bullshit, but enough brilliance enetered into pop culture to make the effort worthwhile. Now that education and the written word have been replaced by self-indulgence and audio-visual images, bullshit prevails. Rather than learn about their craft and its place in cultural history, actors spend their time in a gym or plastic surgeon's office, conforming to the appearance straight camp associates with their gender, to better serve as elements in mass-produced images that dazzle the eye and numb the brain, for uneducated audiences with absurdly low standards of adulthood. Today, at the start of the twenty-first century, the most popular culture consists of straight camp images rendered in a comic book style that in my youth was limited to what teenagers doodled in the margins of their notebooks . . . and for all I know still doodle . . . or are notebooks obsolete?"

"Not yet," I said. "Then you see today's shooter as someone steeped in straight camp?"

"The same as a gay man dressing up as a chorus girl is steeped in gay camp," he said. "Both represent attempts to live out what are essentially visual exaggerations. The shooter posted online videos of himself in his room, which he'd remade into a replica of the hero's lair. He dressed like the hero and acted out scenes from the film."

Robert snorted.

"What better example of our low standard of adulthood? When I was his age, I was reading Eugene O'Neill. This seventeen-year-old, in our technologically advanced society, behaves like a child playing cops and robbers. But it typifies what's happened over the last fifty years. Thanks to the self-indulgence ethos, after puberty, people cease growing to devote themselves either to sex, drugs, and rock and roll or the superstitious materialism driving consumer Capitalism. The education, acculturation, heightened senses, and ennobled faculties once symbolizing adulthood have practically vanished. *Iron Backbone* also spawned a video game this kid played incessantly, and has sites devoted to it where he posted fan fiction featuring himself as the hero's sidekick, a character not in the movie. Just like the camp chorus girl, he latched onto a handful of traits exaggerated by media representation and transformed them into a closed, hermetic kingdom. Then, when his kingdom conflicted with those of his peers—domains defined in the main by sports and partying—they responded to his alien qualities with verbal abuse."

"The derision defense," I said.

"Which the shooter countered with destruction, thus bringing his fantasy world to life and solving his real-world problems by picking up a gun and blowing people's heads off. You may consider it an extreme example; I find it typifies the trends of the last half-century or so. Isolation, ignorance, and indifference to the perspectives of others have replaced education and the arts as the foundation of society. We touched on the absurdity of philosophers whose advocacy of self-indulgence and opposition to empathy works against the learning necessary for philosophy in the first place."

"Yes."

"Hedonists like Epicurus are more and more often cited to support the self-indulgence ethos, along with that of self-centeredness."

"Because in order to be truly self-indulgent, you have to be unconcerned with the consequences of your actions on others," I said.

"Precisely. There's Rousseau, with his notion of original man as a solitary being stalking a primeval wilderness. But if Rousseau believed in the value and freedom of isolation, why did he write books, and who was he writing them for? Author and reader imply a relationship antithetical to isolation. Then there's Machiavelli and Nietzsche, whose contempt for empathy are widely cited. But rejecting empathy means rejecting an essential component for learning, for cultivating the brain. They're advocating a lifestyle that would produce individuals incapable of comprehending their texts. Further, if they followed a program of total self-centeredness, the ideal statesman Machiavelli posits, and Nietzsche's superman would inevitably deteriorate into blithering idiots, a phenomenon clearly illustrated by history's dismal parade of isolated and demented dictators. Then you have sociobiologists who reduce humans to blind, unthinking genetic impulses."

"Seems to me you've been referring to genetic or biological traits often enough to make your arguments."

"But for me, biological traits are the foundation for the intellectual faculties that complicate and enrich our experience of the world and life. Popular sociobiology would encourage people to ignore their complex abilities to indulge in blind, biological instincts. These are just a few examples of how intellectual laziness turns the desire to know into the exact opposite of true learning."

"How do you see that happening?"

"One of the tragic offshoots of the human desire to know is the unspoken belief that we, or exceptionally intelligent members of our species, can perceive and elucidate one or more abstract, super-human, or extra-human force dominating human destiny. Religion, philosophy, science, economics, and whatever others you might name are more representative of the human desire to touch the universal than they are proof of contact. More commonly, they serve as the mainspring for the dynamic between active and passive narcissists."

"How?"

"Since the forces in question fail to reveal themselves in a way that everyone can see or comprehend, the widespread desire to understand them becomes fertile ground for the growth of intermediaries."

"What do you mean by intermediaries?"

"A broad class ranging from scientists and philosophers to con men and crackpots who claim to have perceived a universal force in its entirety, or at least enough to deduce from it a series of rules and regulations to guide human life, individually and collectively."

"Preachers, pundits, and self-appointed messiahs," I said, "interpreting abstract principles the same way cultural critics interpret ambiguous artworks."

"Precisely," he said. "Active narcissists satisfy their egos with the assumed ability to understand such forces, and to mediate between them and the rest of humanity. Passive narcissists satisfy their egos by believing in, and therefore partaking of the active's superior knowledge. Currently, the most fashionable forces for interpretation are God—an old standby—biology, and what Scotty and I called the Magic Marketplace. Referencing God to justify moral and legal measures is too long-standing a habit for comment. Sociobiology, Social Darwinism, eugenics, and others of that class come from a desire to distill a clear direction for human life from biological principles. The Magic Marketplace is the belief that a collective satisfaction of short-term desires via continuous buying and selling decides the course of human destiny for the best, or the greater good, to use a current catchphrase. Instead of a culture where education and creativity play a role, ours is dominated by active narcissists claiming to know what God wants, what natural selection wants, or what the Magic Marketplace wants, for a population of passive narcissists craving an easily understood set of rules to obey. This isn't very far from the shamans of prehistory or the staff that interpreted the vague mutterings of the Delphic oracle for the Ancient Greeks. But as more individuals submit to the principles of whatever superhuman force they look to for guidance, interpreted by intermediaries more often than not appearing as talking heads on TVs and computers, the less likely they are to develop the active habits of mind that truly improve the quality of life."

"And lead to the creation of art."

"Not incidentally," he said. "In fact, one of the ways art helps cultivate the faculties is by contrasting abstract principles with the irreducible specificity of lived experience. Today, the allure of abstract principles and the solitary self-indulgence possible with audio-visual media, have made isolation, lack of empathy, and contempt for the things cultivated minds create the essence of freedom. The good life is that of an armchair adventurer obtaining chemical jolts from exploitative imagery in the seclusion of a living room, bedroom, or wherever, a way of being as far removed from Renaissance Man as possible. It's reminiscent of another study I read about some years ago. Electrodes were implanted in the brains of lab rats to stimulate their pleasure centers whenever the rats pressed a certain button. They were then given a choice between a button that dispensed food and a button that stimulated their pleasure centers. They chose pleasure over nutrition until they died of starvation."

"Then, as isolation led to the deaths of the king's infants, and the preference for pleasure killed the lab rats, you consider the prevalence of audio-visual pleasure in the modern world an equal harbinger of death?"

"If not physical death, certainly the death of culture," he said. "As with the lab rats, the pleasure of audio-visual media consumes every spare moment of the day. As with the king's quest to resurrect humanity's pure, primeval language by isolating his infants, the current habit of locating pure, primeval freedom in isolation removes key incentives for intellectual and moral growth. Together, they discourage people from cultivating their innate potentials, leaving many emotionally and intellectually stunted . . . and civilization rapidly devolving into a society of sociopaths."

"Really?"

"A neat oxymoron, don't you think?"

He sipped his tea, bitter and triumphant in his conclusions.

"I mean, you really believe we're devolving into a society of sociopaths?"

"If you accept my definition of a sociopath as someone unwilling or unable to use the intellectual endowments enabling one mind to tap into the inner world of another," he said. "We live in a time when extreme torture is considered entertainment, religious cults sexually abuse children or use them as suicide bombers, and serial killers are venerated in many quarters."

"Behaviors abundant in the past, too," I said, "along with cultural traditions of suffering as spectacle. Ancient Rome had gladiatorial contests and executions by wild animals. In fact, public executions were popular spectacles for centuries. The French *Grand Guignol* theatre lasted for more than half the twentieth century, attracting a devoted audience with staged images of gore and violent death . . ."

"The difference is," he said. "Those past spectacles occurred infrequently, at least in contrast to the permanent supply available with modern media. They were still framed by periods of everyday life. They also occurred in societies where learning was neither pervasive nor very advanced. I don't know the exact rates of literacy, but I'm sure they were much less than after the advent of the printing press."

"Meaning people had less chance to develop heightened senses or ennobled faculties."

"Even then, there were some with enough of both to decry the bloodiness of their culture: Seneca, for instance, inveighed against the excesses of Ancient Rome. The same widespread absence of learning was also true of the medieval centuries when public executions and other forms of blood sport were popular. The *Grand Guignol* was a theatrical genre operating within the limitations of all genres. It also began in the late nineteenth century when repetitive mass media was beginning to take hold, although again, it would've been framed for most spectators by periods lived in the wider world of their five senses. As for real-life acts, until recently, they were seen for what they are, serious moral failings. We also can't take their pervasiveness in history at face value."

"Why not?"

"Given the extent to which empathy plays a part in essential human abilities like language, everyday kindness and compassion were possibly taken for granted in the past, too tightly woven into the fabric of daily existence for chroniclers to consider them worth noting, except in extraordinary cases as in the lives of saints. They may have emphasized examples of cruelty because they were such glaring instances of inhumanity, of what happens when people lack a natural sense of empathy. I still recall the outrage that confronted the revelation of atrocities committed during World War II. Today, advocates of violence rely on this possibly incomplete, possibly biased historical record to support their beliefs. Moral failings are becoming the norm, accepted with a shrug and a smirk rather than censure. This is the great tragedy of the present. After a brief period when the advantages of literacy and education were available to more people than ever before, the reign of audio-visual media and smart devices are returning us to an earlier condition, one in which individuals are prevented by circumstance and discouraged by dogma from cultivating their most human traits. Even our standards of beauty efface rather than enhance one's humanity. People inflate their musculature and undergo plastic surgeries to conform to straight camp's visual exaggerations of gender until, rather than youthful, healthy homo-sapiens, they end up resembling the inanimate, uniform copies that pop out of a mold in a doll factory."

I laughed.

"You agree?" he said.

"I've seen enough of those living dolls around L.A. the last few months.

But unrealistic standards of beauty were present before film and TV, in ancient statuary, in aristocratic portraiture . . .”

“Hence my comment about visual media appealing to narcissists,” he said. “The artifacts you mention were created mainly to stoke their likenesses’ vanity, along with the admiration of the people they ruled. Yet I find even those portraits lack today’s relentless emphasis on transforming from a three-dimensional human into a two-dimensional image of one.”

“Probably because the purpose of such images has changed from an expression of power wielded by an elite to advertisements for the cosmetics and fashion industries.”

“A function making their effects all the more detrimental since it convinces more people they can attain what the images imply.”

“What do they imply?”

“Like the ecstasies of audio-visual media, they represent a near-hysterical, yet ultimately vain yearning to escape time, a yearning inevitably arising in a society that no longer encourages people to appreciate their place in time or the things time can bring them.”

“What things?”

“Knowledge, wisdom sometimes, the recollection of experiences sorrowful and joyous . . . everything that seasons both body and mind. Until a few decades ago, unreal standards of beauty in magazines and films were part of a society in which education and the arts also mattered. Today we’re urged to sacrifice the mind for the sake of a pristine body or the image of one. The problem with this is, as I’ve said, the brain, not the body, unites our perceptions of existence and ultimately arbitrates the quality of our lives.”

“Nostalgia also represents a yearning to escape time.”

“Is that an accusation?” he said, amused rather than offended.

“You have described your past in glowing terms.”

“I suppose. But before defending myself, I’ll have to know more about the charge. As with murder, there are different degrees of nostalgia, reflecting their import.”

“What might they be?”

“First, and most innocuous, is personal nostalgia. We who live in time, or maybe I should say we who are aware of living in time, are inevitably prone to it. The things lending savor to existence create more intense and lasting impressions when our senses and our faculties are young and most receptive to them. And if we find bliss at any stage in life, we can’t avoid looking back on that time with fondness.”

"What are the less innocuous forms?"

"They're what we might call cultural nostalgia. This is as inevitable as personal nostalgia for a species that strives to replicate its culture across generations. The irony here is that fixing culture in works of art increases the prevalence and malignancy of the nostalgia capable of being attached to it."

"I'm surprised to hear you recognize a downside to art."

"The downside is in the approach to it. The achievements in politics, philosophy, science, and art that have been handed down, and the comparable skills of their numerous chroniclers, are the bedrock of the learning that cultivates our faculties. They become malignant if we imagine they represent the entire historical era in which they occurred. Individuals or small groups living in equally circumscribed areas—like Ancient Athens or Renaissance Italy—are usually responsible for the greatest accomplishments of the past. Thanks to the fascination they exert, those looking back on these people and events often extend their dazzling sheen to the general socio-political conditions obtaining at the time, recasting it as a lost golden age or near-earthy paradise."

"Because romanticizing the past enables one to evade the uncertainty of the present," I said. "One dreams about it being an easier, simpler time, or a greater time, since one knows exactly what happens and what doesn't, and can imagine returning to it armed with that foreknowledge, rather than being plunged into the uncertainty endured by everyone alive in a given present."

"Unquestionably. The security felt when looking back at these periods combines with the glamour of events occurring in them to make history an ideal fodder for anyone wishing to evade experiencing time in the present. Then, as in a subsection of media's hall of mirrors, the fantasy is reproduced and extended by still other cultural products."

"What products do you mean?"

"Oh, legends passed from generation to generation by bards or enacted in quasi-religious ceremonies for preliterate societies, and by novelists and historians in literate societies. All such chroniclers are prone to romanticizing exploits of past individuals or groups, elevating them into emblematic standards of the era in which they lived for an audience wishing to escape the troublesomeness of the present. A handful of legends led the Ancient Greeks to imagine their earliest history was a golden age that decayed into a less marvelous silver age and then into the most debased age, their own. I also remember reading a volume of Ancient Egyptian literature that included a piece from 5,000 BC in which a character bemoaned the deterioration of general conditions from when he was a boy. Everything he railed about, the usual human failings like dishonesty, deviousness, and greed were certainly common in his youth, yet as with most people, he was too wrapped up in the thrill of discovering what it meant to be alive to attach the same significance to them."

"And these extrapolations are handed down until they attain the status of myth or received truth," I said.

"Despite correctives attempted by other cultural products, some quite as canonical as the fantasies," he said. "I'm sure you know *Don Quixote* depicts cultural nostalgia as a form of madness, in which an old man's sense of reality derives from old chivalric romances. But though the fallacy is obvious, it remains widespread, perhaps more so since, like narcissism, visual media is better suited to it than any other form of transmission."

"Because images imply rather than explicate, and are abstracted from time?"

"Partly," he said, "although selective or openly biased visual representations of the past are as old as literary and theatrical versions. Decorative arts like paintings and sculpture are excellent vehicles for cultural nostalgia. Paintings fix moments of glory for warriors or moments of leisure among groups of men and women in Arcadian gardens in such vivid terms they can convince viewers to extend what they see to the conditions obtaining for everyone in the historical period represented. An Impressionist painting, say, can lull viewers into believing that in Renoir's France, everyone spent their time strolling about colorful sunlit gardens in formal wear. Further, since images require less effort to comprehend, offering their implied ideas in one swift, uncritical glance, they reach more people. This is truer now for two reasons."

"One being that audio-visual media has replaced literacy."

"And the second being that socio-cultural changes from around the middle of the 1800s, and certainly since the introduction of film in the 1890s, have lent roughly every decade a unique audio-visual signature, signatures that in the past would have persisted for several decades, if not centuries."

"What do you mean by audio-visual signatures?"

"Fashions in dress and décor, the design of everyday objects from kitchenware to transportation, styles in music and slang," he said. "Each decade for the last hundred and fifty years or so has boasted such distinctive styles that when one or another is depicted, from the Wild West to the 1960s, they create the illusion of their being periods in which people lived and died for generations, rather than brief spans in which most of those alive in one lived to witness two or three or others. A person born at the end of the Wild West, for instance, may well have lived into the 1950s. But since the intervening decades are so distinct in terms of their audio-visual record, it would seem such an individual should rival Methuselah in longevity. This abstraction from time is further exacerbated by the number of films and TV shows set in the past. For instance, if you determined to watch all the westerns ever filmed, it would take longer than the actual Wild West lasted in real-time."

"Making it easier to turn historical fantasies into personal kingdoms to inhabit," I said.

"Something observable everywhere you look," he said. "How many people affect what cowboys wore in the Wild West or styles of the 1950s, embodying a nostalgic wish to take up permanent residence in an era during which nobody existed permanently—at least, nobody who grew to adulthood?"

"Just as today's shooter dressed up as a character in his favorite film."

"Indeed. What with adopting styles of the past and aping those in fantasy films, it sometimes seems as if human society has become a giant costume party."

"Yet you're uncompromising in your preference for art from the past."

"Only because it does what all great art does, or should do, despite bearing the stylistic residue of its era. Criticizing a Renoir painting as a historical document doesn't detract from Renoir's talent, or from the capacity of his work to help cultivate our senses and faculties."

This reminded me of what I said to David about nostalgia. But, at that moment, the image of Lena Crenshaw's old apartment loomed larger in my mind.

"Another of my clients had her apartment decorated like a Victorian Valentine's card. She said she'd earned the right to live her fantasies after forty years as a nurse."

"Whether or not anyone has the right to inhabit a fantasy world is debatable, and probably hinges on the extent to which they confuse fantasy with reality. Then again, as with the blanket skepticism toward mass media, resistance to cultural nostalgia can lead to the opposite prejudice: rejecting all past cultural products because one only sees in them the residue of their time. An insightful play is derided for its quaint slang phrases or a well-acted film laughed at for images of old cars or rotary-dial telephones."

"Mainly, though, the impulse is to romanticize the past."

"Because, as your client admitted, it's a fantasy, and fantasies are comforting. People escape the uncertain present with selective images of past epochs from Medieval Romances to sitcom images of middle-class family life in the 1950s. The same products also tend to focus on members of the elite classes of their era, enabling later audiences to imagine sharing the power and luxuries enjoyed by that elite. This, of course, is another romantic fallacy since, statistically speaking, had they been born in the era they romanticize, they likely would've counted among the disadvantaged majority, along with enduring negative conditions like lack of sanitation and the prevalence of disease that affected everybody. But as with the Renoir painting, those negative conditions are conveniently outside the frame, and therefore outside the minds of viewers."

"Which also makes cultural nostalgia the ideal vehicle for straight camp," I said, "by performing the same sleight of hand for past episodes of violence."

"Or sleight of eyes, more exactly," he said. "But it's true. Armchair adventurers sit for hours viewing the gladiatorial contests of Ancient Rome, gunfights in the Wild West, and every battle from the Trojan War to the Wars of the Roses to the two World Wars, all abstracted from the wider conditions obtaining in the times they occurred, and their long-term consequences. And like viewers who valorize past periods because the exclusionary imagery of various artworks narrows their focus enough for them to imagine living among a privileged, visible majority rather than the less visible, underprivileged majority, armchair adventurers indulge in the comforting fantasy of being among the triumphant, unscathed survivors of a given conflict rather than one of its numerous casualties."

"So cultural nostalgia constructs an image of the past shorn of its disadvantages, imbued with the sense of security that comes from hindsight, focusing on the genteel manners and luxuries of an elite, or on conflicts that excite but never mortally threaten straight camp fans, the whole existing in a limbo abstracted from the flow of time in which it played a part."

"Yet the lure of these obviously unreal fantasies is such that, today especially, you'll find many a demented latter-day Don Quixote proposing to legislate into being whatever fantasies of the past appeal to them."

"Probably nostalgia's most malignant aspect," I said, "goading its adherents into imposing their fantasies on others."

"And why I plead innocent to any but its most benign form," he said.

"I'll admit I'm nostalgic for the times I was in love and happy in my work, but I'd never confuse a period of personal happiness with a general golden age concurrent to it. If I'm nostalgic for anything else, it's for the approach to existence that was more prevalent in my youth, one valuing education and the arts and the ennobled faculties they develop. Following that approach led to most of the satisfaction I've found in life, personally and professionally. If my account leaves me open to accusations of nostalgia, it's because I can't help pitying younger people who have less chance of finding something similar under the current regime of mindless self-indulgence as a reward for adherence to religious, political, and economic dogma."

I broached an idea that had struck me earlier. "I've noticed your two main criticisms of culture concern repetition and lack of empathy."

"Naturally, since both restrict brain function."

"How do you figure?"

"I'm not a neuroscientist, obviously, but this is how I understand it based on what I've read. When we learn, the neurons in our brains link up, forming a chain or pathway that fixes the information we've acquired. Learning that two plus two is four establishes a specific series of connections between neurons."

"Yes."

"Now, when we learn, a certain amount of repetition is necessary to establish and reinforce these neural pathways. Kids learning math, at least in my youth, repeated equations to fix them in their neurons. But neural paths aren't rigid. After we learn one and one is two, we go on to learn two minus one is one because the neural pathway can change to accommodate new information or new ways of thinking about the information embedded there."

"You're talking about neural plasticity."

"Yes. But in order to benefit from it, our neurons must remain pliable enough to accommodate fresh information. Constantly reiterating an idea or worldview reinforces neural pathways at the expense of their plasticity, limiting our ability to learn. This is why repetition in culture is, for me, both boring and dangerous."

"So much for repetition. What about empathy, and its lack?"

"Empathy falls to a set of brain cells called mirror neurons whose purpose is to reflect signs of interior states in others, producing a simulation of that state that allows us to understand what they're experiencing: not precisely, of course, but enough for us to respond. They're what enable us to become parts of each other, since learning via spoken and written language would be impossible unless something in us granted us access to the thoughts of others. And since they're neurons, they're capable of the same plasticity as other neurons. This allows us not only to expand our store of knowledge but our capacity for empathy, which in turn creates our sense of morality. Pretty much every society has some version of what we call the Golden Rule: do unto others as you would have them do unto you; never judge someone unless you've walked a mile in their shoes. These precepts wouldn't just be impossible without mirror neurons; they're also an oblique encouragement to exercise them. This was what I meant when I said human rights are an issue of intellect as much as emotion. Anything restricting our capacity for empathy restricts a part of our brains essential for both learning and morality."

"I see."

"The ethos of mindless self-indulgence, limiting the mind to its own pleasures and pains; to dulled perceptions of time and the consequences of one's actions; exacerbated by the isolation created by technology, all oppose the exercise of our natural empathy, which is why I consider the modern world a society of sociopaths, or budding sociopaths. It also explains why I prefer art to philosophy."

"Why?"

"Philosophical and scientific systems, by virtue of their pretense to universality, can only devolve into a set of precepts embodied in rigid neural pathways. This reduces brain function to memorizing the precepts of the system, and individuals to functional, utilitarian units whose purpose is to carry out the precepts. Art presents us with a unique arrangement of elements, while narrative art traces the unique events befalling unique characters and their unique responses to them. This grounds me in a reality of varied human experiences, exercises the neural plasticity that allows me to continue learning, and maintains me as what I hope has been a reasonably moral human being."

"I see."

"But like I said, technology is quickly rendering this way of being obsolete, and with it are disappearing the associated benefits that improve the quality—and qualities—of life."

"Like what?"

"As older people grow accustomed to technology, organizations like *Heart and Hands* will become obsolete. They'll have what they need delivered to them from stores by anonymous deliverers or robots, and there'll be less chance for people like you and me to meet."

"And if that hadn't happened, I would've had less reason to visit the Argonaut, and I probably wouldn't have met David."

"See what happens when people enter more fully into the temporal sequences of life?" He sighed. "I know many changes—in medicine most of all—have improved things in lots of ways over the past fifty years. But I'm glad I grew up in a time and place where education, the arts, and the need to interact with others enabled me to realize my potentials, even if the result was less than I hoped for at the start. I met interesting people, read great books, saw great plays and great art, and heard great music, all of which enriched my existence immeasurably. Much of the best of what civilization offered became part of me because I was taught to be curious enough and willing enough to welcome it into my private kingdom, and in return, my kingdom and I became steadily more than we were before."

"Yet you've shrunk your kingdom down, too, to this sun-drenched shoe-box, as you called it."

He chuckled, perhaps flattered by my remembering the phrase. "A process that unfolded over two decades and wasn't entirely voluntary."

"How'd it happen?"

"I've told you Jeremy left me wary of any new relationships. For companionship, I relied on my oldest friends, some single like me, others in long-term partnerships. Then AIDS reared its ugly head, scaring me off casual encounters, as it did most others. From the 1980s to the 1990s, it spirited away many of my L.A. friends and severed a good half of my New York connections, for whom Mag served as my mourner by proxy. I lived in a state of fearful suspended animation, like other gay men, worried lest the virus were incubating inside me, suspense punctuated by periods of sorrow and meeting friends at rapidly shrinking parties where we discussed those who'd died like soldiers in a lengthy war recalling their fallen brethren."

"You were still only in your fifties. That seems a little young to give up on love."

"Perhaps," he said. "But after having my heart broken twice and with AIDS all around, I thought it better, or less risky to let my desires atrophy as I had my paternal instincts. If Coleridge captured what being swept off my feet as a young man had been like, another British poet, Ernest Dowson, supplied the couplet that best expressed my later state of mind:

Love, that was songful, with a broken lute
In grass of graveyards goeth murmuring

"My surviving friends and I also discussed the changes in culture and media, sharing the uncomfortable position of being aesthetes in an age of advancing barbarism, treading the grass of art's graveyard, as it were. I had my first heart attack in 1998, at age sixty-three. I recovered enough to continue acting, though by then, age had forced me to join the ranks of character actors, playing a succession of contrast parts."

"What's a contrast part?"

"One that directly contrasts with the actor's appearance," he said, "commonly, its children delivering adult wisecracks, or older people spouting raunchy innuendoes or the slang indigenous to the under thirty crowd. My doctor recommended exercise for my heart, and I followed a mild regimen until arthritis encroached on my mobility. After my second heart attack, at seventy, the advice was to retire. I'd been living in my shoebox since 1988, so I became resigned to spending my last days here, with trips to the market or to visit friends. During the last ten years, my friends either died or became too infirm for visits, relegating the remnants of our relationships to phone calls. The rest, you know. My arthritis eventually forbade me from roaming outside, and you appeared. But though I rarely interact with people anymore, the joy of reading remains. I exercise my mind on ideas and sensations recorded by some of the most interesting individuals the human race has ever produced, which I find more worthy of my remaining time than gazing at a series of insipid reality shows or meaningless competitions. Fascinating people still become part of me, and I'm still becoming more than I was."

"I'm glad you have that pleasure."

"As am I," he said. "Aside from love, it's what I wish most for you when you're my age."

My phone rang.

"It's David," I said and answered. "Hi."

"Hey. Are we still on for tonight?"

"Sure. Why?"

"It's six-thirty. You usually phone by now."

"Crap. I'm sorry. Robert and I were talking."

Robert yelled: "Sorry, David."

David laughed and said, "Tell him I figured as much."

"If I leave now, I can shower and have everything ready by eight, maybe."

"Why don't I get pizza? We can do dinner night tomorrow."

"Are you sure?"

"Sure. I'll see you in an hour at your place?"

"Great."

"Bye."

I returned the phone to my pocket.

"Was he disappointed," Robert said, "or angry?"

"Neither. I was supposed to cook dinner tonight."

"When did you start cooking?"

"David's sister's been giving us lessons."

"Good," he said, "though I'm sure they're not as thrilling as they were with Paolo. She's a caterer, isn't she?"

"Was," I said. "We decided cooking for ourselves would be healthier and more economical than relying on take-out. I've been practicing this last week."

"I'm sorry I ruined it. You should've stopped me."

"I didn't want to. And it gives me an extra day to prepare. I'm planning a nice intimate chicken Florentine, but there's every chance we'll be ordering take-out again."

"I'm sure you'll do fine. You'd better get going. I don't want to interfere with you two more than I already have."

I carried my empty glass to the kitchen and placed it in the dishwasher. Returning to the living room, I found him with the book of sonnets open on his lap.

"I'll see you next week. Call if you need anything."

"Have fun tonight."

"I will," I said. "I have one final question, though."

"What's that?"

"If you're opposed to censorship and dogma, how do you imagine the problems you've outlined might be corrected, or are they insoluble?"

"Things can be improved, I think. It would involve adopting a standard of adulthood that values education for its own sake, one that encourages an understanding of both the world and the self. Only by understanding yourself, what you are as a human being, and your place in time, rather than being just a superficial catalog of likes, dislikes, and desires, can you see through and escape the culture of repetitive exploitation. I've often felt one way to encourage this would be to teach the rudiments of cognitive science at the high school level. Adolescence is the age when self-reflection takes hold in earnest. What better aid to it than understanding how the brain works? Perhaps it would encourage more to appreciate and cultivate their uniquely human abilities, including the aptitude for language and everything else that enters into art. And it would require a notion of freedom that's greater than isolated self-indulgence."

"Sounds reasonable," I said, "if most likely impracticable. I'm also wondering if what you said about accuracy not being the purpose of memory means everything you've told me has been inaccurate."

"I'm sure inaccuracies crept in here and there. But again, what I remember most is how events and people made me feel, since my reactions to them led me from one step in my life to another, ultimately creating the person telling you about them. Anecdotes are the substance of every human life, and that's what I've offered you: experiences and observations drawn from my particular existence, not what's left after they've been subjected to the homogenizing, dogmatic generalizations of preachers, pundits, scientists, philosophers or, heaven help us, the categories and genres beloved by cultural critics. Some generalizations have provided a welcome context for things that are important to me, making them easier to comprehend. But I've always maintained a strict line of demarcation between what's theirs and what's mine."

"I see," I said, and hesitated.

"You have a third final question?"

"No," I said, "it's more like a confession."

"Well, take heart, my son, and unburden yourself," he said, and by way of explanation added: "I played Father O'Malley in our high school drama club's adaptation of *Going My Way*."

"Oh. First, let me say I know what you meant before, about wanting to reach people in the past."

He smiled tolerantly. "How could you? You're too young."

"I also need to apologize."

"For what?"

"What I said to you when we first met about me joining *H&H* because I felt sorry for the older people I saw around. Jeremy's . . ."

"Don't give it a thought. What's that got to do with people from your past?"

"I didn't tell you exactly why I volunteered."

The admission left him unperturbed. "Why did you?"

"Ten years ago, when I came out to my mom, she told me her dad's brother had been gay."

"Indeed?" Robert said.

"His name was Lawrence. He was deeply closeted, at least to his family and childhood friends."

"Par for the course for my generation."

"He dated a few girls in high school and, after leaving for college, kept everyone at home in the dark about his love life. Later, he joined a law firm in Pittsburgh. For the next seven years, he'd come back for holidays and send letters but he only ever discussed his work. One day my grandfather went to Pittsburgh on business. He showed up at Lawrence's unannounced and found him in a compromising position with another man."

"What happened?"

"The family disowned him. He never found a life partner. During my sophomore year in college, he died of a heart attack. Nobody knew for six days, until his neighbors noticed a strange smell coming from his apartment. The coroner also found signs of malnutrition, which she felt contributed to his heart failing. His neighbors told the police he didn't go out much. A few picked up groceries for him from time to time, but if they didn't see him or he didn't contact them, they just assumed he was okay."

"When you get older, you feel less and less like bothering people, maybe because you feel less and less like people bothering you. Present company excepted, of course."

"My mom showed me a picture of him as a senior in high school, the last one the family had of him before they cut ties."

"What was he like?"

"Average, I guess: dark hair, dark eyes, slim," I said. "But he had a friendly, lopsided smile that made me wish I'd gotten to know him. I wanted to hear what being gay had been like for him, and I wanted him to know someone else in the family shared that trait."

"I imagine it would've made a big difference to both of you."

"Then I realized if I'd come out a few years earlier, I might've had the chance. I knew I was gay when I was fourteen, but I didn't tell my mom until after college."

"Were you worried about her reaction?"

"Not exactly. She's not judgmental. It's just that after my dad left, it was my job not to do anything to upset or worry her. I saw what she'd gone through with him, and I didn't want to cause her more stress, which is what I assumed dealing with my sexuality would do. Having boyfriends in college convinced me to stop living the lie. When I told her, it turned out to be one of the least stressful moments of my life."

"Fortunately for you."

"I know. That's when she told me about her uncle. If I'd come out to her earlier, I'd have heard about him while he was still alive. I could've contacted him and visited, seen how he was living, and he wouldn't have died the way he did." I paused, fighting the regret that overwhelmed me whenever I talked about Lawrence. "Sometimes, like you said, usually at night, I see the man with that lopsided smile, alone and hungry day after day, and I want to reach back to him for us to be parts of each other's lives."

"If your mother's not judgmental, why didn't she contact him?"

"She was always working and being a single mother. She also said she and her two cousins grew up after Lawrence had been banished. Their elders rarely mentioned him. When they did, it was only to hint at some insurmountable reason for his absence. They grew up seeing him as a distant, slightly sinister legend rather than a flesh-and-blood relation. He stayed that way for them until he died."

"Then I and the rest of your clients are essentially surrogates for your great-uncle?"

"Partly, I guess . . . I hope that's not too weird."

"On the contrary, I'm honored, and it's a long time since I've been that. Besides, I've served as a surrogate before for my lovelorn *Grandview Park* fans. And you're lucky."

"Why?"

"You and David both have seen the damage time wreaks while you're still young enough to profit from it. Most people, as I've said, drift from one indulgence to another, facing the truth only when they glance at a mirror or attend a funeral. You've been warned. Be aware of time and what happens when you allow it to pass without attending to its contents because what it contains is your life and the lives of whomever you love."

"I'll try." I gathered the flattened shopping bags and started for the door.

"Paul."

I turned round. "Yes?"

"Your great-uncle would have adored you and been very, very proud."

"Thanks."

He opened his sonnets, and I headed to my car.

Back home, the glittering facets of Erich Jacobson's transformative L.A. decade dimmed beside the darker world Robert had depicted. Rather than work on the outline, I flipped through Carol Quigley's diary, brooding over her and Jacobson's affair and her early widowhood; Robert's failed romances; my great-uncle Lawrence's fate, the possible impossibility of love and our opposing desire to become parts of each other.

David arrived at seven with pizza and salad. "Were you working?"

"No, thinking."

He placed the boxes on the table. "About the draft?"

"No," I said, "my talk with Robert."

"It must have been something."

"Yeah, it was."

He opened the pizza box and sniffed its contents. "Margot's boyfriend picked her up at the store tonight. You should see him." He snapped open the plastic salad box.

"Why?"

"He's the tallest person I've ever met."

"Taller than your dad?"

"Believe it or not. His shoulders are broader, too, and he's got a head like a St. Bernard. Margot says he's from Minnesota, but I think he slid down a beanstalk."

He breezed into the kitchen and breezed back carrying napkins, forks, and plates.

"It's just as well you postponed cooking dinner," he said as he set the table. "It gives me a chance to practice before I tackle the pasta primavera I have planned for you. Just don't tell Marge. She'd be pissed if she knew we're ignoring her lessons."

I shifted to a chair at the table. He stood beside me like a waiter and portioned the salad onto our plates. When he sat down, and before we began eating, I briefly related what Robert told me that afternoon.

He listened and afterward said, "I'm not surprised you lost track of time."

"No matter what happens," I said, "I want you to know how glad I am you've become part of me."

"I'm glad you're part of me, too."

15.

Six months after beginning the draft, I completed *Transformation: Erich Jacobson in Los Angeles 1936–1946*. Robert reacted equivocally to the announcement.

"Congratulations. Are you pleased with the results?"

"Very."

"Where do you go from here?"

"That's what David and his family would like to know."

"Especially now that you've exorcised the specter of Cretin Corey like the nameless narrator vanquished the spirit of Rebecca."

"Who?"

"Rebecca, in the DuMaurier novel and Hitchcock film of the same name."

"Oh, yeah," I said, after rifling my memory for the plot. "The day after I submitted the manuscript, we took off for another weekend at his sister's. He said it was to celebrate, but I think they wanted to grill me about my plans."

"Have you any?"

"Nothing definite," I said. "UCLA is grateful that I convinced Barbara Marcus to place her mom's documents in their archives, especially since they figure so prominently in the monograph. They may offer me a position. Then again, I may find another subject to write about. Or maybe I'll take some time to weigh my options. I've enough to live on for a while, and I need a breather after all that research and writing."

"Do your options include relocating?"

"Probably not. I never imagined I'd make such a nice life here, or any kind of life for that matter. If I could convince my mother to fly out now and again, it'd be perfect."

"I know it's selfish to want you around . . ."

"Not at all. I've enjoyed our talks. A lot of what you've said has made me more appreciative of what I have, especially David."

"I'm glad. And it makes it easier to ask you a favor I've absolutely no right to ask."

"What's that?"

"Would you consider acting as my guardian?"

"Your guardian?"

"I have the medical directives in place. A do not resuscitate order and the like. But it's always possible a stroke or Alzheimer's or something else may leave me without self-determination. You've heard of the abuse that happens in nursing homes, especially to people without relatives to watch over them. My only family are cousins back east whom I've never even met. I'd only be a nuisance to them, especially since there's no money involved. I don't want to be tossed onto a human garbage heap. You're the only one I can trust to prevent that from happening. Will you?"

"Of course."

"Then again, another heart attack may spare us the necessity."

"Don't say that."

"Why not? I don't want you forced to make decisions for me, and I don't fancy a long, drawn-out death as a borderline vegetable."

"Let's take the future day by day, okay?"

"A privilege accorded only to people my age," he said.

A week later, in the presence of a lawyer and a notary, I signed papers naming me Robert's legal guardian, without financial remuneration, in the event he became mentally incapacitated.

Transformation caused a stir among the elite circle of Harold Herring aficionados, both scholars and laymen. Three months after it appeared, Jacobson's great-niece Ingrid proposed I compile his official biography. David and I lay in bed that night, discussing her offer.

"You have to do it," he said, "if for the prestige alone."

"I can do a lot of the research online, but it'll still mean going to Denmark to talk to people and search the archives there, not to mention the suff Ingrid says she has. Who knows where it'll lead? You've seen how easy it is for one or two pieces of information to take me down a lengthy byway. I'd rather stay here."

"I'd rather you stayed here, too. But it's too good an opportunity."

"Opportunities are about getting what you want," I said. "I want to be with you."

"More than you want to be the world's foremost authority on Erich Jacobson?"

"Yes."

He rubbed his leg against mine. "We can video chat and text, and I can probably manage a weekend trip or two."

"As long as you promise that when I get back, we'll pick up where we left off," I said, "by which I mean where we are this moment."

"And after five days in bed, we'll go to Marge's for the weekend. What'll you do about your apartment?"

"I don't know. I can't afford to pay rent on a place I'm not living in."

"What about moving in with me?"

"Really?"

"Yeah. I thought about asking you before, but now it's perfect. You can keep your stuff here while you're away."

"I don't have much, apart from my books."

"Space isn't important," he said.

"As long as there's enough for a few rounds of Popcorn Tag, and its ancillary amusements," I said. "I hate leaving *H&H*, though. I've gotten pretty attached to those people."

"I could take over for you."

"Are you kidding?"

"I may have brought it up to keep you talking that day in the Argonaut, but I really was thinking about volunteering with them. With Margot handling the store and you being away, I'll have the time. And it'll make me feel a little nearer to you while you're gone."

The arrangement satisfied Robert. "I'd like to get to know David better," he said.

"Can I trust you with him?"

He practically hooted with laughter. "You can't imagine I have a snowman's chance in Death Valley of luring him away from you. What are you worried about?"

"I don't want you prying into his past with Corey and quizzing him . . ."

"My butting in will consist entirely of giving you advice in private. After that, you're on your own. Just remember, with his protective family looking out for him, you should have someone on your side."

"You didn't tell me the truth about your paternal instincts," I said, thinking now that his persistent mistrust of David stemmed from a desire for someone to need his advice. "They haven't entirely atrophied."

"You're welcome to whatever's left of them."

"Thanks. But I'm sure I'm on a secure footing with him and his family."

"Well, if you run into any trouble . . ."

"I know I'll have someone to turn to."

Preparations for the trip crowded the next few weeks. David and I transferred my things to his place; I briefed him on my *H&H* clients and traded emails with contacts in Denmark: acquaintances of Jacobson and his family, and officials at institutions holding relevant documents. Marge and Brad held a *bon voyage* weekend for me at their house, and the following Monday, I flew to Copenhagen.

Ingrid welcomed me with kind words about *Transformation* and full confidence in my ability to paint a well-rounded portrait of her great-uncle. I began by sorting the documents in her possession, twelve boxes jammed with items ranging from appointment books to patient notes. One box contained letters from friends in Los Angeles that provided the other half of the correspondence I had read back home, including Carol Quigley's letters to him. I expected nothing more of equal or greater importance until, as if fulfilling David's long-ago prediction, the tenth box discharged a bombshell.

Scrawled across the backsides of what at first appeared to be a miscellany of bills, bank statements, and business letters, I found the manuscript for a fifth Harold book called *Atomic Herring*. The plot involved Harold acquiring super swimming speed after an encounter with an atomic-powered submarine, which enabled him to extricate both humans and fellow fish from various dicey situations. The dates on the papers, May 1955 to January 1956, placed the book's composition in the midst of an escalating Cold War, explaining its title and subject, yet Ingrid and I agreed it retained enough universal appeal to transcend the antiquated adjective 'atomic.' I convinced her to postpone publication until I completed the biography for the books to support each other's sales.

Three days after *Atomic Herring* surfaced, David landed in Copenhagen for the weekend. We toured the attractions work forced me to ignore and spent long evenings in his hotel room, a far fancier setting than the flat I had sublet. Despite talking every night since my departure, I waited for our in-person reunion to mention the manuscript.

"You must've shit a brick," he said as we lay twined beneath the satin comforter on the hotel bed.

"Enough to repave Marge and Brad's walkway," I said. "And it's as good as the others. I don't know why he never published it."

"He didn't tell anybody about it or talk about it in his letters?"

"No. It's like he wrote it and forgot it."

"Then the trip's been a bigger success than you expected."

"To find *Atomic Herring*, yes. The records of his practice are a different matter. He had some seriously disturbed patients."

"You knew he was a psychoanalyst."

"I know, but it's different thinking about his patients in the abstract. Probing the details makes them almost too real."

"You knew about Mona Jackson."

"But not much about her condition. The records he kept of his L.A. patients weren't available. I was hoping to find them here, but the files start where he started after he got back in 1946."

"What's bothering you about them?"

"Well, for one, he treated a young man who was obsessed with cemeteries."

"Necrophilia?"

"No. He wasn't interested in corpses, only cemeteries. He'd spend as much time as he could in them. He'd camp out in mausoleums and got into a few altercations with mourners who found him sleeping on their relatives' graves. Then there was a woman who suffered from what Jacobson termed a vegetable compulsion."

"A what?"

"She kept buying vegetables."

"What's wrong with that?"

"She didn't eat them. She kept them around the house, like art objects."

"They must've rotted."

"They did. She bought fresh ones but didn't throw the others out. Her neighbors kept complaining about the smell and the bugs."

"I'll bet."

"The one who really bothers me is a patient he refers to as Greta E."

"Do I even want to know?"

"She had obsessive fantasies about torturing and killing the children and animals in her neighborhood. He described her as a sadist incapable of knowing love. Reading his notes, I realized she was the prototype for Electra Eel."

"You're kidding. Electra never struck me as a sadist."

As promised, David read the Harold corpus prior to my finishing *Transformation* and afterward read them to his nephews. He apologized for kidding me and pronounced them "really cool."

"She wasn't, but she illustrates what he considered Greta's problem. Electra used her electricity not only as protection against predators but to drive away others who might like her, because she was afraid or didn't know how to be liked. He believed Greta E. did the same, viewing any kindly emotion as a threat and relying on violence, or dreams of violence, to protect her from it."

"Did he manage to treat any of them?"

"Not very successfully. Psychiatry was in its infancy back then, both in terms of therapy and medication. He was basically fumbling for solutions. Greta continued with him until she died at sixty-seven. She never stopped dreaming about murder and torture, though she never acted on it, which I suppose is to his credit. Today, of course, rather than a psycho, she'd probably be considered a model individualist and have her own podcast."

"Lower your voice a bit, and I'd swear I was listening to Robert."

"He's not always wrong, you know," I said, repeating what Robert once said to me about Grantland.

"Few people are," David said. "Any chance Greta's last initial stands for Eel?"

"I doubt it," I said, grateful for the laugh.

"And weren't you hoping to find more connections between his life and books?"

"Sure. I just hate linking *Harold Herring Meets Electra Eel* to such a dark case history."

"Maybe rather than the case history darkening the book, you can emphasize how Jacobson turned a dark case history into a meaningful story."

This approach, while obvious, never occurred to me. I tweaked his nose. "Not just a pretty face, are you?"

He laughed. "Any other discoveries?"

"Carol Quigley's letters to him, which are pretty much how she summarized them in her diary. Nothing else significant seems to have happened in the decades bracketing his sojourn in Los Angeles."

"I guess you'll have to focus on the affair again."

"Fleshed out with extensive quotations from his and Carol's letters," I said. "The good thing is it means there's less reason for me to stay here. I've got all the interviews recorded and scans of the necessary documents on my computer. I can work from them at home."

"Seriously?"

I reveled in his delight. "I've two more archives to search, but unless there's another bombshell lurking somewhere, I'll be ready to head back in a few weeks."

"That'd be great. Mark and Adrian will be relieved. They keep asking where you are and when you'll be back. They're afraid you're gone for good."

"Didn't you explain to them?"

"As best I could. They're impressed you're writing about the guy who wrote the Harold books, but they're not clear on what researching a biography entails."

"Call them later, and I'll talk to them. How's the *H&H* work?"

"Good. I see why you liked it."

"How's Robert?"

"Less maudlin than when I first met him. He's been telling me about his days in New York. He can be really funny."

"I know."

"You didn't tell me he's such a good cook, either."

"How do you know?"

"He never cooked for you during all those visits?"

"No. Why'd he cook for you?"

"I happened to show up a half hour late, and he was making a zucchini frittata for lunch. I told him it smelled delicious, and he had me try it."

"Did he tell you where he got the recipe?"

"Yeah, Paolo. He gave it to me, and I passed it on to Marge. She went crazy over it. I'm surprised he never made it for you."

"I guess because I was never late."

"Which goes to show promptness isn't always a virtue. I'll make it for you when you get back. I'd rather it be our thing, anyway."

"We're assembling quite a litany of 'our things,' aren't we?" I said.

"My mom was right about you and Robert. He told me talking to you gave him a more balanced view of his life."

"I think he just needed a sounding board, and I was handy. Or maybe I channeled Jacobson's analytic listening skills."

David nestled his head on my shoulder. "For future reference, listen when I talk, but keep the analyses to a minimum."

"I will if you will."

I returned two weeks earlier than scheduled and barely unpacked before we left for another weekend at Marge and Brad's, which as usual, included Tom and Delia. The first night, after dinner, I recounted my trip, illustrated by pictures and videos, and dispensed souvenirs.

The following Monday, I began writing the biography, working from the moment David left in the morning until he returned at six. A few evenings, he found me asleep at my desk, the computer screen bathing me in radiation, after which he insisted I leave the apartment for at least two hours each day. I met him at Brahmin's Banquet for lunch and joined him on his *H&H* deliveries. My former clients welcomed me back and quizzed me about my trip and my work.

The day we showed up together at Robert's, he greeted me with, "How's the bio coming, Paul?"

"Slowly but surely."

"He spends every waking minute at his computer," David said. "If I'm not careful, he'll end up looking like a pale, bug-eyed cave-dweller from a horror movie."

"I have to assemble a lot of diverse material. Imagine doing a jigsaw puzzle without a copy of the completed image to guide you," I said.

"Sounds excruciating," Robert said. "I always liked working from an established text, though there were always the edits and additions that occur during rehearsals."

David carried the shopping bags into the kitchen, allowing Robert and me to talk while he stored the groceries.

"David tells me there were no more skeletons in Jacobson's closet," Robert said.

"No, but after seeing where he lived, I can pad out the text with some nice scenic descriptions. He was also an early adherent of psychoanalysis, which means I can focus for a while on his conflicts with the medical establishment. And there's the story of his love child. I only touched on it in *Transformation,* to explain why he wrote the Harold books and how it influenced their content. In the biography, I'll go into it more deeply, how it affected his life, and Carol's and Barbara's."

"Someone will want to film it, mark my words," Robert said, his tone leaving me uncertain whether his words constituted a prediction of good fortune or a prophecy of doom. "How did his family react to you locating their unknown relative?"

"I introduced Ingrid and Barbara during a video chat. They were on the way to becoming fast friends when I left."

"Good."

"David says you've been regaling him with your stories."

"He's been about as good an audience. And it was the only way I could get him to stop talking about you."

"I'm sure he didn't . . ."

"Incessantly," Robert said. "At least, it seemed incessant. Only real love narrows your focus that sharply."

"I assume you approve of him now?"

"I just wanted to make sure he was good for you."

"We're good for each other. Among other improvements, I've convinced him to cut his cologne consumption in half, and he's gotten me to be less reticent."

"Good for you both. Have you been doing anything other than working since you got back?"

I described David's program of therapeutic socializing, during which he entered with empty shopping bags and we prepared to leave.

"I wish you luck with the biography," Robert said.

"Thanks."

"Will you be coming around again?"

"Absolutely. I've missed our talks, and I haven't forgotten my legal duties."

"I'd rather have you here to talk than discharge a legal duty."

"Me too. I'll see you next week."

Fourteen months later, Ingrid turned *Atomic Herring* over to an editor the same day I delivered the manuscript of my biography, titled *The Fish and the Analyst*, to mine. *Atomic* appeared before the bio and became a moderate bestseller. *Fish and Analyst* sold nicely, thanks to the recovered Harold novel. As Robert predicted, the tale of Jacobson's affair and long-lost daughter drew interest from producers alert for real-life tearjerkers to film, eventually becoming a drama called *Aftermath of Betrayal,* airing with considerable success on the streaming service Fan Basics. And as David predicted, the bio established me as the recognized expert on Erich Jacobson. Colleges and universities invited me to lecture, and several tendered me offers to teach. I turned them down to pursue a story I had stumbled on while rooting among Oliver Castle's papers.

When Jacobson arrived at Paramount, Castle assigned Martin Atwater, a scribe from the script department, to advise him on scriptwriting. As a matter of course, I searched Atwater's name and discovered a box of his papers also residing at UCLA. Among them, I found a packet of twenty personal letters and his diary, which chronicled an intriguing private life.

Atwater worked in the script department from 1927 to 1958. He lived in Glendale with his wife Edna and their four children until, in 1948, he fell in love with a new male recruit to the department, with whom he carried on an affair that lasted until Atwater's death in 1979, at age seventy-seven. I discussed my intent to relate Atwater's story with David, who showed interest, and with Robert, who said, "The name's familiar. Was he a thin fellow with white hair and blue eyes? His lover was Tyler something . . . Tyler Appleton, correct?"

"Yes. Did you know them?"

"They appeared at gatherings among the older gay crowd in the 1970s. I often spotted them at Cukor's house. What's he doing in the archive?"

"Appleton donated his papers after Atwater died. Most concern daily operations in the script department, which makes them a boon for anyone researching the film industry or the specific films he worked on. Appleton may not have been aware any personal papers were among the rest when he donated them."

"Or he secretly hoped their story would be told."

"Could be," I said. "What were they like?"

"Tyler was an aging social butterfly. Martin drifted around the edges, sipping a drink, watching and listening."

"Wallflowers often attract social butterflies," David said with a glance at me.

"True," Robert said, "but I think the discretion imposed by his double life ended up obscuring his personality. He always looked slightly haunted. I heard his wife knew about the two of them early on. Perhaps he was burdened by guilt."

"I take it you didn't know them well?"

"No, they were of a different generation. Tyler gladly held forth about the old studio system if you asked him, and dished all the behind-the-scenes dirt about the movies I loved as a kid. On the other hand, you had to coax Martin to open up, even a little. Tyler was protective of him for that reason. How do you think Martin's descendants will react to you dredging up their affair?"

"I contacted his granddaughter, April. She identifies as pansexual. She's all for it."

"You shouldn't have much trouble, then. I'll be eager to read about them."

"You'll get the first copy after David."

Atwater proved an easier subject than Jacobson, mainly because I had the crucial material near to hand. The letters and diary, written fitfully over twenty-six years, portrayed a man beset by guilt, as Robert suspected, yet who adored his children and lover and cared very much about his wife. April's father Armand, youngest of the four Atwater children, supplied Edna's diary, which with her archived letters to Martin, presented her side of the story. Understandably, she had been dismayed to discover her husband falling in love with another man and struggled to understand why he preferred Tyler until a worldly-wise friend counseled her that it boiled down to a matter of taste. She told Edna, "Some people like spinach, and some people don't. It's no more profound than that, dear."

"The only sensible way to look at it," Robert said after I repeated the comment to him, "and the exact opposite of how most Molehill Men approach sexuality."

Upon recovering her self-esteem, Edna turned her attention to their children. She worked with Martin to preserve the illusion of happily married parents, celebrating their birthdays and graduations and comforting them during illnesses and other crises. Martin spent most evenings with Tyler under the pretense of working late, while Edna acquired a steady lover in a local bank teller who later died in the Korean War, followed by two more affairs, the first lasting five years, the second two and a quarter. Balancing separate love lives with joint family duties eventually steered the couple past acrimony to a functional relationship that ultimately settled into a genuinely warm friendship. Martin commiserated with Edna over her first lover's death and her later breakups, while Edna lent an ear to Martin during rocky times with Tyler. After Armand, their youngest, left for college Martin more or less moved in with Tyler, yet the Atwaters never officially divorced, and Martin's legal residence remained the house he had shared with Edna.

Encouraged by April and impressed by my credentials as Jacobson's biographer, the four Atwater children allowed Edna's diary and a smattering of other letters in their hands to surrender their secrets. They also granted me interviews, although each told a similar story. They only learned the truth after Edna's diary surfaced following her death. Despite an initial shock, it explained things that had mystified them in their youth, yet since they always felt loved, they ultimately reconciled to the reality of their parent's marriage.

The night after my interview with the last of the Atwater children, I outlined the story to David while he loaded the dishwasher, and I wiped down the kitchen counter.

"Amazing how people adjusted to unorthodox relationships back then," he said, "Jacobson and his friend's wife and now these three."

"Yeah. People cling to the idea of a prim, pure past either to lionize or demonize it, but when you take a closer look, you find it's just as complex as the present."

"I couldn't live a lie like they did. I'd suffocate."

"So would I. But it'll make fascinating reading. I'm just not sure how to treat Martin. I wish I knew if he'd been attracted to men before his marriage."

"He doesn't say anything about it anywhere?"

"No. Edna's diary doesn't mention it, either."

"Does it make much difference?"

"I think so. If he'd never been attracted to men before Tyler, I could cut him some slack. If he knew and married Edna without mentioning it, he deliberately deceived her."

"Weren't marriages of convenience common for gays back then?"

"Sure. But it wasn't fair if she didn't know that's what it was."

"From what you've said, they got along pretty well later on. Even their kids made peace with it, so maybe it wasn't as traumatic as you imagine."

"Maybe. Maybe it reminds me too much of my father leaving."

"You can't let your personal life influence how you treat theirs."

"I know. It's a compelling story either way. There could be another film in it."

"You're on a roll," he said, rather pointedly directing his attention to a stock pot that resisted fitting on the bottom rack of the dishwasher.

"You don't seem too pleased about me getting another big check from a production company."

"I'm always happy for you."

"Why not be happy for us both?"

He stood and closed the dishwasher. "I can't help thinking I may not be the best fit for you."

"Not the best fit?" I said. "Your lines taper perfectly, and you certainly don't need lengthening."

An involuntary smile appeared and faded away. "Seriously, you've been doing better these last few years than either of us could have imagined. I'm still just a guy with a bookstore."

"And an allied online business."

His brow contracted, striking the cerulean sheen from his eyes. "They don't compare with what you've accomplished. It was different when you were researching *Transformation*. I thought it'd be an obscure monograph for academics, like you said it would."

"And you're sorry it wasn't?"

"Of course not. But it was a lot less intimidating."

"Intimidating? I do what I do because I like it, not to lord it over anybody. The subjects interest me, and sharing them with others makes me happy. I'm with you for the same reason. You make me happy, and I want to make you happy. Do I?"

"Yes," he said, leaning forward until our foreheads touched. "But you could still do better."

"If you say I'm making you feel the way rich old Corey did, I'll strangle you."

He laughed, to my relief. "As long as you're sure," he said.

Hearing his doubts break down, I proceeded to demolish them. "I'll prove how sure I am. Marry me."

His head snapped back. "What?"

"Marry me."

"Are you kidding?"

"No. I was planning to ask when I was done with Atwater, but it's better now if it keeps you from becoming a martyr to my two-book career."

"You really want to marry me?"

"If you want to marry me."

His eyes brightened and the smile crinkled. "Yeah, I do."

The decision reduced us to a sloppy mix of laughter, sobs, and embraces. After we blotted away the tears and phlegm, I said:

"Let's call my mom."

"Why yours first?"

"It's three hours later in Pennsylvania. She's probably ready for bed."

David acquiesced, and we phoned her.

"Hello, Paul."

"Hi, Mom. You're on speaker."

"Hi, Mrs. Heywood," David said.

"Hello, David. Is everything okay?"

"Absolutely," David said. "Your son just popped the question."

I turned to him. "Hey."

"If we call your mom first, I get to break the news."

"You're getting married?" she said.

"Yes."

"Oh Paul, I'm so glad. I was worried you'd only live together."

"No worries, Mom. I was up to my neck in work and couldn't think about much else."

"When's the ceremony?"

"We haven't discussed it yet," David said. "I'm still reeling from the proposal."

"You mean he only just asked you?"

"About ten minutes ago."

"And I'm the first to know?"

"Lucky you live in another time zone," I said, "otherwise it'd have been a coin toss."

"Would you like me to tell the relatives and your friends here?"

"I'll send them a message tomorrow," I said. "I'm still working on my next subject. I'd appreciate it if you could keep them from distracting me with questions and congratulations."

"I will. I'm so happy for you, Paul, for you both."

"Thanks," David said.

"Better start preparing for the flight out here," I said. "No sense waiting to stoke your courage."

"I forgot," she said, her joy momentarily damped. "Well, I'll be there."

"I know," I said. "I don't want to keep you. You must be ready for bed."

"I am, and I haven't gone to bed happier since the day I found out I was pregnant with you. Goodnight. Love you both."

"Love you too."

"Okay," I said after hanging up, "Turnabout's fair play. Call your parents, but I get to tell them."

"You're going to be one of those bossy spouses, aren't you?"

Delia answered after the second ring. "Hello, David."

"Hi, Mom. Is Dad there?"

"Yes."

"Get him to the phone and put it on speaker. You're on speaker here."

We heard a faint "Tom, David wants to talk to us," followed by muffled shuffling.

"What's going on?" Tom said.

"Paul has something to tell you," David said.

"What?"

"You're about to get another son-in-law," I said.

"Really?" Delia gasped.

"You're finally going to make an honest man out of our boy?" Tom said.

"If you approve," I said. "Should I ask for his hand first?"

"You can have it gladly," he said. "When did it happen?"

"About twenty minutes ago."

"I'm so happy for you," Delia said. "You'll have to call Marge."

We hung up with Tom and Delia, phoned Marge, and had her call everyone to the phone. The news created a sensation. Mark and Adrian whooped in the background, eliciting agitated barks from Chop.

"Where are you having the ceremony?" Marge said after the commotion died down.

"We've only just gotten engaged," David said.

"How about having it here?"

"At your house?" I said.

"Sure. I've always thought this would be a perfect spot for a wedding. We can put folding chairs on the lawn and have the lake as a backdrop for the ceremony."

"If you can promise good weather, we'll take it," David said.

"How many people will there be?" she said.

"I don't know," David said. "We haven't thought about it."

"What about food? I've got some great hors d'oeuvre recipes . . ."

"You aren't going to cater?" David said.

"Why not? Now that the boys are almost teenagers, I'm thinking about getting back into the business. It'll be good practice."

"My wedding's not going to be a test case for you," David said.

"I'm a ten-year veteran of the trade, Davy, not a novice who has to prove herself. What do you think, Paul?"

"Oh, no," I said, "I may be an only child, but I've been warned about sibling rivalry. I'm going to be a nice, polite in-law and stay out of it."

"Come on," Marge said.

"Okay," I said. "I know you're a good cook and can imagine you're a great caterer. But this is your brother's wedding. You should be having fun, not working."

David nodded his approval.

"Very diplomatic," Marge said. "At least let me give you the names of the best people to do it . . . the second best, at any rate."

"Fine," David said, "and we'll talk about using the house later. For the moment, just be happy for us."

"You know I am."

During these exchanges, I heard a low murmur in the background, followed by stifled laughter. Marge and Brad said goodbye, after which Mark and Adrian yelled, "Goodnight, Uncle Davy! Goodnight, Uncle Paul!"

David ended the call and pocketed his phone.

"Brad told them to call me Uncle Paul," I said.

"Better get used to it unless you'd rather have them call you Uncle Pauly."

Two days later, David and I delivered groceries and broke the news to Robert.

"Congratulations. I wondered what was taking you so long."

"Paul's blaming his work," David said.

"And David's insecurities," I said. "He's worried he might not be good enough for me after how well I was rewarded for finding Jacobson's daughter, even though his dad's been rooting for me from the start."

"Let's not forget your mom adores me, too," David said.

"True, but my mom's a pushover."

"Enough," Robert said. "There's only so much amorous arguing I can stomach. When's the wedding?"

"We're thinking in a few months," I said.

"Professor Paul wants to wait until he's done with his research," David said, "then we can enjoy a honeymoon before he tackles the dual existence of Martin Atwater."

"Not a bad title," I said, "*The Dual Existence of Martin Atwater*."

"A little too near *The Three Faces of Eve*, don't you think?" Robert said.

"Maybe just *Dual Existence*," I said. "It's specific enough to catch the attention yet vague enough to spark curiosity."

"Perhaps add an explanatory subtitle," Robert said, "like 'how one man balanced two loves in old Hollywood.' I'd buy that."

"Come on," David said. "We're not through with the wedding yet."

"Have you given any thought to where you're going for a honeymoon?" Robert said.

"David's never been back east. I was thinking of Cape Cod." I turned to David. "Robert grew up in Massachusetts."

"Cape Cod would be ideal," Robert said, "if you go in summer. The New England weather in any other season is uncertain at best."

"That'd make us June brides," David said.

"June grooms," Robert corrected.

"I suppose there's little point asking if you'll attend the ceremony," I said.

"Not with my arthritis. I'll be content with the hours of video footage you'll have to show me."

David, Marge, and Delia spent the next four months planning the wedding while I prepared the pieces of Atwater's puzzle for assembly on returning from the Cape. Every evening, after leaving the fragments of Martin, Tyler, and Edna sprawled on my desk, David reviewed the latest decisions with me for final approval.

The one element beyond any wedding planner's control cooperated on the day. A thin mist hovering over Lake Bellow at dawn dissipated by seven, leaving a cloudless sky under which Tom, Brad, Mark, Adrian, David, and I deployed five rows of folding chairs on the lawn facing the lake. The previous afternoon, a wooden platform had been built a few yards from the shore; after clearing it of the morning dew, Marge and Delia adorned its sides with voluminous flower arrangements in tall papier-mâché holders. The caterers invaded Marge's kitchen at nine-thirty, and guests began arriving at twelve. My mom and a handful of friends had flown in from Pennsylvania. Lena Crenshaw, aided by her niece, and Danielle Cray, alone among my clients, attended. Rene Arlington's green and red traffic-signal tones advertised her presence wherever she wandered. Per the invitations, everyone dressed casually, except for Chop, who had a black bow tie spooled around his collar.

A cool breeze off the lake ruffled the flowers and our hair as we exchanged vows to a recording of a string orchestra playing "Wait Till You See Him." Following our first married kiss and the accompanying applause, Tom, Brad, and some of our friends cleared away the chairs for the reception. Guests milled around in the house, on the porch, over the lawn, and along the shore, while waiters snaked among them with trays of appetizers and drinks. The caterers erected a buffet table near the porch at three-thirty, and carried out a five-tier wedding cake. After the ritual cake-cutting, more music played, and people danced. David and I left for the airport at six-thirty and arrived in Boston in time to collapse in a boutique hotel room on Newbury Street.

The next day we explored the city before riding the ferry to Provincetown, at the very tip of Cape Cod, where we checked into the top room of a small bed and breakfast, with a view of the ocean and a secluded beach ringed with sand dunes topped by patches of tall, waving grass.

"Robert was right," David said as we feasted on strawberries and champagne at a table by our window, "this is perfect for a honeymoon."

The days passed quickly. We spent the weekend after our return at Marge and Brad's, discussing the trip and handing out souvenirs: lobster-fronted tee shirts for Mark and Adrian, lobster neckties for Brad and Tom, a seafood cookbook for Marge and a pink coral necklace for Delia.

The next Wednesday, we screened footage of the ceremony for Robert, routing it from our phones to his TV. He followed the images avidly while we identified people for him.

"Lovely," he said and, a moment later, chuckled. "Seventy-five percent of your guests are recording it on their phones. Nothing's real anymore until it's filtered through a screen."

The scene shifted to David and I feeding each other slices of wedding cake at the reception.

"I'm glad you dispensed with the tired trope of mashing it in each other's faces."

"The temptation was acute," David said.

I pointed out Lena Crenshaw and Danielle Cray. "She's the one who saw you in *Long Day's Journey into Night*," I said.

"It's nice putting faces to their names after what you've told me about them," he said.

Scenes of people dancing, including my mother, followed.

"You never told me your mother danced," Robert said.

"I didn't know she could. I think she's been corrupted by her bingo cronies."

Shots of Cape Cod displaced the wedding.

"The same as when I was young," Robert said.

"Did you go there often?" David said.

"A week each summer with my parents. How'd you like it?"

"I'll take the first excuse to go back. My parents, my sister, and her family want to go, too."

The footage ended.

"What'd you think?" I said.

"You're off to a good start."

"I wish you could've been there," I said.

"It would've been too uncomfortable. What'll you do now that you're back?'

"Finish the Atwater book."

"What about you, David?"

"Go back to the Argonaut and my deliveries," David said.

"With me tagging along," I said, "for the deliveries, at least."

"Good," Robert said.

Composing Atwater's story again transformed me into a hermit, except for several weekends at Marge and Brad's and following David on his *H&H* rounds, during which Robert invariably enquired about my progress.

Three months after completion, the book appeared under the title *Dual Existence* and, thanks to the publishers, with an even more provocative, or absurd, subtitle than the one Robert suggested: *the life of a sexual double agent*. I presented Robert with a copy. He chuckled over the subtitle and read it in two days.

"You've done a remarkable job. I never would've guessed there was so much to the grizzled introvert who hovered on the fringes of my world forty years ago."

The book also caused a flurry of interest among the general public.

"Not surprisingly," Robert said. "Moralists love scandal."

The next year Fan Basics adapted the book into a film titled *Lovers and Liars* that reduced the complex individual I had painstakingly reconstructed into an angst-ridden bisexual in period costume. I fumed over the changes during one of David's deliveries.

"Films always reduce," Robert said, "since they lack the ability of words to depict the finer shades of being and have to compress their stories into a few short hours. But it may encourage more of the few literate people left in the world to read the book."

"Robert believes civilization is on the brink of collapse," I explained to David.

"Oh, Paul," Robert sighed, "Civilization collapsed years ago. Everyone was just too busy watching football to notice."

Selling the rights to *Dual Existence* enabled David and me to buy a house, a cottage built in 1948 by an architect in thrall to Frank Lloyd Wright. David closed down the Argonaut to sell books solely online, and since we now spent both our working and free time at home, we relied more and more on Marge's cooking lessons. Marge had resumed catering, and her success with us inspired her to post a series of online cooking classes to publicize her business, which attracted several million views and culminated in a publisher's offer for her to compile a cookbook.

Adjusting to life as a married homeowner distracted me from an unavailing search for a subject.

"Why not Robert," David said, "or do you think he'd object?"

"I thought about it, but he destroyed all his personal effects."

"Too bad he didn't record his conversations with the people he met, like he told my mom."

Recalling that day reminded me of the novelist Fiona Vale, who had since been on my lengthy future reading list.

Cornflower Blue corroborated their praise. Reading Vale's other works, I learned her only extant biography had been written thirty years ago, which decided me on her for my next project. Robert's recollections provided me with numerous sources to consult about her life in New York. I spent two years researching and writing; learning enough about medieval amulets to accurately describe the collection Robert had mentioned consumed four and a half months. The book, like my first treatise on Jacobson, appealed to a limited market, and, unlike the earlier two books, lacked the dramatic qualities that ushered Jacobson's and Atwater's stories from the page into Robert's vilified audio-visual media, yet it earned me several awards and considerable praise, not least among which I counted Robert's and Delia's.

The next year I spent toying with subjects for another book. Atwater's papers had mentioned a minor modernist poet named Charles Bunting, who wrote five film scripts for Paramount during the 1940s. Wondering how and why an avant-garde poet ended up a hack in a mainstream film studio settled me on him for my next project, provisionally titled *Poet in the Pleasure Dome*, the title another nod to Coleridge—this time his *Kubla Khan*—and, by extension, Robert. During one visit, I mentioned it to him on the chance he had read any of Bunting's work.

"I don't recall the name."

"I'm not surprised," I said. "He wasn't particularly distinguished."

He paused before speaking again. "Actually, Paul, I've been forgetting things a little too often lately."

"Have you told your doctor?"

"Not yet," he said and sighed. "This may be where your guardianship begins."

"Make an appointment and let me know what he says, or would you prefer me to call?"

"No, I'll do it."

His doctor referred him to a specialist who diagnosed the onset of Alzheimer's.

Robert relocated to a nursing facility catering to retired actors. He had one room with one window, four beige walls, an adjustable hospital bed, and a single, slender closet. He sold all his furniture but for those few pieces his new shoebox managed to accommodate: his bedside table and Doric column lamp, cherry writing table and chair, and his recliner. Against the plain walls and utilitarian bed, the familiar furnishings turned the room into a sad hybrid of the individual and the indifferent, muting the one direct statement of his identity: the framed headshot on his writing desk.

Apart from a dozen favorites, he handed his books over to David and me. "Keep what you want and sell the rest," he said.

He participated in the facility's social activities for the first year and a half. Then, as his arthritis and Alzheimer's advanced, he became confined to his room, dividing his time between the bed and the recliner and, his nurses assured me, contentedly rereading his books. I visited three times a week or more, often with David, for continuity and companionship, to maintain his supply of Velma's and Bub's Tubs, monitor his care, and, as I soon realized, to witness the gradual dissolution of the person he had spent more than seven decades becoming.

We talked as before: he in the recliner and me on the writing desk chair, or he in the upraised bed and me in the recliner, with David on the extra chair or seated cross-legged on the floor, when he accompanied me. The first year, Robert seemed only slightly less alert than in his apartment, the few signs of his condition being a tendency to repeat stories he told me before—sometimes several in a single afternoon—and the infrequent irruption of random comments like, "I should phone Nate Grant and see if he's gotten any interesting scripts," or "the only thing I can't stand about New York are these damned pigeons." I listened patiently to the stories, pleased by his pleasure in telling them, and had learned enough about Alzheimer's to assent to the irrelevancies and guide him back to our original topic. I also told him about studies I had been stumbling over more and more frequently, correlating art with brain function. They validated much of what he had told me, and though the debate continued about reducing art to biology, it seemed clear the greater sense of well-being belonged to Renaissance rather than Utilitarian Man. He listened, gratified, yet forgot everything by the following visit.

During the next several months, his astute gaze became like that of a lost child, bewildered and fearful, searching for outside guidance to help him perform basic tasks like dressing. He also dirifted with increased frequency from lucidity to an inner reality that, judging by what he said, combined his actual memories with episodes from favorite novels and various parts he had played.

During one visit, he lay partially upright in bed, blankets up to his chest and hands folded over his stomach. He quietly consumed his Bub's Tub while I filled him in on my latest project, the history of an obscure TV horror anthology show from the 1950s called *Menace* that Tom told me about. After he set the empty tub under the Doric column beside him, I handed him a copy of Marge's recently published cookbook. The book included my great-grandmother's recipe for stuffed cabbage, one of two dozen of her recipes my mother sent after I proved adept enough in the kitchen to prepare them, and the recipe for Robert's zucchini frittata that Marge received from David. The original and heart-healthy versions appeared on facing pages, beside glamorous photos of the finished products and a line crediting the recipe to Robert above an inset reproduction of his triad photo with Maggie and Grayson. Robert studied the pages, nodding and smiling.

"A final gleam in the public eye for me," he said

The frittata reminded him that he had been playing in *Measure for Measure* while dating Paolo. He quoted speeches from the play for ten minutes, as sharp as he had ever been in his apartment.

When he finished, I said, "It's almost six. I have to get home. I'll be back in a day or two."

"Okay, Paul."

"Do you need anything?"

"No, I'm fine. Tell David I said hi."

"I will."

I slipped on my jacket and walked to the door. As I touched the handle, he said, "Terry?"

I turned. He stared at me yet looked at someone else, a figure standing clearly before him, as if perhaps between two ragged ends of crumbling nitrate. "Yes?" I said as calmly as possible.

"I love you, Terry."

His voice conveyed all the earnest, desperate yearning of a first adolescent crush, and I realized that considering Terry's ambivalence to their physical encounters, Robert probably never told him he loved him.

I returned to the bed and laid a hand on his. "I love you too, Robert."

He smiled, squeezed my fingers, and closed his eyes as if my touch had lulled him to sleep. I removed my hand and stepped back.

His eyes opened again, fixing on me a politely inquisitive stare like the one that had appraised my academic dishevelment my first day in his apartment. "What time are we having dinner?"

"I'm not sure," I said.

"Will you ask the other nurse?"

"Yes, of course."

"Thank you. Will you be working this floor from now on?"

"I think so."

"I hope to see you again."

"Me too."

I arrived home in tears.

David stood at the stove stirring a pot of spaghetti sauce, a blue and white striped dish towel slung over his shoulder, the steaming air around him a mix of sweaty *October Mist* and simmering garlic. I described what had happened.

"Maybe it's for the best," he said.

"I can't believe you just said that."

"Why? Didn't you tell me he once said our memories exist to preserve how we felt about people and events?"

"Yeah . . ."

"So now he relives the important people and events from his past. Isn't that better than staring at a TV or those awful tan walls?"

"I suppose. But he's important to me, too. I'm starting to miss him."

"I know." He lowered the heat under the pot, wiped his hands on the towel, and tossed it on the counter. "Let's dance."

"What?"

"Play David and Paul's dance mix," he commanded our voice-activated audio system.

The mix began with a favorite of Robert's: Ernesto Lecuona's "Always in My Heart." David's arms circled me, and we revolved around the kitchen floor. The third revolution disclosed our two children, Alice and Andrew, standing in the doorway, grinning at their dads.

The same children started kindergarten today, and I note with terror how, despite my best efforts, time increasingly eludes me. Robert exists in a twilight state now. I stop in at the nursing home on Mondays, Wednesdays, and Fridays, less to visit than supervise his treatment. As I told David, he deserves whatever dignity I can wrest from the healthcare industry.

The more time escapes me, the more I imagine treading my own private path among Dowson's grass of graveyards. Then, the words by Tennyson that Robert quoted recur to me and, like Robert, I review all those of whom, merely by existing and following my propensities in love and in work, I became a part: the readers at book signings or who post comments online praising my efforts on behalf of Erich Jacobson, Martin Atwater, Fiona Vale, and Charles Bunting; Barbara Quigley and Ingrid Andersson, who bonded after I introduced them and who, with April Atwater, benefited financially from the sale of their relatives' stories; Danielle and Lena and the other clients whose final years I enlivened with what Danielle once called my 'gentle inquisitiveness;' Tom and Delia, Marge and Brad, and Mark and Adrian, who allot me a valued place in their family circle; and David and Alice and Andrew, who turn to me for the affection and support obtainable only from a spouse and a parent.

I also consider how those I have met became a part of me. Barbara, Ingrid, April, and my readers assure me my work possesses value beyond satisfying mere intellectual curiosity. My *H&H* clients provided me with a more intimate, personal view of the past, one that continues to inform my research and increases my appreciation for what I enjoy in the present. The positive examples of marriage Tom and Delia, and Marge and Brad set counteracted that of my parents while, following our shaky start, Mark and Adrian bolstered my confidence to tackle parenthood. David overcame my reticence, released my playful side, and, with Alice and Andrew, awakened a capacity for devotion I never imagined I possessed.

Becoming parts of these people, and them becoming parts of me, created a far more complex person than the one who disembarked at Los Angeles airport a decade ago. I learned things and discovered capabilities I never suspected, and by doing so, I not only arrived at a condition I may tentatively term happiness, I find that by continuing to learn and discover, I experience a gratifying sensation of realized potentials and life lived.

Robert, of course, remains an important part of me as well. Thanks to his influence, from his observations on being human to his unwittingly setting in motion the events leading to my extended family, my love shall continue songful, despite whatever grassy graveyards I tread in the future. And I like to think that, in some way, my becoming a part of him provides a reciprocal comfort.

Paul Heywood
May–August 2019

Felix Anderson is the pseudonym for a writer
living in Rhode Island.

www.ingramcontent.com/pod-product-compliance
Lightning Source LLC
Chambersburg PA
CBHW050920030726

47503CB00007BB/2381